December 2006.

For Nina,

JACK LONDON'S
GOLDEN STATE

With much love

on your birthday

Mary &c Jim

x xx

JACK LONDON'S

SELECTED CALIFORNIA WRITINGS

GOLDEN STATE

Edited by GERALD HASLAM

HEYDAY BOOKS
Berkeley, California

Library of Congress Cataloging-in-Publication Data

London, Jack, 1876–1916.
Jack London's Golden State : selected California writings / edited by Gerald Haslam.
p.   cm.
Includes bibliographical references (p.   ).
ISBN 1-890771-02-3
1. California Literary collections. 2. California—Civilization. I. Haslam, Gerald W. II. Title.
PS3523.046A6 1999
818′.5209—dc21

99-20437
CIP

Cover Photo: Helen Abbott
Cover Art: Jennifer Beckman
Cover Design: David Bullen Design
Interior Design: Raina Rippel
Printing and Binding: Publishers Press, Salt Lake City, Utah

Orders, inquiries, and correspondence should be addressed to:
Heyday Books
P. O. Box 9145, Berkeley, CA 94709
510/549-3564, Fax 510/549-1889
heyday@heydaybooks.com

Printed in the United States of America

10 9 8 7 6 5 4 3 2 1

For Loki, my favorite new Californian

Contents

Introduction

"I don't care if the whole present, all I possess, were swept away from me—I will build a new present; if I am left naked and hungry tomorrow—before I give in I will go naked and hungry; if I were a woman I would prostitute myself to all men that I would succeed—in short, I will."
—Jack London, 1898

Jack London has been described as "a figure impossible save in California in the opening decade of the twentieth century." That may not have been intended as a compliment, but London's literary accomplishments made it clear that he was worth a regiment of critics. As biographer Earle Labor summarizes, "No major figure in American literature struggled against greater odds, none fought uphill with more spectacular success, and none achieved wider popularity."

Unlike the work of many of his contemporaries, today much of London's writing remains accessible and fresh because he helped invent what we think of as modern American prose. Unencumbered by formal literary training, he went his own way, selected his own subjects, and produced a startling body of work: not only novels and stories, but varied nonfiction, drama, and lively reportage. He became, according to writer Bruce Watson, *"the* American author for the new century—bold, scandalous, self-assured."

Jack London was born in 1876, the illegitimate son of a spiritualist Flora Wellman and, most likely, of wandering lecturer and free-love advocate William Chaney, who abandoned Flora. She later married a kindly widower named John London. After a period of living on farms and ranches, the Londons settled in Oakland. When Flora was defrauded of the family's money in a real estate scheme, her thirteen-year-old son went to work.

Fortunately, by then "two small things [had] happened to me," Jack reported, "...that practically directed the entire course of my life." He had stumbled on a copy of Ouida's novel *Signa* which "put in me an ambition to get beyond the skyline of my narrow California valley and opened up to me the possibilities of the world of art." The other was the influence of Oakland's city librarian, Ina Coolbrith—the state's Poet Laureate—who encouraged and directed the youngster's reading: "It was this world of books, now accessible, that practically gave me the basis of my education."

Jack completed grade school in 1891, worked for a time in a cannery, then became, in his own words, "a salmon fisher, an oyster pirate, a schooner sailor, a fish patrolman, a longshoreman, and a general sort of bay-faring adventurer—a boy in years and a man among men." At seventeen, after seven months on a seal-hunting schooner and only a grammar school graduate, he won a writing competition sponsored by the San Francisco *Morning Call* with "Story of a Typhoon off the Coast of Japan." That manuscript exhibited elements of the descriptive power and passion that would later characterize London's professional style.

After hoboing in 1894—an experience he would recount in *The Road*—Jack attended Oakland High School and concurrently joined the Henry Clay Debating Society, where he was exposed to the stimulating ideas of such thinkers as Adam Smith, Charles Darwin, Immanuel Kant, Friedrich Nietzsche, and Herbert Spencer. The latter's Social Darwinism—the notion that socially elect classes or peoples possess biological superiority—would especially influence London's later writing. But the not-so-gay nineties also shaped London's perspective, for that decade featured infamous economic inequities, a deep depression, labor violence, and the growth of social and economic consciousness; it was during this time that another idea became even more important to him.

On Christmas day of 1895, the *San Francisco Examiner* featured an article by the nineteen-year-old London headlined, "What Socialism Is—The Boy Socialist Describes the Meaning and Intent of the New Philosophy." Observes biographer Clarice Stasz, "Socialism to him then was really a way to protest the social injustices he had seen in his brief life, combined with anticapitalism, an attack on the trusts he thought responsible for the inequities." That was, in any case, the symbolic marriage of London and Socialism, a union that enjoyed much bliss and endured spats before coming apart. Toward the end of his life, Jack told a reporter, "Socialism has cost me hundreds of thousands of dollars. When the time comes I'm going to stay right on my ranch at Glen Ellen and let the revolution go to blazes."

Between bliss and divorce, however, London truly and passionately supported the economic philosophy, and became its boldest and most effective American spokesman. In 1905, for instance, he would challenge an audience of well-to-do New Yorkers: "You have mismanaged the world, and it shall be taken from you!...Consider our hands! They are strong hands, and even now they are reaching forth for all you have, and they will take it, take it by the power of their strong hands; take it from your feeble grasp."

It has been reported that Vladimir Ilyich Lenin, the founder of Soviet Russia, was reading an essay by London when he died. Little wonder, since Jack's portrayals of the downtrodden and oppressed in books such as *Martin Eden* or *The People of the Abyss* or *The Road*, or in his socialist essays and stories, are uniformly unrelenting. His major rival as the most famous American socialist of the time, novelist and politician Upton Sinclair, described London as "one of the great revolutionary figures of our history...one of the greatest writers and one of the greatest souls that America has given to the world."

The same year his socialist manifesto had been published in the *San Francisco Examiner*, young Jack crammed to take the entrance examination at the University of California, Berkeley. He was admitted as a special student, but he remained only a single semester. He later explained, "The student refuses to sit under a professor who lectures after the fashion of the kindergarten. It drives him mad to have all things and the most obvious things explained at length." In terms of actual experiences, London was likely better educated than many of his teachers.

He soon returned to "real life." At that time, Teddy Roosevelt had warned the nation of a "relaxation of fiber that tends to accompany civilization," and like many thoughtful people, Jack came to fear that Americans were losing their toughness. He had been denied a part in the opening of the Great West, but he found his own frontier in 1897 in the Alaskan gold rush, and once more tested himself. He struck it rich there—not with gold but with material for fiction.

"It was in the Klondike I found myself," Jack later admitted. That led to what many consider to be among his or anybody's finest stories, a set of naturalistic tales in which frail human beings struggled to endure amidst the indifferent wilderness Jack called "The White Silence." His story of that title was published in the venerable *Overland Monthly* in 1899; it led George Hamlin Fitch, the *San Francisco Chronicle's* literary critic, to claim, "I would rather have written 'The White Silence' than anything that has appeared in fiction in the last ten years."

In 1900, the promising author married Bess Maddern and also published his first collection of stories, *The Son of the Wolf.* No reviewer suspected that the career of who would eventually become America's most widely read, most frequently translated writer had just been fully launched. At that time, curiously enough, a literary aestheticism that stressed beautiful words rather than hard-hitting subjects was in vogue. Jack, a young man who had known life in the raw, alienated himself from some critics when he asserted that literary form had no value "unless it clothe pregnant substance, great substance." He remained throughout his career a prototypical two-fisted intellectual, a tough-yet-sensitive man who had, by dint of much toil, risen from the working class. His entire career seemed to deny literature's lingering effete image.

Equally important, London brought unusual perspectives to his writing, having actually seen society not only from the bottom up but from the West out: blue-collar California, with all its pluses and minuses, was a constant point of departure and frame of reference. He was the first major American author grounded in the Golden State—almost half of his books are set in the Bay Area. Jack not only revealed some of California's virtues, locales, and situations in his writing, but also exposed some of California's problems, such as its persistent nativism and racism, as well as its stark economic imbalances.

London's first great hit was the enduring *The Call of the Wild*, published in 1903; it brought him worldwide celebrity and the possibility of financial security. He followed that with another success, *The Sea-Wolf*, in 1904, written as his personal life turned turbulent. Jack's marriage to Bess, which had produced daughters Joan and Becky but little harmony, was coming apart, and he was involved with Charmian Kitteridge, the woman who would become his second wife. Amidst this turmoil he produced in *The Sea-Wolf* what Ambrose Bierce called "a rattling good story," one of the best novels of the sea ever written.

Novelist Philip José Farmer has explained the necessity of "telling a story as if it were fuel for a fire." London certainly shared that passion, so his books were often forums for his ideas. Of *The Sea-Wolf*, for example, he told Charmian that he had created Wolf Larsen—one of American literature's most memorable characters—as a Nietzschean superman (*Übermensch*), "anti-social in his tendencies, and in these days of our complex society and sociology he cannot be successful in his hostile aloofness."

Jack could breathe life into abstractions as few other authors have. One of his enduring motifs was atavism—the tapping of primitive, inborn capacities. That notion baffled some folks and was considered regressive by others. In *The Call of the Wild*, however, London used it as a powerful element of plot when a Santa Clara ranch dog, Buck, strips his civilized veneer in order to survive in elemental circumstances:

> *...not only did he learn by experience, but instincts long dead became alive again. The domesticated generations fell from him. In vague ways he remembered back to the youth of the breed, to the time the wild dogs ranged in packs through the primeval forests and killed their meat as they ran it down. It was no task for him to learn to fight with the cut and slash and the quick wolf snap. In this manner he had fought forgotten ancestors. They quickened the old life within him, and the old tricks which they had stamped into the heredity of the breed were his tricks.*

As was true of many city-bound working folks and intellectuals early in the twentieth century, London also came to distrust urban life and industrialization. His portraits of the dehumanization of workers in cities could be grim indeed, as in "The Apostate." For Johnny, the young protagonist—born on the floor of a mill—"There had never been a time when he had not been in intimate relationship with machines. Machinery had almost been bred into him." Jack refused to sugarcoat his portrayals of exploitation and suffering.

Eventually, the author began to yearn for the country and its healing power; from his 1905 purchase of property in the hills west of Glen Ellen, until his death eleven years later on what he had come to call "Beauty Ranch," Jack became a country gentleman and a highly regarded agriculturist. His writing about rural settings tended toward romanticism, and he explained, "mine is not *realism*, but is *idealized realism*."

In his pastoral novel of 1913, *The Valley of the Moon*, he asserted, "All the natural world was right, and sensible, and beneficent. It was the man-world that was wrong, and mad, and horrible." The poverty and exploitation he had seen in cities made such observations axiomatic for him.

London straddled several worlds during his career, just as he straddled two centuries: wealth-poverty, nature-science, rural-urban, male-female, and still others. He also grew and changed as a person, so that contemporary readers quickly sense that London-1899 and London-1910 are by no means the same. His evolving attitudes toward equality within marriage, as well as toward women in general, for instance, seem to reveal a man whose views were dramatically shifting.

Stylistically, Jack London lived on the cusp of nineteenth and twentieth centuries, and his vigorous prose helped shape the techniques that would characterize American fiction after the First World War. Despite occasional flourishes early in his career that hearkened to magazine conventions of the mid-1800s, his language became unusually direct, vigorous, and compelling. His sense of humor remains much underrated, as "Navigating Four Horses North of the Bay" illustrates. London also developed a considerable knack for both recognizing (Ed Morrell in *The Star Rover*) and creating (Felipe Rivera in "The Mexican") memorable characters.

When it came to writing of a scrap or a chase or a competition—of action of all kinds—he set a high standard. In the aforementioned "Navigating Four Horses North of the Bay," for example, he evoked a pleasant wagon journey this way:

> *You are swinging a sharp, down-grade, mountain curve, at a fast trot. The rock wall is the outside of the curve. The inside of the curve is a precipice. The continuance of the curve is a narrow unrailed bridge. You hit the curve, throwing the leaders against the wall and making the pole-horse work. The leaders are hugging the wall like nestling doves. But the moment comes in the evolution when the leaders must shoot out ahead. They really must shoot, or else they'll hit the wall and miss the bridge.*

He was a gifted writer of physical descriptions as well, as this evocation of the San Francisco Bay Area in "The Golden Poppy" demonstrates:

> *This field blazes on the rim of the Piedmont Hills. Beneath lies all the world. In the distance, across the silver sweep of bay, San Francisco*

smokes on her many hills like a second Rome. Not far away, Mount Tamalpais thrusts a rugged shoulder into the sky; and midway between is the Golden Gate, where sea mists love to linger. From the poppy field we often see the shimmering blue of the Pacific beyond, and the busy ships that go forever out and in.

London's action sequences read as well as Ernest Hemingway's, while his evocations of landscape and nature rival John Steinbeck's. He was truly a benchmark writer.

Along with *The Call of the Wild* and *The Sea-Wolf, White Fang,* published in 1906, was a great commercial success. Despite that, London often found himself scrambling for paychecks—as his collected letters illustrate—because he lived an expensive life. Always a sailor, for instance, Jack spent over $35,000—a fabulous sum then—to build his boat the *Snark* in 1906–07. Then, seeking what he called "big moments in living," he sailed her for two years, visiting Hawaii and the South Seas, a journey that stimulated some wonderful writing in *South Sea Tales* and *The Cruise of the Snark,* both published in 1911.

He also spent considerable money buying and improving his slice of Sonoma County, developing Beauty Ranch as a model of modern agriculture and husbandry. Jack said, "I realize that much of California's romance is passing away, and I intend to see to it that I, at least, shall preserve as much of that romance as is possible for me." Toward the end of his career, he produced three novels with distinctly Californian settings: *Burning Daylight, The Valley of the Moon,* and *The Little Lady of the Big House,* of which *The Valley of the Moon* was the most successful; Lawrence Clark Powell, in his book, *California Classics,* notes, "it is a passionate book, its characters sharply drawn, and it is purely Californian."

That set of uniquely regional works shows an artist in the thrall of the agrarian vision that dominated the final stage of his life. "In the solution of the great economic problems of the present age," he told Charmian, "I see a return to the soil. I go into farming, because my philosophy and research have taught me to recognize that a return to the soil is the basis of economics." It was also a new challenge that produced a degree of personal contentment, but his deceptively fragile body was by then breaking down.

Damaged by tropical diseases and personal excesses, wracked by chronic ailments, Jack London died somewhat mysteriously and far too soon at his ranch on November 22, 1916. His route from the urban Bay Area of his youth to rural Sonoma County of his mature years—a mere fifty miles—had been circuitous and adventuresome, and this had made him the most popular American author of his time and an international celebrity. It had also established a continuing pattern of working-class emergence into lofty literary levels that has come to characterize California's artistic fluorescence.

Jack participated in and came to represent many of his home state's several myths—a roustabout, a rebel, a rowdy—never quite tame despite his accomplishments: In the eyes of many, he *was* California. At the time he was writing, the Golden State was considered a distant, alien place, a continent away from the nation's center of power. Then, as now, it boasted a multicultural and multi-ethnic population unlike any other in America. Additionally, it already hosted a fun-house mixture of political, social, and religious groups, as well as the aforementioned blatant exploitation of workers, and both racial and ethnic discrimination; London's home state wasn't an ideal society. Still, many of its citizens did believe they had escaped eastern conventions and old-world limitations. As a result, an enriched sense of the possible enhanced life on what was then called "the far coast."

Unlike many other writers, the Oakland boy didn't flee to New York once he became famous, but remained in California—a decision that both disturbed and baffled some critics. This is likely the basis for continued assertions that his strengths and weaknesses are the strengths and weaknesses of California, when in fact, London's qualities are his own, but often set in the Golden State. As biographer Stasz observes, "What the rest of the country had failed to recognize before Jack's appearance was the degree of literacy and culture in California." He became the West Coast's

literary avatar, setting a high standard indeed for future generations because Jack may have been as richly talented as any
American author has ever been.

Ironically, he remained throughout his life a literary out-
sider, seen as a rude westerner and radical, never part of the trendy
elite. He has been disdained by some not only due to his regional identification and politics, but also to his popularity; a socialist
westerner with that many readers can't be important, or so some
critics have suggested. That is as silly as suggesting Jack is a great
author merely *because* of those things.

He was actually an author who broke barriers and set stan-
dards for the next century, combining sophisticated ideas with
lively action and straightforward language. When his work, like
that of other artists, is judged by its highest levels of achievement—*The Call of the Wild*, say, or any number of his short stories
and essays—Jack London remains a literary treasure not only of
his native state but of the world. In a 1900 letter to his friend
Cloudesly Jones, the young writer had explained that he sought to
"create things that live, and breathe, and grip men, and cause reading lamps to burn overtime."

It's a century later, and lamps are still burning...overtime.

Gerald Haslam
April 1999

A CALIFORNIA
PERSPECTIVE

Jack London by Himself

The memoir that follows appeared as a pamphlet, as well as the pref-
ace to The Star Rover *(1915), one of London's most controversial nov-*
els. The author wasn't shy about presenting his own life, or even in
assessing it. In this autobiographical essay, he summarizes who and
what he was, how he saw himself, and the forces that created him.

I was born in San Francisco in 1876. At fifteen I was a man
among men, and if I had a spare nickel I spent it on beer instead
of candy, because I thought it was more manly to buy beer. Now,
when my years are doubled, I am out on a hunt for the boyhood
which I never had, and I am less curious than at any other time of
my life. Guess I'll find that boyhood. Almost the first things I realized were responsibilities. I have no recollection of being taught to
read or write—I could do both at the age of five—but I know that
my first school was in Alameda before I went out on a ranch with
my folks, and as a ranch boy worked hard from my eighth year.

The second school where I tried to pick up a little learning
was an irregular hit-or-miss affair at San Mateo. Each class sat in a
separate desk, but there were days when we did not sit at all, for
the master used to get drunk very often, and then one of the older
boys would thrash him. To even things up, the master would then
thrash the younger lads, so you can think what sort of school it
was. There was no one belonging to me, or associated with me in
any way, who had literary tastes or ideas; the nearest I can make to
it is that my grandfather was a circuit rider, a Welshman, known as
"Priest" Jones in the backwoods, where his enthusiasm led him to
scatter the Gospel.

One of my earliest and strongest impressions was of the ignorance of other people. I had read and absorbed Washington Irving's *Alhambra* before I was nine, but could never understand how it was that the other ranchers knew nothing about it. Later I concluded that this ignorance was peculiar to the country, and felt that those who lived in cities would not be so dense. One day a man from the city came to the ranch; he wore shiny shoes and a cloth coat, and I felt that here was a good chance for me to exchange thoughts with an enlightened mind. From the bricks of an old fallen chimney I had built an Alhambra of my own; towers, terraces, and all were complete, and chalk inscriptions marked the different sections. Here I led the city man and questioned him about *The Alhambra*, but he was as ignorant as the men on the ranch, and then I consoled myself with the thought that there were only two clever people in the world—Washington Irving and myself.

My other reading-matter at that time consisted mainly of dime novels, borrowed from the hired men, and newspapers in which the servants gloated over the adventures of poor but virtuous shop-girls.

Through reading such stuff, my mind was necessarily ridiculously conventional, but being very lonely, I read everything that came my way, and was greatly impressed by Ouida's story, *Signa*, which I devoured regularly for a couple of years. I never knew the finish until I grew up, for the closing chapters were missing from my copy, so I kept on dreaming with the hero, like him, unable to see Nemesis at the end. My work on the ranch at one time was to watch the bees, and as I sat under a tree from sunrise till late in the afternoon, waiting for the swarming, I had plenty of time to read and dream. Livermore Valley was very flat, and even the hills around were then to me devoid of interest, and the only incident to break in on my visions was when I gave the alarm of swarming, and the ranch folk rushed out with pots, pans, and buckets of water. I think the opening line of *Signa* was, "It was only a little lad, yet he had dreams of becoming a great musician, and having all Europe at his feet." Well, I was only a little lad, too, but why could not I become what "Signa" dreamed of being?

Life on a California ranch was then to me the dullest possible existence, and every day I thought of going out beyond the skyline to see the world. Even then there were whispers, art promptings; my mind inclined to things beautiful, although my environment was unbeautiful. The hills and valley around were eyesores and aching pits, and I never loved them till I left them.

Before I was eleven I left the ranch and came to Oakland, where I spent so much of my time in the Free Public Library, eagerly reading everything that came to my hand, that I developed the first stages of St. Vitus's dance from lack of exercise. Disillusions quickly followed, as I learned more of the world. At this time I made my living as a newsboy, selling papers in the streets; and from then on until I was sixteen I had a thousand and one different occupations—work and school, school and work—and so it ran.

Then the adventurelust was strong within me, and I left home. I didn't run, I just left—went out in the bay, and joined the oyster pirates. The days of the oyster pirates are now past, and if I had got my dues for piracy, I would have been given five hundred years in prison. Later, I shipped as a sailor on a schooner, and also took a turn at salmon fishing. Oddly enough, my next occupation was on a fish patrol, where I was entrusted with the arrest of any violators of the fishing laws. Numbers of the lawless Chinese, Greeks, and Italians were at that time engaged in illegal fishing, and many a patrolman paid his life for his interference. My only weapon on duty was a steel table-fork, but I felt fearless and a man when I climbed over the side of a boat to arrest some marauder.

Subsequently I shipped before the mast and sailed for the Japanese coast on a seal-hunting expedition, later going on to the Bering Sea. After sealing for seven months I came back to California and took odd jobs at coal shoveling and longshoring, and also in a jute factory, when I worked from six in the morning till seven at night. I had planned to join the same lot for another

sealing trip the following year, but somehow I missed them. They
sailed away on the *Mary Thomas,* which was lost with all hands.

In my fitful schooldays I had written the usual compositions,
which had been praised in the usual way, and while working in
the jute mills I still made an occasional try. The factory occupied
thirteen hours of my days and, being young and husky, I wanted
a little time for myself, so there was little left for composition. The
San Francisco Call offered a prize for a descriptive article. My mother urged me to try for it, and I did, taking for my subject,
"Typhoon off the Coast of Japan." Very tired and sleepy, and
knowing I had to be up at half-past five, I began the article at midnight and worked straight on until I had written two thousand
words, the limit of the article, but with my idea only half worked
out. The next night, under the same conditions, I continued,
adding another two thousand words before I had finished, and
then the third night I spent in cutting out the excess, so as to bring
the article within the conditions of the contest. The first prize
came to me, and the second and third went to students of the
Stanford and Berkeley Universities.

My success in the *San Francisco Call* competition seriously
turned my thoughts to writing, but my blood was still too hot for
a settled routine, so I practically deferred literature, beyond writing a little gush for the *Call,* which that journal promptly rejected.

I tramped all through the United States, from California to
Boston, and up and down, returning to the Pacific Coast by way
of Canada, where I got into jail and served a term for vagrancy,
and the whole tramping experience made me become a Socialist.
Previously, I had been impressed by the dignity of labor, and,
without having read Carlyle or Kipling, I had formulated a Gospel
of work which put theirs in the shade. Work was everything. It was
sanctification and salvation. The pride I took in a hard day's work
well done would be inconceivable to you. I was as faithful a wage-
slave as ever a capitalist exploited. In short, my joyous individual-
ism was dominated by the orthodox bourgeois ethics. I had
fought my way from the open West, where the men bulked big

and the job hunted the man, to the congested labor centers of the eastern states, where men were small potatoes and hunted the job for all they were worth, and I found myself looking upon life from a new and totally different angle. I saw the workers in the shambles at the bottom of the Social Pit. I swore I would never again do a hard day's work with my body except where I was absolutely compelled to, and I have been busy ever since running away from hard bodily labor.

In my nineteenth year, I returned to Oakland and started at the High School, which ran the usual school magazine. This publication was a weekly—no, I guess a monthly—one, and I wrote stories for it: very little imaginary, just recitals of my sea and tramping experiences. I remained there a year, doing janitor work as a means of livelihood, and leaving eventually because the strain was more than I could bear. At this time, my socialistic utterances had attracted considerable attention, and I was known as the "Boy Socialist," a distinction that brought about my arrest for street-talking. After leaving the High School, in three months' cramming by myself, I took the three years' work for that time and entered the University of California. I hated to give up the hope of university education, and worked in a laundry and with my pay to help me keep on. This was the only time I worked because I loved it, but the task was too much, and when halfway through my freshman year I had to quit.

I worked away ironing shirts and other things in the laundry, and wrote in all my spare time. I tried to keep on at both, but often fell asleep with the pen in my hand. Then I left the laundry and wrote all the time, and lived and dreamed again. After three months' trial I gave up writing, having decided that I was a failure, and left for the Klondike to prospect for gold. At the end of the year, owing to an outbreak of scurvy, I was compelled to come out, and on a homeward journey of 1,900 miles in an open boat made the only notes of the trip. It was in the Klondike I found myself. There nobody talks. Everybody thinks. You get your true perspective. I got mine.

While I was in the Klondike my father died, and the burden of the family fell on my shoulders. Times were bad in California, and I could get no work. While trying for it, I wrote "Down the River," which was rejected. During the wait for this rejection, I wrote a twenty-thousand-word serial for a news company, which was also rejected. Pending each rejection, I still kept on writing fresh stuff. I did not know what an editor looked like. I did not know a soul who had ever published anything. Finally a story was accepted by a California magazine, for which I received five dollars. Soon afterward *The Black Cat* offered me forty dollars for a story. Then things took a turn, and I shall probably not have to shovel coal for a living for some time to come, although I have done it, and could do it again.

My first book was published in 1900. I could have made a good deal at newspaper work; but I had sufficient sense to refuse to be a slave to that man-killing machine, for such I hold a newspaper to be to a young man in his framing period. Not until I was well on my feet as a magazine writer did I do much work for a newspaper. I am a believer in regular work, and never wait for an inspiration. Temperamentally, I am not only careless and irregular, but melancholy; still I have fought both down. The discipline I had as a sailor had full effect on me. Perhaps my old sea days are also responsible for the regularity and limitations of my sleep. Five and a half hours is the precise average I allow myself, and no circumstance has yet arisen in my life that can keep me awake when the time comes to "turn in."

I am very fond of sport, and delight in boxing, fencing, swimming, riding, yachting, and even kite-flying. Although primarily of the city, I like to be near it rather than in it. The country, though, is the best, the only natural life.

from The Sea-Wolf

The first few pages of one of London's successful novels of 1904 introduce the story's intellectual, prissy narrator, Humphrey Van Weyden, who becomes the foil of the unforgettable Wolf Larsen. These pages also illustrate the vigorous prose style that characterized so much of the author's writing. London, who had been overboard in the San Francisco Bay more than once, well knew the effects of its chill waters and swift currents. As a journeyman sailor, he was also familiar with the ferry accidents that occasionally occurred on those rough waters. This scene benefits from his wide experience.

I scarcely know where to begin, though I sometimes facetiously place the cause of it all to Charley Furuseth's credit. He kept a summer cottage in Mill Valley, under the shadow of Mount Tamalpais, and never occupied it except when he loafed through the winter months and read Nietzsche and Schopenhauer to rest his brain. When summer came on, he elected to sweat out a hot and dusty existence in the city and to toil incessantly. Had it not been my custom to run up to see him every Saturday afternoon and to stop over till Monday morning, this particular January Monday morning would not have found me afloat on San Francisco Bay.

Not but that I was afloat in a safe craft, for the *Martinez* was a new ferry-steamer, making her fourth or fifth trip on the run between Sausalito and San Francisco. The danger lay in the heavy fog which blanketed the bay, and of which, as a landsman, I had little apprehension. In fact, I remember the placid exaltation with which I took up my position on the forward upper deck, directly beneath the pilot-house, and allowed the mystery of the fog to lay hold of my imagination. A fresh breeze was blowing, and for a time I was alone in the moist obscurity—yet not alone, for I was dimly conscious of the presence of the pilot, and of what I took to be the captain, in the glass house above my head.

I remember thinking how comfortable it was, this division of labor which made it unnecessary for me to study fogs, winds, tides, and navigation, in order to visit my friend who lived across an arm of the sea. It was good that men should be specialists, I mused. The peculiar knowledge of the pilot and captain sufficed for many thousands of people who knew no more of the sea and navigation than I knew. On the other hand, instead of having to devote my energy to the learning of a multitude of things, I concentrated it upon a few particular things, such as, for instance, the analysis of Poe's place in American literature—an essay of mine, by the way, in the current *Atlantic*. Coming aboard, as I passed through the cabin, I had noticed with greedy eyes a stout gentleman reading the *Atlantic*, which was open at my very essay. And there it was again, the division of labor, the special knowledge of the pilot and captain which permitted the stout gentleman to read my special knowledge on Poe while they carried him safely from Sausalito to San Francisco.

A red-faced man, slamming the cabin door behind him and stumping out on the deck, interrupted my reflections, though I made a mental note of the topic for use in a projected essay which I had thought of calling "The Necessity for Freedom: A Plea for the Artist." The red-faced man shot a glance up at the pilot-house, gazed around at the fog, stumped across the deck and back (he evidently had artificial legs), and stood still by my side, legs wide apart, and with an expression of keen enjoyment on his face. I was not wrong when I decided that his days had been spent on the sea.

"It's nasty weather like this here that turns heads gray before their time," he said, with a nod toward the pilot-house.

"I had not thought there was any particular strain," I answered. "It seems as simple as A, B, C. They know the direction by compass, the distance, and the speed. I should not call it any-thing more than mathematical certainty."

"Strain!" he snorted. "Simple as A, B, C! Mathematical cer-tainty!"

He seemed to brace himself up and lean backward against the air as he stared at me. "How about this here tide that's rushin' out through the Golden Gate?" he demanded, or bellowed, rather. "How fast is she ebbin'? What's the drift, eh? Listen to that, will you? A bellbuoy, and we're a-top of it! See'em alterin' the course!"

From out of the fog came the mournful tolling of a bell, and I could see the pilot turning the wheel with great rapidity. The bell, which had seemed straight ahead, was now sounding from the side. Our own whistle was blowing hoarsely, and from time to time the sound of other whistles came to us from out of the fog.

"That's a ferry-boat of some sort," the newcomer said, indi-cating a whistle off to the right. "And there! D'ye hear that? Blown by mouth. Some scow schooner, most likely. Better watch out, Mr. Schooner-man. Ah, I thought so. Now hell's a-poppin' for somebody!"

The unseen ferry-boat was blowing blast after blast, and the mouth-blown horn was tooting in terror-stricken fashion.

"And now they're payin' their respects to each other and tryin' to get clear," the red-faced man went on, as the hurried whistling ceased.

His face was shining, his eyes flashing with excitement, as he translated into articulate language the speech of the horns and sirens. "That's a steam siren a-goin' it over there to the left. And you hear that fellow with a frog in his throat—a steam schooner as near as I can judge, crawlin' in from the Heads against the tide."

A shrill little whistle, piping as if gone mad, came from directly ahead and from very near at hand. Gongs sounded on the *Martinez.* Our paddle-wheels stopped, their pulsing beat died away, and then they started again. The shrill little whistle, like the chirping of a cricket amid the cries of great beasts, shot through the fog from more to the side and swiftly grew faint and fainter. I looked to my companion for enlightenment.

"One of them dare-devil launches," he said. "I almost wish we'd sunk him, the little rip! They're the cause of more trouble. And what good are they? Any jackass gets aboard one and runs it from hell to breakfast, blowin' his whistle to beat the band and tellin' the rest of the world to look out for him, because he's comin' and can't look out for himself! Because he's comin'! And you've got to look out, too! Right of way! Common decency! They don't know the meanin' of it!"

I felt quite amused at his unwarranted choler, and while he stumped indignantly up and down I fell to dwelling upon the romance of the fog. And romantic it certainly was—the fog, like the gray shadow of infinite mystery, brooding over the whirling speck of earth; and men, mere motes of light and sparkle, cursed with an insane relish for work, riding their steeds of wood and steel through the heart of the mystery, groping their way blindly through the Unseen, and clamoring and clanging in confident speech the while their hearts are heavy with incertitude and fear.

The voice of my companion brought me back to myself with a laugh. I too had been groping and floundering, the while I thought I rode clear-eyed through the mystery.

"Hello; somebody comin' our way," he was saying. "And d'ye hear that? He's comin' fast. Walking right along. Guess he don't hear us yet. Wind's in wrong direction."

The fresh breeze was blowing right down upon us, and I could hear the whistle plainly, off to one side and a little ahead.

"Ferry-boat?" I asked.

He nodded, then added, "Or he wouldn't be keepin' up such a clip." He gave a short chuckle. "They're gettin' anxious up there."

I glanced up. The captain had thrust his head and shoulders out of the pilot-house, and was staring intently into the fog as though by sheer force of will he could penetrate it. His face was anxious, as was the face of my companion, who had stumped over to the rail and was gazing with a like intentness in the direction of the invisible danger.

Then everything happened, and with inconceivable rapidity. The fog seemed to break away as though split by a wedge, and the bow of a steamboat emerged, trailing fog-wreaths on either side like seaweed on the snout of Leviathan. I could see the pilot-house and a white-bearded man leaning partly out of it, on his elbows. He was clad in a blue uniform, and I remember noting how trim and quiet he was. His quietness, under the circumstances, was terrible. He accepted Destiny, marched hand in hand with it, and coolly measured the stroke. As he leaned there, he ran a calm and speculative eye over us, as though to determine the precise point of the collision, and took no notice whatever when our pilot, white with rage, shouted, "Now you've done it!"

On looking back, I realize that the remark was too obvious to make rejoinder necessary.

"Grab hold of something and hang on," the red-faced man said to me. All his bluster had gone, and he seemed to have caught the contagion of preternatural calm. "And listen to the women scream," he said grimly—almost bitterly, I thought, as though he had been through the experience before.

The vessels came together before I could follow his advice. We must have been struck squarely amidships, for I saw nothing, the strange steamboat having passed beyond my line of vision. The *Martinez* heeled over, sharply, and there was a crashing and rending of timber. I was thrown flat on the wet deck, and before I could scramble to my feet I heard the scream of the women. This it was, I am certain—the most indescribable of blood-curdling sounds—that threw me into a panic. I remembered the life-preservers stored in the cabin, but was met at the door and swept backward by a wild rush of men and women. What happened in the next few minutes I do not recollect, though I have a clear remembrance of pulling down life-preservers from the overhead racks, while the red-faced man fastened them about the bodies of a hysterical group of women. This memory is as distinct and sharp as that of any picture I have seen. It is a picture, and I can see it now—the jagged edges of the hole in the side of the cabin, through which the gray fog swirled and eddied; the empty uphol-stered seats, littered with all the evidences of sudden flight, such as packages, hand satchels, umbrellas, and wraps; the stout gen-tleman who had been reading my essay, encased in cork and can-vas, the magazine still in his hand, and asking me with monot-onous insistence if I thought there was any danger; the red-faced man, stumping gallantly around on his artificial legs and buck-ling life-preservers on all comers; and finally, the screaming bed-lam of women.

This it was, the screaming of the women, that most tried my nerves. It must have tried, too, the nerves of the red-faced man, for I have another picture which will never fade from my mind. The stout gentleman is stuffing the magazine into his overcoat pocket and looking on curiously. A tangled mass of women, with drawn, white faces and open mouths, is shrieking like a chorus of lost souls; and the red-faced man, his face now purplish with wrath, and with arms extended overhead as in the act of hurling thun-derbolts, is shouting, "Shut up! Oh, shut up!"

I remember the scene impelled me to sudden laughter, and in the next instant I realized I was becoming hysterical myself; for these were women of my own kind, like my mother and sisters, with the fear of death upon them and unwilling to die. And I remember that the sounds they made reminded me of the squeal-ing of pigs under the knife of the butcher, and I was struck with horror at the vividness of the analogy. These women, capable of the most sublime emotions, of the tenderest sympathies, were open-mouthed and screaming. They wanted to live, they were helpless, like rats in a trap, and they screamed.

The horror of it drove me out on deck. I was feeling sick and squeamish, and sat down on a bench. In a hazy way I saw and heard men rushing and shouting as they strove to lower the boats. It was just as I had read descriptions of such scenes in books. The tackles jammed. Nothing worked. One boat lowered away with the plugs out, filled with women and children and then with water, and capsized. Another boat had been lowered by one end, and still hung in the tackle by the other end, where it had been abandoned. Nothing was to be seen of the strange steamboat which had caused the disaster, though I heard men saying that she would undoubtedly send boats to our assistance.

I descended to the lower deck. The *Martinez* was sinking fast, for the water was very near. Numbers of the passengers were leaping overboard. Others, in the water, were clamoring to be taken aboard again. No one heeded them. A cry arose that we were sinking. I was seized by the consequent panic, and went over the side in a surge of bodies. How I went over I do not know, though I did know, and instantly, why those in the water were so desirous of getting back on the steamer. The water was cold—so cold that it was painful. The pang, as I plunged into it, was as quick and sharp as that of fire. It bit to the marrow. It was like the grip of death. I gasped with the anguish and shock of it, filling my lungs before the life-preserver popped me to the surface. The taste of the salt was strong in my mouth, and I was strangling with the acrid stuff in my throat and lungs.

But it was the cold that was most distressing. I felt that I could survive but a few minutes. People were struggling and floundering in the water about me. I could hear them crying out to one another. And I heard, also, the sound of oars. Evidently the strange steamboat had lowered its boats. As the time went by I marveled that I was still alive. I had no sensation whatever in my lower limbs, while a chilling numbness was wrapping about my heart and creeping into it. Small waves, with spiteful foaming crests, continually broke over me and into my mouth, sending me off into more strangling paroxysms.

The noises grew indistinct, though I heard a final and despairing chorus of screams in the distance and knew that the *Martinez* had gone down. Later—how much later I have no knowledge—I came to myself with a start of fear. I was alone. I could hear no calls or cries—only the sound of the waves, made weirdly hollow and reverberant by the fog. A panic in a crowd, which partakes of a sort of community of interest, is not so terrible as a panic when one is by oneself; and such a panic I now suffered. Whither was I drifting? The red-faced man had said that the tide was ebbing through the Golden Gate. Was I, then, being carried out to sea? And the life-preserver in which I floated? Was it not liable to go to pieces at any moment? I had heard of such things being made of paper and hollow rushes which quickly became saturated and lost all buoyancy. And I could not swim a stroke. And I was alone, floating, apparently, in the midst of a gray primordial vastness. I confess that a madness seized me, that I shrieked aloud as the women had shrieked, and beat the water with my numb hands.

How long this lasted I have no conception, for a blankness intervened, of which I remember no more than one remembers of troubled and painful sleep. When I aroused, it was as after centuries of time; and I saw, almost above me and emerging from the fog, the bow of a vessel, and three triangular sails, each shrewdly lapping the other and filled with wind. Where the bow cut the water there was a great foaming and gurgling, and I seemed directly in its path. I tried to cry out, but was too exhausted. The bow plunged down, just missing me and sending a swash of water clear over my head. Then the long, black side of the vessel began slipping past, so near that I could have touched it with my hands. I tried to reach it, in a mad resolve to claw into the wood with my nails, but my arms were heavy and lifeless. Again I strove to call out, but made no sound.

The stern of the vessel shot by, dropping, as it did so, into a hollow between the waves; and I caught a glimpse of a man standing at the wheel, and of another man who seemed to be doing little else than smoke a cigar. I saw the smoke issuing from his lips as he slowly turned his head and glanced out over the water in my direction. It was a careless, unpremeditated glance, one of those haphazard things men do when they have no immediate call to do anything in particular, but act because they are alive and must do something.

But life and death were in that glance. I could see the vessel being swallowed up in the fog; I saw the back of the man at the wheel, and the head of the other man turning, slowly turning, as his gaze struck the water and casually lifted along it toward me. His face wore an absent expression, as of deep thought, and I became afraid that if his eyes did light upon me he would nevertheless not see me. But his eyes did light upon me, and looked squarely into mine; and he did see me, for he sprang to the wheel, thrusting the other man aside, and whirled it round and round, hand over hand, at the same time shouting orders of some sort. This vessel seemed to go off at a tangent to its former course and leapt almost instantly from view into the fog.

I felt myself slipping into unconsciousness, and tried with all the power of my will to fight above the suffocating blankness and darkness that was rising around me. A little later I heard the stroke of oars, growing nearer and nearer, and the calls of a man. When he was very near I heard him crying, in vexed fashion, "Why in hell don't you sing out?" This meant me, I thought, and then the blankness and darkness rose over me.

I seemed swinging in a mighty rhythm through orbit vastness. Sparkling points of light spluttered and shot past me. They were stars, I knew, and flaring comets, that peopled my flight among the suns. As I reached the limit of my swing and prepared to rush back on the counter swing, a great gong struck and thundered. For an immeasurable period, lapped in the rippling of placid centuries, I enjoyed and pondered my tremendous flight.

But a change came over the face of the dream, for a dream I told myself it must be. My rhythm grew shorter and shorter. I was jerked from swing to counter swing with irritating haste. I could scarcely catch my breath, so fiercely was I impelled through the

heavens. The gong thundered more frequently and more furious-
ly. I grew to await it with a nameless dread. Then it seemed as
though I were being dragged over rasping sands, white and hot in
the sun. This gave place to a sense of intolerable anguish. My skin
was scorching in the torment of fire. The gong clanged and
knelled. The sparkling points of light flashed past me in an interminable stream, as though the whole sidereal system were dropping into the void. I gasped, caught my breath painfully, and
opened my eyes. Two men were kneeling beside me, working over
me. My mighty rhythm was the lift and forward plunge of a ship
on the sea. The terrific gong was a frying-pan, hanging on the wall,
that rattled and clattered with each leap of the ship. The rasping,
scorching sands were a man's hard hands chafing my naked chest.
I squirmed under the pain of it, and half lifted my head. My chest
was raw and red, and I could see tiny blood globules starting
through the torn and inflamed cuticle.

"That'll do, Yonson," one of the men said. "Carn't yer see
you've bloomin' well rubbed all the gent's skin orf?"

The man addressed as Yonson, a man of the heavy
Scandinavian type, ceased chafing me, and arose awkwardly to his
feet. The man who had spoken to him was clearly a Cockney, with
the clean lines and weakly pretty, almost effeminate, face of the
man who has absorbed the sound of Bow Bells with his mother's
milk. A draggled muslin cap on his head and a dirty gunny-sack
about his slim hips proclaimed him cook of the decidedly dirty
ship's galley in which I found myself.

"An' 'ow yer feelin' now, sir?" he asked, with the subservient
smirk which comes only of generations of tip-seeking ancestors.

For reply, I twisted weakly into a sitting posture, and was
helped by Yonson to my feet. The rattle and bang of the frying-pan
was grating horribly on my nerves. I could not collect my
thoughts. Clutching the woodwork of the galley for support—and
I confess the grease with which it was scummed put my teeth on
edge—I reached across a hot cooking-range to the offending uten-
sil, unhooked it, and wedged it securely into the coal-box.

The cook grinned at my exhibition of nerves, and thrust into my hand a steaming mug with an "'Ere, this'll do yer good." It was a nauseous mess,—ship's coffee,—but the heat of it was revivifying. Between gulps of the molten stuff I glanced down at my raw and bleeding chest and turned to the Scandinavian.

"Thank you, Mr. Yonson," I said, "but don't you think your measures were rather heroic?"

It was because he understood the reproof of my action, rather than of my words, that he held up his palm for inspection. It was remarkably calloused. I passed my hand over the horny projections, and my teeth went on edge once more from the horrible rasping sensation produced.

"My name is Johnson, not Yonson," he said, in very good, though slow, English, with no more than a shade of accent to it.

There was mild protest in his pale blue eyes, and withal a timid frankness and manliness that quite won me to him.

"Thank you, Mr. Johnson," I corrected, and reached out my hand for his.

He hesitated, awkward and bashful, shifted his weight from one leg to the other, then blunderingly gripped my hand in a hearty shake.

"Have you any dry clothes I may put on?" I asked the cook.

"Yes, sir," he answered, with cheerful alacrity. "I'll run down an' tyke a look over my kit, if you've no objections, sir, to wearin' my things."

He dived out of the galley door, or glided rather, with a swiftness and smoothness of gait that struck me as being not so much cat-like as oily. In fact, this oiliness, or greasiness, as I was later to learn, was probably the most salient expression of his personality.

"And where am I?" I asked Johnson, whom I took, and rightly, to be one of the sailors. "What vessel is this, and where is she bound?"

"Off the Farallones, heading about sou'west," he answered, slowly and methodically, as though groping for his best English, and rigidly observing the order of my queries. "The schooner *Ghost*, bound seal-hunting to Japan."

"And who is the captain? I must see him as soon as I am dressed."

Johnson looked puzzled and embarrassed. He hesitated while he groped in his vocabulary and framed a complete answer. "The cap'n is Wolf Larsen, or so men call him. I never heard his other name. But you better speak soft with him. He is mad this morning. The mate—"

But he did not finish. The cook had glided in.

"Better sling yer 'ook out of 'ere, Yonson," he said. "The old man'll be wantin' yer on deck, an' this ayn't no d'y to fall foul of 'im."

Johnson turned obediently to the door, at the same time, over the cook's shoulder, favoring me with an amazingly solemn and portentous wink, as though to emphasize his interrupted remark and the need for me to be softspoken with the captain.

Hanging over the cook's arm was a loose and crumpled array of evil-looking and sour-smelling garments.

"They was put aw'y wet, sir," he vouchsafed explanation. "But you'll 'ave to make them do till I dry yours out by the fire."

Clinging to the woodwork, staggering with the roll of the ship, and aided by the cook, I managed to slip into a rough woollen undershirt. On the instant my flesh was creeping and crawling from the harsh contact. He noticed my involuntary twitching and grimacing, and smirked:

"I only 'ope yer don't ever 'ave to get used to such as that in this life, 'cos you've got a bloomin' soft skin, that you 'ave, more like a lydy's than any I know of. I was bloomin' well sure you was a gentleman as soon as I set eyes on yer."

I had taken a dislike to him at first, and as he helped to dress me this dislike increased. There was something repulsive about his touch. I shrank from his hand; my flesh revolted. And between this and the smells arising from various pots boiling and bubbling on the galley fire, I was in haste to get out into the fresh air.

Further, there was the need of seeing the captain about what arrangements could be made for getting me ashore.

A cheap cotton shirt, with frayed collar and a bosom discolored with what I took to be ancient blood-stains, was put on me amid a running and apologetic fire of comment. A pair of workman's brogans encased my feet, and for trousers I was furnished with a pair of pale blue, washed-out overalls, one leg of which was fully ten inches shorter than the other. The abbreviated leg looked as though the devil had there clutched for the Cockney's soul and missed the shadow for the substance.

"And whom have I to thank for this kindness?" I asked, when I stood completely arrayed, a tiny boy's cap on my head, and for coat a dirty, striped cotton jacket which ended at the small of my back and the sleeves of which reached just below my elbows.

The cook drew himself up in a smugly humble fashion, a deprecating smirk on his face. Out of my experience with stewards on the Atlantic liners at the end of the voyage, I could have sworn he was waiting for his tip. From my fuller knowledge of the creature I now know that the posture was unconscious. A hereditary servility, no doubt, was responsible.

"Mugridge, sir," he fawned, his effeminate features running into a greasy smile. "Thomas Mugridge, sir, an' at yer service."

"All right, Thomas," I said. "I shall not forget you—when my clothes are dry."

A soft light suffused his face and his eyes glistened, as though somewhere in the deeps of his being his ancestors had quickened and stirred with dim memories of tips received in former lives.

"Thank you, sir," he said, very gratefully and very humbly indeed.

Precisely in the way that the door slid back, he slid aside, and I stepped out on deck. I was still weak from my prolonged immersion. A puff of wind caught me, and I staggered across the moving deck to a corner of the cabin, to which I clung for support. The schooner, heeled over far out from the perpendicular, was bowing

and plunging into the long Pacific roll. If she were heading southwest as Johnson had said, the wind, then, I calculated, was blowing
nearly from the south. The fog was gone, and in its place the sun
sparkled crisply on the surface of the water. I turned to the east,
where I knew California must lie, but could see nothing save low-
lying fog-banks—the same fog, doubtless, that had brought about
the disaster to the *Martinez* and placed me in my present situation.
To the north, and not far away, a group of naked rocks thrust
above the sea, on one of which I could distinguish a lighthouse.
In the southwest, and almost in our course, I saw the pyramidal
loom of some vessel's sails.

Having completed my survey of the horizon, I turned to my
more immediate surroundings. My first thought was that a man
who had come through a collision and rubbed shoulders with
death merited more attention than I received. Beyond a sailor at
the wheel who stared curiously across the top of the cabin, I
attracted no notice whatever.

Everybody seemed interested in what was going on amidships. There, on a hatch, a large man was lying on his back. He was
fully clothed, though his shirt was ripped open in front. Nothing
was to be seen of his chest, however, for it was covered with a mass
of black hair, in appearance like the furry coat of a dog. His face
and neck were hidden beneath a black beard, intershot with gray,
which would have been stiff and bushy had it not been limp and
draggled and dripping with water. His eyes were closed, and he
was apparently unconscious; but his mouth was wide open, his
breast heaving as though from suffocation as he labored noisily
for breath. A sailor, from time to time and quite methodically, as
a matter of routine, dropped a canvas bucket into the ocean at the
end of a rope, hauled it in hand under hand, and sluiced its contents over the prostrate man.

Pacing back and forth the length of the hatchway, and savagely chewing the end of a cigar, was the man whose casual glance
had rescued me from the sea. His height was probably five feet ten
inches, or ten and a half; but my first impression, or feel of the

man, was not of this, but of his strength. And yet, while he was of massive build, with broad shoulders and deep chest, I could not characterize his strength as massive. It was what might be termed a sinewy, knotty strength, of the kind we ascribe to lean and wiry men, but which, in him, because of his heavy build, partook more of the enlarged gorilla order. Not that in appearance he seemed in the least gorillalike. What I am striving to express is this strength itself, more as a thing apart from his physical semblance. It was a strength we are wont to associate with things primitive, with wild animals, and the creatures we imagine our tree-dwelling proto-types to have been—a strength savage, ferocious, alive in itself, the essence of life in that it is the potency of motion, the elemental stuff itself out of which the many forms of life have been molded; in short, that which writhes in the body of a snake when the head is cut off, and the snake, as a snake, is dead, or which lingers in a shapeless lump of turtle-meat and recoils and quivers from the prod of a finger.

Such was the impression of strength I gathered from this man who paced up and down. He was firmly planted on his legs; his feet struck the deck squarely and with surety; every movement of a muscle, from the heave of the shoulders to the tightening of the lips about the cigar, was decisive, and seemed to come out of a strength that was excessive and overwhelming. In fact, though this strength pervaded every action of his, it seemed but the adver-tisement of a greater strength that lurked within, that lay dormant and no more than stirred from time to time, but which might arouse, at any moment, terrible and compelling, like the rage of a lion or the wrath of a storm.

The cook stuck his head out of the galley door and grinned encouragingly at me, at the same time jerking his thumb in the direction of the man who paced up and down by the hatchway. Thus I was given to understand that he was the captain, the "Old Man," in the cook's vernacular, the individual whom I must inter-view and put to the trouble of somehow getting me ashore. I had half started forward, to get over with what I was certain would be a stormy five minutes, when a more violent suffocating paroxysm seized the unfortunate person who was lying on his back. He wrenched and writhed about convulsively. The chin, with the damp black beard, pointed higher in the air as the back muscles stiffened and the chest swelled in an unconscious and instinctive effort to get more air. Under the whiskers, and all unseen, I knew that the skin was taking on a purplish hue.

The captain, or Wolf Larsen, as men called him, ceased pacing and gazed down at the dying man. So fierce had this final struggle become that the sailor paused in the act of flinging more water over him and stared curiously, the canvas bucket partly tilted and dripping its contents to the deck. The dying man beat a tattoo on the hatch with his heels, straightened out his legs, and stiffened in one great tense effort, and rolled his head from side to side. Then the muscles relaxed, the head stopped rolling, and a sigh, as of profound relief, floated upward from his lips. The jaw dropped, the upper lip lifted, and two rows of tobacco discolored teeth appeared. It seemed as though his features had frozen into a diabolical grin at the world he had left and outwitted.

Then a most surprising thing occurred. The captain broke loose upon the dead man like a thunderclap. Oaths rolled from his lips in a continuous stream. And they were not namby-pamby oaths, or mere expressions of indecency. Each word was a blasphemy, and there were many words. They crisped and crackled like electric sparks. I had never heard anything like it in my life, nor could I have conceived it possible. With a turn for literary expression myself, and a penchant for forcible figures and phrases, I appreciated, as no other listener, I dare say, the peculiar vividness and strength and absolute blasphemy of his metaphors. The cause of it all, as near as I could make out, was that the man, who was a mate, had gone on a debauch before leaving San Francisco, and then had the poor taste to die at the beginning of the voyage and leave Wolf Larsen short-handed.

It should be unnecessary to state, at least to my friends, that I was shocked. Oaths and vile language of any sort had always been repellent to me. I felt a wilting sensation, a sinking at the heart, and, I might just as well say, a giddiness. To me, death had always been invested with solemnity and dignity. It had been peaceful in its occurrence, sacred in its ceremonial. But death in its more sordid and terrible aspects was a thing with which I had been unacquainted till now. As I say, while I appreciated the power of the terrific denunciation that swept out of Wolf Larsen's mouth, I was inexpressibly shocked. The scorching torrent was enough to wither the face of the corpse. I should not have been surprised if the wet black beard had frizzled and curled and flared up in smoke and flame. But the dead man was unconcerned. He continued to grin with a sardonic humor, with a cynical mockery and defiance. He was master of the situation.

from The Scarlet Plague

This 1915 novel's narrator, James Howard Smith, is a professor of English at the University of California and one of the few survivors of a plague that devastates civilization in 2013. In this excerpt he recounts the desperation of those trying to survive in the chemistry building on the university's campus. As the plot progresses, however, educated and refined people turn out to be too soft to endure. Instead, atavism reigns: "a large, dark hairy man, heavy-jawed, slant-browed, fierce-eyed." This story, inspired in part by Edgar Allan Poe's "The Masque of the Red Death," nevertheless ends with nature's vigor intact even as humans fade.

"I was a young man when the Plague came—twenty-seven years old; and I lived on the other side of San Francisco Bay, in Berkeley. You remember those great stone houses, Edwin, when we came down the hills from Contra Costa? That was where I lived, in those stone houses. I was a professor of English literature."

Much of this was over the heads of the boys, but they strove to comprehend dimly this tale of the past.

"What was them stone houses for?" Hare-Lip queried.

"You remember when your dad taught you to swim?" The boy nodded. "Well, in the University of California—that is the name we had for the houses—we taught young men and women how to think, just as I have taught you now, by sand and pebbles and shells, to know how many people lived in those days. There was very much to teach. The young men and women we taught were called students. We had large rooms in which we taught. I talked to them, forty or fifty at a time, just as I am talking to you

26

now. I told them about the books other men had written before their time, and even, sometimes, in their time—"

"Was that all you did?—just talk, talk, talk?" Hoo-Hoo demanded. "Who hunted your meat for you? and milked the goats? and caught the fish?"

"A sensible question, Hoo-Hoo, a sensible question. As I have told you, in those days food-getting was easy. We were very wise. A few men got the food for many men. The other men did other things. As you say, I talked. I talked all the time, and for this food was given me—much food, fine food, beautiful food, food that I have not tasted in sixty years and shall never taste again. I sometimes think the most wonderful achievement of our tremendous civilization was food—its inconceivable abundance, its infinite variety, its marvellous delicacy. O my grandsons, life was life in those days, when we had such wonderful things to eat."

This was beyond the boys, and they let it slip by, words and thoughts, as a mere senile wandering in the narrative.

"Our food-getters were called *freemen*. This was a joke. We of the ruling classes owned all the land, all the machines, everything. These food-getters were our slaves. We took almost all the food they got, and left them a little so that they might eat, and work, and get us more food—"

"I'd have gone into the forest and got food for myself," Hare-Lip announced, "and if any man tried to take it away from me, I'd have killed him."

The old man laughed.

"Did I not tell you that we of the ruling class owned all the land, all the forest, everything? Any food-getter who would not get food for us, him we punished or compelled to starve to death. And very few did that. They preferred to get food for us, and make clothes for us, and prepare and administer to us a thousand—a musselshell, Hoo-Hoo—a thousand satisfactions and delights. And I was Professor Smith in those days—Professor James Howard Smith. And my lecture courses were very popular—that is, very many of the young men and women liked to hear me talk about the books other men had written.

"And I was very happy, and I had beautiful things to eat. And my hands were soft, because I did no work with them, and my body was clean all over and dressed in the softest garments—" He surveyed his mangy goat-skin with disgust. "We did not wear such things in those days. Even the slaves had better garments. And we were most clean. We washed our faces and hands often every day. You boys never wash unless you fall into the water or go in swimming."

"Neither do you, Granser," Hoo-Hoo retorted.

"I know, I know. I am a filthy old man. But times have changed. Nobody washes these days, and there are no conveniences. It is sixty years since I have seen a piece of soap. You do not know what soap is, and I shall not tell you, for I am telling the story of the Scarlet Death. You know what sickness is. We called it a disease. Very many of the diseases came from what we called germs. Remember that word—germs...

"The Scarlet Death broke out in San Francisco. The first death came on a Monday morning. By Thursday they were dying like flies in Oakland and San Francisco. They died everywhere—in their beds, at their work, walking along the street. It was on Tuesday that I saw my first death—Miss Collbran, one of my students, sitting right there before my eyes, in my lecture-room. I noticed her face while I was talking. It had suddenly turned scarlet. I ceased speaking and could only look at her, for the first fear of the plague was already on all of us and we knew that it had come. The young women screamed and ran out of the room. So did the young men run out, all but two. Miss Collbran's convulsions were very mild and lasted less than a minute. One of the young men fetched her a glass of water. She drank only a little of it, and cried out:

"'My feet! All sensation has left them.'

"After a minute she said, 'I have no feet. I am unaware that I have any feet. And my knees are cold. I can scarcely feel that I have knees.'

"She lay on the floor, a bundle of notebooks under her head. And we could do nothing. The coldness and the numbness crept up past her hips to her heart, and when it reached her heart she was dead. In fifteen minutes, by the clock—I timed it—she was dead, there, in my own classroom, dead. And she was a very beautiful, strong, healthy young woman. And from the first sign of the plague to her death only fifteen minutes elapsed. That will show you how swift was the Scarlet Death.

"Yet in those few minutes I remained with the dying woman in my classroom, the alarm had spread over the university; and the students, by thousands, all of them, had deserted the lecture-room and laboratories. When I emerged, on my way to make my report to the President of the Faculty, I found the university deserted. Across the campus were several stragglers hurrying for their homes. Two of them were running.

"President Hoag, I found in his office, all alone, looking very old and very gray, with a multitude of wrinkles in his face that I had never seen before. At the sight of me, he pulled himself to his feet and tottered away to the inner office, banging the door after him and locking it. You see, he knew I had been exposed, and he was afraid. He shouted to me through the door to go away. I shall never forget my feelings as I walked down the silent corridors and out across that deserted campus. I was not afraid. I had been exposed, and I looked upon myself as already dead. It was not that, but a feeling of awful depression that impressed me. Everything had stopped. It was like the end of the world to me— my world. I had been born within sight and sound of the university. It had been my predestined career. My father had been a professor there before me, and his father before him. For a century and a half had this university, like a splendid machine, been running steadily on. And now, in an instant, it had stopped. It was like seeing the sacred flame die down on some thrice-sacred altar. I was shocked, unutterably shocked.

"When I arrived home, my housekeeper screamed as I entered, and fled away. And when I rang, I found the housemaid had likewise fled. I investigated. In the kitchen I found the cook on the point of departure. But she screamed, too, and in her haste dropped a suitcase of her personal belongings and ran out of the house and across the grounds, still screaming. I can hear her scream to this day. You see, we did not act in this way when ordinary diseases smote us. We were always calm over such things, and sent for the doctors and nurses who knew just what to do. But this was different. It struck so suddenly, and killed so swiftly, and never missed a stroke. When the scarlet rash appeared on a person's face, that person was marked by death. There was never a known case of a recovery.

"I was alone in my big house. As I have told you often before, in those days we could talk with one another over wires or through the air. The telephone bell rang, and I found my brother talking to me. He told me that he was not coming home for fear of catching the plague from me, and that he had taken our two sisters to stop at Professor Bacon's home. He advised me to remain where I was, and wait to find out whether or not I had caught the plague.

"To all of this I agreed, staying in my house and for the first time in my life attempting to cook. And the plague did not come out on me. By means of the telephone I could talk with whomsoever I pleased and get the news. Also, there were the newspapers, and I ordered all of them to be thrown up to my door so that I could know what was happening with the rest of the world.

"New York City and Chicago were in chaos. And what happened with them was happening in all the large cities. A third of the New York police were dead. Their chief was also dead, likewise the mayor. All law and order had ceased. The bodies were lying in the streets unburied. All railroads and vessels carrying food and such things into the great city had ceased running, and mobs of the hungry poor were pillaging the stores and warehouses. Murder and robbery and drunkenness were everywhere. Already the people had fled from the city by millions—at first the rich, in their private motor-cars and dirigibles, and then the great mass of the population, on foot, carrying the plague with them, themselves starving and pillaging the farmers and all the towns and villages on the way.

"The man who sent this news, the wireless operator, was alone with his instrument on the top of a lofty building. The people remaining in the city—he estimated them at several hundred thousand—had gone mad from fear and drink, and on all sides of him great fires were raging. He was a hero, that man who stayed by his post—an obscure newspaperman, most likely.

"For twenty-four hours, he said, no transatlantic airships had arrived, and no more messages were coming from England. He did state, though, that a message from Berlin—that's in Germany—announced that Hoffmeyer, a bacteriologist of the Metchnikoff School, had discovered the serum for the plague. That was the last word, to this day, that we of America ever received from Europe. If Hoffmeyer discovered the serum, it was too late, or otherwise, long ere this, explorers from Europe would have come looking for us. We can only conclude that what happened in America happened in Europe, and that, at the best, some several score may have survived the Scarlet Death on that whole continent.

"For one day longer the dispatches continued to come from New York. Then they, too, ceased. The man who had sent them, perched in his lofty building, had either died of the plague or been consumed in the great conflagrations he had described as raging around him. And what had occurred in New York had been duplicated in all the other cities. It was the same in San Francisco, and Oakland, and Berkeley. By Thursday the people were dying so rapidly that their corpses could not be handled, and dead bodies lay everywhere. Thursday night the panic outrush for the country began. Imagine, my grandsons, people, thicker than the salmon-run you have seen on the Sacramento river, pouring out of the cities by millions, madly over the country, in vain attempt to escape the ubiquitous death. You see, they carried the germs with them. Even the airships of the rich, fleeing for mountain and desert fastnesses, carried the germs.

"Hundreds of these airships escaped to Hawaii, and not only did they bring the plague with them, but they found the plague already there before them. This we learned, by the dispatches, until all order in San Francisco vanished, and there were no operators left at their posts to receive or send. It was amazing, astounding, this loss of communication with the world. It was exactly as if the world had ceased, been blotted out. For sixty years that world has no longer existed for me. I know there must be such places as New York, Europe, Asia, and Africa; but not one word has been heard of them—not in sixty years. With the coming of the Scarlet Death the world fell apart, absolutely, irretrievably. Ten thousand years of culture and civilization passed in the twinkling of an eye, 'lapsed like foam.'

"I was telling about the airships of the rich. They carried the plague with them and no matter where they fled, they died. I never encountered but one survivor of any of them—Mungerson. He was afterwards a Santa Rosan, and he married my eldest daughter. He came into the tribe eight years after the plague. He was then nineteen years old, and he was compelled to wait twelve years more before he could marry. You see, there were no unmarried women, and some of the older daughters of the Santa Rosans were already bespoken. So he was forced to wait until my Mary had grown to sixteen years. It was his son, Gimp-Leg, who was killed last year by the mountain lion.

"Mungerson was eleven years old at the time of the plague. His father was one of the Industrial Magnates, a very wealthy, powerful man. It was on his airship, the *Condor*, that they were fleeing, with all the family, for the wilds of British Columbia, which is far to the north of here. But there was some accident, and they were wrecked near Mount Shasta. You have heard of that mountain. It is far to the north. The plague broke out amongst them, and this boy of eleven was the only survivor. For eight years he was alone, wandering over a deserted land and looking vainly for his own kind. And at last, travelling south, he picked up with us, the Santa Rosans.

"But I am ahead of my story. When the great exodus from the cities around San Francisco Bay began, and while the telephones were still working, I talked with my brother. I told him this flight from the cities was insanity, that there were no symptoms of the plague in me, and that the thing for us to do was to isolate ourselves and our relatives in some safe place. We decided on the Chemistry Building, at the university, and we planned to lay in a supply of provisions, and by force of arms to prevent any other persons from forcing their presence upon us after we had retired to our refuge.

"All this being arranged, my brother begged me to stay in my own house for at least twenty-four hours more, on the chance of the plague developing in me. To this I agreed, and he promised to come for me next day. We talked on over the details of the provisioning and the defending of the Chemistry Building until the telephone died. It died in the midst of our conversation. That evening there were no electric lights, and I was alone in my house in the darkness. No more newspapers were being printed, so I had no knowledge of what was taking place outside. I heard sounds of rioting and of pistol shots, and from my windows I could see the glare in the sky of some conflagration in the direction of Oakland. It was a night of terror. I did not sleep a wink. A man—why and how I do not know—was killed on the sidewalk in front of the house. I heard the rapid reports of an automatic pistol, and a few minutes later the wounded wretch crawled up to my door, moaning and crying out for help. Arming myself with two automatics, I went to him. By the light of a match I ascertained that while he was dying of the bullet wounds, at the same time the plague was on him. I fled indoors, whence I heard him moan and cry out for half an hour longer.

"In the morning, my brother came to me. I had gathered into a handbag what things of value I purposed taking, but when I saw his face I knew that he would never accompany me to the Chemistry Building. The plague was on him. He intended shaking my hand, but I went back hurriedly before him.

"Look at yourself in the mirror," I commanded.

"He did so, and at sight of his scarlet face, the color deepening as he looked at it, he sank down nervelessly in a chair.

"'My God!' he said. 'I've got it. Don't come near me. I am a dead man.'

"Then the convulsions seized him. He was two hours in dying, and he was conscious to the last, complaining about the coldness and loss of sensation in his feet, his calves, his thighs, until at last it was his heart and he was dead.

"That was the way the Scarlet Death slew. I caught up my handbag and fled. The sights in the streets were terrible. One stumbled on bodies everywhere. Some were not yet dead. And even as you looked, you saw men sink down with the death fastened upon them. There were numerous fires burning in Berkeley, while Oakland and San Francisco were apparently being swept by vast conflagrations. The smoke of the burning filled the heavens, so that the midday was as a gloomy twilight, and, in the shifts of wind, sometimes the sun shone through dimly, a dull red orb. Truly, my grandsons, it was like the last days of the end of the world.

"There were numerous stalled motor cars, showing that the gasoline and the engine supplies of the garages had given out. I remember one such car. A man and a woman lay back dead in the seats, and on the pavement near it were two more women and a child. Strange and terrible sights there were on every hand. People slipped by silently, furtively, like ghosts—white-faced women carrying infants in their arms; fathers leading children by the hand singly, and in couples, and in families—all fleeing out of the city of death. Some carried supplies of food, others blankets and valuables, and there were many who carried nothing.

"There was a grocery store—a place where food was sold. The man to whom it belonged—I knew him well—a quiet, sober, but stupid and obstinate fellow, was defending it. The windows and doors had been broken in, but he, inside, hiding behind a counter, was discharging his pistol at a number of men on the sidewalk who were breaking in. In the entrance were several bodies—of men, I decided, whom he had killed earlier in the day. Even as I looked on from a distance, I saw one of the robbers break the windows of the adjoining store, a place where shoes were sold, and deliberately set fire to it. I did not go to the groceryman's assistance. The time for such acts had already passed. Civilization was crumbling, and it was each for himself.

"I went away hastily, down a cross-street, and at the first corner I saw another tragedy. Two men of the working-class had caught a man and a woman with two children, and were robbing them. I knew the man by sight, though I had never been introduced to him. He was a poet whose verses I had long admired. Yet I did not go to his help, for at the moment I came upon the scene there was a pistol shot, and I saw him sinking to the ground. The woman screamed, and she was felled with a fist-blow by one of the brutes. I cried out threateningly, whereupon they discharged their pistols at me and I ran away around the corner. Here I was blocked by an advancing conflagration. The buildings on both sides were burning, and the street was filled with smoke and flame. From somewhere in that murk came a woman's voice calling shrilly for help. But I did not go to her. A man's heart turned to iron amid such scenes, and one heard all too many appeals for help.

"Returning to the corner, I found the two robbers were gone. The poet and his wife lay dead on the pavement. It was a shocking sight. The two children had vanished—whither I could not tell. And I knew, now, why it was that the fleeing persons I encountered slipped along so furtively and with such white faces. In the midst of our civilization, down in our slums and labor-ghettos, we had bred a race of barbarians, of savages; and now, in the time of our calamity, they turned upon us like the wild beasts they were and destroyed us. And they destroyed themselves as well. They inflamed themselves with strong drink and committed a thousand atrocities, quarreling and killing one another in the general madness. One group of workingmen I saw, of the better sort, who had banded together, and, with their women and children in their midst, the sick and aged in litters and being carried, and with a number of horses pulling a truckload of provisions, they were fighting their way out of the city. They made a fine spectacle as they came down the street through the drifting smoke, though they nearly shot me when I first appeared in their path. As they went by, one of their leaders shouted out to me in apologetic explanation. He said they were killing the robbers and looters on sight, and that they had thus banded together as the only means by which to escape the prowlers.

"It was here that I saw for the first time what I was soon to see so often. One of the marching men had suddenly shown the unmistakable mark of the plague. Immediately those about him drew away, and he, without a remonstrance, stepped out of his place to let them pass on. A woman, most probably his wife, attempted to follow him. She was leading a little boy by the hand. But the husband commanded her sternly to go on, while others laid hands on her and restrained her from following him. This I saw, and I saw the man also, with his scarlet blaze of face, step into a doorway on the opposite side of the street. I heard the report of his pistol, and saw him sink lifeless to the ground.

"After being turned aside twice again by advancing fires, I succeeded in getting through to the university. On the edge of the campus I came upon a party of university folk who were going in the direction of the Chemistry Building. They were all family men, and their families were with them, including the nurses and the servants. Professor Badminton greeted me, and I had difficulty in recognizing him. Somewhere he had gone through flames, and his beard was singed off. About his head was a bloody bandage, and his clothes were filthy. He told me he had been cruelly beaten by prowlers, and that his brother had been killed the previous night, in the defense of their dwelling.

"Midway across the campus, he pointed suddenly to Mrs. Swinton's face. The unmistakable scarlet was there. Immediately all the other women set up a screaming and began to run away from her. Her two children were with a nurse, and these also ran with the women. But her husband, Doctor Swinton, remained with her.

"'Go on, Smith,' he told me. 'Keep an eye on the children. As for me, I shall stay with my wife. I know she is as already dead, but I can't leave her. Afterwards, if I escape, I shall come to the Chemistry Building, and do you watch for me and let me in.'

"I left him bending over his wife and soothing her last moments, while I ran to overtake the party. We were the last to be admitted to the Chemistry Building. After that, with our automatic rifles we maintained our isolation. By our plans, we had arranged for a company of sixty to be in this refuge. Instead, every one of the number originally planned had added relatives and friends and whole families until there were over four hundred souls. But the Chemistry Building was large, and, standing by itself, was in no danger of being burned by the great fires that raged everywhere in the city.

"A large quantity of provisions had been gathered, and a food committee took charge of it, issuing rations daily to the various families and groups that arranged themselves into messes. A number of committees were appointed, and we developed a very efficient organization. I was on the committee of defense, though for the first day no prowlers came near. We could see them in the distance, however, and by the smoke of their fires knew that several camps of them were occupying the far edge of the campus. Drunkenness was rife, and often we heard them singing ribald songs or insanely shouting. While the world crashed to ruin about them and all the air was filled with the smoke of its burning, these low creatures gave rein to their bestiality and fought and drank and died. And after all, what did it matter? Everybody died anyway, the good and the bad, the efficients and the weaklings, those that loved to live and those that scorned to live. They passed. Everything passed.

"When twenty-four hours had gone by and no signs of the plague were apparent, we congratulated ourselves and set about digging a well. You have seen the great iron pipes which in those days carried water to all the city-dwellers. We feared that the fires in the city would burst the pipes and empty the reservoirs. So we tore up the cement floor of the central court of the Chemistry Building and dug a well. There were many young men, under-graduates, with us, and we worked night and day on the well. And our fears were confirmed. Three hours before we reached water, the pipes went dry.

"A second twenty-four hours passed, and still the plague did not appear among us. We thought we were saved. But we did not know what I afterwards decided to be true, namely, that the peri-od of the incubation of the plague germs in a human's body was a matter of a number of days. It slew so swiftly when once it man-ifested itself, that we were led to believe that the period of incu-bation was equally swift. So, when two days had left us unscathed, we were elated with the idea that we were free of the contagion.

"But the third day disillusioned us. I can never forget the night preceding it. I had charge of the night guards from eight to twelve, and from the roof of the building I watched the passing of all man's glorious works. So terrible were the local conflagrations that all the sky was lighted up. One could read the finest print in the red glare. All the world seemed wrapped in flames. San Francisco spouted smoke and fire from a score of vast conflagra-tions that were like so many active volcanoes. Oakland, San Leandro, Hayward—all were burning; and to the northward, clear to Point Richmond, other fires were at work. It was an awe-inspir-ing spectacle. Civilization, my grandsons, civilization was passing in a sheet of flame and a breath of death. At ten o'clock that night, the great powder magazines at Point Pinole exploded in rapid suc-cession. So terrific were the concussions that the strong building rocked as in an earthquake, while every pane of glass was broken. It was then that I left the roof and went down the long corridors, from room to room, quieting the alarmed women and telling them what had happened.

"An hour later, at a window on the ground floor, I heard pandemonium break out in the camps of the prowlers. There were cries and screams, and shots from many pistols. As we afterward conjectured, this fight had been precipitated by an attempt on the part of those that were well to drive out those that were sick. At any rate, a number of the plague-stricken prowlers escaped across the campus and drifted against our doors. We warned them back, but they cursed us and discharged a fusillade from their pistols. Professor Merryweather, at one of the windows, was instantly killed, the bullet striking him squarely between the eyes. We opened fire in turn, and all the prowlers fled away with the exception of three. One was a woman. The plague was on them and they were reckless. Like foul fiends, there in the red glare from the skies, with faces blazing, they continued to curse us and fire at us. One of the men I shot with my own hand. After that the other man and the woman, still cursing us, lay down under our windows, where we were compelled to watch them die of the plague.

"The situation was critical. The explosions of the powder magazines had broken all the windows of the Chemistry Building, so that we were exposed to the germs from the corpses. The sanitary committee was called upon to act, and it responded nobly. Two men were required to go out and remove the corpses, and this meant the probable sacrifice of their own lives, for, having performed the task, they were not to be permitted to re-enter the building. One of the professors, who was a bachelor, and one of the undergraduates volunteered. They bade good-bye to us and went forth. They were heroes. They gave up their lives that four hundred others might live. After they had performed their work, they stood for a moment, at a distance, looking at us wistfully. Then they waved their hands in farewell and went away slowly across the campus toward the burning city.

"And yet it was all useless. The next morning the first one of us was smitten with the plague—a little nurse-girl in the family of Professor Stout. It was no time for weak-kneed, sentimental policies.

On the chance that she might be the only one, we thrust her forth from the building and commanded her to be gone. She went away slowly across the campus, wringing her hands and crying pitifully. We felt like brutes, but what were we to do? There were four hundred of us, and individuals had to be sacrificed...."

Navigating Four Horses
North of the Bay

Jack London's sense of humor has been rarely noted by critics. In this essay, originally published in the September 1911 issue of Sunset Magazine, *he offers his version of the rough-hewn wit that character-ized much western writing in the nineteenth century. His style borders on the tall-tale tradition: after the horses bite, kick, surge, tangle reins, and nearly send the whole gang over a precipice, London observes, "a boat would never act that way." All this is accomplished within the context of wonderful descriptive writing that gives readers a picture of Sonoma, Mendocino, and Humboldt counties as they were early in the twentieth century—wild and inviting.*

"Huh! Drive four horses! I wouldn't sit behind you—not for a thousand dollars—over them mountain roads."

So said Henry, and he ought to have known, for he drives four horses himself.

Said another Glen Ellen friend: "What? London? He drive four horses? Can't drive one!"

And the best of it is that he was right. Even after managing to get a few hundred miles with my four horses, I don't know how to drive one. Just the other day, swinging down a steep mountain road and rounding an abrupt turn, I came full tilt on a horse and buggy being driven by a woman up the hill. We could not pass on the narrow road, where was only a foot to spare, and my horses did not know how to back, especially uphill. About two hundred yards down the hill was a spot where we could pass. The driver of the buggy said she didn't dare back down because she was not sure of the brake. And as I didn't know how to tackle one horse, I didn't try it. So we unhitched her horse and backed down by hand. Which was very well, till it came to hitching the horse to the buggy again. She didn't know how. I didn't either, and I had depended on her knowledge. It took us about half an hour, with frequent debates and consultations, though it is an absolute certainty that never in its life was that horse hitched in that particular way.

No; I can't harness up one horse. But I can four, which compels me to back up again to get to my beginning. Having selected Sonoma Valley for our abiding place, Charmian and I decided it was about time we knew what we had in our own country and the neighboring ones. How to do it was the first question. Among our many weaknesses is the one of being old-fashioned. We don't mix with gasoline very well. And, as true sailors should, we naturally gravitate toward horses. Being one of those lucky individuals who carries his office under his hat, I should have to take a typewriter and a load of books along. This put saddle horses out of the running. Charmian suggested driving a span. She had faith in me; besides, she could drive a span herself. But when I thought of the many mountains to cross and of crossing them for three months with a poor, tired span, I vetoed the proposition and said we'd have to come back to gasoline after all. This she vetoed just as emphatically, and a deadlock obtained until I received inspiration.

"Why not drive four horses?" I said.

"But you don't know how to drive four horses," was her objection.

I threw my chest out and my shoulders back. "What man has done, I can do," I proclaimed grandly. "And please don't forget that when we sailed on the *Snark* I knew nothing of navigation, and that I taught myself as I sailed."

"Very well," she said. (And there's faith for you!) "They shall be four saddle horses, and we'll strap our saddles on behind the rig."

It was my turn to object. "Our saddle horses are not broken to harness."

"Then break them."

And what I knew about horses, much less about breaking them, was just about as much as any sailor knows. Having been kicked, bucked off, fallen over backward upon, and thrown out and run over, on very numerous occasions, I had a mighty vigorous respect for horses; but a wife's faith must be lived up to, and I went at it.

King was a polo pony from St. Louis, and Prince a many-gaited love-horse from Pasadena. The hardest thing was to get them to dig in and pull. They frolicked along on the levels and galloped down the hills, but when they struck an up-grade and felt the weight of the breaking-cart, they stopped and turned around and looked at me. But I passed them, and my troubles began. Milda was fourteen years old, an unadulterated bronco, and in temperament was a combination of mule and jackrabbit blended equally. If you pressed your hand on her flank and told her to get over, she lay down on you. If you got her by the head and told her to back, she walked forward over you. And if you got behind her and shoved and told her to "Giddap!" she sat down on you. Also, she wouldn't walk. For endless weary miles I strove with her, but never could I get her to walk a step. Finally, she was a manger-glutton. No matter how near or far from the stable, when six o'clock came around, she bolted for home and never missed the directest cross road. Many times I rejected her.

The fourth and most rejected horse of all was the Outlaw. From the age of three to seven she had defied all horse-breakers and broken a number of them. Then a long, lanky cowboy, with a fifty-pound saddle and a Mexican bit, had got her proud goat. I was the next owner. She was my favorite riding-horse. Charmian said I'd have to put her in as a wheeler where I would have more control over her. Now Charmian had a favorite riding mare called Maid. I suggested Maid as a substitute. Charmian pointed out that my mare was a branded range horse, while hers was a thorough-bred, and that the legs of her mare would be ruined forever if she were driven for three months. I acknowledged her mare's thoroughbredness, and at the same time defied her to find any thoroughbred with as small and delicately-viciously pointed ears as my Outlaw. She indicated Maid's exquisitely thin shin bone. I measured the Outlaw's. It was equally thin, although, I insinuated, possibly more durable. This stabbed Charmian's pride. Of course her thoroughbred Maid, carrying the blood of "Old Lexington, Morella, and a streak of the super-enduring Morgan," could run, walk, and work my unregistered Outlaw into the ground; and that was the very precise reason why such a paragon of a saddle animal should not be degraded by harness.

So it was that Charmian remained obdurate, until, one day, I got her behind the Outlaw for a forty-mile drive. For every inch of those forty miles the Outlaw kicked and jumped, in between the kicks and jumps finding time and space in which to seize its teammate by the back of the neck and attempt to drag it to the ground. Another trick the Outlaw developed during that drive was suddenly to turn at right angles in the traces and endeavor to butt its teammate over the grade. Reluctantly and nobly did Charmian give in and consent to the use of Maid. The Outlaw's shoes were pulled off, and she was turned out on the range.

Finally, the four horses were hooked to the rig—a light Studebaker trap. With two hours and a half of practice, in which the excitement was not abated by several jack-poles and numerous kicking matches, I announced myself as ready for the start. Came the morning, and Prince, who was to have been a wheeler with Maid, showed up with a badly kicked shoulder. He did not exactly show up; we had to find him, for he was unable to walk. His leg swelled and continually swelled during the several days we waited for him. Remained only the Outlaw. In from pasture she came, shoes were nailed on, and she was harnessed into the wheel. Friends and relatives strove to press accident policies on me, but Charmian climbed up alongside, and Nakata got into the rear seat with the typewriter—Nakata, who sailed cabin-boy on the *Snark* for two years and who has shown himself afraid of nothing, not even of me and my amateur jamborees in experimenting with new modes of locomotion. And we did very nicely, thank you, especially after the first hour or so, during which time the Outlaw had kicked about fifty various times, chiefly to the damage of her own legs and the paintwork, and after she had bitten a couple of hundred times, to the damage of Maid's neck and Charmian's temper. It was hard enough to have her favorite mare in the harness without also enduring the spectacle of its being eaten alive.

Our leaders were joys. King being a polo pony and Milda a rabbit, they rounded curves beautifully and darted ahead like coyotes out of the way of the wheelers. Milda's besetting weakness was a frantic desire not to have the lead-bar strike her hocks. When this happened, one of three things occurred: either she sat down on the lead-bar, kicked it up in the air until she got her back under it, or exploded in a straight-ahead, harness-disrupting jump. Not until she carried the lead-bar clean away and danced a breakdown on it and the traces did she behave decently. Nakata and I made the repairs with good old-fashioned bale-rope, which is stronger than wrought iron any time, and we went on our way.

In the meantime I was learning—I shall not say to tool a four-in-hand—but just simply to drive four horses. Now it is all right enough to begin with four work-horses pulling a load of several tons. But to begin with four light horses, all running, and a light rig that seems to outrun them—well, when things happen they happen quickly. My weakness was total ignorance. In particular, my fingers lacked training, and I made the mistake of depending on my eyes to handle the reins. This brought me up against a disastrous optical illusion. The bight of the off lead-line, being longer and heavier than that of the off wheel-line, hung lower. In a moment requiring quick action, I invariably mistook the two lines. Pulling on what I thought was the wheel-line, in order to straighten the team, I would see the leaders swing abruptly around into a jack-pole. Now for sensations of sheer impotence, nothing can compare with a jack-pole, when the horrified driver beholds his leaders prancing gaily up the road and his wheelers jogging steadily down the road, all at the same time and all harnessed together and to the same rig.

I no longer jack-pole, and I don't mind admitting how I got out of the habit. It was my eyes that enslaved my fingers into ill practices. So I shut my eyes and let the fingers go it alone. Today my fingers are independent of my eyes and work automatically. I do not see what my fingers do. They just do it. All I see is the satisfactory result.

Still we managed to get over the ground that first day—down sunny Sonoma Valley to the old town to Sonoma, founded by General Vallejo as the remotest outpost on the northern frontier for the purpose of holding back the Gentiles, as the wild Indians of those days were called. Here history was made. Here the last Spanish mission was reared; here the Bear flag was raised; and here Kit Carson, and Frémont, and all our early adventurers, came and rested in the days before the days of gold.

We swung on over the low rolling hills, through miles of dairy farms and chicken ranches where every blessed hen is white, and down the slopes to Petaluma Valley. Here, in 1776, Captain Quiros came up Petaluma Creek from San Pablo Bay in quest of an outlet to Bodega Bay on the coast. And here, later, the Russians, with Alaskan hunters, carried skin boats across from Fort Ross to poach for sea otters on the Spanish preserve of San Francisco Bay. Here, too, still later, General Vallejo built a fort, which still stands—one of the finest examples of Spanish adobe that remain to us. And here, at the old fort, to bring the chronicle up to date, our horses proceeded to make peculiarly personal history with astonishing success and dispatch. King, our peerless polo-pony leader, went lame. So hopelessly lame did he go that no expert, then and afterward, could determine whether the lameness was in his frogs, hoofs, legs, shoulders, or head. Maid picked up a nail and began to limp. Milda, figuring the day already sufficiently spent and maniacal with manger gluttony, began to rabbit-jump. All that held her was the bale-rope. And the Outlaw, game to the last, exceeded all previous exhibitions of skin-removing, paint-marring, and horse-eating.

At Petaluma we rested over while King was returned to the ranch and Prince sent to us. Now Prince had proved himself an excellent wheeler, yet he had to go into the lead and let the Outlaw retain his old place. There is an axiom that a good wheeler is a poor leader. I object to the last adjective. A good wheeler makes an infinitely worse kind of a leader than that. I know...now. I ought to know. Since that day I have driven Prince a few hundred miles in the lead. He is neither any better nor any worse than the first mile he ran in the lead; and his worst is even extremely worse than what you are thinking. Not that he is vicious. He is merely a good-natured rogue who shakes hands for sugar, steps on your toes out of sheer excessive friendliness, and just goes on loving you in your harshest moments.

But he won't get out of the way. Also, whenever he is reproved for being in the wrong, he accuses Milda of it and bites the back of her neck. So bad has this become that whenever I yell "Prince!" in a loud voice, Milda immediately rabbit-jumps to the side, straight ahead, or sits down on the lead-bar. All of which is quite disconcerting. Picture it yourself. You are swinging a sharp, down-grade, mountain curve, at a fast trot. The rock wall is the outside of the curve. The inside of the curve is a precipice. The continuance of the curve is a narrow, unrailed bridge. You hit the curve, throwing the leaders in against the wall and making the pole-horse do the work. All is lovely. The leaders are hugging the wall like nestling doves. But the moment comes in the evolution when the leaders must shoot out ahead. They really must shoot, or else they'll hit the wall and miss the bridge. Also, behind them are the wheelers, and the rig, and you have just eased the brake in order to put sufficient snap into the maneuver. If ever teamwork is required, now is the time. Milda tries to shoot. She does her best, but Prince, bubbling over with roguishness, lags behind. He knows the trick. Milda is half a length ahead of him. He times it to the fraction of a second. Maid, in the wheel, over-running him, naturally bites him. This disturbs the Outlaw, who has been behaving beautifully, and she immediately reaches across for Maid. Simultaneously, with a fine display of firm conviction that it's all Milda's fault, Prince sinks his teeth into the back of Milda's defenseless neck. The whole thing has occurred in less than a second. Under the surprise and pain of the bite, Milda either jumps ahead to the imminent peril of harness and lead-bar, or smashes into the wall, stops short with the lead-bar over her back, and emits a couple of hysterical kicks. The Outlaw invariably selects this moment to remove paint. And after things are untangled and you have had time to appreciate the close shave, you go up to Prince and reprove him with your choicest vocabulary. And Prince, gazelle-eyed and tender, offers to shake hands with you for sugar. I leave it to any one: a boat would never act that way.

We have some history north of the bay. Nearly three centuries and a half ago, that doughty pirate and explorer, Sir Francis Drake, combing the Pacific for Spanish galleons, anchored in the bight formed by Point Reyes, on which today is one of the richest dairy regions in the world. Here, less than two decades after Drake, Sebastien Carmenon piled up on the rocks with a silkladen galleon from the Philippines. And in this same bay of Drake, long afterward, the Russian fur-poachers rendezvoused their *bidarkas* and stole in through the Golden Gate to the forbidden waters of San Francisco Bay.

Farther up the coast, in Sonoma County, we pilgrimaged to the sites of the Russian settlements. At Bodega Bay, south of what today is called Russian River, was their anchorage, while north of the river they built their fort. And much of Fort Ross still stands. Log bastions, church, and stables hold their own, and so well, with rusty hinges creaking, that we warmed ourselves at the hundred-years-old double fireplace and slept under the hand-hewn roof beams still held together by spikes of hand-wrought iron.

We went to see where history had been made, and we saw scenery as well. One of our stretches in a day's drive was from beautiful Inverness on Tomales Bay, down the Olema Valley to

Bolinas Bay, along the eastern shore of that body of water to Willow Camp, and up over the sea-bluffs, around the bastions of Tamalpais, and down to Sausalito. From the head of Bolinas Bay to Willow Camp the drive on the edge of the beach, and actually, for half-mile stretches, in the waters of the bay itself, was a delightful experience. The wonderful part was to come. Very few San Franciscans, much less Californians, know of that drive from Willow Camp, to the south and east, along the poppy-blown cliffs, with the sea thundering in the sheer depths hundreds of feet below and the Golden Gate opening up ahead, disclosing smoky San Francisco on her many hills. Far off, blurred on the breast of the sea, can be seen the Farallones, which Sir Francis Drake passed on a southwest course in the thick of a fog that robbed him of the glory of discovering San Francisco Bay.

It was on this part of the drive that I decided at last I was learning real mountain-driving. To confess the truth, for delicious titillation of one's nerve, I have since driven over no mountain road that was worse, or better, rather, than that piece.

And then the contrast! From Sausalito, over excellent park-like boulevards, through the splendid redwoods and homes of Mill Valley, across the blossomed hills of Marin County, along the knoll-studded picturesque marshes, past San Rafael resting warmly among her hills, over the divide and up the Petaluma Valley, and on to the grassy feet of Sonoma Mountain and home. We covered fifty-five miles that day. Not so bad, eh, for Prince the Rogue, the paint-removing Outlaw, the thin-shanked thoroughbred, and the rabbit-jumper? And they came in cool and dry, ready for their mangers and the straw.

Oh, we didn't stop. We considered we were just starting, and that was many weeks ago. We have kept on, going over six counties which are comfortably large, even for California, and we are still going. We have twisted and doubled, crisscrossed our tracks, made fascinating and lengthy drives into the interior valleys in the hearts of Napa and Lake counties, travelled the coast for hundreds of miles on end, and are now in Eureka, on Humboldt Bay, which was discovered by accident by the gold-seekers, who were trying to find their way to and from the Trinity diggings. Even here, the white man's history preceded them, for dim tradition says that the Russians once anchored here and hunted sea otter before the first Yankee trader rounded the Horn, or the first Rocky Mountain trapper thirsted across the "Great American Desert" and trickled down the snowy Sierra to the sun-kissed land. No, we are not resting our horses here on Humboldt Bay. We are writing this, gorging on abalones and mussels, digging clams, and catching record-breaking sea trout and rock cod in the intervals in which we are not sailing, motorboating, and swimming in the most temperately equable climate we have ever experienced.

These comfortably large counties! They are veritable empires. Take Humboldt, for instance. It is three times as large as Rhode Island, one and one half times as large as Delaware, almost as large as Connecticut, and half as large as Massachusetts. The pioneer has done his work in this north-of-the-bay region, the foundations are laid, and all is ready for the inevitable inrush of population and adequate development of resources which so far have been no more than skimmed, and casually and carelessly skimmed at that. This region of the six counties alone will some day support a population of millions. In the meanwhile, O you home-seekers, you wealth-seekers, and, above all, you climate-seekers, now is the time to get in on the ground floor.

Robert Ingersoll once said that the genial climate of California would in a fairly brief time evolve a race resembling the Mexicans, and that in two or three generations the Californians would be seen of a Sunday morning on their way to a cockfight with a rooster under each arm. Never was made a rasher generalization, based on so absolute an ignorance of facts. It is to laugh. Here is a climate that breeds vigor, with just sufficient geniality to prevent the expenditure of most of that vigor in fighting the elements. Here is a climate where a man can work three hundred sixty-five days in the year without the slightest hint of enervation, and where for three hundred sixty-five nights he must perforce sleep under blankets. What more can one say? I consider myself somewhat of a climate expert, having adventured among most of the climates of five out of the six zones. I have not yet been in the Antarctic, but whatever climate obtains there will not deter me from drawing the conclusion that nowhere is there a climate to compare with that of this region. Maybe I am as wrong as Ingersoll was. Nevertheless I take my medicine by continuing to live in this climate. Also, it is the only medicine I ever take.

But to return to the horses. There is some improvement. Milda has actually learned to walk. Maid has proved her thoroughbredness by never tiring on the longest days, and, while being the strongest and highest spirited of all, by never causing any trouble save for an occasional kick at the Outlaw. And the Outlaw rarely gallops, no longer butts, only periodically kicks, comes in to the pole and does her work without attempting to vivisect Maid's medulla oblongata, and—marvel of marvels—is really and truly getting lazy. But Prince remains the same incorrigible, loving and lovable rogue as always.

And the country we've been over! The drives through Napa and Lake counties! One, from Sonoma Valley, via Santa Rosa, we could not refrain from taking several ways, and on all the ways we found the roads excellent for machines as well as horses. One route, and a more delightful one for an automobile cannot be found, is out from Santa Rosa, past old Altruria and Mark West Springs, then to the right and across to Calistoga in Napa Valley. By keeping to the left, the drive holds on up the Russian River Valley, through the miles of the noted Asti Vineyards to Cloverdale, and then by way of Pieta, Witter, and Highland Springs to Lakeport. Still another way we took was down Sonoma Valley, skirting San Pablo Bay, and up the lovely Napa Valley. From Napa were side excursions through Pope and Berryessa valleys, on to Aetna Springs, and into Lake County, crossing the famous Langtry Ranch.

More valley from Ukiah to Willits, and then we turned westward through the virgin Sherwood Forest of magnificent redwood, stopping at Alpine for the night and continuing on through Mendocino County to Fort Bragg and "salt water." We also came to Fort Bragg up the coast from Fort Ross, keeping our coast journey intact from the Golden Gate. The coast weather was cool and delightful, the coast driving superb. Especially in the Fort Ross section did we find the roads thrilling, while all the way along we followed the sea. At every stream the road skirted dizzy cliff edges, dived down into lush growths of forest and ferns, and climbed out along the cliff edges again. The way was lined with flowers—wild lilac, wild roses, poppies, and lupines. Such lupines!—giant clumps of them of every lupine-shade and color. And it was along the Mendocino roads that Charmian caused many delays by insisting on getting out to pick the wild blackberries, strawberries, and thimbleberries which grew so profusely. And ever we caught peeps, far down, of steam schooners loading lumber in the rocky coves; ever we skirted the cliffs, day after day, crossing stretches of rolling farm lands and passing through thriving villages and saw-mill towns. Memorable was our launch-trip from Mendocino City up Big River, where the steering gears of the launches work the reverse of anywhere else in the world; where we saw a stream of logs, of six to twelve and fifteen feet in diameter, which filled the riverbed for miles to the obliteration of any sign of water; and where we were told of a white or albino redwood tree. We did not see this last, so cannot vouch for it.

All the streams were filled with trout, and more than once we saw side-hill salmon on the slopes. No, side-hill salmon is not a peripatetic fish; it is a deer out of season. But the trout! At Gualala Charmian caught her first one. Once before in my life I had caught two...on angleworms. On occasion I had tried fly and spinner and never got a strike, and I had come to believe that all this talk of fly-fishing was just so much nature-faking. But on the Gualala River I caught trout—a lot of them—on fly and spinner; and I was beginning to feel quite an expert, until Nakata, fishing on bottom with a pellet of bread for bait, caught the biggest trout of all. I now affirm there is nothing in science nor in art.

Nevertheless, since that day poles and baskets have been added to our baggage, we tackle every stream we come to, and we no longer are able to remember the grand total of our catch.

At Usal, many hilly and picturesque miles north of Fort Bragg, we turned again into the interior of Mendocino, crossing the ranges and coming out in Humboldt County on the south fork of Eel River at Garberville. Throughout the trip, from Marin County north, we had been warned of "bad roads ahead." Yet we never found those bad roads. We seemed always to be just ahead of them or behind them. The farther we came the better the roads seemed, though this was probably due to the fact that we were learning more and more what four horses and a light rig could do on a road. And thus do I save my face with all the counties. I refuse to make invidious road comparisons. I can add that while, save in rare instances on steep pitches, I have trotted my horses down all the grades, I have never had one horse fall down nor have I had to send the rig to a blacksmith shop for repairs.

Also, I am learning to throw leather. If any tyro thinks it is easy to take a short-handled, long-lashed whip, and throw the end of that lash just where he wants it, let him put on automobile goggles and try it. On reconsideration, I would suggest the substitution of a wire fencing-mask for the goggles. For days I looked at that whip. It fascinated me, and the fascination was composed mostly of fear. At my first attempt, Charmian and Nakata became afflicted with the same fascination, and for a long time afterward, whenever they saw me reach for the whip, they closed their eyes and shielded their heads with their arms.

Here's the problem. Instead of pulling honestly, Prince is lagging back and maneuvering for a bite at Milda's neck. I have four reins in my hands. I must put these four reins into my left hand, properly gather the whip handle and the bight of the lash in my right hand, and throw that lash past Maid without striking her and into Prince. If the lash strikes Maid, her thoroughbredness will go up in the air, and I'll have a case of horse hysteria on my hands for the next half hour. But follow. The whole problem is not yet stated.

Suppose that I miss Maid and reach the intended target. The instant the lash cracks, the four horses jump, Prince most of all, and his jump, with spread wicked teeth, is for the back of Milda's neck. She jumps to escape—which is her second jump, for the first one came when the lash exploded. The Outlaw reaches for Maid's neck, and Maid, who has already jumped and tried to bolt, tries to bolt harder. And all this infinitesimal fraction of time I am trying to hold the four animals with my left hand, while my whip-lash, writhing through the air, is coming back to me. Three simultaneous things I must do: keep hold of the four lines with my left hand; slam on the brake with my foot; and on the rebound catch that flying lash in the hollow of my right arm and get the bight of it safely into my right hand. Then I must get two of the four lines back into my right hand and keep the horses from running away or going over the grade. Try it some time. You will find life anything but wearisome. Why, the first time I hit the mark and made the lash go off like a revolver shot, I was so astounded and delighted that I was paralyzed. I forgot to do any of the multitudinous other things, tangled the whip-lash in Maid's harness, and was forced to call upon Charmian for assistance. And now, confession. I carry a few pebbles handy. They're great for reaching Prince in a tight place. But just the same I'm learning that whip every day, and before I get home I hope to discard the pebbles. And as long as I rely on pebbles, I cannot truthfully speak of myself as "tooling a four-in-hand."

From Garberville, where we ate eel to repletion and got acquainted with the aborigines, we drove down the Eel River Valley for two days through the most unthinkably glorious body of redwood timber to be seen anywhere in California. From Dyerville on to Eureka we caught glimpses of railroad construction and of great concrete bridges in the course of building, which advertised that at last Humboldt County is to be linked to the rest of the world.

We still consider our trip is just begun. As soon as this is mailed from Eureka, it's heigh-ho! for the horses and pull on. We shall continue up the coast, turn in for the Hoopa Reservation and the gold mines, and shoot down the Trinity and Klamath rivers in Indian canoes to Requa. After that, we shall go on through Del Norte County and into Oregon. The trip so far has justified us in taking the attitude that we won't go home until the winter rains drive us in. And, finally, I am going to try the experiment of putting the Outlaw in the lead and relegating Prince to his old position in the near wheel. I won't need any pebbles then.

Demetrios Contos

It can reasonably be argued that Jack London became an adult when, in his mid-teens, he worked as an oyster pirate on San Francisco Bay, stealing the mollusks from commercial beds. That was in many ways his first frontier experience. He followed it with a stint on the other side of the law, working with Charley Le Grant on the Fish Patrol at Carquinez Straits, where the following story is set. Jack knew well both the place and the men who plied it, and "Demetrios Contos"— which was included in Tales of the Fish Patrol *(1905)—recaptures not only the rigor of their lives and the quality of their contests, but the complexity and honor of their relationships.*

It must not be thought, from what I have told of the Greek fishermen, that they were altogether bad. Far from it. But they were rough men, gathered together in isolated communities and fighting with the elements for a livelihood. They lived far away from the law and its workings, did not understand it, and thought it tyranny. Especially did the fish laws seem tyrannical. And because of this, they looked upon the men of the fish patrol as their natural enemies.

We menaced their lives, or their living, which is the same thing, in many ways. We confiscated illegal traps and nets, the materials of which had cost them considerable sums and the making of which required weeks of labor. We prevented them from catching fish at many times and seasons, which was equivalent to preventing them from making as good a living as they might have made had we not been in existence. And when we captured them, they were brought into the courts of law, where heavy cash fines were collected from them. As a result, they hated us vindictively.

As the dog is the natural enemy of the cat, the snake of man, so were we of the fish patrol the natural enemies of the fishermen.

But it is to show that they could act generously as well as hate bitterly that this story of Demetrios Contos is told. Demetrios Contos lived in Vallejo. Next to Big Alec, he was the largest, bravest, and most influential man among the Greeks. He had given us no trouble, and I doubt if he would ever have clashed with us had he not invested in a new salmon boat. This boat was the cause of all the trouble. He had had it built upon his own model, in which the lines of the general salmon boat were somewhat modified.

To his high elation he found his new boat very fast—in fact, faster than any other boat on the bay or rivers. Forthwith he grew proud and boastful: and, our raid with the *Mary Rebecca* on the Sunday salmon fishers having wrought fear in their hearts, he sent a challenge up to Benicia. One of the local fishermen conveyed it to us; it was to the effect that Demetrios Contos would sail up from Vallejo on the following Sunday, and in the plain sight of Benicia set his net and catch salmon, and that Charley Le Grant, patrolman, might come and get him if he could. Of course Charley and I had heard nothing of the new boat. Our own boat was pretty fast, and we were not afraid to have a brush with any other that happened along.

Sunday came. The challenge had been bruited abroad, and the fishermen and sea-faring folk of Benicia turned out to a man, crowding Steamboat Wharf till it looked like the grandstand at a football match. Charley and I had been skeptical, but the fact of the crowd convinced us that there was something in Demetrios Contos's dare.

In the afternoon, when the sea-breeze had picked up in strength, his sail hove into view as he bowled along before the wind. He tacked a score of feet from the wharf, waved his hand theatrically, like a knight about to enter the lists, received a hearty cheer in return, and stood away into the Straits for a couple of hundred yards. Then he lowered sail, and, drifting the boat sidewise by

means of the wind, proceeded to set his net. He did not set much
of it, possibly fifty feet; yet Charley and I were thunderstruck at the
man's effrontery. We did not know at the time, but we learned afterward, that the net he used was old and worthless. It *could* catch fish,
true; but a catch of any size would have torn it to pieces.

Charley shook his head and said:

"I confess, it puzzles me. What if he has out only fifty feet?
He could never get it in if we once started for him. And why does
he come here anyway, flaunting his law-breaking in our faces?
Right in our home town, too."

Charley's voice took on an aggrieved tone, and he continued
for some minutes to inveigh against the brazenness of Demetrios
Contos.

In the meantime, the man in question was lolling in the
stem of his boat and watching the net floats. When a large fish is
meshed in a gill-net, the floats by their agitation advertise the fact.
And they evidently advertised it to Demetrios, for he pulled in
about a dozen feet of net, and held aloft for a moment, before he
flung it into the bottom of the boat a big, glistening salmon. It was
greeted by the audience on the wharf with round after round of
cheers. This was more than Charley could stand.

"Come on, lad," he called to me; and we lost no time jumping into our salmon boat and getting up sail.

The crowd shouted warning to Demetrios, and as we darted
out from the wharf we saw him slash his worthless net clear with
a long knife. His sail was all ready to go up, and a moment later it
fluttered in the sunshine. He ran aft, drew in the sheet, and filled
on the long tack toward the Contra Costa Hills.

By this time we were not more than thirty feet astern.
Charley was jubilant. He knew our boat was fast, and he knew,
further, that in fine sailing few men were his equals. He was confident that we should surely catch Demetrios, and I shared his
confidence. But somehow we did not seem to gain.

It was a pretty sailing breeze. We were gliding sleekly through
the water, but Demetrios was slowly sliding away from us. And not

only was he going faster, but he was eating into the wind a fraction of a point closer than we. This was sharply impressed upon us when he went about under the Contra Costa Hills and passed us on the other tack fully one hundred feet dead to windward.

"Whew!" Charley exclaimed. "Either that boat is a daisy, or we've got a five-gallon coal-oil can fast to our keel!"

It certainly looked it one way or the other. And by the time Demetrios made the Sonoma Hills, on the other side of the Straits, we were so hopelessly outdistanced that Charley told me to slack off the sheet, and we squared away for Benicia. The fishermen on Steamboat Wharf showered us with ridicule when we returned and tied up. Charley and I got out and walked away, feeling rather sheepish, for it is a sore stroke to one's pride when he thinks he has a good boat and knows how to sail it, and another man comes along and beats him.

Charley mooned over it for a couple of days; then word was brought to us, as before, that on the next Sunday Demetrios Contos would repeat his performance. Charley roused himself. He had our boat out of the water, cleaned and repainted its bottom, made a trifling alteration about the center-board, overhauled the running gear, and sat up nearly all of Saturday night sewing on a new and much larger sail. So large did he make it, in fact, that additional ballast was imperative, and we stowed away nearly five hundred extra pounds of old railroad iron in the bottom of the boat.

Sunday came, and with it came Demetrios Contos, to break the law defiantly in open day. Again we had the afternoon sea-breeze, and again Demetrios cut loose some forty or more feet of his rotten net, and got up sail and under way under our very noses. But he had anticipated Charley's move, and his own sail peaked higher than ever, while a whole extra cloth had been added to the after leech.

It was nip and tuck across to the Contra Costa Hills, neither of us seeming to gain or to lose. But by the time we had made the return tack to the Sonoma Hills, we could see that, while we footed it at about equal speed, Demetrios had eaten into the wind the least bit more than we. Yet Charley was sailing our boat as finely and delicately as it was possible to sail it, and getting more out of it than he ever had before.

Of course, he could have drawn his revolver and fired at Demetrios; but we had long since found it contrary to our natures to shoot at a fleeing man guilty of only a petty offence. Also a sort of tacit agreement seemed to have been reached between the patrolmen and the fishermen. If we did not shoot while they ran away, they, in turn, did not fight if we once laid hands on them. Thus Demetrios Contos ran away from us, and we did no more than try our best to overtake him, and, in turn, if our boat proved faster than his, or was sailed better, he would, we knew, make no resistance when we caught up with him.

With our large sails and the healthy breeze romping up the Carquinez Straits, we found that our sailing was what is called "ticklish." We had to be constantly on the alert to avoid a capsize, and while Charley steered I held the main-sheet in my hand with but a single turn round a pin, ready to let go at any moment. Demetrios, we could see, sailing his boat alone, had his hands full.

But it was a vain undertaking for us to attempt to catch him. Out of his inner consciousness he had evolved a boat that was better than ours. And though Charley sailed fully as well, if not the least bit better, the boat he sailed was not so good as the Greek's.

"Slack away the sheet," Charley commanded; and as our boat fell off before the wind, Demetrios's mocking laugh floated down to us.

Charley shook his head, saying, "It's no use. Demetrios has the better boat. If he tries his performance again, we must meet it with some new scheme."

This time it was my imagination that came to the rescue.

"What's the matter," I suggested, on the Wednesday following, "with my chasing Demetrios in the boat next Sunday, while you wait for him on the wharf at Vallejo when he arrives?"

Charley considered it a moment and slapped his knee.

"A good idea! You're beginning to use that head of yours. A credit to your teacher, I must say."

"But you mustn't chase him too far," he went on, the next moment, "or he'll head out into San Pablo Bay instead of running home to Vallejo, and there I'll be, standing lonely on the wharf and waiting in vain for him to arrive."

On Thursday Charley registered an objection to my plan.

"Everybody'll know I've gone to Vallejo, and you can depend upon it that Demetrios will know, too. I'm afraid we'll have to give up the idea."

This objection was only too valid, and for the rest of the day I struggled under my disappointment. But that night a new way seemed to open to me, and in my eagerness I awoke Charley from a sound sleep.

"Well," he grunted, "what's the matter? House afire?"

"No," I replied, "but my head is. Listen to this. On Sunday you and I will be around Benicia up to the very moment Demetrios's sail heaves into sight. This will lull everybody's suspicions. Then, when Demetrios's sail does heave in sight, do you stroll leisurely away and up-town. All the fishermen will think you're beaten and that you know you're beaten."

"So far, so good," Charley commented, while I paused to catch breath.

"And very good indeed," I continued proudly. "You stroll carelessly up-town, but when you're once out of sight you leg it for all you're worth for Dan Maloney's. Take the little mare of his, and strike out on the county road for Vallejo. The road's in fine condition, and you can make it in quicker time than Demetrios can beat all the way down against the wind."

"And I'll arrange right away for the mare, first thing in the morning," Charley said, accepting the modified plan without hesitation.

"But, I say," he said, a little later, this time waking *me* out of a sound sleep.

I could hear him chuckling in the dark.

"I say, lad, isn't it rather a novelty for the fish patrol to be taking to horseback?"

"Imagination," I answered. "It's what you're always preaching—'keep thinking one thought ahead of the other fellow, and you're bound to win out.'"

"He! he!" he chuckled. "And if one thought ahead, including a mare, doesn't take the other fellow's breath away this time, I'm not your humble servant, Charley Le Grant."

"But can you manage the boat alone?" he asked, on Friday. "Remember, we've a ripping big sail on her."

I argued my proficiency so well that he did not refer to the matter again till Saturday, when he suggested removing one whole cloth from the after leech. I guess it was the disappointment written on my face that made him desist; for I, also, had a pride in my boat-sailing abilities, and I was almost wild to get out alone with the big sail and go tearing down the Carquinez Straits in the wake of the flying Greek.

As usual, Sunday and Demetrios Contos arrived together. It had become the regular thing for the fishermen to assemble on Steamboat Wharf to greet his arrival and to laugh at our discomfiture. He lowered sail a couple of hundred yards out and set his customary fifty feet of rotten net.

"I suppose this nonsense will keep up as long as his old net holds out," Charley grumbled, with intention, in the hearing of several of the Greeks.

"Den I give-a heem my old-a net-a," one of them spoke up, promptly and maliciously.

"I don't care," Charley answered. "I've got some old net myself he can have—if he'll come around and ask for it."

They all laughed at this, for they could afford to be sweet-tempered with a man so badly outwitted as Charley was.

"Well, so long, lad," Charley called to me a moment later. "I think I'll go up-town to Maloney's."

"Let me take the boat out?" I asked.

"If you want to," was his answer, as he turned on his heel and walked slowly away.

Demetrios pulled two large salmon out of his net, and I jumped into the boat. The fishermen crowded around in a spirit of fun, and when I started to get up sail, overwhelmed me with all sorts of jocular advice. They even offered extravagant bets to one another that I would surely catch Demetrios, and two of them, styling themselves the committee of judges, gravely asked permission to come along with me to see how I did it.

But I was in no hurry. I waited to give Charley all the time I could, and I pretended dissatisfaction with the stretch of the sail and slightly shifted the small tackle by which the huge sprit forces up the peak. It was not until I was sure that Charley had reached Dan Maloney's and was on the little mare's back, that I cast off from the wharf and gave the big sail to the wind. A stout puff filled it and suddenly pressed the lee gunwale down till a couple of buckets of water came inboard. A little thing like this will happen to the best small-boat sailors, and yet, though I instantly let go of the sheet and righted, I was cheered sarcastically, as though I had been guilty of a very awkward blunder.

When Demetrios saw only one person in the fish patrol boat, and that one a boy, he proceeded to play with me. Making a short tack out, with me not thirty feet behind, he returned, with his sheet a little free, to Steamboat Wharf. And there he made short tacks, and turned and twisted and ducked around, to the great delight of his sympathetic audience. I was right behind him all the time, and I dared to do whatever he did, even when he squared away before the wind and jibed his big sail over—a most dangerous trick with such a sail in such a wind.

He depended upon the brisk sea breeze and the strong ebb tide, which together kicked up a nasty sea, to bring me to grief. But I was on my mettle, and never in all my life did I sail a boat better than on that day. I was keyed up to concert pitch, my brain was working smoothly and quickly, my hands never fumbled once, and it seemed that I almost divined the thousand little things which a small-boat sailor must be taking into consideration every second.

It was Demetrios who came to grief instead. Something went wrong with his center-board, so that it jammed in the case and would not go all the way down. In a moment's breathing space, which he had gained from me by a clever trick, I saw him working impatiently with the center-board, trying to force it down. I gave him little time, and he was compelled quickly to return to the tiller and sheet.

The center-board made him anxious. He gave over playing with me, and started on the long beat to Vallejo. To my joy, on the first long tack across, I found that I could eat into the wind just a little bit closer than he. Here was where another man in the boat would have been of value to him; for, with me but a few feet astern, he did not dare let go the tiller and run amidships to try to force down the center-board.

Unable to hang on as close in the eye of the wind as formerly, he proceeded to slack his sheet a trifle and to ease off a bit, in order to outfoot me. This I permitted him to do till I had worked to windward, when I bore down upon him. As I drew close, he feinted at coming about. This led me to shoot into the wind to forestall him. But it was only a feint, cleverly executed, and he held back to his course while I hurried to make up lost ground.

He was undeniably smarter than I when it came to maneuvering. Time after time I all but had him, and each time he tricked me and escaped. Besides, the wind was freshening constantly, and each of us had his hands full to avoid capsizing. As for my boat, it could not have been kept afloat but for the extra ballast. I sat cocked over the weather gunwale, tiller in one hand and sheet in the other; and the sheet, with a single turn around a pin, I was very often forced to let go in the severer puffs. This allowed the sail to spill the wind, which was equivalent to taking off so much driving power, and of course I lost ground. My consolation was that Demetrios was as often compelled to do the same thing.

The strong ebb tide, racing down the Straits in the teeth of the wind, caused an unusually heavy and spiteful sea, which dashed aboard continually. I was dripping wet, and even the sail was wet half-way up the after leech. Once I did succeed in outmaneuvering Demetrios, so that my bow bumped into him amidships. Here was where I should have had another man. Before I could run forward and leap aboard, he shoved the boats apart with an oar, laughing mockingly in my face as he did so.

We were now at the mouth of the Straits, in a bad stretch of water. Here the Vallejo Straits and the Carquinez Straits rushed directly at each other. Through the first flowed all the water of Napa River and the great tidelands; through the second flowed all the water of Suisun Bay and the Sacramento and San Joaquin rivers. And where such immense bodies of water, flowing swiftly, clashed together, a terrible tide-rip was produced. To make it worse, the wind howled up San Pablo Bay for fifteen miles and drove in a tremendous sea upon the tide-rip.

Conflicting currents tore about in all directions, colliding, forming whirlpools, sucks, and boils, and shooting up spitefully into hollow waves which fell aboard as often from leeward as from windward. And through it all, confused, driven into a madness of motion, thundered the great smoking seas from San Pablo Bay.

I was as wildly excited as the water. The boat was behaving splendidly, leaping and lurching through the welter like a race-horse. I could hardly contain myself with the joy of it. The huge sail, the howling wind, the driving seas, the plunging boat—I, a pygmy, a mere speck in the midst of it, was mastering the elemental strife, flying through it and over it, triumphant and victorious.

And just then, as I roared along like a conquering hero, the boat received a frightful smash and came instantly to a dead stop. I was flung forward and into the bottom. As I sprang up I caught a fleeting glimpse of a greenish, barnacle-covered object, and knew it at once for what it was, that terror of navigation, a sunken pile. No man may guard against such a thing. Water-logged and floating just beneath the surface, it was impossible to sight it in the troubled water in time to escape.

The whole bow of the boat must have been crushed in, for in a few seconds the boat was half full. Then a couple of seas filled it, and it sank straight down, dragged to bottom by the heavy ballast. So quickly did it all happen that I was entangled in the sail and drawn under. When I fought my way to the surface, suffocating, my lungs almost bursting, I could see nothing of the oars. They must have been swept away by the chaotic currents. I saw Demetrios Contos looking back from his boat, and heard the vindictive and mocking tones of his voice as he shouted exultantly. He held steadily on his course, leaving me to perish.

There was nothing to do but to swim for it, which, in that wild confusion, was at the best a matter of but a few moments. Holding my breath and working with my hands, I managed to get off my heavy sea-boots and my jacket. Yet there was very little breath I could catch to hold, and I swiftly discovered that it was not so much a matter of swimming as of breathing.

I was beaten and buffeted, smashed under by the great San Pablo whitecaps, and strangled by the hollow tide-rip waves, which flung themselves into my eyes, nose, and mouth. Then the strange sucks would grip my legs and drag me under, to spout me up in some fierce boiling, where, even as I tried to catch my breath, a great whitecap would crash down upon my head.

It was impossible to survive any length of time. I was breathing more water than air, and drowning all the time. My senses began to leave me, my head to whirl around. I struggled on, spasmodically, instinctively, and was barely half conscious when I felt myself caught by the shoulders and hauled over the gunwale of a boat.

For some time I lay across a seat where I had been flung, face downward, and with the water running out of my mouth. After a while, still weak and faint, I turned around to see who was my rescuer. And there, in the stern, sheet in one hand and tiller in the other, grinning and nodding good-naturedly, sat Demetrios

Contos. He had intended to leave me to drown—he said so afterward—but his better self had fought the battle, conquered, and sent him back to me.

"You all-a right?" he asked.

I managed to shape a "yes" on my lips, though I could not yet speak.

"You sail-a de boat verr-a good-a," he said. "So good-a as a man."

A compliment from Demetrios Contos was a compliment indeed, and I keenly appreciated it, though I could only nod my head in acknowledgment.

We held no more conversation, for I was busy recovering and he was busy with the boat. He ran in to the wharf at Vallejo, made the boat fast, and helped me out. Then it was, as we both stood on the wharf, that Charley stepped out from behind a net-rack and put his hand on Demetrios Contos's arm.

"He saved my life, Charley," I protested, "and I don't think he ought to be arrested."

A puzzled expression came into Charley's face, which cleared immediately after, in a way it had when he made up his mind.

"I can't help it, lad," he said kindly. "I can't go back on my duty, and it's plain duty to arrest him. Today is Sunday; there are two salmon in his boat which he caught today. What else can I do?"

"But he saved my life," I persisted, unable to make any other argument.

Demetrios Contos's face went black with rage when he learned Charley's judgment. He had a sense of being unfairly treated. The better part of his nature had triumphed, he had performed a generous act and saved a helpless enemy, and in return the enemy was taking him to jail.

Charley and I were out of sorts with each other when we went back to Benicia. I stood for the spirit of the law and not the letter; but by the letter Charley made his stand. As far as he could see, there was nothing else for him to do. The law said distinctly that no salmon should be caught on Sunday. He was a patrolman, and it was his duty to enforce that law. That was all there was to it. He had done his duty, and his conscience was clear. Nevertheless, the whole thing seemed unjust to me, and I felt very sorry for Demetrios Contos.

Two days later we went down to Vallejo to the trial. I had to go along as a witness, and it was the most hateful task that I ever performed in my life when I testified on the witness stand to seeing Demetrios catch the two salmon Charley had captured him with.

Demetrios had engaged a lawyer, but his case was hopeless. The jury was out only fifteen minutes, and returned a verdict of guilty. The judge sentenced Demetrios to pay a fine of one hundred dollars or go to jail for fifty days.

Charley stepped up to the clerk of the court. "I want to pay that fine," he said, at the same time placing five twenty-dollar gold pieces on the desk. "It—it was the only way out of it, lad," he stammered, turning to me.

The moisture rushed into my eyes as I seized his hand. "I want to pay—" I began.

"To pay your half?" he interrupted. "I certainly shall expect you to pay it."

In the meantime Demetrios had been informed by his lawyer that his fee likewise had been paid by Charley.

Demetrios came over to shake Charley's hand, and all his warm Southern blood flamed in his face. Then, not to be outdone in generosity, he insisted on paying his fine and lawyer's fee himself, and flew half-way into a passion because Charley refused to let him.

More than anything else we ever did, I think, this action of Charley's impressed upon the fishermen the deeper significance of the law. Also Charley was raised high in their esteem, while I came in for a little share of praise as a boy who knew how to sail a boat. Demetrios Contos not only never broke the law again, but he became a very good friend of ours, and on more than one occasion he ran up to Benicia to have a gossip with us.

URBAN CHALLENGES

The Apostate

America has produced few short-story writers better than Jack London at his best. In "The Apostate," which appeared in When God Laughs and Other Stories *(1911), he reveals the desolate existence of a young "work-beast." The author had himself briefly toiled in a jute mill, an experience he never forgot; here he employs that setting to bring to life Johnny, a boy described as "a twisted and stunted and nameless piece of a life," who finally—though perhaps futilely—asserts himself. This evocation of life near the bottom of the working-class is relentless in its denial of romanticization; as the author observed, "it is better to be a hobo than an urban slave."*

Now I wake me up to work;
I pray the Lord I may not shirk.
If I should die before the night
I pray the Lord my work's all right.
> *Amen.*

"If you don't git up, Johnny, I won't give you a bite to eat!"

The threat had no effect on the boy. He clung stubbornly to sleep, fighting for its oblivion as the dreamer fights for his dream. The boy's hands loosely clenched themselves, and he made feeble, spasmodic blows at the air. These blows were intended for his mother, but she betrayed practised familiarity in avoiding them as she shook him roughly by the shoulder.

"Lemme 'lone!"

It was a cry that began, muffled, in the deeps of sleep, that swiftly rushed upward, like a wail, into passionate belligerence, and that died away and sank down into an inarticulate whine. It was a bestial cry, as of a soul in torment, filled with infinite protest and pain.

But she did not mind. She was a sad-eyed, tired-faced woman, and she had grown used to this task, which she repeated every day of her life. She got a grip on the bed-clothes and tried to strip them down; but the boy, ceasing his punching, clung to them desperately. In a huddle, at the foot of the bed, he still remained covered. Then she tried dragging the bedding to the floor. The boy opposed her. She braced herself. Hers was the superior weight, and the boy and bedding gave, the former instinctively following the latter in order to shelter against the chill of the room that bit into his body.

As he toppled off the edge of the bed it seemed that he must fall head-first to the floor. But consciousness fluttered up in him. He righted himself and for a moment perilously balanced. Then he struck the floor on his feet. On the instant his mother seized him by the shoulders and shook him. Again his fists struck out, this time with more force and directness. At the same time his eyes opened. She released him. He was awake.

"All right," he mumbled.

She caught up the lamp and hurried out, leaving him in darkness.

"You'll be docked," she warned back to him.

He did not mind the darkness. When he had got into his clothes, he went out into the kitchen. His tread was very heavy for so thin and light a boy. His legs dragged with their own weight, which seemed unreasonable because they were such skinny legs. He drew a broken-bottomed chair to the table.

"Johnny!" his mother called sharply.

He arose as sharply from the chair, and, without a word, went to the sink. It was a greasy, filthy sink. A smell came up from the outlet. He took no notice of it. That a sink should smell was to him part of the natural order, just as it was a part of the natural order that the soap should be grimy with dishwater and hard to lather. Nor did he try very hard to make it lather. Several splashes of the cold water from the running faucet completed the function. He did not wash his teeth. For that matter he had never seen a toothbrush, nor did he know that there existed beings in the world who were guilty of so great a foolishness as tooth washing.

"You might wash yourself wunst a day without bein' told," his mother complained.

She was holding a broken lid on the pot as she poured two cups of coffee. He made no remark, for this was a standing quarrel between them, and the one thing upon which his mother was hard as adamant. "Wunst" a day it was compulsory that he should wash his face. He dried himself on a greasy towel, damp and dirty and ragged, that left his face covered with shreds of lint.

"I wish we didn't live so far away," she said, as he sat down. "I try to do the best I can. You know that. But a dollar on the rent is such a savin', an' we've more room here. You know that."

He scarcely followed her. He had heard it all before, many times. The range of her thought was limited, and she was ever harking back to the hardship worked upon them by living so far from the mills.

"A dollar means more grub," he remarked sententiously. "I'd sooner do the walkin' an' git the grub."

He ate hurriedly, half chewing the bread and washing the unmasticated chunks down with coffee. The hot and muddy liquid went by the name of coffee. Johnny thought it was coffee—and excellent coffee. That was one of the few of life's illusions that remained to him. He had never drunk real coffee in his life.

In addition to the bread, there was a small piece of cold pork. His mother refilled his cup with coffee. As he was finishing the bread, he began to watch if more was forthcoming. She intercepted his questioning glance.

"Now, don't be hoggish, Johnny," was her comment. "You've had your share. Your brothers an' sisters are smaller'n you."

He did not answer the rebuke. He was not much of a talker. Also, he ceased his hungry glancing for more. He was uncomplaining, with a patience that was as terrible as the school in which it had been learned. He finished his coffee, wiped his mouth on the back of his hand, and started to rise.

"Wait a second," she said hastily. "I guess the loaf kin stand you another slice—a thin un."

There was legerdemain in her actions. With all the seeming of cutting a slice from the loaf for him, she put loaf and slice back in the bread box and conveyed to him one of her own two slices. She believed she had deceived him, but he had noted her sleight-of-hand. Nevertheless, he took the bread shamelessly. He had a philosophy that his mother, what of her chronic sickliness, was not much of an eater anyway.

She saw that he was chewing the bread dry, and reached over and emptied her coffee cup into his.

"Don't set good somehow on my stomach this morning," she explained.

A distant whistle, prolonged and shrieking, brought both of them to their feet. She glanced at the tin alarm clock on the shelf. The hands stood at half-past five. The rest of the factory world was just arousing from sleep. She drew a shawl about her shoulders, and on her head put a dingy hat, shapeless and ancient.

"We've got to run," she said, turning the wick of the lamp and blowing down the chimney.

They groped their way out and down the stairs. It was clear and cold, and Johnny shivered at the first contact with the outside air. The stars had not yet begun to pale in the sky, and the city lay in blackness. Both Johnny and his mother shuffled their feet as they walked. There was no ambition in the leg muscles to swing the feet clear of the ground.

After fifteen silent minutes, his mother turned off to the right.

"Don't be late," was her final warning from out of the dark that was swallowing her up.

He made no response, steadily keeping on his way. In the factory quarter, doors were opening everywhere, and he was soon one of a multitude that pressed onward through the dark. As he entered the factory gate the whistle blew again. He glanced at the east.

Across a ragged skyline of housetops a pale light was beginning to creep. This much he saw of the day as he turned his back upon it and joined his work gang.

He took his place in one of many long rows of machines. Before him, above a bin filled with small bobbins, were large bobbins revolving rapidly. Upon these he wound the jute-twine of the small bobbins. The work was simple. All that was required was celerity. The small bobbins were emptied so rapidly, and there were so many large bobbins that did the emptying, that there were no idle moments.

He worked mechanically. When a small bobbin ran out, he used his left hand for a brake, stopping the large bobbin and at the same time, with thumb and forefinger, catching the flying end of twine. Also, at the same time, with his right hand, he caught up the loose twine-end of a small bobbin. These various acts with both hands were performed simultaneously and swiftly. Then there would come a flash of his hands as he looped the weaver's knot and released the bobbin. There was nothing difficult about weaver's knots. He once boasted he could tie them in his sleep. And for that matter, he sometimes did, toiling centuries long in a single night at tying an endless succession of weaver's knots.

Some of the boys shirked, wasting time and machinery by not replacing the small bobbins when they ran out. And there was an overseer to prevent this. He caught Johnny's neighbor at the trick, and boxed his ears.

"Look at Johnny there—why ain't you like him?" the overseer wrathfully demanded.

Johnny's bobbins were running full blast, but he did not thrill at the indirect praise. There had been a time...but that was long ago, very long ago. His apathetic face was expressionless as he listened to himself being held up as a shining example. He was the perfect worker. He knew that. He had been told so, often. It was a commonplace, and besides it didn't seem to mean anything to him any more. From the perfect worker he had evolved into the perfect machine. When his work went wrong, it was with him as with the machine, due to faulty material. It would have been as possible for a perfect nail-die to cut imperfect nails as for him to make a mistake.

And small wonder. There had never been a time when he had not been in intimate relationship with machines. Machinery had almost been bred into him, and at any rate he had been brought up on it. Twelve years before, there had been a small flutter of excitement in the loom room of this very mill. Johnny's mother had fainted. They stretched her out on the floor in the midst of the shrieking machines. A couple of elderly women were called from their looms. The foreman assisted. And in a few minutes there was one more soul in the loom room than had entered by the doors. It was Johnny, born with the pounding, crashing roar of the looms in his ears, drawing with his first breath the warm, moist air that was thick with flying lint. He had coughed that first day in order to rid his lungs of the lint; and for the same reason he had coughed ever since.

The boy alongside of Johnny whimpered and sniffed. The boy's face was convulsed with hatred for the overseer who kept a threatening eye on him from a distance; but every bobbin was running full. The boy yelled terrible oaths into the whirling bobbins before him; but the sound did not carry half a dozen feet, the roaring of the room holding it in and containing it like a wall.

Of all this Johnny took no notice. He had a way of accepting things. Besides, things grow monotonous by repetition, and this particular happening he had witnessed many times. It seemed to him as useless to oppose the overseer as to defy the will of a machine. Machines were made to go in certain ways and to perform certain tasks. It was the same with the overseer.

But at eleven o'clock there was excitement in the room. In an apparently occult way the excitement instantly permeated everywhere. The one-legged boy who worked on the other side of Johnny bobbed swiftly across the floor to a bin truck that stood empty. Into this he dived out of sight, crutch and all. The superintendent of the mill was coming along, accompanied by a young man. He was well dressed and wore a starched shirt—a gentleman, in Johnny's classification of men, and also "the Inspector."

He looked sharply at the boys as he passed along. Sometimes he stopped and asked questions. When he did so, he was compelled to shout at the top of his lungs, at which moments his face was ludicrously contorted with the strain of making himself heard. His quick eye noted the empty machine alongside of Johnny's, but he said nothing. Johnny also caught his eye, and he stopped abruptly. He caught Johnny by the arm to draw him back a step from the machine; but with an exclamation of surprise he released the arm.

"Pretty skinny," the superintendent laughed anxiously.

"Pipe stems," was the answer. "Look at those legs. The boy's got the rickets—incipient, but he's got them. If epilepsy doesn't get him in the end, it will be because tuberculosis gets him first."

Johnny listened, but did not understand. Furthermore he was not interested in future ills. There was an immediate and more serious ill that threatened him in the form of the inspector.

"Now, my boy, I want you to tell me the truth," the inspector said, or shouted, bending close to the boy's ear to make him hear. "How old are you?"

"Fourteen," Johnny lied, and he lied with the full force of his lungs. So loudly did he lie that it started him off in a dry, hacking cough that lifted the lint which had been settling in his lungs all morning.

"Looks sixteen at least," said the superintendent.

"Or sixty," snapped the inspector.

"He's always looked that way."

"How long?" asked the inspector, quickly.

"For years. Never gets a bit older."

"Or younger, I dare say. I suppose he's worked here all those years?"

"Off and on—but that was before the new law was passed," the superintendent hastened to add.

"Machine idle?" the inspector asked, pointing at the unoccupied machine beside Johnny's, in which the part-filled bobbins were flying like mad.

"Looks that way." The superintendent motioned the overseer to him and shouted in his ear and pointed at the machine. "Machine's idle," he reported back to the inspector.

They passed on, and Johnny returned to his work, relieved in that the ill had been averted. But the one-legged boy was not so fortunate. The sharp-eyed inspector haled him out at arm's length from the bin truck. His lips were quivering, and his face had all the expression of one upon whom was fallen profound and irremediable disaster. The overseer looked astounded, as though for the first time he had laid eyes on the boy, while the superintendent's face expressed shock and displeasure.

"I know him," the inspector's aide said. "He's twelve years old. I've had him discharged from three factories inside the year. This makes the fourth."

He turned to the one-legged boy. "You promised me, word and honor, that you'd go to school."

The one-legged boy burst into tears. "Please, Mr. Inspector, two babies died on us, and we're awful poor."

"What makes you cough that way?" the inspector demanded, as though charging him with crime.

And as in denial of guilt, the one-legged boy replied: "It ain't nothin'. I jes' caught a cold last week, Mr. Inspector, that's all."

In the end the one-legged boy went out of the room with the inspector, the latter accompanied by the anxious and protesting superintendent. After that monotony settled down again. The long morning and the longer afternoon wore away and the whistle blew for quitting time. Darkness had already fallen when Johnny passed out through the factory gate. In the interval the sun had made a golden ladder of the sky, flooded the world with its gracious warmth, and dropped down and disappeared in the west behind a ragged skyline of housetops.

Supper was the family meal of the day—the one meal at which Johnny encountered his younger brothers and sisters. It partook of the nature of an encounter to him, for he was very old, while they were distressingly young. He had no patience with their excessive and amazing juvenility. He did not understand it. His own childhood was too far behind him. He was like an old and irritable man, annoyed by the turbulence of their young spirits that was to him arrant silliness. He glowered silently over his food, finding compensation in the thought that they would soon have to go to work. That would take the edge off of them and make them sedate and dignified—like him. Thus it was, after the fashion of the human, that Johnny made of himself a yardstick with which to measure the universe.

During the meal, his mother explained in various ways and with infinite repetition that she was trying to do the best she could; so that it was with relief, the scant meal ended, that Johnny shoved back his chair and arose. He debated for a moment between bed and the front door, and finally went out the latter. He did not go far. He sat down on the stoop, his knees drawn up and his narrow shoulders drooping forward, his elbows on his knees and the palms of his hands supporting his chin.

As he sat there, he did no thinking. He was just resting. So far as his mind was concerned, it was asleep. His brothers and sisters came out, and with other children played noisily about him. An electric globe on the corner lighted their frolics. He was peevish and irritable, that they knew; but the spirit of adventure lured them into teasing him. They joined hands before him, and, keeping time with their bodies, chanted in his face weird and uncomplimentary doggerel. At first he snarled curses at them—curses he had learned from the lips of various foremen. Finding this futile, and remembering his dignity, he relapsed into dogged silence.

His brother Will, next to him in age, having just passed his tenth birthday, was the ringleader. Johnny did not possess particularly kindly feelings toward him. His life had early been embittered by continual giving over and giving way to Will. He had a definite feeling that Will was greatly in his debt and was ungrateful about it. In his own playtime, far back in the dim past, he had been robbed of a large part of that playtime by being compelled to take care of Will. Will was a baby then, and then, as now, their mother had spent her days in the mills. To Johnny had fallen the part of little father and little mother as well.

Will seemed to show the benefit of the giving over and the giving way. He was well built, fairly rugged, as tall as his elder brother and even heavier. It was as though the life-blood of the one had been diverted into the other's veins. And in spirits it was the same. Johnny was jaded, worn out, without resilience, while his younger brother seemed bursting and spilling over with exuberance.

The mocking chant rose louder and louder. Will leaned closer as he danced, thrusting out his tongue. Johnny's left arm shot out and caught the other around the neck. At the same time he rapped his bony fist to the other's nose. It was a pathetically bony fist, but that it was sharp to hurt was evidenced by the squeal of pain it produced. The other children were uttering frightened cries, while Johnny's sister, Jennie, had dashed into the house.

He thrust Will from him, kicked him savagely on the shins, then reached for him and slammed him face downward in the dirt. Nor did he release him till the face had been rubbed into the dirt several times. Then the mother arrived, an anemic whirlwind of solicitude and maternal wrath.

"Why can't he leave me alone?" was Johnny's reply to her upbraiding. "Can't he see I'm tired?"

"I'm as big as you," Will raged in her arms, his face a mess of tears, dirt, and blood. "I'm as big as you now, an' I'm goin' to git bigger. Then I'll lick you—see if I don't."

"You ought to be to work, seein' how big you are," Johnny snarled. "That's what's the matter with you. You ought to be to work. An' it's up to your ma to put you to work."

"But he's too young," she protested. "He's only a little boy."

"I was younger'n him when I started to work."

Johnny's mouth was open, further to express the sense of unfairness that he felt, but the mouth closed with a snap. He turned gloomily on his heel and stalked into the house and to bed. The door of his room was open to let in warmth from the kitchen. As he undressed in the semi-darkness he could hear his mother talking with a neighbor woman who had dropped in. His mother was crying, and her speech was punctuated with spiritless sniffles.

"I can't make out what's gittin' into Johnny," he could hear her say. "He didn't used to be this way. He was a patient little angel.

"An' he is a good boy " she hastened to defend. "He's worked faithful, an' he did go to work too young. But it wasn't my fault. I do the best I can, I'm sure."

Prolonged sniffling from the kitchen, and Johnny murmured to himself as his eyelids closed down, "You betcher life I've worked faithful."

The next morning he was torn bodily by his mother from the grip of sleep. Then came the meager breakfast, the tramp through the dark, and the pale glimpse of day across the housetops as he turned his back on it and went in through the factory gate. It was another day, of all the days, and all the days were alike.

And yet there had been variety in his life—at the times he changed from one job to another, or was taken sick. When he was six, he was little mother and father to Will and the other children still younger. At seven he went into the mills—winding bobbins. When he was eight, he got work in another mill. His new job was marvelously easy. All he had to do was to sit down with a little stick in his hand and guide a stream of cloth that flowed past him. This stream of cloth came out of the maw of a machine, passed over a hot roller, and went on its way elsewhere. But he sat always in the one place, beyond the reach of daylight, a gas-jet flaring over him, himself part of the mechanism.

He was very happy at that job, in spite of the moist heat, for he was still young and in possession of dreams and illusions. And wonderful dreams he dreamed as he watched the steaming cloth streaming endlessly by. But there was no exercise about the work, no call upon his mind, and he dreamed less and less, while his mind grew torpid and drowsy. Nevertheless, he earned two dollars a week, and two dollars represented the difference between acute starvation and chronic underfeeding.

But when he was nine, he lost his job. Measles was the cause of it. After he recovered, he got work in a glass factory. The pay was better, and the work demanded skill. It was piece-work, and the more skillful he was, the bigger wages he earned. Here was incentive. And under this incentive he developed into a remarkable worker.

It was simple work, the tying of glass stoppers into small bottles. At his waist he carried a bundle of twine. He held the bottles between his knees so that he might work with both hands. Thus, in a sitting position and bending over his own knees, his narrow shoulders grew humped and his chest was contracted for ten hours each day. This was not good for the lungs, but he tied three hundred dozen bottles a day.

The superintendent was very proud of him, and brought visitors to look at him. In ten hours three hundred dozen bottles passed through his hands, This meant that he had attained machine-like perfection. All waste movements were eliminated. Every motion of his thin arms, every movement of a muscle in the thin fingers, was swift and accurate. He worked at high tension, and the result was that he grew nervous. At night his muscles twitched in his sleep, and in the daytime he could not relax and rest. He remained keyed up and his muscles continued to twitch. Also he grew sallow and his lint-cough grew worse. Then pneumonia laid hold of the feeble lungs within the contracted chest, and he lost his job in the glass-works.

Now he had returned to the jute mills where he had first begun with winding bobbins. But promotion was waiting for him. He was a good worker. He would next go on the starcher, and later he would go into the loom room. There was nothing after that except increased efficiency.

The machinery ran faster than when he had first gone to work, and his mind ran slower. He no longer dreamed at all, though his earlier years had been full of dreaming. Once he had been in love. It was when he first began guiding the cloth over the hot roller, and it was with the daughter of the superintendent. She was much older than he, a young woman, and he had seen her at a distance only a paltry half-dozen times. But that made no difference. On the surface of the cloth stream that poured past him, he pictured radiant futures wherein he performed prodigies of toil, invented miraculous machines, won to the mastership of the mills, and in the end took her in his arms and kissed her soberly on the brow.

But that was all in the long ago, before he had grown too old and tired to love. Also, she had married and gone away, and his mind had gone to sleep. Yet it had been a wonderful experience, and he used often to look back upon it as other men and women look back upon the time they believed in fairies. He had never believed in fairies nor Santa Claus; but he had believed implicitly in the smiling future his imagination had wrought into the steaming cloth stream.

He had become a man very early in life. At seven, when he drew his first wages, began his adolescence. A certain feeling of independence crept up in him, and the relationship between him and his mother changed. Somehow, as an earner and breadwinner, doing his own work in the world, he was more like an equal with her. Manhood, full-blown manhood, had come when he was eleven, at which time he had gone to work on the night shift for six months. No child works on the night shift and remains a child.

There had been several great events in his life. One of these had been when his mother bought some California prunes. Two others had been the two times when she cooked custard. Those had been events. He remembered them kindly. And at that time his mother had told him of a blissful dish she would sometime make—"floating island," she had called it, "better than custard." For years he had looked forward to the day when he would sit down to the table with floating island before him, until at last he had relegated the idea of it to the limbo of unattainable ideals.

Once he found a silver quarter lying on the sidewalk. That, also, was a great event in his life, withal a tragic one. He knew his duty on the instant the silver flashed on his eyes, before even he had picked it up. At home, as usual, there was not enough to eat, and home he should have taken it as he did his wages every Saturday night. Right conduct in this case was obvious; but he never had any spending of his money, and he was suffering from candy hunger. He was ravenous for the sweets that only on red-letter days he had ever tasted in his life.

He did not attempt to deceive himself. He knew it was sin, and deliberately he sinned when he went on a fifteen-cent candy debauch. Ten cents he saved for a future orgy; but not being accustomed to the carrying of money, he lost the ten cents. This occurred at the time when he was suffering all the torments of conscience, and it was to him an act of divine retribution. He had a frightened sense of the closeness of an awful and wrathful God. God had seen, and God had been swift to punish, denying him even the full wages of sin.

In memory he always looked back upon that event as the one great criminal deed of his life, and at the recollection his conscience always awoke and gave him another twinge. It was the one skeleton in his closet. Also, being so made and circumstanced, he looked back upon the deed with regret. He was dissatisfied with the manner in which he had spent the quarter. He could have invested it better, and, out of his later knowledge of the quickness of God, he would have beaten God out by spending the whole quarter at one fell swoop. In retrospect he spent the quarter a thousand times, and each time to better advantage.

There was one other memory of the past, dim and faded, but stamped into his soul everlasting by the savage feet of his father. It was more like a nightmare than a remembered vision of a concrete thing—more like the race-memory of man that makes him fall in his sleep and that goes back to his arboreal ancestry.

This particular memory never came to Johnny in broad daylight when he was wide awake. It came at night, in bed, at the moment that his consciousness was sinking down and losing itself in sleep. It always aroused him to frightened wakefulness, and for the moment, in the first sickening start, it seemed to him that he lay crosswise on the foot of the bed. In the bed were the vague forms of his father and mother. He never saw what his father looked like. He had but one impression of his father, and that was that he had savage and pitiless feet.

His earlier memories lingered with him, but he had no late memories. All days were alike. Yesterday or last year were the same as a thousand years—or a minute. Nothing ever happened. There were no events to mark the march of time. Time did not march. It stood always still. It was only the whirling machines that moved, and they moved nowhere—in spite of the fact that they moved faster.

When he was fourteen, he went to work on the starcher. It was a colossal event. Something had at last happened that could be remembered beyond a night's sleep or a week's payday. It marked an era. It was a machine Olympiad, a thing to date from. "When I went to work on the starcher," or, "after," or "before I went to work on the starcher," were sentences often on his lips.

He celebrated his sixteenth birthday by going into the loom room and taking a loom. Here was an incentive again, for it was piece-work. And he excelled, because the clay of him had been moulded by the mills into the perfect machine. At the end of three months he was running two looms, and, later, three and four.

At the end of his second year at the looms he was turning out more yards than any other weaver, and more than twice as much as some of the less skillful ones. And at home things began to prosper as he approached the full stature of his earning power. Not, however, that his increased earnings were in excess of need. The children were growing up. They ate more. And they were going to school, and schoolbooks cost money. And somehow, the faster he worked, the faster climbed the prices of things. Even the rent went up, though the house had fallen from bad to worse disrepair.

He had grown taller, but with his increased height he seemed leaner than ever. Also, he was more nervous. With the nervousness increased his peevishness and irritability. The children had learned by many bitter lessons to fight shy of him. His mother respected him for his earning power, but somehow her respect was tinctured with fear.

There was no joyousness in life for him. The procession of the days he never saw. The nights he slept away in twitching unconsciousness. The rest of the time he worked, and his consciousness was machine consciousness. Outside this his mind was a blank. He had no ideals, and but one illusion; namely, that he drank excellent coffee. He was a work-beast. He had no mental life whatever; yet deep down in the crypts of his mind, unknown to him, were being weighed and sifted every hour of his toil, every movement of his hands, every twitch of his muscles, and preparations were making for a future course of action that would amaze him and all his little world.

It was in the late spring that he came home from work one night aware of unusual tiredness. There was a keen expectancy in the air as he sat down to the table, but he did not notice. He went through the meal in moody silence, mechanically eating what was before him. The children um'd and ah'd and made smacking noises with their mouths. But he was deaf to them.

"D'ye know what you're eatin'?" his mother demanded at last, desperately.

He looked vacantly at the dish before him, and vacantly at her.

"Floatin' island," she announced triumphantly.

"Oh," he said.

"Floating island!" the children chorused loudly.

"Oh," he said. And after two or three mouthfuls, he added, "I guess I ain't hungry tonight."

He dropped the spoon, shoved back his chair, and arose wearily from the table.

"An' I guess I'll go to bed."

His feet dragged more heavily than usual as he crossed the kitchen floor. Undressing was a Titan's task, a monstrous futility, and he wept weakly as he crawled into bed, one shoe still on. He was aware of a rising, swelling something inside his head that made his brain thick and fuzzy. His lean fingers felt as big as his wrist, while in the ends of them was a remoteness of sensation vague and fuzzy like his brain. The small of his back ached intolerably. All his bones ached. He ached everywhere. And in his head began the shrieking, pounding, crashing, roaring of a million looms. All space was filled with flying shuttles. They darted in and out, intricately, amongst the stars. He worked a thousand looms himself, and ever they speeded up, faster and faster, and his brain unwound, faster and faster, and became the thread that fed the thousand flying shuttles.

He did not go to work next morning. He was too busy weaving colossally on the thousand looms that ran inside his head. His mother went to work, but first she sent for the doctor. It was a severe attack of *la grippe,* he said. Jennie served as nurse and carried out his instructions.

It was a very severe attack, and it was a week before Johnny dressed and tottered feebly across the floor. Another week, the doctor said, and he would be fit to return to work. The foreman of the loom room visited him on Sunday afternoon, the first day of his convalescence. The best weaver in the room, the foreman told his mother. His job would be held for him. He could come back to work a week from Monday.

"Why don't you thank 'im, Johnny?" his mother asked anxiously.

"He's ben that sick he ain't himself yet," she explained apologetically to the visitor.

Johnny sat hunched up and gazing steadfastly at the floor. He sat in the same position long after the foreman had gone. It was warm outdoors, and he sat on the stoop in the afternoon. Sometimes his lips moved. He seemed lost in endless calculations.

Next morning, after the day grew warm, he took his seat on the stoop. He had pencil and paper this time with which to continue his calculations, and he calculated painfully and amazingly.

"What comes after millions?" he asked at noon, when Will came home from school. "An' how d'ye work 'em?"

That afternoon he finished his task. Each day, but without paper and pencil, he returned to the stoop. He was greatly absorbed in the one tree that grew across the street. He studied it for hours at a time, and was unusually interested when the wind swayed its branches and fluttered its leaves. Throughout the week he seemed lost in a great communion with himself. On Sunday, sitting on the stoop, he laughed aloud, several times, to the perturbation of his mother, who had not heard him laugh in years.

Next morning, in the early darkness, she came to his bed to rouse him. He had had his fill of sleep all week, and awoke easily. He made no struggle, nor did he attempt to hold on to the bedding when she stripped it from him. He lay quietly, and spoke quietly.

"It ain't no use, ma."

"You'll be late," she said, under the impression that he was still stupid with sleep.

"I'm awake, ma, an' I tell you it ain't no use. You might as well lemme alone. I ain't goin' to git up."

"But you'll lose your job!" she cried.

"I ain't goin' to git up," he repeated in a strange, passionless voice.

She did not go to work herself that morning. This was sickness beyond any sickness she had ever known. Fever and delirium she could understand; but this was insanity. She pulled the bedding up over him and sent Jennie for the doctor.

When that person arrived, Johnny was sleeping gently, and gently he awoke and allowed his pulse to be taken.

"Nothing the matter with him," the doctor reported. "Badly debilitated, that's all. Not much meat on his bones."

"He's always been that way," his mother volunteered.

"Now go 'way, ma, an' let me finish my snooze."

Johnny spoke sweetly and placidly, and sweetly and placidly he rolled over on his side and went to sleep.

At ten o'clock he awoke and dressed himself. He walked out into the kitchen, where he found his mother with a frightened expression on her face.

"I'm goin' away, ma," he announced, "an' I jes' want to say good-bye."

She threw her apron over her head and sat down suddenly and wept. He waited patiently.

"I might a-known it," she was sobbing.

"Where?" she finally asked, removing the apron from her head and gazing up at him with a stricken face in which there was little curiosity.

"I don't know—anywhere."

As he spoke, the tree across the street appeared with dazzling brightness on his inner vision. It seemed to lurk just under his eyelids, and he could see it whenever he wished.

"An' your job?" she quavered.

"I ain't never goin' to work again."

"My God, Johnny!" she wailed, "don't say that!"

What he had said was blasphemy to her. As a mother who hears her child deny God, was Johnny's mother shocked by his words.

"What's got into you, anyway?" she demanded, with a lame attempt at imperativeness.

"Figures," he answered. "Jes' figures. I've ben doin' a lot of figurin' this week, an' it's most surprisin'."

"I don't see what that's got to do with it," she sniffled.

Johnny smiled patiently, and his mother was aware of a distinct shock at the persistent absence of his peevishness and irritability.

"I'll show you," he said. "I'm plum' tired out. What makes me tired? Moves. I've ben movin' ever since I was born. I'm tired of movin', an' I ain't goin' to move anymore. Remember when I worked in the glass-house? I used to do three hundred dozen a day. Now I reckon I made about ten different moves to each bottle. That's thirty-six thousan' moves a day. Ten days, three hundred an' sixty thousan' moves a day. One month, one million an' eighty thousan' moves. Chuck out the eighty thousan'—" he spoke with the complacent beneficence of a philanthropist—"chuck out the eighty thousan', that leaves a million moves a month—twelve million moves a year.

"At the looms I'm movin' twic'st as much. That makes twenty-five million moves a year, an' it seems to me I've ben a movin' that way 'most a million years.

"Now this week I ain't moved at all. I ain't made one move in hours an' hours. I tell you it was swell, jes' settin' there, hours an' hours, an' doin' nothin'. I ain't never ben happy before. I never had any time. I've ben movin' all the time. That ain't no way to be happy. An' I ain't goin' to do it anymore. I'm jes' goin' to set, an' set, an' rest, an' rest, and then rest some more."

"But what's goin' to come of Will an' the children?" she asked despairingly.

"That's it, 'Will an' the children,'" he repeated.

But there was no bitterness in his voice. He had long known his mother's ambition for the younger boy, but the thought of it no longer rankled. Nothing mattered anymore. Not even that.

"I know, ma, what you've ben plannin' for Will—keepin' him in school to make a bookkeeper out of him. But it ain't no use, I've quit. He's got to go to work."

"An' after I have brung you up the way I have," she wept, starting to cover her head with the apron and changing her mind.

"You never brung me up," he answered with sad kindliness. "I brung myself up, ma, an' I brung up Will. He's bigger'n me, an' heavier, an' taller. When I was a kid, I reckon I didn't git enough to eat. When he come along an' was a kid, I was workin' an' earnin' grub for him too. But that's done with. Will can go to work, same as me, or he can go to hell, I don't care which. I'm tired. I'm goin' now. Ain't you goin' to say good-bye?"

She made no reply. The apron had gone over her head again, and she was crying. He paused a moment in the doorway.

"I'm sure I done the best I knew how," she was sobbing.

He passed out of the house and down the street. A wan delight came into his face at the sight of the lone tree. "Jes' ain't goin' to do nothin'," he said to himself, half aloud, in a crooning tone.

He glanced wistfully up at the sky, but the bright sun dazzled and blinded him.

It was a long walk he took, and he did not walk fast. It took him past the jute mill. The muffled roar of the loom room came to his ears, and he smiled. It was a gentle, placid smile. He hated no one, not even the pounding, shrieking machines. There was no bitterness in him, nothing but an inordinate hunger for rest.

The houses and factories thinned out and the open spaces increased as he approached the country. At last the city was behind him, and he was walking down a leafy lane beside the railroad track. He did not walk like a man. He did not look like a man. He was a travesty of the human. It was a twisted and stunted and nameless piece of life that shambled like a sickly ape, arms loose-hanging, stoop-shouldered, narrow-chested, grotesque and terrible.

He passed by a small railroad station and lay down in the grass under a tree. All afternoon he lay there. Sometimes he dozed, with muscles that twitched in his sleep. When awake, he lay without movement, watching the birds or looking up at the sky through the branches of the tree above him. Once or twice he laughed aloud, but without relevance to anything he had seen or felt.

After twilight had gone, in the first darkness of the night, a freight train rumbled into the station. When the engine was switching cars on to the side-track, Johnny crept along the side of the train. He pulled open the side door of an empty boxcar and awkwardly and laboriously climbed in. He closed the door. The engine whistled. Johnny was lying down, and in the darkness he smiled.

from John Barleycorn

Jack London was a heavy drinker. Biographer Clarice Stasz suggests that John Barleycorn *(1913) was an attempt at self-therapy: "Doubtless he thought that by describing the problem with brutal frankness and analyzing its course, he could control it." Perhaps more importantly, this tough, confessional book also reveals how alcohol dulls the hardship endured by those Jack called "work-beasts"—the exploited laboring class—and how it came to define masculinity among them, with the tavern their solace. The following excerpt introduces readers to the saloons and the pressure to drink Jack knew even as a boy in Oakland.*

This physical loathing for alcohol I have never got over. But I have conquered it. To this day I reconquer it every time I take a drink. The palate never ceases to rebel, and the palate can be trusted to know what is good for the body. But men do not knowingly drink for the effect alcohol produces on the body. What they drink for is the brain-effect; and if it must come through the body, so much the worse for the body.

And yes, despite my physical loathing for alcohol, the brightest spots in my child life were the saloons. Sitting on the heavy potato wagons, wrapped in fog, feet stinging from inactivity, the horses plodding slowly along the deep road through the sandhills, one bright vision made the way never too long. The bright vision was the saloon at Colma, where my father, or whoever drove, always got out to get a drink. And I got out to warm by the great stove and get a soda cracker. Just one soda cracker, but a fabulous luxury. Saloons were good for something. Back behind the plodding horses, I would take an hour in consuming that one cracker. I took the smallest of nibbles, never losing a crumb, and chewed the nibble till it became the thinnest and most delectable of pastes. I never voluntarily swallowed this paste. I just tasted it, and went on tasting it, turning it over with my tongue, spreading it on the inside of one check, then on the inside of the other check, until, at the end, it eluded me and in tiny drops and oozelets slipped and dribbled down my throat. Horace Fletcher had nothing on me when it came to soda crackers.

I liked saloons. Especially I liked the San Francisco saloons. They had the most delicious dainties for the taking—strange breads and crackers, cheeses, sausages, sardines—wonderful foods that I never saw on our meager home table. And once, I remember, a barkeeper mixed me a sweet temperance drink of syrup and soda water. My father did not pay for it. It was the barkeeper's treat, and he became my ideal of a good, kind man. I dreamed daydreams of him for years. Although I was seven years old at the time, I can see him now with undiminished clearness, though I never laid eyes on him but that one time. The saloon was south of Market Street in San Francisco. It stood on the west side of the street. As you entered, the bar was on the left. On the right, against the wall, was the free-lunch counter. It was a long, narrow room, and at the rear, beyond the beer kegs on tap, were small round tables and chairs. The barkeeper was blue-eyed, and had fair, silky hair peeping out from under a black silk skull-cap. I remember he wore a brown Cardigan jacket, and I know precisely the spot, in the midst of the array of bottles, from which he took the bottle of red-colored syrup. He and my father talked long, and I sipped my sweet drink and worshiped him. And for years afterward I worshiped the memory of him.

Despite my two disastrous experiences, here was John Barleycorn, prevalent and accessible everywhere in the community, luring and drawing me. Here were connotations of the saloon making deep indentations in a child's mind. Here was a child, forming its first judgments of the world, finding the saloon a delightful and desirable place. Stores, nor public buildings, nor all the dwellings of men ever opened their doors to me and let me warm by their fires or permitted me to eat the food of the gods from narrow shelves against the wall. Their doors were ever closed to me; the saloon's doors were ever open. And always and everywhere I found saloons, on highway and byway, up narrow alleys and on busy thoroughfares, bright-lighted and cheerful, warm in winter and in summer dark and cool. Yes, the saloon was a mighty fine place, and it was more than that.

By the time I was ten years old, my family had abandoned ranching and gone to live in the city. And here, at ten, I began on the streets as a newsboy. One of the reasons for this was that we needed the money. Another reason was that I needed the exercise. I had found my way to the Free Public Library, and was reading myself into nervous prostration. On the poor ranches on which I had lived there had been no books. In ways truly miraculous, I had been lent four books, marvelous books, and them I had devoured. One was the life of Garfield; the second, Paul du Chaillu's African travels; the third, a novel by Ouida with the last forty pages missing; and the fourth, Irving's *Alhambra*. This last had been lent me by a schoolteacher. I was not a forward child. Unlike Oliver Twist, I was incapable of asking for more. When I returned the *Alhambra* to the teacher I hoped she would lend me another book. And because she did not—most likely she deemed me unappreciative— I cried all the way home on the three-mile tramp from the school to the ranch. I waited and yearned for her to lend me another book. Scores of times I nerved myself almost to the point of asking her, but never quite reached the necessary pitch of effrontery.

And then came the city of Oakland, and on the shelves of that Free Library I discovered all the great world beyond the skyline. Here were thousands of books as good as my four wonder-books, and some were even better. Libraries were not concerned with children in those days, and I had strange adventures. I remember, in the catalog, being impressed by the title, *The Adventures of Peregrine Pickle*. I filled an application blank and the librarian handed me the collected and entirely unexpurgated works of Smollet in one huge volume. I read everything, but principally history and adventure, and all the old travels and voyages. I read mornings, afternoons, and nights. I read in bed, I read at table, I read as I walked to and from school, and I read at recess while the other boys were playing. I began to get the "jerks." To everybody I replied: "Go away. You make me nervous."

And so, at ten, I was out on the streets, a newsboy. I had no time to read. I was busy getting exercise and learning how to fight, busy learning forwardness, and brass and bluff. I had an imagination and a curiosity about all things that made me plastic. Not least among the things I was curious about was the saloon. And I was in and out of many a one. I remember, in those days, on the east side of Broadway between Sixth and Seventh, from corner to corner, there was a solid block of saloons.

In the saloons life was different. Men talked with great voices, laughed great laughs, and there was an atmosphere of greatness. Here was something more than common every day where nothing happened. Here life was always very live, and, sometimes, even lurid, when blows were struck, and blood was shed, and big policemen came shouldering in. Great moments, these, for me, my head filled with all the wild and valiant fighting of the gallant adventures on sea and land. There were no big moments when I trudged along the street throwing my papers in at doors. But in the saloons, even the sots, stupefied, sprawling across the tables or in the sawdust, were objects of mystery and wonder.

And more, the saloons were right. The city fathers sanctioned them and licensed them. They were not the terrible places I heard boys deem them who lacked my opportunities to know. Terrible they might be, but then that only meant they were terribly wonderful, and it is the terribly wonderful that a boy desires to know. In the same way pirates, and shipwrecks, and battles were terrible; and what healthy boy wouldn't give his immortal soul to participate in such affairs?

Besides, in saloons I saw reporters, editors, lawyers, judges, whose names and faces I knew. They put the seal of social approval on the saloon. They verified my own feeling of fascination in the saloon. They, too, must have found there that something different, that something beyond, which I sensed and groped after. What it was, I did not know; yet there it must be, for there men focused like buzzing flies about a honey pot. I had no sorrows, and the world was very bright, so I could not guess that what these men sought was forgetfulness of jaded toil and stale grief.

Not that I drank at that time. From ten to fifteen I rarely tasted liquor, but I was intimately in contact with drinkers and drinking places. The only reason I did not drink was because I didn't like the stuff. As the time passed, I worked as boy-helper on an ice-wagon, set up pins in a bowling alley with a saloon attached, and swept out saloons at Sunday picnic grounds.

Big jovial Josie Harper ran a roadhouse at Telegraph Avenue and Thirty-ninth Street. Here for a year I delivered an evening paper, until my route was changed to the waterfront and tenderloin of Oakland. The first month, when I collected Josie Harper's bill, she poured me a glass of wine. I was ashamed to refuse, so I drank it. But after that I watched the chance when she wasn't around so as to collect from her barkeeper.

The first day I worked in the bowling alley, the barkeeper, according to custom, called us boys up to have a drink after we had been setting up pins for several hours. The others asked for beer. I said I'd take ginger ale. The boys snickered, and I noticed the barkeeper favored me with a strange, searching scrutiny. Nevertheless he opened a bottle of ginger ale. Afterward, back in the alleys, in the pauses between games, the boys enlightened me. I had offended the barkeeper. A bottle of ginger ale cost the saloon ever so much more than a glass of steam beer; and it was up to me, if I wanted to hold my job, to drink beer. Besides, beer was food. I could work better on it. There was no food in ginger ale. After that, when I couldn't sneak out of it, I drank beer and wondered what men found in it that was so good. I was always aware that I was missing something.

What I really liked in those days was candy. For five cents I could buy five "cannon-balls"—big lumps of the most delicious lastingness. I could chew and worry a single one for an hour. Then there was a Mexican who sold big slabs of brown chewing-taffy for five cents each. It required a quarter of a day to properly absorb one of them. And many a day I made my entire lunch off of one of those slabs. In truth, I found food there, but not in beer.

from Martin Eden

Often considered London's most controversial and most autobio-graphical novel, this 1909 chronicle of a young man's move from inno-cence to enlightenment draws on the author's early years. Martin is a bright but crude sailor who falls under the spell of an upper-class woman and radically changes his life in order to become worthy of her. He eventually decides to become a writer, but suffers rejection from many editors and the young woman as well. During this period, the frustrated and impoverished young man takes a job in a resort hotel's laundry, the scene from chapter XVII, the first excerpt included here. The second excerpt, from chapter XLII, follows Martin back to his rowdy, working-class haunts, where, it becomes clear, Martin's eventu-al success as an author does not bring him happiness in the end.

Martin learned to do many things. In the course of the first week, in one afternoon, he and Joe accounted for the two hundred white shirts. Joe ran the tiler, a machine wherein a hot iron was hooked on a steel string which furnished the pressure. By this means he ironed the yoke, wristbands, and neckband, setting the latter at right angles to the shirt, and put the glossy finish on the bosom. As fast as he finished them, he flung the shirts on a rack between him and Martin, who caught them up and "backed" them. This task consisted of ironing all the unstarched portions of the shirts.

It was exhausting work, carried on, hour after hour, at top speed. Out on the broad verandas of the hotel, men and women, in cool white, sipped iced drinks and kept their circulation down. But in the laundry the air was sizzling. The huge stove roared red hot and white hot, while the irons, moving over the damp cloth, sent up clouds of steam. The heat of these irons was different from that used by housewives. An iron that stood the ordinary test of a wet finger was too cold for Joe and Martin, and such a test was useless. They went wholly by holding the irons close to their cheeks, gauging the heat by some secret mental process that Martin admired but could not understand. When the fresh irons proved too hot, they hooked them on iron rods and dipped them into cold water. This again required a precise and subtle judgment. A fraction of a second too long in the water and the fine and silken edge of the proper heat was lost, and Martin found time to marvel at the accuracy he developed—an automatic accuracy, founded upon criteria that were machinelike and unerring.

But there was little time in which to marvel. All Martin's consciousness was concentrated in the work. Ceaselessly active, head and hand, an intelligent machine, all that constituted him a man was devoted to furnishing that intelligence. There was no room in his brain for the universe and its mighty problems. All the broad and spacious corridors of his mind were closed and hermetically sealed. The echoing chamber of his soul was a narrow room, a conning tower, whence were directed his arm and shoulder muscles, his ten nimble fingers, and the swift-moving iron along its steaming path in broad, sweeping strokes, just so many strokes and no more, just so far with each stroke and not a fraction of an inch farther, rushing along interminable sleeves, sides, backs, and tails, and tossing the finished shirts, without rumpling, upon the receiving frame. And even as his hurrying soul tossed, it was reaching for another shirt. This went on, hour after hour, while outside all the world swooned under the overhead California sun. But there was no swooning in that superheated room. The cool guests on the verandas needed clean linen.

The sweat poured from Martin. He drank enormous quantities of water, but so great was the heat of the day and of his exertions, that the water sluiced through the interstices of his flesh and out at all his pores. Always, at sea, except at rare intervals, the work he performed had given him ample opportunity to commune with himself. The master of the ship had been lord of Martin's time; but here the manager of the hotel was lord of Martin's thoughts as well. He had no thoughts save for the nerve-racking, body-destroying toil. Outside of that it was impossible to think. He did not know that he loved Ruth. She did not even exist, for his driven soul had no time to remember her. It was only when he crawled to bed at night, or to breakfast in the morning, that she asserted herself to him in fleeting memories.

"This is hell, ain't it?" Joe remarked once.

Martin nodded, but felt a rasp of irritation. The statement had been obvious and unnecessary. They did not talk while they worked. Conversation threw them out of their stride, as it did this time, compelling Martin to miss a stroke of his iron and to make two extra motions before he caught his stride again.

On Friday morning the washer ran. Twice a week they had to put through hotel linen—the sheets, pillow-slips, spreads, table-cloths and napkins. This finished, they buckled down to "fancy starch." It was slow work, fastidious and delicate, and Martin did not learn it so readily. Besides, he could not take chances. Mistakes were disastrous.

"See that," Joe said, holding up a filmy corset-cover that he could have crumpled from view in the hand. "Scorch that an' it's twenty dollars out of your wages."

So Martin did not scorch that, and eased down on his muscular tension, though nervous tension rose higher than ever, and he listened sympathetically to the other's blasphemies as he toiled and suffered over the beautiful things that women wear when they do not have to do their own laundrying. "Fancy starch" was Martin's nightmare, and it was Joe's, too. It was "fancy starch" that robbed them of their hard-won minutes. They toiled at it all day. At seven in the evening they broke off to run the hotel linen through the mangle. At ten o'clock, while the hotel guests slept, the two laundrymen sweated on at "fancy starch" till midnight, till one, till two. At half-past two they knocked off.

Saturday morning it was "fancy starch," and odds and ends, and at three in the afternoon the week's work was done.

"You ain't a-goin' to ride them seventy miles into Oakland on top of this?" Joe demanded, as they sat on the stairs and took a triumphant smoke.

"Got to," was the answer.

"What are you goin' for?—a girl?"

"No; to save two and a half on the railroad ticket. I want to renew some books at the library."

"Why don't you send 'em down an' up by express? That'll cost only a quarter each way."

Martin considered it.

"An' take a rest tomorrow," the other urged. "You need it. I know I do. I'm plumb tuckered out."

He looked it. Indomitable, never resting, fighting for seconds and minutes all week, circumventing delays and crushing down obstacles, a font of resistless energy, a high-driven human motor, a demon for work, now that he had accomplished the week's task he was in a state of collapse. He was worn and haggard, and his handsome face drooped in lean exhaustion. He puffed his cigarette spiritlessly, and his voice was peculiarly dead and monotonous. All the snap and fire had gone out of him. His triumph seemed a sorry one.

"An' next week we got to do it all over again," he said sadly. "An' what's the good of it all, hey? Sometimes I wish I was a hobo. They don't work, an' they get their livin'. Gee! I wish I had a glass of beer; but I can't get up the gumption to go down to the village an' get it. You'll stay over, an' send your books down by express, or else you're a damn fool."

"But what can I do here all day Sunday?" Martin asked.

"Rest. You don't know how tired you are. Why, I'm that tired Sunday I can't even read the papers. I was sick once—typhoid. In the hospital two months an' a half. Didn't do a tap of work all that time. It was beautiful."

"It was beautiful," he repeated dreamily, a minute later.

Martin took a bath, after which he found that the head laundryman had disappeared. Most likely he had gone for the glass of beer, Martin decided, but the half-mile walk down to the village to find out seemed a long journey to him. He lay on his bed with his shoes off, trying to make up his mind. He did not reach out for a book. He was too tired to feel sleepy, and he lay, scarcely thinking, in a semi-stupor of weariness, until it was time for supper. Joe did not appear for that function, and when Martin heard the gardener remark that most likely he was ripping the slats off the bar, Martin understood. He went to bed immediately afterward, and in the morning decided that he was greatly rested. Joe being still absent, Martin procured a Sunday paper and lay down in a shady nook under the trees. The morning passed, he knew not how. He did not sleep, nobody disturbed him, and he did not finish the paper. He came back to it in the afternoon, after dinner, and fell asleep over it.

So passed Sunday, and Monday morning he was hard at work, sorting clothes, while Joe, a towel bound tightly around his head, with groans and blasphemies, was running the washer and mixing soft-soap.

"I simply can't help it," he explained. "I got to drink when Saturday night comes around."

Another week passed, a great battle that continued under the electric lights each night and that culminated on Saturday afternoon at three o'clock, when Joe tasted his moment of wilted triumph and then drifted down to the village to forget. Martin's Sunday was the same as before. He slept in the shade of the trees, toiled aimlessly through the newspaper, and spent long hours lying on his back, doing nothing, thinking nothing. He was too dazed to think, though he was aware that he did not like himself. He was self-repelled as though he had undergone some degradation or was intrinsically foul. All that was godlike in him was blotted out. The spur of ambition was blunted; he had no vitality with which to feel the prod of it. He was dead. His soul seemed dead. He was a beast, a work-beast. He saw no beauty in the sunshine sifting down through the green leaves, nor did the azure vault of the sky whisper as of old and hint of cosmic vastness and secrets trembling to disclosure. Life was intolerably dull and stupid, and its taste was bad in his mouth. A black screen was drawn across his mirror of inner vision, and fancy lay in a darkened sick-room where entered no ray of light. He envied Joe, down in the village, rampant, tearing the slats off the bar, his brain gnawing with maggots, exulting in maudlin ways over maudlin things, fantastically and gloriously drunk and forgetful of Monday morning and the week of deadening toil to come.

A third week went by, and Martin loathed himself, and loathed life. He was oppressed by a sense of failure. There was reason for the editors refusing his stuff. He could see that clearly now, and laugh at himself and the dreams he had dreamed. Ruth returned his "Sea Lyrics" by mail. He read her letter apathetically. She did her best to say how much she liked them and that they were beautiful. But she could not lie, and she could not disguise the truth from herself. She knew they were failures, and he read her disapproval in every perfunctory and unenthusiastic line of her letter. And she was right. He was firmly convinced of it as he read the poems over. Beauty and wonder had departed from him, and as he read the poems he caught himself puzzling as to what he had had in mind when he wrote them. His audacities of phrase struck him as grotesque, his felicities of expression were monstrosities and everything was absurd, unreal, and impossible. He would have burned the "Sea Lyrics" on the spot, had his will been strong enough to set them aflame. There was the engine-room, but the exertion of carrying them to the furnace was not worthwhile. All his exertion was used in washing other persons' clothes. He did not have any left for private affairs.

He resolved that when Sunday came he would pull himself together and answer Ruth's letter. But Saturday afternoon, after work was finished and he had taken a bath, the desire to forget overpowered him. "I guess I'll go down and see how Joe's getting on," was the way he put it to himself; and in the same moment he knew that he lied. But he did not have the energy to consider the lie. If he had had the energy, he would have refused to consider the lie, because he wanted to forget. He started for the village slowly and casually, increasing his pace in spite of himself as he neared the saloon.

"I thought you was on the water-wagon," was Joe's greeting.

Martin did not deign to offer excuses, but called for whiskey, filling his own glass brimming before he passed the bottle.

"Don't take all night about it," he said roughly.

The other was dawdling with the bottle, and Martin refused to wait for him, tossing the glass off in a gulp and refilling it.

"Now, I can wait for you," he said grimly, "but hurry up."

Joe hurried, and they drank together.

"The work did it, eh?" Joe queried.

Martin refused to discuss the matter.

"It's fair hell, I know," the other went on, "but I kind of hate to see you come off the wagon, Mart. Well, here's how!"

Martin drank on silently, biting out his orders and invitations and awing the barkeeper, an effeminate country youngster with watery blue eyes and hair parted in the middle.

"It's something scandalous the way they work us poor devils," Joe was remarking. "If I didn't bowl up, I'd break loose an' burn down the shebang. My bowlin' up is all that saves 'em, I can tell you that."

But Martin made no answer. A few more drinks, and in his brain he felt the maggots of intoxication beginning to crawl. Ah, it was living, the first breath of life he had breathed in three weeks. His dreams came back to him. Fancy came out of the darkened room and lured him on, a thing of flaming brightness. His mirror of vision was silver-clear, a flashing, dazzling palimpsest of imagery. Wonder and beauty walked with him, hand-in-hand, and all power was his. He tried to tell it to Joe, but Joe had visions of his own, infallible schemes whereby he would escape the slavery of laundry-work and become himself the owner of a great steam laundry.

"I tell yeh, Mart, they won't be no kids workin' in my laundry—not on yer life. An' they won't be no workin' a livin' soul after six p.m. You hear me talk! They'll be machinery enough an' hands enough to do it all in decent workin' hours, an' Mart, s'help me, I'll make yeh superintendent of the whole shebang—the whole of it, all of it. Now here's the scheme. I get on the water-wagon an' save my money for two years—save an' then—"

But Martin turned away, leaving him to tell it to the barkeeper, until that worthy was called away to furnish drinks to two farmers who, coming in, accepted Martin's invitation. Martin dispensed royal largess, inviting everybody up, farm hands, a stableman, and the gardener's assistant from the hotel, the barkeeper, and the furtive hobo who slid in like a shadow and like a shadow hovered at the end of the bar....

One day Martin became aware that he was lonely. He was healthy and strong, and had nothing to do. The cessation from writing and studying, the death of Brissenden, and the estrangement from Ruth had made a big hole in his life; and his life refused to be pinned down to good living in cafés and the smoking of Egyptian cigarettes. It was true the South Seas were calling to him, but he had a feeling that the game was not yet played out in the United States. Two books were soon to be published, and he had more books that might find publication. Money could be made out of them, and he would wait and take a sackful of it into the South Seas. He knew a valley and a bay in the Marquesas that he could buy for a thousand Chili dollars. The valley ran from the horseshoe, land-locked bay to the tops of the dizzy, cloud-capped peaks and contained perhaps ten thousand acres. It was filled with tropical fruits, wild chickens, and wild pigs, with an occasional herd of wild cattle, while high up among the peaks were herds of wild goats harried by packs of wild dogs. The whole place was wild. Not a human lived in it. And he could buy it and the bay for a thousand Chili dollars.

The bay, as he remembered it, was magnificent, with water deep enough to accommodate the largest vessel afloat, and so safe that the South Pacific Directory recommended it as the best careening place for ships for hundreds of miles around. He would buy a schooner—one of those yachtlike, coppered crafts that sailed like witches—and go trading copra and pearling among the islands. He would make the valley and the bay his headquarters. He would build a patriarchal grass house like Tati's, and have it and the valley and the schooner filled with dark-skinned servitors. He would entertain there the factor of Taiohæ, captains of wandering traders, and all the best of the South Pacific riffraff. He would keep open house and entertain like a prince. And he would forget the books he had opened and the world that had proved an illusion.

To do all this he must wait in California to fill the sack with money. Already it was beginning to flow in. If one of the books made a strike, it might enable him to sell the whole heap of manuscripts. Also he could collect the stories and the poems into books, and make sure of the valley and the bay and the schooner. He would never write again. Upon that he was resolved. But in the meantime, awaiting the publication of the books, he must do something more than live dazed and stupid in the sort of uncaring trance into which he had fallen.

He noted, one Sunday morning, that the Bricklayers' Picnic took place that day at Shell Mound Park, and to Shell Mound Park he went. He had been to the working-class picnics too often in his earlier life not to know what they were like, and as he entered the park he experienced a recrudescence of all the old sensations. After all, they were his kind, these working people. He had been born among them, he had lived among them, and though he had strayed for a time, it was well to come back among them.

"If it ain't Mart!" he heard someone say, and the next moment a hearty hand was on his shoulder. "Where you ben all the time? Off to sea? Come on an' have a drink."

It was the old crowd in which he found himself—the old crowd, with here and there a gap, and here and there a new face. The fellows were not bricklayers, but, as in the old days, they attended all Sunday picnics for the dancing, and the fighting, and the fun. Martin drank with them, and began to feel really human once more. He was a fool to have ever left them, he thought; and he was very certain that his sum of happiness would have been greater had he remained with them and let alone the books and the people who sat in the high places. Yet the beer seemed not so good as of yore. It didn't taste as it used to taste. Brissenden had spoiled him for steam beer, he concluded, and wondered if, after all, the books had spoiled him for companionship with these friends of his youth. He resolved that he would not be so spoiled, and he went on to the dancing pavilion. Jimmy, the plumber, he met there, in the company of a tall, blond girl who promptly forsook him for Martin.

"Gee, it's like old times," Jimmy explained to the gang that gave him the laugh as Martin and the blonde whirled away in a waltz. "An' I don't give a rap. I'm too damned glad to see 'm back. Watch 'm waltz, eh? It's like silk. Who'd blame any girl?"

But Martin restored the blonde to Jimmy, and the three of them, with half a dozen friends, watched the revolving couples and laughed and joked with one another. Everybody was glad to see Martin back. No book of his had been published, he carried no fictitious value in their eyes. They liked him for himself. He felt like a prince returned from exile, and his lonely heart burgeoned in the geniality in which it bathed. He made a mad day of it, and was at his best. Also, he had money in his pockets, and, as in the old days when he returned from sea with a payday, he made the money fly.

Once, on the dancing-floor, he saw Lizzie Connolly go by in the arms of a young workingman; and, later, when he made the round of the pavilion, he came upon her sitting by a refreshment table. Surprise and greetings over, he led her away into the grounds, where they could talk without shouting down the music. From the instant he spoke to her, she was his. He knew it. She showed it in the proud humility of her eyes, in every caressing movement of her proudly carried body, and in the way she hung upon his speech. She was not the young girl as he had known her. She was a woman, now, and Martin noted that her wild, defiant beauty had improved, losing none of its wildness, while the defiance and the fire seemed more in control. "A beauty, a perfect beauty," he murmured admiringly under his breath. And he knew she was his, that all he had to do was to say "Come," and she would go with him over the world wherever he led.

Even as the thought flashed through his brain he received a heavy blow on the side of his head that nearly knocked him down. It was a man's fist, directed by a man so angry and in such haste that the fist had missed the jaw for which it was aimed. Martin turned as he staggered, and saw the fist coming at him in a wild swing. Quite as a matter of course he ducked and the fist flew harmlessly past, pivoting the man who had driven it. Martin hooked with his left, landing on the pivoting man with the weight of his body behind the blow. The man went to the ground sidewise, leaped to his feet, and made a mad rush. Martin saw his passion-distorted face and wondered what could be the cause of the fellow's anger. But while he wondered, he shot in a straight left, the weight of his body behind the blow. The man went over backward and fell in a crumpled heap. Jimmy and others of the gang were running toward them.

Martin was thrilling all over. This was the old days with a vengeance, with their dancing, and their fighting, and their fun. While he kept a wary eye on his antagonist, he glanced at Lizzie. Usually the girls screamed when the fellows got to scrapping but she had not screamed. She was looking on with bated breath, leaning slightly forward, so keen was her interest, one hand pressed to her breast, her cheek flushed, and in her eyes a great and amazed admiration.

The man had gained his feet and was struggling to escape the restraining arms that were laid on him.

"She was waitin' for me to come back!" he was proclaiming to all and sundry "She was waitin' for me to come back, an' then that fresh guy comes buttin' in. Let go o' me, I tell yeh. I'm goin' to fix 'm."

"What's eatin' yer?" Jimmy was demanding, as he helped hold the young fellow back. "That guy's Mart Eden. He's nifty with his mits, lemme tell you that, an' he'll eat you alive if you monkey with 'm."

"He can't steal her on me that way," the other interjected.

"He licked the Flyin' Dutchman, an' you know *him*," Jimmy went on expostulating. "An' he did it in five rounds. You couldn't last a minute against him. See?"

This information seemed to have a mollifying effect, and the irate young man favored Martin with a measuring stare.

"He don't look it," he sneered; but the sneer was without passion.

"That's what the Flyin' Dutchman thought," Jimmy assured him. "Come on, now, let's get outa this. There's lots of other girls. Come on."

The young fellow allowed himself to be led away toward the pavilion, and the gang followed after him.

"Who is he?" Martin asked Lizzie. "And what's it all about, anyway?"

Already the zest of combat, which of old had been so keen and lasting, had died down, and he discovered that he was self-analytical, too much so to live, single heart and single hand, so primitive an existence.

Lizzie tossed her head.

"Oh, he's nobody," she said. "He's just ben keepin' company with me.

"I had to, you see," she explained after a pause. "I was gettin' pretty lonesome. But I never forgot." Her voice sank lower, and she looked straight before her. "I'd throw 'm down for you anytime."

Martin, looking at her averted face, knowing that all he had to do was to reach out his hand and pluck her, fell to pondering whether, after all, there was any real worth in refined, grammatical English, and, so, forgot to reply to her.

"You put it all over him," she said tentatively, with a laugh.

"He's a husky young fellow, though," he admitted generously, "If they hadn't taken him away, he might have given me my hands full."

"Who was that lady friend I seen you with that night?" she asked abruptly.

"Oh, just a lady friend," was his answer.

"It was a long time ago," she murmured contemplatively. "It seems like a thousand years."

But Martin went no further into the matter. He led the conversation off into other channels. They had lunch in the restaurant, where he ordered wine and expensive delicacies and afterward he danced with her and with no one but her, till she was tired. He was a good dancer, and she whirled around and around with him in a heaven of delight, her head against his shoulder, wishing that it could last forever. Later in the afternoon they strayed off among the trees, where, in the good old fashion, she sat down while he sprawled on his back, his head in her lap. He lay and dozed, while she fondled his hair, looked down on his closed eyes, and loved him without reserve. Looking up suddenly, he read the tender advertisement in her face. Her eyes fluttered down, then they opened and looked into his with soft defiance.

"I've kept straight all these years," she said, her voice so low that it was almost a whisper.

In his heart Martin knew that it was the miraculous truth. And his heart pleaded a great temptation. It was in his power to make her happy. Denied happiness himself, why should he deny happiness to her? He could marry her and take her down to dwell in the grass-walled castle in the Marquesas. The desire to do it was so strong, but stronger still was the imperative command of his nature not to do it. In spite of himself he was still faithful to Love. The old days of license and easy living were gone. He could not

bring them back, nor could he go back to them. He was changed—
how changed he had not realized until now.

"I am not a marrying man, Lizzie," he said lightly.

The hand caressing his hair paused perceptibly, then went on
with the same gentle stroke. He noticed her face harden, but it was
with the hardness of resolution, for still the soft color was in her
checks, and she was all glowing and melting.

"I did not mean that—" she began, then faltered. "Or anyway
I don't care.

"I don't care," she repeated. "I'm proud to be your friend. I'd
do anything for you. I'm made that way, I guess."

Martin sat up. He took her hand in his. He did it deliberately, with warmth but without passion; and such warmth chilled her.

"Don't let's talk about it," she said.

"You are a great and noble woman," he said. "And it is I who
should be proud to know you. And I am, I am. You are a ray of light
to me in a very dark world, and I've got to be straight with you, just
as straight as you have been."

"I don't care whether you're straight with me or not. You
could do anything with me. You could throw me in the dirt an'
walk on me. An' you're the only man in the world that can," she
added with a defiant flash. "I ain't taken care of myself ever since I
was a kid for nothin'."

"And it's just because of that that I'm not goin' to," he said
gently. "You are so big and generous that you challenge me to
equal generousness. I'm not marrying, and I'm not—well, loving
without marrying, though I've done my share of that in the past.
I'm sorry I came here today and met you. But it can't be helped
now, and I never expected it would turn out this way.

"But look here, Lizzie. I can't begin to tell you how much I
like you. I do more than like you. I admire and respect you. You are
magnificent, and you are magnificently good. But what's the use of
words? Yet there's something I'd like to do. You've had a hard life;
let me make it easy for you." (A joyous light welled into her eyes,

then faded out again.) "I'm pretty sure of getting hold of some money soon—lots of it."

In that moment he abandoned the idea of the valley and the bay, the grass-walled castle and the trim, white schooner. After all, what did it matter? He could go away, as he had done so often, before the mast, on any ship bound anywhere.

"I'd like to turn it over to you. There must be something you want—to go to school or business college. You might like to study and be a stenographer. I could fix it for you. Or maybe your father and mother are living—I could set them up in a grocery store or something. Anything you want, just name it, and I can fix it for you."

She made no reply, but sat, gazing straight before her, dry-eyed and motionless, but with an ache in the throat which Martin divined so strongly that it made his own throat ache. He regretted that he had spoken. It seemed so tawdry what he had offered her— mere money—compared with what she offered him. He offered her an extraneous thing with which he could part without a pang, while she offered him herself, along with disgrace and shame, and sin, and all her hopes of heaven.

"Don't let's talk about it," she said with a catch in her voice that she changed to a cough. She stood up. "Come on, let's go home. I'm all tired out."

The day was done, and the merrymakers had nearly all departed. But as Martin and Lizzie emerged from the trees they found the gang waiting for them. Martin knew immediately the meaning of it. Trouble was brewing. The gang was his bodyguard. They passed out through the gates of the park with, straggling in the rear, a second gang, the friends that Lizzie's young man had collected to avenge the loss of his lady. Several constables and special police officers, anticipating trouble, trailed along to prevent it, and herded the two gangs separately aboard the train for San Francisco. Martin told Jimmy that he would get off at Sixteenth Street Station and catch the electric car into Oakland. Lizzie was very quiet and without interest in what was impending. The train pulled in to Sixteenth Street Station, and the walking electric car could be seen, the conductor of which was impatiently clanging the gong.

"There she is," Jimmy counselled. "Make a run for it, an' we'll hold 'em back. Now you go! Hit her up!"

The hostile gang was temporarily disconcerted by the maneuver, then it dashed from the train in pursuit. The staid and sober Oakland folk who sat upon the car scarcely noted the young fellow and the girl who ran for it and found a seat in front on the outside. They did not connect the couple with Jimmy, who sprang on the steps, crying to the motorman:

"Slam on the juice, old man, and beat it outa here!"

The next moment Jimmy whirled about, and the passengers saw him land his fist on the face of a running man who was trying to board the car. But fists were landing on faces the whole length of the car. Thus, Jimmy and his gang, strung out on the long, lower steps, met the attacking gang. The car started with a great clanging of its gong, and, as Jimmy's gang drove off the last assailants they, too, jumped off to finish the job. The car dashed on, leaving the flurry of combat far behind, and its dumfounded passengers never dreamed that the quiet young man and the pretty working-girl sitting in the corner on the outside seat had been the cause of the row.

Martin had enjoyed the fight, with a recrudescence of the old fighting thrills. But they quickly died away, and he was oppressed by a great sadness. He felt very old—centuries older than those careless, carefree young companions of his other days. He had travelled far, too far to go back. Their mode of life, which had once been his, was now distasteful to him. He was disappointed in it all. He had developed into an alien. As the steam beer had tasted raw, so their companionship seemed raw to him. He was too far removed. Too many thousands of opened books yawned between them and him. He had exiled himself. He had travelled in the vast realm of intellect until he could no longer return home. On the other hand, he was human, and his gregarious need for companionship remained unsatisfied. He had found no new home. As the gang could not understand him, as his own family could not understand him, as the bourgeoisie could not understand him, so this girl beside him, whom he honored high, could not understand him nor the honor he paid her. His sadness was not untouched with bitterness as he thought it over.

"Make it up with him," he advised Lizzie, at parting, as they stood in front of the workingman's shack in which she lived, near Sixth and Market. He referred to the young fellow whose place he had usurped that day.

"I can't—now," she said.

"Oh, go on," he said jovially. "All you have to do is whistle and he'll come running."

"I didn't mean that," she said simply.

And he knew what she had meant.

She leaned toward him as he was about to say good night. But she leaned not imperatively, not seductively, but wistfully and humbly. He was touched to the heart. His large tolerance rose up in him. He put his arms around her, and kissed her, and knew that upon his own lips rested as true a kiss as man ever received.

"My God!" she sobbed. "I could die for you. I could die for you."

She tore herself from him suddenly and ran up the steps. He felt a quick moisture in his eyes.

"Martin Eden," he communed. "You're not a brute, and you're a damn poor Nietzscheman. You'd marry her if you could and fill her quivering heart full with happiness. But you can't, you can't. And it's a damn shame.

"'A poor old tramp explains his poor old ulcers,'" he muttered, remembering his Henley. "'Life is, I think, a blunder and a shame.' It is—a blunder and a shame."

The Story of an Eyewitness

As was true for so many Bay Area residents, the terrible earthquake of April 18, 1906, was an unforgettable event in London's life. Jack and his wife, Charmian, were asleep at their ranch when it occurred. They rode to the top of Sonoma Mountain that morning, seeing great clouds of smoke from distant San Francisco and nearby Santa Rosa, both of which were devastated. The couple then travelled to San Francisco so that Jack could cover events for Collier's Weekly, *a major national magazine. By the time they arrived the city was in flames, and London's reportage remains a defining document of the disaster. The excerpt that follows appeared in the May 5, 1906, issue of the journal.*

The earthquake shook down in San Francisco hundreds of thousands of dollars' worth of walls and chimneys. But the conflagration that followed burned up hundreds of millions of dollars' worth of property. There is no estimating within hundreds of millions the actual damage wrought. Not in history has a modern imperial city been so completely destroyed. San Francisco is gone. Nothing remains of it but memories and a fringe of dwelling-houses on its outskirts. Its industrial section is wiped out. Its business section is wiped out. Its social and residential section is wiped out. The factories and warehouses, the great stores and newspaper buildings, the hotels and the palaces of the nabobs, are all gone. Remains only the fringe of dwelling-houses on the outskirts of what was once San Francisco.

Within an hour after the earthquake shock the smoke of San Francisco's burning was a lurid tower visible a hundred miles away.

115

And for three days and nights this lurid tower swayed in the sky, reddening the sun, darkening the day, and filling the land with smoke.

On Wednesday morning at a quarter past five came the earthquake. A minute later the flames were leaping upward. In a dozen different quarters south of Market Street, in the working-class ghetto, and in the factories, fires started. There was no opposing the flames. There was no organization, no communication. All the crowning adjustments of a twentieth-century city had been smashed by the earthquake. The streets were humped into ridges and depressions, and piled with the debris of fallen walls. The steel rails were twisted into perpendicular and horizontal angles. The telephone and telegraph systems were disrupted. And the great water mains had burst. All the shrewd contrivances and safeguards of man had been thrown out of gear by thirty seconds' twitching of the earth-crust.

By Wednesday afternoon, inside of twelve hours, half the heart of the city was gone. At that time I watched the vast conflagration from out on the bay. It was dead calm. Not a flicker of wind stirred. Yet from every side wind was pouring in upon the city. East, west, north, and south, strong winds were blowing upon the doomed city. The heated air rising made an enormous suck. Thus did the fire of itself build its own colossal chimney through the atmosphere. Day and night this dead calm continued, and yet, near to the flames, the wind was often half a gale, so mighty was the suck.

Wednesday night saw the destruction of the very heart of the city. Dynamite was lavishly used, and many of San Francisco's proudest structures were crumbled by man himself into ruins, but there was no withstanding the onrush of the flames. Time and again successful stands were made by the firefighters, and every time the flames flanked around on either side, or came up from the rear, and turned to defeat the hard-won victory.

An enumeration of the buildings destroyed would be a directory of San Francisco. An enumeration of the buildings undestroyed would be a line and several addresses. An enumeration of the deeds of heroism would stock a library and bankrupt the Carnegie Medal Fund. An enumeration of the dead—will never be made. All vestiges of them were destroyed by the flames. The number of the victims of the earthquake will never be known. South of Market Street, where the loss of life was particularly heavy, was the first to catch fire.

Remarkable as it may seem, Wednesday night, while the whole city crashed and roared into ruin, was a quiet night. There were no crowds. There was no shouting and yelling. There was no hysteria, no disorder. I passed Wednesday night in the path of the advancing flames, and in all those terrible hours I saw not one woman who wept, not one man who was excited, not one person who was in the slightest degree panic-stricken.

Before the flames, throughout the night, fled tens of thousands of homeless ones. Some were wrapped in blankets. Others carried bundles of bedding and dear household treasures. Sometimes a whole family was harnessed to a carriage or delivery wagon that was weighted down with their possessions. Baby buggies, toy wagons, and go-carts were used as trucks, while every other person was dragging a trunk. Yet everybody was gracious. The most perfect courtesy obtained. Never, in all San Francisco's history, were her people so kind and courteous as on this night of terror.

All night these tens of thousands fled before the flames. Many of them, the poor people from the labor ghetto, had fled all day as well. They had left their homes burdened with possessions. Now and again they lightened up, flinging out upon the street clothing and treasures they had dragged for miles.

They held on longest to their trunks, and over these trunks many a strong man broke his heart that night. The hills of San Francisco are steep, and up these hills, mile after mile, were the trunks dragged. Everywhere were trunks, with across them lying their exhausted owners, men and women. Before the march of the flames were flung picket lines of soldiers. And a block at a time, as the flames advanced, these pickets retreated. One of their tasks was to keep the trunk-pullers moving. The exhausted creatures, stirred on by the menace of bayonets, would arise and struggle up the steep pavements, pausing from weakness every five or ten feet.

Often, after surmounting a heart-breaking hill, they would find another wall of flame advancing upon them at right angles and be compelled to change anew the line of their retreat. In the end, completely played out, after toiling for a dozen hours like giants, thousands of them were compelled to abandon their trunks. Here the shopkeepers and soft members of the middle class were at a disadvantage. But the working-men dug holes in vacant lots and backyards and buried their trunks.

At nine o'clock Wednesday evening I walked down through the very heart of the city. I walked through miles and miles of magnificent buildings and towering skyscrapers. Here was no fire. All was in perfect order. The police patrolled the streets. Every building had its watchman at the door. And yet it was doomed, all of it. There was no water. The dynamite was giving out. And at right angles two different conflagrations were sweeping down upon it.

At one o'clock in the morning I walked down through the same section. Everything still stood intact. There was no fire. And yet there was a change. A rain of ashes was falling. The watchmen at the doors were gone. The police had been withdrawn. There were no firemen, no fire engines, no men fighting with dynamite. The district had been absolutely abandoned. I stood at the corner of Kearney and Market, in the very innermost heart of San Francisco. Kearney Street was deserted.

Half a dozen blocks away it was burning on both sides. The street was a wall of flame. And against this wall of flame, silhouetted sharply, were two United States cavalrymen sitting on their horses, calmly watching. That was all. Not another person was in sight. In the intact heart of the city two troopers sat on their horses and watched.

Surrender was complete. There was no water. The sewers had long since been pumped dry. There was no dynamite. Another fire had broken out further uptown, and now from three sides conflagrations were sweeping down. The fourth side had been burned earlier in the day. In that direction stood the tottering walls of the Examiner building, the burned-out Call building, the smoldering ruins of the Grand Hotel, and the gutted, devastated, dynamited Palace Hotel.

The following will illustrate the sweep of the flames and the inability of men to calculate their spread. At eight o'clock Wednesday evening I passed through Union Square. It was packed with refugees. Thousands of them had gone to bed on the grass. Government tents had been set up, supper was being cooked, and the refugees were lining up for free meals.

At half-past one in the morning three sides of Union Square were in flames. The fourth side, where stood the great St. Francis Hotel, was still holding out. An hour later, ignited from top and sides, the St. Francis was flaming heavenward. Union Square, heaped high with mountains of trunks, was deserted. Troops, refugees, and all had retreated.

It was at Union Square that I saw a man offering a thousand dollars for a team of horses. He was in charge of a truck piled high with trunks from some hotel. It had been hauled here into what was considered safety, and the horses had been taken out. The flames were on three sides of the Square, and there were no horses.

Also, at this time, standing beside the truck, I urged a man to seek safety in flight. He was all but hemmed in by several conflagrations. He was an old man and he was on crutches. Said he: "Today is my birthday. Last night I was worth thirty thousand dollars. I bought five bottles of wine, some delicate fish, and other things for my birthday dinner. I have had no dinner, and all I own are these crutches."

I convinced him of his danger and started him limping on his way. An hour later, from a distance, I saw the truckload of trunks burning merrily in the middle of the street.

On Thursday morning, at a quarter past five, just twenty-four hours after the earthquake, I sat on the steps of a small residence on Nob Hill. With me sat Japanese, Italians, Chinese, and negroes—

a bit of the cosmopolitan flotsam of the wreck of the city. All about were the palaces of the nabob pioneers of '49. To the east and south, at right angles, were advancing two mighty walls of flame.

I went inside with the owner of the house on the steps of which I sat. He was cool and cheerful and hospitable. "Yesterday morning," he said, "I was worth six hundred thousand dollars. This morning this house is all I have left. It will go in fifteen minutes." He pointed to a large cabinet. "That is my wife's collection of china. This rug upon which we stand is a present. It cost fifteen hundred dollars. Try that piano. Listen to its tone. There are few like it. There are no horses. The flames will be here in fifteen minutes."

Outside, the old Mark Hopkins residence, a palace, was just catching fire. The troops were falling back and driving the refugees before them. From every side came the roaring of flames, the crashing of walls, and the detonations of dynamite.

I passed out of the house. Day was trying to dawn through the smoke-pall. A sickly light was creeping over the face of things. Once only the sun broke through the smoke-pall, blood-red, and showing a quarter its usual size. The smoke-pall itself, viewed from beneath, was a rose color that pulsed and fluttered with lavender shades. Then it turned to mauve and yellow and dun. There was no sun. And so dawned the second day on stricken San Francisco.

An hour later I was creeping past the shattered dome of the City Hall. Than it there was no better exhibit of the destructive force of the earthquake. Most of the stone had been shaken from the great dome, leaving standing the naked framework of steel. Market Street was piled high with the wreckage, and across the wreckage lay the overthrown pillars of the City Hall shattered into short cross-wise sections.

This section of the city, with the exception of the Mint and the Post Office, was already a waste of smoking ruins. Here and there through the smoke, creeping warily under the shadows of tottering walls, emerged occasional men and women. It was like the meeting of the handful of survivors after the day of the end of the world.

On Mission Street lay a dozen steers, in a neat row stretching across the street, just as they had been struck down by the flying ruins of the earthquake. The fire had passed through afterward and roasted them. The human dead had been carried away before the fire came. At another place on Mission Street I saw a milk wagon. A steel telegraph pole had smashed down sheer through the driver's seat and crushed the front wheels. The milk cans lay scattered around.

All day Thursday and all Thursday night, all day Friday and Friday night, the flames still raged.

Friday night saw the flames finally conquered, though not until Russian Hill and Telegraph Hill had been swept and three-quarters of a mile of wharves and docks had been licked up.

The great stand of the firefighters was made Thursday night on Van Ness Avenue. Had they failed here, the comparatively few remaining houses of the city would have been swept. Here were the magnificent residences of the second generation of San Francisco nabobs, and these, in a solid zone, were dynamited down across the path of the fire. Here and there the flames leaped the zone, but these fires were beaten out, principally by the use of wet blankets and rugs.

San Francisco, at the present time, is like the crater of a volcano, around which are camped tens of thousands of refugees. At the Presidio alone are at least twenty thousand. All the surrounding cities and towns are jammed with the homeless ones, where they are being cared for by the relief committees. The refugees were carried free by the railroads to any point they wished to go, and it is estimated that over one hundred thousand people have left the peninsula on which San Francisco stood. The Government has the situation in hand, and, thanks to the immediate relief given by the whole United States, there is not the slightest possibility of a famine. The bankers and businessmen have already set about making preparations to rebuild San Francisco.

from The Road

"If the sea had served as Jack London's Harvard," writes biographer Earle Labor, "The Road—and by this he meant the railroad—was his Yale." Like many young working-class men of his generation, Jack rode the rails for a spell. In 1894, he joined the California contingent of "Coxey's Army" of the unemployed, then left it for his own adventures. He ended up serving thirty days for vagrancy in the Erie County, New York Penitentiary, a defining experience. "I had been reborn, but not renamed," he later wrote, "and I was running around to find out what manner of thing I was. I ran back to California and opened the books." The segment of The Road *(1907) that follows reveals some essentials of the young tramp's initiation.*

Every once in a while, in newspapers, magazines, and biographical dictionaries, I run upon sketches of my life, wherein, delicately phrased, I learn that it was in order to study sociology that I became a tramp. This is very nice and thoughtful of the biographers, but it is inaccurate. I became a tramp—well, because of the life that was in me, of the wanderlust in my blood that would not let me rest. Sociology was merely incidental; it came afterward, in the same manner that a wet skin follows a ducking. I went on The Road because I couldn't keep away from it; because I hadn't the price of the railroad fare in my jeans; because I was so made that I couldn't work all my life on one same shift; because—well, just because it was easier to than not to.

It happened in my own town, in Oakland, when I was sixteen. At that time I had attained a dizzy reputation in my chosen circle of adventurers, by whom I was known as the Prince of the Oyster Pirates. It is true, those immediately outside my circle, such as honest bay-sailors, longshoremen, yachtsmen, and the legal owners of the oysters, called me "tough," "hoodlum," "smoudge," "thief," "robber," and various other not nice things—all of which was complimentary and but served to increase the dizziness of the high place in which I sat. At that time I had not read *Paradise Lost,* and later, when I read Milton's "Better to reign in hell than serve in heaven," I was fully convinced that great minds run in the same channels.

It was at this time that the fortuitous concatenation of events sent me upon my first adventure on The Road. It happened that there was nothing doing in oysters just then; that at Benicia, forty miles away, I had some blankets I wanted to get; and that at Port Costa, several miles from Benicia, a stolen boat lay at anchor in charge of the constable. Now this boat was owned by a friend of mine, by name Dinny McCrea. It had been stolen and left at Port Costa by Whiskey Bob, another friend of mine. (Poor Whiskey Bob! Only last winter his body was picked up on the beach shot full of holes by nobody knows whom.) I had come down from "up river" some time before, and reported to Dinny McCrea the whereabouts of his boat; and Dinny McCrea had promptly offered ten dollars to me if I should bring it down to Oakland to him.

Time was heavy on my hands. I sat on the dock and talked it over with Nickey the Greek, another idle oyster pirate. "Let's go," said I, and Nickey was willing. He was broke. I possessed fifty cents and a small skiff. The former I invested and loaded into the latter in the form of crackers, canned corned beef, and a ten-cent bottle of French mustard. (We were keen on French mustard in those days.) Then, late in the afternoon, we hoisted our small spritsail and started. We sailed all night, and next morning, on the first of a glorious flood-tide, a fair wind behind us, we came booming up the Carquinez Straits to Port Costa. There lay the stolen boat, not twenty-five feet from the wharf. We ran alongside and doused our little spritsail. I sent Nickey forward to lift the anchor, while I began casting off the gaskets.

A man ran out on the wharf and hailed us. It was the constable. It suddenly came to me that I had neglected to get a written authorization from Dinny McCrea to take possession of his boat. Also, I knew that the constable wanted to charge at least twenty-five dollars in fees for capturing the boat from Whiskey Bob and subsequently taking care of it. And my last fifty cents had been blown in for corned beef and French mustard, and the reward was only ten dollars anyway. I shot a glance forward to Nickey. He had the anchor up-and-down and was straining at it. "Break her out," I whispered to him, and turned and shouted back to the constable. The result was that he and I were talking at the same time, our spoken thoughts colliding in midair and making gibberish.

The constable grew more imperative, and perforce I had to listen. Nickey was heaving on the anchor till I thought he'd burst a blood vessel. When the constable got done with his threats and warnings, I asked him who he was. The time he lost in telling me enabled Nickey to break out the anchor. I was doing some quick calculating. At the feet of the constable a ladder ran down the dock to the water, and to the ladder was moored a skiff. The oars were in it. But it was padlocked. I gambled everything on that padlock. I felt the breeze on my cheek, saw the surge of the tide, looked at the remaining gaskets that confined the sail, ran my eyes up the halyards to the blocks and knew that all was clear, and then threw off all dissimulation.

"In with her!" I shouted to Nickey, and sprang to the gaskets, casting them loose and thanking my stars that Whiskey Bob had tied them in square-knots instead of "grannies."

The constable had slid down the ladder and was fumbling with a key at the padlock. The anchor came aboard and the last gasket was loosed at the same instant that the constable freed the skiff and jumped to the oars.

"Peak-halyards!" I commanded my crew, at the same time swinging on to the throat-halyards. Up came the sail on the run. I belayed and ran aft to the tiller.

"Stretch her!" I shouted to Nickey at the peak. The constable was just reaching for our stern. A puff of wind caught us, and we shot away. It was great. If I'd had a black flag, I know I'd have run it up in triumph. The constable stood up in the skiff, and paled the glory of the day with the vividness of his language. Also, he wailed for a gun. You see, that was another gamble we had taken.

Anyway, we weren't stealing the boat. It wasn't the constable's. We were merely stealing his fees, which was his particular form of graft. And we weren't stealing the fees for ourselves, either; we were stealing them for my friend, Dinny McCrea.

Benicia was made in a few minutes, and a few minutes later my blankets were aboard. I shifted the boat down to the far end of Steamboat Wharf, from which point of vantage we could see anybody coming after us. There was no telling. Maybe the Port Costa constable would telephone to the Benicia constable. Nickey and I held a council of war. We lay on deck in the warm sun, the fresh breeze on our cheeks, the flood-tide rippling and swirling past. It was impossible to start back to Oakland till afternoon, when the ebb would begin to run. But we figured that the constable would have an eye out on the Carquinez Straits when the ebb started, and that nothing remained for us but to wait for the following ebb, at two o'clock next morning, when we could slip by Cerberus in the darkness.

So we lay on deck, smoked cigarettes, and were glad that we were alive. I spat over the side and gauged the speed of the current.

"With this wind, we could run this flood clear to Rio Vista," I said.

"And it's fruit time on the river," said Nickey.

"And low water on the river," said I. "It's the best time of the year to make Sacramento."

We sat up and looked at each other. The glorious west wind was pouring over us like wine. We both spat over the side and gauged the current. Now I contend that it was all the fault of that flood-tide and fair wind. They appealed to our sailor instinct. If it had not been for them, the whole chain of events that was to put me upon The Road would have broken down.

We said no word, but cast off our moorings and hoisted sail. Our adventures up the Sacramento River are no part of this narrative. We subsequently made the city of Sacramento and tied up at a wharf. The water was fine, and we spent most of our time in swimming. On the sandbar above the railroad bridge we fell in with a bunch of boys likewise in swimming. Between swims we lay on the bank and talked. They talked differently from the fellows I had been used to herding with. It was a new vernacular. They were road-kids, and with every word they uttered the lure of The Road laid hold of me more imperiously.

"When I was down in Alabama," one kid would begin; or, another, "Coming up on the C. & A. from K.C."; whereat, a third kid, "On the C. & A. there ain't no steps to the 'blinds.'" And I would lie silently in the sand and listen. "It was at a little town in Ohio on the Lake Shore and Michigan Southern," a kid would start; and another, "Ever ride the Cannonball on the Wabash?"; and yet another, "Nope, but I've been on the White Mail out of Chicago." "Talk about railroadin'—wait till you hit the Pennsylvania, four tracks, no water tanks, take water on the fly, that's goin' some." "The Northern Pacific's a bad road now." "Salinas is on the hog; the bulls is horstile." "I got pinched at El Paso, along with Moke Kid." "Talkin' of poke-outs, wait till you hit the French country out of Montreal—not a word of English—you say, 'Mongee, Madame, mongee, no spika da French,' an' rub your stomach an' look hungry, an' she gives you a slice of sow-belly an' a chunk of dry punk."

And I continued to lie in the sand and listen. These wanderers made my oyster piracy look like thirty cents. A new world was calling to me in every word that was spoken—a world of rods and gunnels, blind baggages and "side-door Pullmans," "bulls" and "shacks," "floppings" and "chewin's," "pinches" and "get-aways," "strong arms" and "bindle-stiffs," "punks" and "profesh." And it all spelled Adventure. Very well; I would tackle this new world. I "lined" myself up alongside those road-kids. I was just as strong as any of them, just as quick, just as nervy, and my brain was just as good.

After the swim, as evening came on, they dressed and went up town. I went along. The kids began "battering the main-stem for light pieces," or, in other words, begging for money on the main street. I had never begged in my life, and this was the hardest thing for me to stomach when I first went on The Road. I had absurd notions about begging. My philosophy, up to that time, was that it was finer to steal than to beg; and that robbery was finer still because the risk and the penalty were proportionately greater. As an oyster pirate I had already earned convictions at the hands of justice, which, if I had tried to serve them, would have required a thousand years in state's prison. To rob was manly; to beg was sordid and despicable. But I developed in the days to come all right, all right, till I came to look upon begging as a joyous prank, a game of wits, a nerve-exerciser.

That first night, however, I couldn't rise to it; and the result was that when the kids were ready to go to a restaurant and eat, I wasn't. I was broke. Meeny Kid, I think it was, gave me the price, and we all ate together. But white I ate, I meditated. The receiver, it was said, was as bad as the thief; Meeny Kid had done the begging, and I was profiting by it. I decided that the receiver was a whole lot worse than the thief, and that it shouldn't happen again. And it didn't. I turned out next day and threw my feet as well as the next one.

Nickey the Greek's ambition didn't run to The Road. He was not a success at throwing his feet, and he stowed away one night on a barge and went down river to San Francisco. I met him, only a week ago, at a pugilistic carnival. He has progressed. He sat in a place of honor at the ringside. He is now a manager of prize-fighters and proud of it. In fact, in a small way, in local sportdom, he is quite a shining light.

"No kid is a road-kid until he has gone over the hill"—such was the law of The Road I heard expounded in Sacramento. All right, I'd go over the hill and matriculate. "The hill," by the way, was the Sierra Nevada. The whole gang was going over the hill on a jaunt, and of course I'd go along. It was French Kid's first adventure on The Road. He had just run away from his people in San Francisco. It was up to him and me to deliver the goods. In passing,

I may remark that my old title of "Prince" had vanished. I had received my "monica." I was now "Sailor Kid," later to be known as "'Frisco Kid," when I had put the Rockies between me and my native state.

At 10:20 p.m. the Central Pacific overland pulled out of the depot at Sacramento for the East—that particular item of time-table is indelibly engraved on my memory. There were about a dozen in our gang, and we strung out in the darkness ahead of the train ready to take her out. All the local road-kids that we knew came down to see us off—also, to "ditch" us if they could. That was their idea of a joke, and there were only about forty of them to carry it out. Their ringleader was a crackerjack road-kid named Bob. Sacramento was his home town, but he'd hit The Road pretty well everywhere over the whole country. He took French Kid and me aside and gave us advice something like this: "We're goin' to try an' ditch your bunch, see? Youse two are weak. The rest of the push can take care of itself. So, as soon as youse two nail a blind, deck her. An'stay on the decks till youse pass Roseville Junction, at which burg the constables are horstile, sloughin' in everybody on sight."

The engine whistled and the overland pulled out. There were three blinds on her—room for all of us. The dozen of us who were trying to make her out would have preferred to slip aboard quiet-ly; but our forty friends crowded on with the most amazing and shameless publicity and advertisement. Following Bob's advice, I immediately "decked her," that is, climbed up on top of the roof of one of the mail-cars. There I lay down, my heart jumping a few extra beats, and listened to the fun. The whole train crew was for-ward, and the ditching went on fast and furious. After the train had run half a mile, it stopped, and the crew came forward again and ditched the survivors. I, alone, had made the train out.

Back at the depot, about him two or three of the push that had witnessed the accident, lay French Kid with both legs off. French Kid had slipped or stumbled—that was all, and the wheels had done the rest. Such was my initiation to The Road. It was two years afterward when I next saw French Kid and examined his "stumps." This was an act of courtesy. "Cripples" always like to have their stumps examined. One of the entertaining sights on The Road is to witness the meeting of two cripples. Their common disability is a fruitful source of conversation; and they tell how it happened, describe what they know of the amputation, pass critical judgment on their own and each other's surgeons, and wind up by withdrawing to one side, taking off bandages and wrappings, and comparing stumps.

But it was not until several days later, over in Nevada, when the push caught up with me, that I learned of French Kid's accident. The push itself arrived in bad condition. It had gone through a train wreck in the snow-sheds; Happy Joe was on crutches with two mashed legs, and the rest were nursing skins and bruises.

In the meantime, I lay on the roof of the mail-car, trying to remember whether Roseville Junction, against which burg Bob had warned me, was the first stop or the second stop. To make sure, I delayed descending to the platform of the blind until after the second stop. And then I didn't descend. I was new to the game, and I felt safer where I was. But I never told the push that I held down the decks the whole night, clear across the Sierra, through snow-sheds and tunnels, and down to Truckee on the other side, where I arrived at seven in the morning. Such a thing was disgraceful, and I'd have been a common laughingstock. This is the first time I have confessed the truth about that first ride over the hill. As for the push, it decided that I was all right, and when I came back over the hill to Sacramento, I was a full-fledged road-kid.

Yet I had much to learn. Bob was my mentor, and he was all right. I remember one evening (it was fair time in Sacramento and we were knocking about and having a good time) when I lost my hat in a fight. There was I bare-headed in the street, and it was Bob to the rescue. He took me to one side from the push and told me what to do. I was a bit timid of his advice. I had just come out of jail, where I had been three days, and I knew that if the police "pinched" me again, I'd get good and "soaked." On the other hand, I couldn't show the white feather. I'd been over the hill, I was running full-fledged with the push, and it was up to me to deliver the goods. So I accepted Bob's advice, and he came along with me to see that I did it up brown.

We took our position on K Street, on the corner, I think, of Fifth. It was early in the evening and the street was crowded. Bob studied the headgear of every Chinaman that passed. I used to wonder how the road-kids all managed to wear "five-dollar Stetson stiff-rims," and now I knew. They got them, the way I was going to get mine, from the Chinese. I was nervous—there were so many people about; but Bob was cool as an iceberg. Several times, when I started forward toward a Chinaman, all nerved and keyed up, Bob dragged me back. He wanted me to get a good hat, and one that fitted. Now a hat came by that was the right size but not new; and, after a dozen impossible hats, along would come one that was new but not the right size. And when one did come by that was new and the right size, the rim was too large or not large enough. My, Bob was finicky. I was so wrought up that I'd have snatched any kind of a head-covering.

At last came the hat, the one hat in Sacramento for me. I knew it was a winner as soon as I looked at it. I glanced at Bob. He sent a sweeping look-about for police, then nodded his head. I lifted the hat from the Chinaman's head and pulled it down on my own. It was a perfect fit. Then I started. I heard Bob crying out, and I caught a glimpse of him blocking the irate Mongolian and tripping him up. I ran on. I turned up the next corner, and around the next. This street was not so crowded as K, and I walked along in quietude, catching my breath and congratulating myself upon my hat and my getaway.

And then, suddenly, around the corner at my back, came the bare-headed Chinaman. With him were a couple more Chinamen, and at their heels were half a dozen men and boys. I sprinted to the next corner, crossed the street, and rounded the following corner. I decided that I had surely played him out, and I dropped into a walk again. But around the corner at my heels came that persistent Mongolian. It was the old story of the hare and the tortoise. He could not run so fast as I, but he stayed with it, plodding along at a shambling and deceptive trot, and wasting much good breath in noisy imprecations. He called all Sacramento to witness the dishonor that had been done him, and a goodly portion of Sacramento heard and flocked at his heels. And I ran on like the hare, and ever that persistent Mongolian, with the increasing rabble, overhauled me. But finally, when a policeman had joined his following, I let out all my links. I twisted and turned, and I swear I ran at least twenty blocks on the straight away. And I never saw that Chinaman again. The hat was a dandy, a brand-new Stetson, just out of the shop, and it was the envy of the whole push. Furthermore, it was the symbol that I had delivered the goods. I wore it for over a year.

Road-kids are nice little chaps—when you get them alone and they are telling you "how it happened"; but take my word for it, watch out for them when they run in pack. Then they are wolves, and like wolves they are capable of dragging down the strongest man. At such times they are not cowardly. They will fling themselves upon a man and hold on with every ounce of strength in their wiry bodies, till he is thrown and helpless. More than once have I seen them do it, and I know whereof I speak. Their motive is usually robbery. And watch out for the "strong arm." Every kid in the push I travelled with was expert at it. Even French Kid mastered it before he lost his legs.

I have strong upon me now a vision of what I once saw in The Willows. The Willows was a clump of trees in a waste piece of land near the railway depot and not more than five minutes walk from the heart of Sacramento. It is nighttime, and the scene is illumined by the thin light of stars. I see a husky laborer in the midst of a pack of road-kids. He is infuriated and cursing them, not a bit afraid, confident of his own strength. He weighs about one hundred and eighty pounds, and his muscles are hard; but he doesn't know what he is up against. The kids are snarling. It is not pretty. They make a rush from all sides, and he lashes out and whirls. Barber Kid is standing beside me. As the man whirls, Barber Kid leaps forward and does the trick. Into the man's back goes his knee; around the man's neck, from behind, passes his right hand, the bone of the wrist pressing against the jugular vein. Barber Kid throws his whole weight backward. It is a powerful leverage. Besides, the man's wind has been shut off. It is the strong arm.

The man resists, but he is already practically helpless. The road-kids are upon him from every side, clinging to arms and legs and body, and like a wolf at the throat of a moose Barber Kid hangs on and drags backward. Over the man goes, and down under the heap. Barber Kid changes the position of his own body, but never lets go. While some of the kids are "going through" the victim, others are holding his legs so that he cannot kick and thresh about. They improve the opportunity by taking off the man's shoes. As for him, he has given in. He is beaten. Also, what of the strong arm at his throat, he is short of wind. He is making ugly choking noises, and the kids hurry. They really don't want to kill him. All is done. At a word all holds are released at once, and the kids scatter, one of them lugging the shoes—he knows where he can get half a dollar for them. The man sits up and looks about him, dazed and helpless. Even if he wanted to, barefooted pursuit in the darkness would be hopeless. I linger a moment and watch him. He is feeling at his throat, making dry, hawking noises, and jerking his head in a quaint way as though to assure himself that the neck is not dislocated. Then I slip away to join the push, and see that man no more—though I shall always see him, sitting there in the starlight, somewhat dazed, a bit frightened, greatly dishevelled, and making quaint jerking movements of head and neck.

Drunken men are the especial prey of the road-kids. Robbing a drunken man they call "rolling a stiff"; and wherever they are, they are on the constant lookout for drunks. The drunk is their particular meat, as the fly is the particular meat of the spider. The rolling of a stiff is ofttimes an amusing sight, especially when the stiff is helpless and when interference is unlikely. At the first swoop the stiff's money and jewelery go. Then the kids sit around their victim in a sort of pow-wow. A kid generates a fancy for the stiff's necktie. Off it comes. Another kid is after underclothes. Off they come, and a knife quickly abbreviates arms and legs. Friendly hoboes may be called in to take the coat and trousers, which are too large for the kids. And in the end they depart, leaving beside the stiff the heap of their discarded rags.

Another vision comes to me. It is a dark night. My push is coming along the sidewalk in the suburbs. Ahead of us, under an electric light, a man crosses the street diagonally. There is something tentative and desultory in his walk. The kids scent the game on the instant. The man is drunk. He blunders across the opposite sidewalk and is lost in the darkness as he takes a shortcut through a vacant lot. No hunting cry is raised, but the pack flings itself forward in quick pursuit. In the middle of the vacant lot it comes upon him. But what is this?—snarling and strange forms, small and dim and menacing, are between the pack and its prey. It is another pack of road-kids, and in the hostile pause we learn that it is their meat, that they have been trailing it a dozen blocks and more and that we are butting in. But it is the world primeval. These wolves are baby wolves. (As a matter of fact, I don't think one of them was over twelve or thirteen years of age. I met some of them afterward, and learned that they had just arrived that day over the hill, and that they hailed from Denver and Salt Lake City.) Our pack flings forward. The baby wolves squeal and screech and fight like little demons. All about the drunken man rages the struggle for the possession of him. Down he goes in the thick of it, and the combat rages over his body after the fashion of the Greeks and Trojans over the body and armor of a fallen hero. Amid cries and tears and wailings the baby wolves are dispossessed, and my pack rolls the stiff. But always I remember the poor stiff and his befuddled amazement at the abrupt eruption of battle in the vacant lot. I see him now, dim in the darkness, titubating in stupid wonder, good-naturedly essaying the role of peacemaker in that multitudinous scrap the significance of which he did not understand, and the really hurt expression on his face when he, unoffending he, was clutched at by many hands and dragged down in the thick of the press.

"Bindle-stiffs" are favorite prey of the road-kids. A bindle-stiff is a working tramp. He takes his name from the roll of blankets he carries, which is known as a "bindle." Because he does work, a bindle-stiff is expected usually to have some small change about him, and it is after that small change that the road-kids go. The best hunting ground for bindle-stiffs is in the sheds, barns, lumber-yards, railroad-yards, etc., on the edges of a city, and the time for hunting is the night, when the bindle-stiff seeks these places to roll up in his blankets and sleep.

"Gay-cats" also come to grief at the hands of the road-kid. In more familiar parlance, gay-cats are short-horns, *chechaquos*, new chums, or tenderfeet. A gay-cat is a newcomer on The Road who is man-grown, or, at least, youth-grown. A boy on The Road, on the other hand, no matter how green he is, is never a gay-cat; he is a road-kid or a "punk," and if he travels with a "profesh," he is known possessively as a "prushun." I was never a prushun, for I did not take kindly to possession. I was first a road-kid and then a pro-fesh. Because I started in young, I practically skipped my gay-cat apprenticeship. For a short period, during the time I was exchang-ing my 'Frisco Kid monica for that of Sailor Jack, I labored under the suspicion of being a gay-cat. But closer acquaintance on the part of those that suspected me quickly disabused their minds, and in a short time I acquired the unmistakable airs and ear-marks of the blowed-in-the-glass profesh. And be it known, here and now, that the profesh are the aristocracy of The Road. They are the lords and masters, the aggressive men, the primordial noblemen, the "blond beasts" so beloved of Nietzsche.

When I came back over the hill from Nevada, I found that some river pirate had stolen Dinny McCrea's boat. (A funny thing at this day is that I cannot remember what became of the skiff in which Nickey the Greek and I sailed from Oakland to Port Costa. I know that the constable didn't get it, and I know that it didn't go with us up the Sacramento River, and that is all I do know.) With the loss of Dinny McCrea's boat, I was pledged to The Road; and when I grew tired of Sacramento, I said good-bye to the push (which, in its friendly way, tried to ditch me from a freight as I left town) and started on a *passear* down the valley of the San Joaquin. The Road had gripped me and would not let me go; and later, when I had voyaged to sea and done one thing and another, I returned to The Road to make longer flights, to be a "comet" and a profesh, and to plump into the bath of sociology that wet me to the skin.

AGRARIAN IDEALS...
PASTORAL ROMANCES

The Golden Poppy

"It is not good to be city folk," London writes in "The Golden Poppy." "Of this I am convinced." This is one of the author's earliest examinations of disenchantment with city life and enchantment with country living. Originally published in the January 1904 edition of The Delineator, *it illustrates the environmental awareness that would become a major theme of some later works. At the time this essay was written, Jack and his first wife, Bess, new parents, were living in a cottage in the Piedmont hills above Oakland, and he was at last becoming a successful writer; these may in fact have been their happiest days together. The East Bay then hosted a group of artists—Xavier Martinez, Yone Noguchi, George Sterling, and Blanche Partington, as well as the venerable Joaquin Miller, among others—and the young author became a lively part of that circle.*

I have a poppy field. That is, by the grace of God and the good-nature of editors, I am enabled to place each month divers gold pieces into a clerical gentleman's hands, and in return for said gold pieces I am each month reinvested with certain proprietary rights in a poppy field. This field blazes on the rim of the Piedmont Hills. Beneath lies all the world. In the distance, across the silver sweep of bay, San Francisco smokes on her many hills like a second Rome. Not far away, Mount Tamalpais thrusts a rugged shoulder into the sky; and midway between is the Golden Gate, where sea mists love to linger. From the poppy field we often see the shimmering blue of the Pacific beyond, and the busy ships that go forever out and in.

"We shall have great joy in our poppy field," said Bess. "Yes," said I; "how the poor city folk will envy when they come to see us, and how we will make all well again when we send them off with great golden armfuls!"

"But those things will have to come down," I added, pointing to numerous obtrusive notices (relics of the last tenant) displayed conspicuously along the boundaries, and bearing, each and all, this legend: "Private Grounds. No Trespassing."

"Why should we refuse the poor city folk a ramble over our field, because, forsooth, they have not the advantage of our acquaintance?"

"How I abhor such things," said Bess; "the arrogant symbols of power."

"They disgrace human nature," said I.

"They shame the generous landscape," she said, "and they are abominable."

"Piggish!" quoth I, hotly. "Down with them!"

We looked forward to the coming of the poppies, did Bess and I, looked forward as only creatures of the city may look who have been long denied. I have forgotten to mention the existence of a house above the poppy field, a squat and wandering bungalow in which we had elected to forsake town traditions and live in fresher and more vigorous ways. The first poppies came, orange-yellow and golden in the standing grain, and we went about glee-fully, as though drunken with their wine, and told each other that the poppies were there. We laughed at unexpected moments, in the midst of silences, and at times grew ashamed and stole forth secret-ly to gaze upon our treasury. But when the great wave of poppy-flame finally spilled itself down the field, we shouted aloud, and danced, and clapped our hands, freely and frankly mad.

And then came the Goths. My face was in a lather, the time of the first invasion, and I suspended my razor in midair to gaze out on my beloved field. At the far end I saw a little girl and a little boy, their arms filled with yellow spoil. Ah, thought I, an unwonted benevolence burgeoning, what a delight to me is their delight! It is sweet that children should pick poppies in my field. All summer shall they pick poppies in my field. But they must be little children, I added as an afterthought, and they must pick from the lower end—this last prompted by a glance at the great golden fellows nodding in the wheat beneath my window. Then the razor descended. Shaving was always an absorbing task, and I did not glance out of the window again until the operation was completed. And then I was bewildered. Surely this was not my poppy field. No—and yes, for there were the tall pines clustering austerely together on one side, the magnolia tree burdened with bloom, and the Japanese quinces splashing the driveway hedge with blood. Yes, it was the field, but no wave of poppy-flame spilled down it, nor did the great golden fellows nod in the wheat beneath my window. I rushed into a jacket and out of the house. In the far distance were disappearing two huge balls of color, orange and yellow, for all the world like perambulating poppies of cyclopean breed.

"Johnny," said I to the nine-year-old son of my sister, "Johnny, whenever little girls come into our field to pick poppies, you must go down to them, and in a very quiet and gentlemanly manner, tell them it is not allowed."

Warm days came, and the sun drew another blaze from the free-bosomed earth. Whereupon a neighbor's little girl, at the behest of her mother, duly craved and received permission from Bess to gather a few poppies for decorative purposes. But of this I was uninformed, and when I descried her in the midst of the field I waved my arms like a semaphore against the sky.

"Little girl!" called I. "Little girl!"

The little girl's legs blurred the landscape as she fled, and in high elation I sought Bess to tell of the potency of my voice. Nobly she came to the rescue, departing forthwith on an expedition of conciliation and explanation to the little girl's mother. But to this day the little girl seeks cover at sight of me, and I know the mother will never be as cordial as she would otherwise have been.

Came dark, overcast days, stiff, driving winds and pelting rains, day on day, without end, and the city folk cowered in their dwelling-places like flood-beset rats; and like rats, half-drowned and gasping, when the weather cleared they crawled out and up the green Piedmont slopes to bask in the blessed sunshine. And they invaded my field in swarms and droves, crushing the sweet wheat into the earth and with lustful hands ripping the poppies out by the roots.

"I shall put up the warnings against trespassing," I said.

"Yes," said Bess, with a sigh. "I'm afraid it is necessary."

The day was yet young when she sighed again: "I'm afraid, O Man, that your signs are of no avail. People have forgotten how to read, these days."

I went out on the porch. A city nymph, in cool summer gown and picture hat, paused before one of my newly reared warnings and read it through with care. Profound deliberation characterized her movements. She was statuesquely tall, but with a toss of the head and a flirt of the skirt she dropped on hands and knees, crawled under the fence, and came to her feet on the inside with poppies in both her hands. I walked down the drive and talked ethically to her, and she went away. Then I put up more signs.

At one time, years ago, these hills were carpeted with poppies. As between the destructive forces and the will "to live," the poppies maintained an equilibrium with their environment. But the city folk constituted a new and terrible destructive force, the equilibrium was overthrown, and the poppies well-nigh perished. Since the city folk plucked those with the longest stems and biggest bowls, and since it is the law of kind to procreate kind, the long-stemmed, big-bowled poppies failed to go to seed, and a stunted, short-stemmed variety remained to the hills. And not only was it stunted and short-stemmed, but sparsely distributed as well. Each day and every day, for years and years, the city folk swarmed over the Piedmont Hills, and only here and there did the genius of the race survive in the form of miserable little flowers, close-clinging and quick-blooming, like children of the slums dragged hastily and precariously through youth to a shrivelled and futile maturity.

On the other hand, the poppies had prospered in my field; and not only had they been sheltered from the barbarians, but also from the birds. Long ago the field was sown in wheat, which went to seed unharvested each year, and in the cool depths of which the poppy seeds were hidden from the keen-eyed songsters. And, further, climbing after the sun through the wheat stalks, the poppies grew taller and taller and more royal even than the primordial ones of the open.

So the city folk, gazing from the bare hills to my blazing, burning field, were sorely tempted, and, it must be told, as sorely fell. But no sorer was their fall than that of my beloved poppies. Where the grain holds the dew and takes the bite from the sun the soil is moist, and in such soil it is easier to pull the poppies out by the roots than to break the stalk. Now the city folk, like other folk, are inclined to move along the line of least resistance, and for each flower they gathered, there were also gathered many crisp-rolled buds and with them all the possibilities and future beauties of the plant for all time to come.

One of the city folk, a middle-aged gentleman, with white hands and shifty eyes, especially made life interesting for me. We called him the "Repeater," what of his ways. When from the porch we implored him to desist, he was wont slowly and casually to direct his steps toward the fence, simulating finely the actions of a man who had not heard, but whose walk, instead, had terminated of itself or of his own volition. To heighten this effect, now and again, still casually and carelessly, he would stoop and pluck another poppy. Thus did he deceitfully save himself the indignity of being put out, and rob us of the satisfaction of putting him out, but he came, and he came often, each time getting away with an able-bodied man's share of plunder.

It is not good to be of the city folk. Of this I am convinced. There is something in the mode of life that breeds an alarming condition of blindness and deafness, or so it seems with the city folk that come to my poppy field. Of the many to whom I have talked ethically not one has been found who ever saw the warnings so conspicuously displayed, while of those called out to from the porch, possibly one in fifty has heard. Also, I have discovered that the relation of city folk to country flowers is quite analogous to that of a starving man to food. No more than the starving man realizes that five pounds of meat is not so good as an ounce, do they realize that five hundred poppies crushed and bunched are less beautiful than two or three in a free cluster, where the green leaves and golden bowls may expand to their full loveliness.

Less forgivable than the unaesthetic are the mercenary. Hordes of young rascals plunder me and rob the future that they may stand on street corners and retail "California poppies, only five cents a bunch!" In spite of my precautions some of them made a dollar a day out of my field. One horde do I remember with keen regret. Reconnoitering for a possible dog, they applied at the kitchen door for "a drink of water, please." While they drank they were besought not to pick any flowers. They nodded, wiped their mouths, and proceeded to take themselves off by the side of the bungalow. They smote the poppy field beneath my windows, spread out fan-shaped six wide, picking with both hands, and ripped a swath of destruction through the very heart of the field. No cyclone travelled faster or destroyed more completely. I shouted after them, but they sped on the wings of the wind, great regal poppies, broken-stalked and mangled, trailing after them or cluttering their wake—the most high-handed act of piracy, I am confident, ever committed off the high seas.

One day I went a-fishing, and on that day a woman entered the field. Appeals and remonstrances from the porch having no effect upon her, Bess despatched a little girl to beg of her to pick no more poppies. The woman calmly went on picking. Then Bess herself went down through the heat of the day. But the woman went on picking, and while she picked she discussed property and proprietary rights, denying Bess's sovereignty until deeds and documents should be produced in proof thereof. And all the time she went on picking, never once overlooking her hand. She was a large woman, belligerent of aspect, and Bess was only a woman and not prone to fisticuffs. So the invader picked until she could pick no more, said "Good-day," and sailed majestically away.

"People have really grown worse in the last several years, I think," said Bess to me in a tired sort of voice that night, as we sat in the library after dinner.

Next day I was inclined to agree with her. "There's a woman and a little girl heading straight for the poppies," said May, a maid about the bungalow. I went out on the porch and waited their advent. They plunged through the pine trees and into the fields, and as the roots of the first poppies were pulled I called to them. They were about a hundred feet away. The woman and the little girl turned to the sound of my voice and looked at me. "Please do not pick the poppies," I pleaded. They pondered this for a minute; then the woman said something in an undertone to the little girl, and both backs jack-knifed as the slaughter recommenced. I shouted, but they had become suddenly deaf. I screamed, and so fiercely that the little girl wavered dubiously. And while the woman went on picking I could hear her in low tones heartening the little girl.

I recollected a siren whistle with which I was wont to summon Johnny, the son of my sister. It was a fearsome thing, of a kind to wake the dead, and I blew and blew, but the jack-knifed backs never unclasped. I do not mind with men, but I have never particularly favored physical encounters with women; yet this woman, who encouraged a little girl in iniquity, tempted me.

I went into the bungalow and fetched my rifle. Flourishing it in a sanguinary manner and scowling fearsomely, I charged upon the invaders. The little girl fled, screaming, to the shelter of the pines, but the woman calmly went on picking. She took not the least notice. I had expected her to run at sight of me, and it was embarrassing. There was I, charging down the field like a wild bull upon a woman who would not get out of the way. I could only slow down, supremely conscious of how ridiculous it all was. At a distance of ten feet she straightened up and deigned to look at me. I came to a halt and blushed to the roots of my hair. Perhaps I really did frighten her (I sometimes try to persuade myself that this is so), or perhaps she took pity on me; but, at any rate, she stalked out of my field with great composure, nay, majesty, her arms brimming with orange and gold.

Nevertheless, thenceforward I saved my lungs and flourished my rifle. Also, I made fresh generalizations. To commit robbery women take advantage of their sex. Men have more respect for property than women. Men are less insistent in crime than women. And women are less afraid of guns than men. Likewise, we conquer the earth in hazard and battle by the virtues of our mothers. We are a race of land-robbers and sea-robbers, we Anglo-Saxons, and small wonder, when we suckle at the breasts of a breed of women such as maraud my poppy field.

Still the pillage went on. Sirens and gun-flourishings were without avail. The city folk were great of heart and undismayed, and I noted the habit of "repeating" was becoming general. What booted it how often they were driven forth if each time they were permitted to carry away their ill-gotten plunder? When one has turned the same person away twice and thrice an emotion arises somewhat akin to homicide. And when one has once become conscious of this sanguinary feeling his whole destiny seems to grip hold of him and drag him into the abyss. More than once I found myself unconsciously pulling the rifle into position to get a sight on the miserable trespassers. In my sleep I slew them in manifold ways and threw their carcasses into the reservoir. Each day the temptation to shoot them in the legs became more luring, and every day I felt my fate calling to me imperiously. Visions of the gallows rose up before me, and with the hemp about my neck I saw stretched out the pitiless future of my children, dark with disgrace and shame. I became afraid of myself, and Bess went about with anxious face, privily beseeching my friends to entice me into taking a vacation. Then, and at the last gasp, came the thought that saved me: *Why not confiscate?* If their forays were bootless, in the nature of things their forays would cease.

The first to enter my field thereafter was a man. I was waiting for him—And, oh joy! it was the "Repeater" himself, smugly complacent with knowledge of past success. I dropped the rifle negligently across the hollow of my arm and went down to him.

"I am sorry to trouble you for those poppies," I said in my oiliest tones, "but really, you know, I must have them."

He regarded me speechlessly. It must have made a great picture. It surely was dramatic. With the rifle across my arm and my suave request still ringing in my ears, I felt like Black Bart, and Jesse James, and Jack Shepard, and Robin Hood, and whole generations of highwaymen.

"Come, come," I said, a little sharply and in what I imagined was the true fashion; "I am sorry to inconvenience you, believe me, but I must have those poppies."

I absently shifted the gun and smiled. That fetched him. Without a word he passed them over and turned his toes toward the fence, but no longer casual and careless was his carriage, nor did he stoop to pick the occasional poppy by the way. That was the last of the "Repeater." I could see by his eyes that he did not like me, and his back reproached me all the way down the field and out of sight.

From that day the bungalow has been flooded with poppies. Every vase and earthen jar is filled with them. They blaze on every mantel and run riot through all the rooms. I present them to my friends in huge bunches, and still the kind city folk come and gather more for me. "Sit down for a moment," I say to the departing guest. And there we sit in the shade of the porch while aspiring city creatures pluck my poppies and sweat under the brazen sun. And when their arms are sufficiently weighted with my yellow glories, I go down with the rifle over my arm and disburden them. Thus have I become convinced that every situation has its compensations.

Confiscation was successful, so far as it went; but I had forgotten one thing; namely, the vast number of the city folk. Though the old transgressors came no more, new ones arrived every day, and I found myself confronted with the titanic task of educating a whole cityful to the inexpediency of raiding my poppy field. During the process of disburdening them I was accustomed to explaining my side of the case, but I soon gave this over. It was a waste of breath. They could not understand. To one lady, who insinuated that I was miserly, I said:

"My dear madam, no hardship is worked upon you. Had I not been parsimonious yesterday and the day before, these poppies would have been picked by the city hordes of that day and the day before, and your eyes, which today have discovered this field, would have beheld no poppies at all. The poppies you may not pick today are the poppies I did not permit to be picked yesterday and the day before. Therefore, believe me, you are denied nothing."

"But the poppies are here today," she said, glaring carnivorously upon their glow and splendor.

"I will pay you for them," said a gentleman, at another time. (I had just relieved him of an armful.) I felt a sudden shame, I know not why, unless it be that his words had just made clear to me that a monetary as well as an aesthetic value was attached to my flowers. The apparent sordidness of my position overwhelmed me, and I said weakly: "I do not sell my poppies. You may have what you have picked." But before the week was out I confronted the same gentleman again. "I will pay you for them." he said. "Yes," I said, "you may pay me for them. Twenty dollars, please." He gasped, looked at me searchingly, gasped again, and silently and sadly put the poppies down. But it remained, as usual, for a woman to attain the sheerest pitch of audacity. When I declined payment and demanded my plucked beauties, she refused to give them up. "I picked these poppies," she said, "and my time is worth money. When you have paid me for my time you may have them." Her cheeks flamed rebellion, and her face, withal a pretty one, was set and determined. Now, I was a man of the hill tribes, and she a mere woman of the city folk, and though it is not my inclination to enter into details, it is my pleasure to state that that bunch of poppies subsequently glorified the bungalow and that the woman departed to the city unpaid. Anyway, they were my poppies.

"They are God's poppies," said the Radiant Young Radical, democratically shocked at sight of me turning city folk out of my field. And for two weeks she hated me with a deathless hatred. I sought her out and explained. I explained at length. I told the story of the poppy as Maeterlink has told the life of the bee. I treated the question biologically, psychologically, and sociologically. I discussed it ethically and aesthetically. I grew warm over it, and impassioned; and when I had done, she professed conversion, but in my heart of hearts I knew it to be compassion.

I fled to other friends for consolation. I retold the story of the poppy. They did not appear supremely interested. I grew excited. They were surprised and pained. They looked at me curiously. "It ill-befits your dignity to squabble over poppies," they said. "It is unbecoming."

I fled away to yet other friends. I sought vindication. The thing had become vital, and I needs must put myself right. I felt called upon to explain, though well knowing that he who explains is lost. I told the story of the poppy over again. I went into the minutest details. I added to it, and expanded. I talked myself hoarse, and when I could talk no more they looked bored. Also, they said insipid things, and soothful things, and things concerning other things, and not at all to the point. I was consumed with anger, and there and then I renounced them all.

At the bungalow I lie in wait for chance visitors. Craftily I broach the subject, watching their faces closely the while to detect first signs of disapprobation, whereupon I empty long-stored vials of wrath upon their heads. I wrangle for hours with whomsoever does not say I am right. I have become like Guy de Maupassant's old man who picked up a piece of string. I am incessantly explaining, and nobody will understand. I have become more brusque in my treatment of the predatory city folk. No longer do I take delight in their disburdenment, for it has become an onerous duty, a wearisome and distasteful task. My friends look askance and murmur pityingly on the side when we meet in the city. They rarely come to see me now. They are afraid. I am an embittered and disappointed man, and all the light seems to have gone out of my life and into my blazing field. So one pays for things.

from The Valley of the Moon

"Life on a California ranch," London wrote of his boyhood, "was then to me the dullest possible existence." By the time he penned those words in 1915, though, he had become an agriculturist of genuine achievement at his spread in Glen Ellen. The following section of The Valley of the Moon *(1913) shows a fictional version of Jack and Charmian—Billy and Saxon, a working-class couple disenchanted with urban life—finding the Sonoma Valley ranch that becomes their haven and challenge. Part of the author's research for Billy and Saxon's trip, by the way, was the journey detailed in "Navigating Four Horses North of the Bay," and readers will recognize some settings and events.*

South they held along the coast, hunting, fishing, swimming, and horse buying. Billy shipped his purchases on the coasting steamers. Through Del Norte and Humboldt counties they went, and through Mendocino into Sonoma—counties larger than Eastern states—threading the giant woods, whipping innumerable trout-streams, and crossing countless rich valleys. Ever Saxon sought the valley of the moon. Sometimes, when all seemed fair, the lack was a railroad, sometimes madroño and manzanita trees, and, usually, there was too much fog.

"We do want a sun cocktail once in a while," she told Billy.

"Yep," was his answer. "Too much fog might make us soggy. What we're after is betwixt an' between, an' we'll have to get back from the coast a ways to find it."

This was in the fall of the year, and they turned their backs on the Pacific at old Fort Ross and entered the Russian River Valley, far below Ukiah, by way of Cazadero and Guerneville. At Santa Rosa, Billy was delayed with the shipping of several horses, so that it was not until afternoon that he drove south and east for Sonoma Valley.

"I guess we'll no more than make Sonoma Valley when it'll be time to camp," he said, measuring the sun with his eye. "This is called Bennett Valley. You cross a divide from it and come out at Glen Ellen. Now this is a mighty pretty valley if anybody should ask you. An' that's some nifty mountain over there."

Rising from rolling stubble fields, Bennett Peak towered hot in the sun, a row of bastion hills leaning against its base. But hills and mountain on that side showed bare and heated, though beautiful with the sunburnt tawniness of California.

They took a turn to the right and began crossing a series of steep foothills. As they approached the mountain there were signs of a greater abundance of water. They drove beside a running stream, and though the vineyards on the hills were summer-dry, the farmhouses in the hollows and on the levels were grouped about with splendid trees.

"Maybe it sounds funny," Saxon observed, "but I'm beginning to love that mountain already. It almost seems as if I'd seen it before, somehow; it's so all-around satisfying—oh!"

Crossing a bridge and rounding a sharp turn, they were suddenly enveloped in a mysterious coolness and gloom. All about them arose stately trunks of redwood. The forest floor was a rosy carpet of autumn fronds. Occasional shafts of sunlight, penetrating the deep shade, warmed the somberness of the grove. Alluring paths led off among the trees and into cozy nooks made by circles of red columns growing around the dust of vanished ancestors— witnessing the titanic proportions of those ancestors by the girth of the circles in which they stood.

Out of the grove they pulled to the steep divide, which was no more than a buttress of Sonoma Mountain. The way led on through rolling uplands and across small dips and canyons, all well wooded and adrip with water. In places the road was muddy from wayside springs.

"The mountain's a sponge," said Billy. "Here it is, the tail end of a dry summer, an' the ground's just leakin' everywhere."

"I know I've never been here before," Saxon communed aloud.

"But it's all so familiar! So I must have dreamed it. And there's madroños—a whole grove! And manzanita! Why, I feel just as if I was coming home. Oh, Billy, if it should turn out to be our valley!"

"Plastered against the side of a mountain?" he queried, with a skeptical laugh.

"No; I don't mean that. I mean on the way to our valley. Because the way—all ways—to our valley must be beautiful. And this—I've seen it all before, dreamed it."

They passed a large and comfortable farmhouse surrounded by wandering barns and cow-sheds, went on under forest arches, and emerged beside a field with which Saxon was instantly enchanted. It flowed in a gentle concave from the road up the mountain, its farther boundary an unbroken line of timber. The field glowed like rough gold in the approaching sunset, and near the middle of it stood a solitary great redwood, with blasted top suggesting a nesting eyrie for eagles. The timber beyond clothed the mountain in solid green to what they took to be the top. But as they drove on, Saxon, looking back upon what she called *her* field, saw the real summit of Sonoma towering beyond, the mountain behind her field a mere spur upon the side of the larger mass.

Ahead and toward the right, across sheer ridges of the mountains, separated by deep green canyons and broadening lower down into rolling orchards and vineyards, they caught their first sight of Sonoma Valley and the wild mountains that rimmed its eastern side. To the left they gazed across a golden land of small hills and valleys. Beyond, to the north, they glimpsed another portion of the valley, and, still beyond, the opposing wall of the valley—a range of mountains, the highest of which reared its red and battered ancient crater against a rosy and mellowing sky. From north to southeast, the mountain rim curved in the brightness of the sun, while Saxon and Billy were already in the shadow of evening. He looked at Saxon, noted the ravished ecstasy of her face, and stopped the horses. All the eastern sky was blushing to rose, which descended upon the mountains, touching them with wine and ruby. Sonoma Valley began to fill with a purple flood, laving the mountain bases, rising, inundating, drowning them in its purple. Saxon pointed in silence, indicating that the purple flood was the sunset shadow of Sonoma Mountain. Billy nodded, then chirruped to the mares, and the descent began through a warm and colorful twilight.

On the elevated sections of the road they felt the cool, delicious breeze from the Pacific, forty miles away; while from each little dip and hollow came warm breaths of autumn earth, spicy with sunburnt grass and fallen leaves and passing flowers.

They came to the rim of a deep canyon that seemed to penetrate to the heart of Sonoma Mountain. Again, with no word spoken, merely from watching Saxon, Billy stopped the wagon. The canyon was wildly beautiful. Tall redwoods lined its entire length. On its farther rim stood three rugged knolls, covered with dense woods of spruce and oak. From between the knolls, a feeder to the main canyon and likewise fringed with redwoods, emerged a smaller canyon. Billy pointed to a stubble-field that lay at the feet of the knolls.

"It's in fields like that I've seen my mares a-pasturing," he said.

They dropped down into the canyon, the road following a stream that sang under maples and alders. The sunset fires, refracted from the cloud-driftage of the autumn sky, bathed the canyon with crimson, in which ruddy-limbed madroños and wine-wooded manzanitas burned and smoldered. The air was aromatic with laurel. Wild grapevines bridged the stream from tree to tree. Oaks of many sorts were veiled in lacy Spanish moss. Ferns and brakes grew lush beside the stream.

"I've got a hunch," said Billy.

"Let me say it first," Saxon begged.

He waited, his eyes on her face as she gazed about her in rapture.

"We've found our valley," she whispered. "Was that it?"

He nodded, but checked speech at sight of a small boy driving a cow up the road, a preposterously big shotgun in one hand, in the other as preposterously big a jackrabbit.

"How far to Glen Ellen?" Billy asked.

"Mile an' a half," was the answer.

"What creek is this?" inquired Saxon.

"Wild Water. It empties into Sonoma Creek, half a mile down."

"Trout?"—this from Billy.

"If you know how to ketch 'em," grinned the boy.

"Deer up the mountain?"

"It ain't open season," the boy evaded.

"I guess you never shot a deer," Billy slyly baited, and was rewarded with, "I got the horns to show."

"Deer sheds their horns," Billy teased on. "Anybody can find 'em."

"I got the meat on mine. It ain't dry yet—"

The boy broke off, gazing with shocked eyes into the pit Billy had dug for him.

"It's all right, sonny," Billy laughed, as he drove on. "I ain't the game-warden. I'm buyin' horses."

More ruddy madroños, more fairy circles of redwoods, and, still beside the singing stream, they passed a gate by the roadside. Before it stood a rural mailbox, on which was lettered "Edmund Hale." Standing under the rustic arch, leaning upon the gate, a man and woman composed a picture so arresting and beautiful that Saxon caught her breath. They were side by side, the delicate hand of the woman curled in the hand of the man, which looked as if made to confer benedictions. His face bore out this impression—a beautiful-browed countenance, with large, benevolent gray eyes under a wealth of white hair that shone like spun glass. He was fair and large; the little woman beside him was daintily wrought. She was saffron brown, as a woman of the white race can well be, with smiling eyes of bluest blue. In quaint sage-green draperies, she seemed a flower, with her small, vivid face irresistibly reminding Saxon of a springtime wake-robin.

Perhaps the picture made by Saxon and Billy was equally arresting and beautiful, as they drove down through the golden end of day. The two couples had eyes only for each other. The little woman beamed joyously. The man's face glowed into the benediction that had trembled there. To Saxon, like the field up the mountain, like the mountain itself, it seemed that she had always known this adorable pair. She knew that she loved them.

"How d'ye do," said Billy.

"You blessed children," said the man. "I wonder if you know how dear you look sitting there."

That was all. The wagon had passed by, rustling down the road which was carpeted with fallen leaves of maple, oak, and alder. Then they came to the meeting of the two creeks.

"Oh, what a place for a home," Saxon cried, pointing across Wild Water. "See, Billy, on that bench there, above the meadow."

"It's a rich bottom, Saxon, and so is the bench rich. Look at the big trees on it. An' they's sure to be springs."

"Drive over," she said.

Forsaking the main road, they crossed Wild Water on a narrow bridge and continued along an ancient, rutted road that ran beside an equally ancient worm fence of split redwood rails. They came to a gate, open and off its hinges, through which the road led out on the bench.

"This is it—I know it," Saxon said with conviction. "Drive in, Billy."

A small, whitewashed farmhouse with broken windows showed through the trees.

"Talk about your madroños—"

Billy pointed to the father of all madroños, six feet in diameter at its base, sturdy and sound, which stood before the house.

They spoke in low tones as they passed around the house under great oak trees and came to a stop before a small barn. They did not wait to unharness. Tying the horses, they started to explore. The pitch from the bench to the meadow was steep yet thickly wooded with oaks and manzanita. As they crashed through the underbrush they startled a score of quail into flight.

"How about game?" Saxon queried.

Billy grinned, and fell to examining a spring which bubbled a clear stream into the meadow. Here the ground was sunbaked and wide open in a multitude of cracks.

Disappointment leaped into Saxon's face, but Billy, crumbling a clod between his fingers, had not made up his mind.

"It's rich," he pronounced. "But—"

He broke off, stared all about, studying the configuration of the meadow, crossed it to the redwood trees beyond, then came back.

"It's no good as it is," he said. "But it's the best ever if it's handled right. All it needs is a little common sense an' a lot of drainage. This meadow's a natural basin not yet filled level. Come on; I'll show you."

They went through the redwoods and came out on Sonoma Creek. At this spot was no singing. The stream poured into a quiet pool. The willows on their side brushed the water. The opposite side was a steep bank. Billy measured the height of the bank with his eye, the depth of the water with a driftwood pole.

"Fifteen feet," he announced. "That allows all kinds of high divin' from the bank."

They followed down the pool. It emptied into a riffle, across exposed bedrock, into another pool. As they looked, a trout flashed into the air and back, leaving a widening ripple on the quiet surface.

"This place was specially manufactured for us," Billy said. "In the morning I'll find out who owns it."

Half an hour later, feeding the horses, he called Saxon's attention to a locomotive whistle.

"You've got your railroad," he said. "That's a train pulling into Glen Ellen, an' it's only a mile from here."

Saxon was dozing off to sleep under the blankets when Billy aroused her.

"Suppose the guy that owns it won't sell?"

"There isn't the slightest doubt," Saxon answered with unruffled certainty. "This is our place. I know it."

All Gold Canyon

Many critics have pointed out the contrasting presentations of the physical environment between London's Northland stories and his later tales set in California, which he called the Southland. Those regions were inherently different, of course, and the author used them to make different points about humans in relation to the web of all life. He found the former setting daunting indeed, writing "Nature has many tricks wherewith she convinces man of his finity...the most tremendous, the most stupefying of all, is the passive phase of the White Silence." On the other hand, he used fecund California wilderness to illustrate not human insignificance, but that "city folk constituted a new and terrible destructive force" that upset the equilibrium of nature. Jack had explored places like the canyon described in this story not long after returning from Alaska in 1898, when he and a friend explored the Mother Lode and the Sierra Nevada, and he had certainly known many prospectors like the one he created in this story. "All Gold Canyon" was included in 1906's Moon Face and Other Stories.

It was the green heart of the canyon, where the walls swerved back from the rigid plan and relieved their harshness of line by making a little sheltered nook and filling it to the brim with sweetness and roundness and softness. Here all things rested. Even the narrow stream ceased its turbulent down-rush long enough to form a quiet pool. Knee-deep in the water, with drooping head and half-shut eyes, drowsed a red-coated, many-antlered buck.

On one side, beginning at the very lip of the pool, was a tiny meadow, a cool, resilient surface of green that extended to the base of the frowning wall. Beyond the pool a gentle slope of earth ran up and up to meet the opposing wall. Fine grass covered the slope—grass that was spangled with flowers, with here and there patches of color, orange and purple and golden. Below, the canyon was shut in. There was no view. The walls leaned together abrupt-ly and the canyon ended in a chaos of rocks, moss-covered and hidden by a green screen of vines and creepers and boughs of trees. Up the canyon rose far hills and peaks, the big foothills, pine-cov-ered and remote. And far beyond, like clouds upon the border of the sky, towered minarets of white, where the Sierra's eternal snows flashed austerely the blazes of the sun.

There was no dust in the canyon. The leaves and flowers were clean and virginal. The grass was young velvet. Over the pool three cottonwoods sent their snowy fluffs fluttering down the quiet air. On the slope the blossoms of the wine-wooded manzanita filled the air with springtime odors, while the leaves, wise with experi-ence, were already beginning their vertical twist against the coming aridity of summer. In the open spaces on the slope, beyond the far-thest shadow-reach of the manzanita, poised the mariposa lilies, like so many flights of jewelled moths suddenly arrested and on the verge of trembling into flight again. Here and there that woods harlequin, the madrõno, permitting itself to be caught in the act of changing its pea-green trunk to madder-red, breathed its fragrance into the air from great clusters of waxen bells. Creamy white were these bells, shaped like lilies-of-the-valley, with the sweetness of perfume that is of the springtime.

There was not a sigh of wind. The air was drowsy with its weight of perfume. It was a sweetness that would have been cloy-ing had the air been heavy and humid. But the air was sharp and thin. It was as starlight transmuted into atmosphere, shot through and warmed by sunshine, and flower-drenched with sweetness.

An occasional butterfly drifted in and out through the patch-es of light and shade. And from all about rose the low and sleepy hum of mountain bees—feasting Sybarites that jostled one anoth-er good-naturedly at the board, nor found time for rough discour-tesy. So quietly did the little stream drip and ripple its way through the canyon that it spoke only in faint and occasional gurgles. The voice of the stream was as a drowsy whisper, ever interrupted by dozings and silences, ever lifted again in the awakenings.

The motion of all things was a drifting in the heart of the canyon. Sunshine and butterflies drifted in and out among the trees. The hum of the bees and the whisper of the stream were a drifting of sound. And the drifting sound and drifting color seemed to weave together in the making of a delicate and intangible fabric which was the spirit of the place. It was a spirit of peace that was not of death, but of smooth-pulsing life, of quietude that was not silence, of movement that was not action, of repose that was quick with existence without being violent with struggle and travail. The spirit of the place was the spirit of the peace of the living, somnolent with the easement and content of prosperity, and undisturbed by rumors of far wars.

The red-coated, many-antlered buck acknowledged the lordship of the spirit of the place and dozed knee-deep in the cool, shaded pool. There seemed no flies to vex him and he was languid with rest. Sometimes his ears moved when the stream awoke and whispered; but they moved lazily, with foreknowledge that it was merely the stream grown garrulous at discovery that it had slept.

But there came a time when the buck's ears lifted and tensed with swift eagerness for sound. His head was turned down the canyon. His sensitive, quivering nostrils scented the air. His eyes could not pierce the green screen through which the stream rippled away, but to his ears came the voice of a man. It was a steady, monotonous, singsong voice. Once the buck heard the harsh clash of metal upon rock. At the sound he snorted with a sudden start that jerked him through the air from water to meadow, and his feet sank into the young velvet, while he pricked his ears and again scented the air. Then he stole across the tiny meadow, pausing once and again to listen, and faded away out of the canyon like a wraith, soft-footed and without sound.

The clash of steel-shod soles against the rocks began to be heard, and the man's voice grew louder. It was raised in a sort of chant and became distinct with nearness, so that the words could be heard:

"Tu'n around an' tu'n yo' face
Untoe them sweet hills of grace.
  (D' pow'rs of sin yo' am scornin'!)
Look about an' look aroun',
Fling yo' sin pack on d' groun'
  (Yo' will meet wid d' Lord in d' mornin'!)"

A sound of scrambling accompanied the song, and the spirit of the place fled away on the heels of the red-coated buck. The green screen was burst asunder, and a man peered out at the meadow and the pool and the sloping sidehill. He was a deliberate sort of man. He took in the scene with one embracing glance, then ran his eyes over the details to verify the general impression. Then, and not until then, did he open his mouth in vivid and solemn approval:

"Smoke of life an' snakes of purgatory! Will you just look at that! Wood an' water an' grass an' a sidehill! A pocket-hunter's delight an' a cayuse's paradise! Cool green for tired eyes! Pink pills for pale people ain't in it. A secret pasture for prospectors and a resting place for tired burros, by damn!"

He was a sandy-complexioned man in whose face geniality and humor seemed the salient characteristics. It was a mobile face, quick-changing to inward mood and thought. Thinking was in him a visible process. Ideas chased across his face like wind-flaws across the surface of a lake. His hair, sparse and unkempt of growth, was as indeterminate and colorless as his complexion. It would seem that all the color of his frame had gone into his eyes, for they were startlingly blue. Also they were laughing and merry eyes, within them much of the naïveté and wonder of the child; and yet, in an unassertive way, they contained much of calm self-reliance and strength of purpose founded upon self-experience and experience of the world.

From out the screen of vines and creepers he flung ahead of him a miner's pick and shovel and gold-pan. Then he crawled out himself into the open. He was clad in faded overalls and black cotton shirt, with hobnailed brogans on his feet, and on his head a hat whose shapelessness and stains advertised the rough usage of wind and rain and sun and camp smoke. He stood erect, seeing wide-eyed the secrecy of the scene and sensuously inhaling the warm, sweet breath of the canyon garden through nostrils that dilated and quivered with delight. His eyes narrowed to laughing slits of blue, his face wreathed itself in joy, and his mouth curled in a smile as he cried aloud:

"Jumping dandelions and happy hollyhocks, but that smells good to me! Talk about your attar o' roses an' cologne factories! They ain't in it."

He had the habit of soliloquy. His quick-changing facial expressions might tell every thought and mood, but the tongue, perforce, ran hard after, repeating, like a second Boswell.

The man lay down on the lip of the pool and drank long and deep of its water. "Tastes good to me," he murmured, lifting his head and gazing across the pool at the sidehill, while he wiped his mouth with the back of his hand. The sidehill attracted his attention. Still lying on his stomach, he studied the hill formation long and carefully. It was a practiced eye that travelled up the slope to the crumbling canyon wall and back and down again to the edge of the pool. He scrambled to his feet and favored the sidehill with a second survey.

"Looks good to me," he concluded, picking up his pick and shovel and gold-pan.

He crossed the stream below the pool, stepping agilely from stone to stone. Where the sidehill touched the water he dug up a shovelful of dirt and put it into the gold-pan. He squatted down, holding the pan in his two hands, and partly immersing it in the stream. Then he imparted to the pan a deft circular motion that sent the water sluicing in and out through the dirt and gravel. The larger and the lighter particles worked to the surface, and these, by a skillful dipping movement of the pan, he spilled out and over the edge. Occasionally, to expedite matters, he rested the pan and with his fingers raked out the large pebbles and pieces of rock.

The contents of the pan diminished rapidly until only fine dirt and the smallest bits of gravel remained. At this stage he began to work very deliberately and carefully. It was fine washing, and he washed fine and finer, with a keen scrutiny and delicate and fastidious touch. At last the pan seemed empty of everything but water; but with a quick semicircular flirt that sent the water flying over the shallow rim into the stream, he disclosed a layer of black sand on the bottom of the pan. So thin was this layer that it was like a streak of paint. He examined it closely. In the midst of it was a tiny golden speck. He dribbled a little water in over the depressed edge of the pan. With a quick flirt he sent the water sluicing across the bottom, turning the grains of black sand over and over. A second tiny golden speck rewarded his effort.

The washing had now become very fine—fine beyond all need of ordinary placer mining. He worked the black sand, a small portion at a time, up the shallow rim of the pan. Each small portion he examined sharply, so that his eyes saw every grain of it before he allowed it to slide over the edge and away. Jealously, bit by bit, he let the black sand slip away. A golden speck, no larger than a pin-point, appeared on the rim, and by his manipulation of the water it returned to the bottom of the pan. And in such fashion another speck was disclosed, and another. Great was his care of them. Like a shepherd he herded his flock of golden specks so that not one should be lost. At last, of the pan of dirt nothing remained but his golden herd. He counted it, and then, after all his labor, sent it flying out of the pan with one final swirl of water.

But his blue eyes were shining with desire as he rose to his feet. "Seven," he muttered aloud, asserting the sum of the specks for which he had toiled so hard and which he had so wantonly thrown away. "Seven," he repeated, with the emphasis of one trying to impress a number on his memory.

He stood still a long while, surveying the hillside. In his eyes was a curiosity, new-aroused and burning. There was an exultance about his bearing and a keenness like that of a hunting animal catching the fresh scent of game.

He moved down the stream a few steps and took a second panful of dirt.

Again came the careful washing, the jealous herding of the golden specks, and the wantonness with which he sent them flying into the stream when he had counted their number.

"Five," he muttered, and repeated, "five."

He could not forbear another survey of the hill before filling the pan farther down the stream. His golden herds diminished. "Four, three, two, two, one," were his memory tabulations as he moved down the stream. When but one speck of gold rewarded his washing, he stopped and built a fire of dry twigs. Into this he thrust the gold-pan and burned it till it was blue-black. He held up the pan and examined it critically. Then he nodded approbation. Against such a color background he could defy the tiniest yellow speck to elude him.

Still moving down the stream, he panned again. A single speck was his reward. A third pan contained no gold at all. Not satisfied with this, he panned three times again, taking his shovels of dirt within a foot of one another. Each pan proved empty of gold, and the fact, instead of discouraging him, seemed to give him satisfaction. His elation increased with each barren washing, until he arose, exclaiming jubilantly:

"If it ain't the real thing, may God knock off my head with sour apples!"

Returning to where he had started operations, he began to pan up the stream. At first his golden herds increased—increased prodigiously. "Fourteen, eighteen, twenty-one, twenty-six," ran his memory tabulations. Just above the pool he struck his richest pan—thirty-five colors.

"Almost enough to save," he remarked regretfully as he allowed the water to sweep them away.

The sun climbed to the top of the sky. The man worked on. Pan by pan he went up the stream, the tally of results steadily decreasing.

"It's just booful, the way it peters out," he exulted when a shovelful of dirt contained no more than a single speck of gold.

And when no specks at all were found in several pans he straightened up and favored the hillside with a confident glance.

"Ah, ha! Mr. Pocket!" he cried out, as though to an auditor hidden somewhere above him beneath the surface of the slope. "Ah, ha! Mr. Pocket! I'm a-comin', I'm a-comin', an' I'm shorely gwine to get yer! You heah me, Mr. Pocket? I'm gwine to get yer as shore as punkins ain't cauliflowers!"

He turned and flung a measuring glance at the sun poised above him in the azure of the cloudless sky. Then he went down the canyon, following the line of shovel holes he had made in filling the pans. He crossed the stream below the pool and disappeared through the green screen. There was little opportunity for the spirit of the place to return with its quietude and repose, for the man's voice, raised in ragtime song, still dominated the canyon with possession.

After a time, with a greater clashing of steel-shod feet on rock, he returned. The green screen was tremendously agitated. It surged back and forth in the throes of a struggle. There was a loud grating and clanging of metal. The man's voice leaped to a higher pitch and was sharp with imperativeness. A large body plunged and panted. There was a snapping and ripping and rending, and amid a shower of falling leaves a horse burst through the screen. On its back was a pack, and from this trailed broken vines and torn creepers. The animal gazed with astonished eyes at the scene into which it had been precipitated, then dropped its head to the grass and began contentedly to graze. A second horse scrambled into view, slipping once on the mossy rocks and regaining equilibrium when its hoofs sank into the yielding surface of the meadow. It was riderless, though on its back was a high-horned Mexican saddle, scarred and discolored by long usage.

The man brought up the rear. He threw off pack and saddle, with an eye to camp location, and gave the animals their freedom to graze. He unpacked his food and got out frying pan and coffee-pot. He gathered an armful of dry wood, and with a few stones made a place for his fire.

"My!" he said, "but I've got an appetite. I could scoff iron-filings an' horseshoe nails an' thank you kindly, ma'am, for a second helpin'."

He straightened up, and, while he reached for matches in the pocket of his overalls, his eyes travelled across the pool to the side-hill. His fingers had clutched the matchbox, but they relaxed their hold and the hand came out empty. The man wavered perceptibly. He looked at his preparations for cooking and he looked at the hill.

"Guess I'll take another whack at her," he concluded, starting to cross the stream.

"They ain't no sense in it, I know," he mumbled apologetically. "But keepin' grub back an hour ain't goin' to hurt none, I reckon."

A few feet back from his first line of test pans he started a second line. The sun dropped down the western sky, the shadows lengthened, but the man worked on. He began a third line of test pans. He was crosscutting the hillside, line by line, as he ascended. The center of each line produced the richest pans, while the ends came where no colors showed in the pan. And as he ascended the hillside the lines grew perceptibly shorter. The regularity with which their length diminished served to indicate that somewhere up the slope the last line would be so short as to have scarcely length at all, and that beyond could come only a point. The design was growing into an inverted V. The converging sides of this V marked the boundaries of the gold-bearing dirt.

The apex of the V was evidently the man's goal. Often he ran his eye along the converging sides and on up the hill, trying to divine the apex, the point where the gold-bearing dirt must cease. Here resided "Mr. Pocket"—for so the man familiarly addressed the imaginary point above him on the slope, crying out:

"Come down out o' that, Mr. Pocket! Be right smart an' agreeable, an' come down!"

"All right," he would add later, in a voice resigned to determination. "All right, Mr. Pocket. It's plain to me I got to come right up an' snatch you out bald-headed. An' I'll do it! I'll do it!" he would threaten still later.

Each pan he carried down to the water to wash, and as he went higher up the hill the pans grew richer, until he began to save the gold in an empty baking-powder can which he carried carelessly in his lap pocket. So engrossed was he in his toil that he did not notice the long twilight of oncoming night. It was not until he tried vainly to see the gold colors in the bottom of the pan that he realized the passage of time. He straightened up abruptly. An expression of whimsical wonderment and awe overspread his face as he drawled:

"Gosh darn my buttons, if I didn't plumb forget dinner!"

He stumbled across the stream in the darkness and lighted his long-delayed fire. Flapjacks and bacon and warmed-over beans constituted his supper. Then he smoked a pipe by the smoldering coals, listening to the night noises and watching the moonlight stream through the canyon. After that he unrolled his bed, took off his heavy shoes, and pulled the blankets up to his chin. His face showed white in the moonlight, like the face of a corpse. But it was a corpse that knew its resurrection, for the man rose suddenly on one elbow and gazed across at his hillside.

"Good night, Mr. Pocket," he called sleepily. "Good night."

He slept through the early gray of morning until the direct rays of the sun smote his closed eyelids, when he awoke with a start and looked about him until he had established the continuity of his existence and identified his present self with the days previously lived.

To dress, he had merely to buckle on his shoes. He glanced at his fireplace and at his hillside, wavered, but fought down the temptation and started the fire.

"Keep yer shirt on, Bill; keep yer shirt on," he admonished himself. "What's the good of rushin'? No use in gettin' all het up an' sweaty. Mr. Pocket'll wait for you. He ain't a-runnin' away before you can get yer breakfast. Now, what you want, Bill, is something fresh in yer bill o' fare. So it's up to you to go an' get it."

He cut a short pole at the water's edge and drew from one of his pockets a bit of line and a draggled fly that had once been a royal coachman.

"Mebbe they'll bite in the early morning," he muttered, as he made his first cast into the pool. And a moment later he was gleefully crying: "What'd I tell you, eh? What'd I tell you?"

He had no reel nor any inclination to waste time, and by main strength, and swiftly, he drew out of the water a flashing ten-inch trout. Three more, caught in rapid succession, furnished his breakfast. When he came to the stepping-stones on his way to his hillside, he was struck by a sudden thought, and paused.

"I'd just better take a hike downstream a ways," he said. "There's no tellin' what cuss may be snoopin' around."

But he crossed over on the stones, and with a "I really oughter take that hike," the need of the precaution passed out of his mind and he fell to work.

At nightfall he straightened up. The small of his back was stiff from stooping toil, and as he put his hand behind him to soothe the protesting muscles, he said:

"Now what d'ye think of that, by damn? I clean forgot my dinner again! If I don't watch out, I'll sure be degeneratin' into a two-meal-a-day crank."

"Pockets is the damnedest things I ever see for makin' a man absentminded," he communed that night, as he crawled into his blankets. Nor did he forget to call up the hillside, "Good night, Mr. Pocket! Good night!"

Rising with the sun, and snatching a hasty breakfast, he was early at work. A fever seemed to be growing in him, nor did the increasing richness of the test pans allay this fever. There was a flush in his cheek other than that made by the heat of the sun, and he was oblivious to fatigue and the passage of time. When he filled a pan with dirt, he ran down the hill to wash it; nor could he forbear running up the hill again, panting and stumbling profanely, to refill the pan.

He was now a hundred yards from the water, and the inverted V was assuming definite proportions. The width of the pay-dirt steadily decreased, and the man extended in his mind's eye the sides of the V to their meeting place far up the hill. This was his goal, the apex of the V, and he panned many times to locate it.

"Just about two yards above that manzanita bush an' a yard to the right," he finally concluded.

Then the temptation seized him. "As plain as the nose on your face," he said, as he abandoned his laborious crosscutting and climbed to the indicated apex. He filled a pan and carried it down the hill to wash. It contained no trace of gold. He dug deep, and he dug shallow, filling and washing a dozen pans, and was unrewarded even by the tiniest golden speck. He was enraged at having yielded to the temptation, and cursed himself blasphemously and pridelessly. Then he went down the hill and took up the crosscutting.

"Slow an' certain, Bill; slow an' certain," he crooned. "Shortcuts to fortune ain't in your line, an' it's about time you know it. Get wise, Bill; get wise. Slow an' certain's the only hand you can play; so go to it, an' keep to it, too."

As the crosscuts decreased, showing that the sides of the V were converging, the depth of the V increased. The gold trace was dipping into the hill. It was only at thirty inches beneath the surface that he could get colors in his pan. The dirt he found at twenty-five inches from the surface, and at thirty-five inches, yielded barren pans. At the base of the V, by the water's edge, he had found the gold colors at the grass roots. The higher he went up the hill, the deeper the gold dipped. To dig a hole three feet deep in order to get one test pan was a task of no mean magnitude; while between the man and the apex intervened an untold number of such holes to be dug. "An' there's no tellin' how much deeper it'll pitch," he sighed, in a moment's pause, while his fingers soothed his aching back.

Feverish with desire, with aching back and stiffening muscles, with pick and shovel gouging and mauling the soft brown earth, the man toiled up the hill. Before him was the smooth slope, spangled with flowers and made sweet with their breath. Behind him was devastation. It looked like some terrible eruption breaking out on the smooth skin of the hill. His slow progress was like that of a slug, befouling beauty with a monstrous trail.

Though the dipping gold trace increased the man's work, he found consolation in the increasing richness of the pans. Twenty cents, thirty cents, fifty cents, sixty cents, were the values of the gold found in the pans, and at nightfall he washed his banner pan, which gave him a dollar's worth of gold dust from a shovelful of dirt.

"I'll just bet it's my luck to have some inquisitive cuss come buttin' in here on my pasture," he mumbled sleepily that night as he pulled the blankets up to his chin.

Suddenly he sat upright. "Bill!" he called sharply. "Now listen to me, Bill; d'ye hear! It's up to you, tomorrow mornin', to mosey round an' see what you can see. Understand? Tomorrow morning, an' don't you forget it!"

He yawned and glanced across at his sidehill. "Good night, Mr. Pocket," he called.

In the morning he stole a march on the sun, for he had finished breakfast when its first rays caught him, and he was climbing the wall of the canyon where it crumbled away and gave footing. From the outlook at the top he found himself in the midst of loneliness. As far as he could see, chain after chain of mountains heaved themselves into his vision. To the east his eyes, leaping the miles between range and range and between many ranges, brought up at last against the white-peaked Sierra—the main crest, where the backbone of the Western world reared itself against the sky. To the north and south he could see more distinctly the cross systems that broke through the main trend of the sea of mountains. To the west the ranges fell away, one behind the other, diminishing and fading into the gentle foothills that, in turn, descended into the great valley which he could not see.

And in all that mighty sweep of earth he saw no sign of man nor of the handiwork of man—save only the torn bosom of the hillside at his feet. The man looked long and carefully. Once, far down his own canyon, he thought he saw in the air a faint hint of smoke. He looked again and decided that it was the purple haze of the hills made dark by a convolution of the canyon wall at its back.

"Hey, you, Mr. Pocket!" he called down into the canyon. "Stand out from under! I'm a-comin' Mr. Pocket! I'm a-comin'!"

The heavy brogans on the man's feet made him appear clumsy-footed, but he swung down from the giddy height as lightly and airily as a mountain goat. A rock, turning under his foot on the edge of the precipice, did not disconcert him. He seemed to know the precise time required for the turn to culminate in disaster, and in the meantime he utilized the false footing itself for the momentary earth contact necessary to carry him into safety. Where the earth sloped so steeply that it was impossible to stand for a second upright, the man did not hesitate. His foot pressed the impossible surface for but a fraction of the fatal second and gave him the bound that carried him onward. Again, where even the fraction of a second's footing was out of the question, he would swing his body past by a moment's handgrip on a jutting knob of rock, a crevice, or a precariously rooted shrub. At last, with a wild leap and yell, he exchanged the face of the wall for an earth slide and finished the descent in the midst of several tons of sliding earth and gravel.

His first pan of the morning washed out over two dollars in coarse gold. It was from the center of the V. To either side the diminution in the values of the pans was swift. His lines of cross-cutting holes were growing very short. The converging sides of the inverted V were only a few yards apart. Their meeting point was only a few yards above him. But the pay streak was dipping deeper and deeper into the earth. By early afternoon he was sinking the test holes five feet before the pans could show the gold trace.

For that matter, the gold trace had become something more than a trace; it was a placer mine in itself, and the man resolved to come back after he had found the pocket and work over the ground. But the increasing richness of the pans began to worry him. By late afternoon the worth of the pans had grown to three and four dollars. The man scratched his head perplexedly and looked a few feet up the hill at the manzanita bush that marked approximately the apex of the V. He nodded his head and said oracularly:

"It's one o' two things, Bill; one o' two things. Either Mr. Pocket's spilled himself all out an' down the hill, or else Mr. Pocket's that damned rich you maybe won't be able to carry him all away with you. And that'd be hell, wouldn't it now?" He chuckled at contemplation of so pleasant a dilemma.

Nightfall found him by the edge of the stream, his eyes wrestling with the gathering darkness over the washing of a five-dollar pan.

"Wisht I had an electric light to go on working," he said.

He found sleep difficult that night. Many times he composed himself and closed his eyes for slumber to overtake him; but his blood pounded with too strong desire, and as many times his eyes opened and he murmured wearily, "Wisht it was sunup."

Sleep came to him in the end, but his eyes were open with the first paling of the stars, and the gray dawn caught him with break-fast finished and climbing the hillside in the direction of the secret abiding place of Mr. Pocket.

The first crosscut the man made, there was space for only three holes, so narrow had become the pay streak and so close was he to the fountainhead of the golden stream he had been follow-ing for four days.

"Be ca'm, Bill; be ca'm," he admonished himself, as he broke ground for the final hole where the sides of the V had at last come together in a point.

"I've got the almighty cinch on you, Mr. Pocket, an' you can't lose me," he said many times as he sank the hole deeper and deeper.

Four feet, five feet, six feet, he dug his way down into the earth. The digging grew harder. His pick grated on broken rock. He examined the rock. "Rotten quartz," was his conclusion as, with the shovel, he cleared the bottom of the hole of loose dirt. He attacked the crumbling quartz with the pick, bursting the disintegrating rock asunder with every stroke.

He thrust his shovel into the loose mass. His eye caught a gleam of yellow. He dropped the shovel and squatted suddenly on his heels. As a farmer rubs the clinging earth from fresh-dug potatoes, so the man, a piece of rotten quartz held in both hands, rubbed the dirt away.

"Sufferin' Sardanopolis!" he cried. "Lumps an' chunks of it! Lumps an' chunks of it!"

It was only half rock he held in his hand. The other half was virgin gold. He dropped it into his pan and examined another piece. Little yellow was to be seen, but with his strong fingers he crumbled the rotten quartz away till both hands were filled with glowing yellow. He rubbed the dirt away from fragment after fragment, tossing them into the gold-pan. It was a treasure hole. So much had the quartz rotted away that there was less of it than there was of gold. Now and again he found a piece to which no rock clung—a piece that was all gold. A chunk, where the pick had laid open the heart of the gold, glittered like a handful of yellow jewels, and he cocked his head at it and slowly turned it around and over to observe the rich play of the light upon it.

"Talk about yer Too Much Gold diggins!" the man snorted contemptuously. "Why, this diggin'd make it look like thirty cents. This diggin is All Gold. An' right here an' now I name this yere canyon 'All Gold Canyon,' b' gosh!"

Still squatting on his heels, he continued examining the fragments and tossing them into the pan. Suddenly there came to him a premonition of danger. It seemed a shadow had fallen upon him, But there was no shadow. His heart had given a great jump up into his throat and was choking him. Then his blood slowly chilled and he felt the sweat of his shirt cold against his flesh.

He did not spring up nor look around. He did not move. He was considering the nature of the premonition he had received, trying to locate the source of the mysterious force that had warned him, striving to sense the imperative presence of the unseen thing that threatened him. There is an aura of things hostile, made manifest by messengers too refined for the senses to know; and this aura he felt, but knew not how he felt it. His was the feeling as when a cloud passes over the sun. It seemed that between him and life had passed something dark and smothering and menacing; a gloom, as it were, that swallowed up life and made for death—his death.

Every force of his being impelled him to spring up and confront the unseen danger, but his soul dominated the panic, and he remained squatting on his heels, in his hands a chunk of gold. He did not dare to look around, but he knew by now that there was something behind him and above him. He made believe to be interested in the gold in his hand. He examined it critically, turned it over and over, and rubbed the dirt from it. And all the time he knew that something behind him was looking at the gold over his shoulder.

Still feigning interest in the chunk of gold in his hand, he listened intently and he heard the breathing of the thing behind him. His eyes searched the ground in front of him for a weapon, but they saw only the uprooted gold, worthless to him now in his extremity. There was his pick, a handy weapon on occasion; but this was not such an occasion. The man realized his predicament. He was in a narrow hole that was seven feet deep. His head did not come to the surface of the ground. He was in a trap.

He remained squatting on his heels. He was quite cool and collected; but his mind, considering every factor, showed him only his helplessness. He continued rubbing the dirt from the quartz fragments and throwing the gold into the pan. There was nothing else for him to do. Yet he knew that he would have to rise up, sooner or later, and face the danger that breathed at his back. The minutes passed, and with the passage of each minute he knew that by so much he was nearer the time when he must stand up, or else—and his wet shirt went cold against his flesh again at the thought—or else he might receive death as he stooped there over his treasure.

Still he squatted on his heels, rubbing dirt from gold and debating in just what manner he should rise up. He might rise up with a rush and claw his way out of the hole to meet whatever threatened on the even footing aboveground. Or he might rise up slowly and carelessly, and feign casually to discover the thing that breathed at his back. His instinct and every fighting fibre of his body favored the mad, clawing rush to the surface. His intellect, and the craft thereof, favored the slow and cautious meeting with the thing that menaced and which he could not see. And while he debated, a loud, crashing noise burst on his ear. At the same instant he received a stunning blow on the left side of the back, and from the point of impact felt a rush of flame through his flesh. He sprang up in the air, but halfway to his feet collapsed. His body crumpled in like a leaf withered in sudden heat, and he came down, his chest across his pan of gold, his face in the dirt and rock, his legs tangled and twisted because of the restricted space at the bottom of the hole. His legs twitched convulsively several times. His body was shaken as with a mighty ague. There was a slow expansion of the lungs, accompanied by a deep sigh. Then the air was slowly, very slowly, exhaled, and his body as slowly flattened itself down into inertness.

Above, revolver in hand, a man was peering down over the edge of the hole. He peered for a long time at the prone and motionless body beneath him. After a while the stranger sat down on the edge of the hole so that he could see into it, and rested the revolver on his knee. Reaching his hand into a pocket, he drew out a wisp of brown paper. Into this he dropped a few crumbs of tobacco. The combination became a cigarette, brown and squat, with the ends turned in. Not once did he take his eyes from the body at the bottom of the hole. He lighted the cigarette and drew its smoke into his lungs with a caressing intake of the breath. He smoked slowly. Once the cigarette went out and he relighted it. And all the while he studied the body beneath him.

In the end he tossed the cigarette stub away and rose to his feet. He moved to the edge of the hole. Spanning it, a hand resting on each edge, and with the revolver still in the right hand, he muscled his body down into the hole. While his feet were yet a yard from the bottom he released his hands and dropped down.

At the instant his feet struck bottom he saw the pocket miner's arm leap out, and his own legs knew a swift, jerking grip that overthrew him. In the nature of the jump his revolver hand was above his head. Swiftly as the grip had flashed about his legs, just as swiftly he brought the revolver down. He was still in the air, his fall in process of completion, when he pulled the trigger. The explosion was deafening in the confined space. The smoke filled the hole so that he could see nothing. He struck the bottom on his back, and like a cat's the pocket miner's body was on top of him. Even as the miner's body passed on top, the stranger crooked in his right arm to fire; and even in that instant the miner, with a quick thrust of elbow, struck his wrist. The muzzle was thrown up and the bullet thudded into the dirt of the side of the hole.

The next instant the stranger felt the miner's hand grip his wrist. The struggle was now for the revolver. Each man strove to turn it against the other's body. The smoke in the hole was clearing. The stranger, lying on his back, was beginning to see dimly. But suddenly he was blinded by a handful of dirt deliberately flung into his eyes by his antagonist. In that moment of shock his grip on the revolver was broken. In the next moment he felt a smashing darkness descend upon his brain, and in the midst of the darkness even the darkness ceased.

But the pocket miner fired again and again, until the revolver was empty. Then he tossed it from him and, breathing heavily, sat down on the dead man's legs.

The miner was sobbing and struggling for breath. "Measly skunk!" he panted; "a-campin' on my trail an' lettin' me do the work, an' then shootin' me in the back!"

He was half crying from anger and exhaustion. He peered at the face of the dead man. It was sprinkled with loose dirt and gravel, and it was difficult to distinguish the features.

"Never laid eyes on him before," the miner concluded his scrutiny. "Just a common an' ordinary thief, damn him! An' he shot me in the back! He shot me in the back!"

He opened his shirt and felt himself, front and back, on his left side.

"Went clean through, and no harm done!" he cried jubilantly. "I'll bet he aimed all right all right; but he drew the gun over when he pulled the trigger—the cuss! But I fixed 'm! Oh, I fixed 'm!"

His fingers were investigating the bullet hole in his side, and a shade of regret passed over his face. "It's goin' to be stiffer'n hell," he said. "An' it's up to me to get mended an' get out o' here."

He crawled out of the hole and went down the hill to his camp. Half an hour later he returned, leading his pack horse. His open shirt disclosed the rude bandages with which he had dressed his wound. He was slow and awkward with his left-hand movements, but that did not prevent his using the arm.

The bight of the pack rope under the dead man's shoulders enabled him to heave the body out of the hole. Then he set to work gathering up his gold. He worked steadily for several hours, pausing often to rest his stiffening shoulder and to exclaim.

"He shot me in the back, the measly skunk! He shot me in the back!"

When his treasure was quite cleaned up and wrapped securely into a number of blanket-covered parcels, he made an estimate of its value.

"Four hundred pounds, or I'm a Hottentot," he concluded. "Say two hundred in quartz an' dirt—that leaves two hundred pounds of gold. Bill! Wake up! Two hundred pounds of gold! Forty thousand dollars! An' it's yourn—all yourn!"

He scratched his head delightedly and his fingers blundered into an unfamiliar groove. They quested along it for several inches. It was a crease through his scalp where the second bullet had ploughed.

He walked angrily over to the dead man.

"You would, would you?" he bullied. "You would, eh? Well, I fixed you good an' plenty, an' I'll give you decent burial, too. That's more'n you'd have done for me."

He dragged the body to the edge of the hole and toppled it in. It struck the bottom with a dull crash, on its side, the face twisted up to the light. The miner peered down at it.

"An' you shot me in the back!" he said accusingly.

With pick and shovel he filled the hole. Then he loaded the gold on his horse. It was too great a load for the animal, and when he had gained his camp he transferred part of it to his saddle horse. Even so, he was compelled to abandon a portion of his outfit— pick and shovel and gold-pan, extra food and cooking utensils, and divers odds and ends.

The sun was at the zenith when the man forced the horses at the screen of vines and creepers. To climb the huge boulders the animals were compelled to uprear and struggle blindly through the tangled mass of vegetation. Once the saddle horse fell heavily and the man removed the pack to get the animal on its feet. After it started on its way again the man thrust his head out from among the leaves and peered up at the hillside.

"The measly skunk!" he said, and disappeared.

There was a ripping and tearing of vines and boughs. The trees surged back and forth, marking the passage of the animals through the midst of them. There was a clashing of steel-shod hoofs on stone, and now and again an oath or a sharp cry of command. Then the voice of the man was raised in song:

> "Tu'n around an' tu'n yo' face
> Untoe them sweet hills of grace.
>   (D' pow'rs of sin yo' am scornin'!)
> Look about an' look aroun',
> Fling yo' sin pack on d' groun'
>   (Yo' will meet wid d' Lord in d' mornin'!)"

The song grew faint and fainter, and through the silence crept back the spirit of the place. The stream once more drowsed and whispered; the hum of the mountain bees rose sleepily. Down through the perfume-weighted air fluttered the snowy fluffs of the cottonwoods. The butterflies drifted in and out among the trees, and over all blazed the quiet sunshine. Only remained the hoof-marks in the meadow and the torn hillside to mark the boisterous trail of the life that had broken the peace of the place and passed on.

from The Iron Heel

Critic Joseph Blotner called The Iron Heel *(1908) "the first apocalyptic novel of the century." The story is ostensibly a copy of the manuscript of Avis Everhard, the widow of Ernest Everhard, who had been leader of the second unsuccessful revolt against the capitalist Oligarchy (the Iron Heel of the title), and it covers the period from 1912–1932. This book has supposedly been edited seven centuries later by a historian named Anthony Meredith. Ernest and other socialists had been elected to Congress, but the Oligarchy suppressed all opposition and eventually executed Everhard. Such a complicated set of premises, along with the book's political radicalism, likely contributed to this highly original novel's lack of commercial success: "It was a labor of love," London later wrote, "and a dead failure as a book." Yet it is still being read, perhaps appreciated more than ever before. In the segment that follows, Avis—freshly out of prison—manages to find a place to hide from the Oligarchy's agents.*

Of myself, during this period, there is not much to say. For six months I was kept in prison, though charged with no crime. I was a *suspect*—a word of fear that all revolutionists were soon to come to know. But our own nascent secret service was beginning to work. By the end of my second month in prison, one of the jailers made himself known as a revolutionist in touch with the organization. Several weeks later, Joseph Parkhurst, the prison doctor who had just been appointed, proved himself to be a member of one of the Fighting Groups.

Thus, throughout the organization of the Oligarchy, our own organization, weblike and spidery, was insinuating itself. And so I was kept in touch with all that was happening in the world without. And furthermore, every one of our imprisoned leaders was in contact with brave comrades who masqueraded in the livery of the Iron Heel. Though Ernest lay in prison three thousand miles away, on the Pacific Coast, I was in unbroken communication with him, and our letters passed regularly back and forth.

The leaders, in prison and out, were able to discuss and direct the campaign. It would have been possible, within a few months, to have effected the escape of some of them; but since imprisonment proved no bar to our activities, it was decided to avoid anything premature. Fifty-two congressmen were in prison, and fully three hundred more of our leaders. It was planned that they should be delivered simultaneously. If part of them escaped, the vigilance of the oligarchs might be aroused so as to prevent the escape of the remainder. On the other hand, it was held that a simultaneous jail-delivery all over the land would have immense psychological influence on the proletariat. It would show our strength and give confidence.

So it was arranged, when I was released at the end of six months, that I was to disappear and prepare a secure hiding-place for Ernest. To disappear was in itself no easy thing. No sooner did I get my freedom than my footsteps began to be dogged by the spies of the Iron Heel. It was necessary that they should be thrown off the track, and that I should win to California. It is laughable, the way this was accomplished.

Already the passport system, modeled on the Russian, was developing. I dared not cross the continent in my own character. It was necessary that I should be completely lost if ever I was to see Ernest again, for by trailing me after he escaped, he would be caught once more. Again, I could not disguise myself as a proletarian and travel. There remained the disguise of a member of the Oligarchy. While the arch-oligarchs were no more than a handful, there were myriads of lesser ones of the type, say, of Mr. Wickson—men, worth a few millions, who were adherents of the arch-oligarchs. The wives and daughters of these lesser oligarchs were legion, and it was decided that I should assume the disguise of such a one. A few years later this would have been impossible, because the passport system was to become so perfect that no man, woman, nor child in all the land was unregistered and unaccounted for in his or her movements.

When the time was ripe, the spies were thrown off my track. An hour later Avis Everhard was no more. At that time one Felice Van Verdighan, accompanied by two maids and a lap-dog, with another maid for the lap-dog, entered a drawing-room on a Pullman, and a few minutes later was speeding west.

The three maids who accompanied me were revolutionists. Two were members of the Fighting Groups, and the third, Grace Holbrook, entered a group the following year, and six months later was executed by the Iron Heel. She it was who waited upon the dog. Of the other two, Bertha Stole disappeared twelve years later, while Anna Roylston still lives and plays an increasingly important part in the Revolution.

Without adventure we crossed the United States to California. When the train stopped at Sixteenth Street Station, in Oakland, we alighted, and there Felice Van Verdighan, with her two maids, her lap-dog, and her lap-dog's maid, disappeared forever. The maids, guided by trusty comrades, were led away. Other comrades took charge of me. Within half an hour after leaving the train I was on board a small fishing boat and out on the waters of San Francisco Bay. The winds baffled, and we drifted aimlessly the greater part of the night. But I saw the lights of Alcatraz where Ernest lay, and found comfort in the thought of nearness to him. By dawn, what with the rowing of the fishermen, we made the Marin Islands. Here we lay in hiding all day, and on the following night, swept on by a flood-tide and a fresh wind, we crossed San Pablo Bay in two hours and ran up Petaluma Creek.

Here horses were ready and another comrade, and without delay we were away through the starlight. To the north I could see the loom of Sonoma Mountain, toward which we rode. We left the old town of Sonoma to the right and rode up a canyon that lay between outlying buttresses of the mountain. The wagon-road became a wood-road, the wood-road became a cow-path, and the cow-path dwindled away and ceased among the upland pastures. Straight over Sonoma Mountain we rode. It was the safest route. There was no one to mark our passing.

Dawn caught us on the northern brow, and in the gray light we dropped down through chaparral into redwood canyons deep and warm with the breath of passing summer. It was old country to me that I knew and loved, and soon I became the guide. The hiding-place was mine. I had selected it. We let down the bars and crossed an upland meadow. Next, we went over a low, oak-covered ridge and descended into a smaller meadow. Again we climbed a ridge, this time riding under red-limbed madroños and manzanitas of deeper red. The first rays of the sun streamed upon our backs as we climbed. A flight of quail thrummed off through the thickets. A big jackrabbit crossed our path, leaping swiftly and silently like a deer. And then a deer, a many-pronged buck, the sun flashing red-gold from neck and shoulders, cleared the crest of the ridge before us and was gone.

We followed in his wake a space, then dropped down a zigzag trail that he disdained into a group of noble redwoods that stood about a pool of water murky with minerals from the mountain side. I knew every inch of the way. Once a writer friend of mine had owned the ranch; but he, too, had become a revolutionist, though more disastrously than I, for he was already dead and gone, and none knew where nor how. He alone, in the days he had lived, knew the secret of the hiding-place for which I was bound. He had bought the ranch for beauty, and paid a round price for it, much to the disgust of the local farmers. He used to tell with great glee how they were wont to shake their heads mournfully at the price, to accomplish ponderously a bit of mental arithmetic, and then to say, "But you can't make six percent on it!"

But he was dead now, nor did the ranch descend to his children. Of all men, it was now the property of Mr. Wickson, who owned the whole eastern and northern slopes of Sonoma Mountain, running from the Spreckels estate to the divide of Bennett Valley. Out of it he had made a magnificent deer park, where, over thousands of acres of sweet slopes and glades and canyons, the deer ran almost in primitive wildness. The people who had owned the soil had been driven away. A state home for the feeble minded had also been demolished to make room for the deer.

To cap it all, Wickson's hunting lodge was a quarter of a mile from my hiding-place. This, instead of being a danger, was an added security. We were sheltered under the very aegis of one of the minor oligarchs. Suspicion, by the nature of the situation, was turned aside. The last place in the world the spies of the Iron Heel would dream of looking for me, and for Ernest when he joined me, was Wickson's deer park.

We tied our horses among the redwoods at the pool. From a cache behind a hollow rotting log my companion brought out a variety of things—a fifty-pound sack of flour, tinned foods of all sorts, cooking utensils, blankets, a canvas tarpaulin, books and writing material, a great bundle of letters, a five-gallon can of kerosene, an oil stove, and, last and most important, a large coil of stout rope. So large was the supply of things that a number of trips would be necessary to carry them to the refuge.

But the refuge was very near. Taking the rope and leading the way, I passed through a glade of tangled vines and bushes that ran between two wooded knolls. The glade ended abruptly at the steep bank of a stream. It was a little stream, rising from springs, and the hottest summer never dried it up. On every hand were tall wooded knolls, a group of them, with all the seeming of having been flung there from some careless Titan's hand. There was no bedrock in them. They rose from their bases hundreds of feet, and they were composed of red volcanic earth, the famous wine-soil of Sonoma. Through these the tiny stream had cut its deep and precipitous channel.

It was quite a scramble down to the stream bed, and, once on the bed, we went downstream perhaps for a hundred feet. And then we came to the great hole. There was no warning of the existence of the hole, nor was it a hole in the common sense of the word. One crawled through tight-locked briers and branches, and found oneself on the very edge, peering out and down through a green screen. A couple of hundred feet in length and width, it was half of that in depth. Possibly because of some fault that had occurred when the knolls were flung together, and certainly helped by freakish erosion, the hole had been scooped out in the course of centuries by the wash of water. Nowhere did the raw earth appear. All was garmented by vegetation, from tiny maiden-hair and gold-back ferns to mighty redwoods and Douglas spruces. These great trees even sprang out from the walls of the hole. Some leaned over at angles as great as forty-five degrees, though the majority towered straight up from the soft and almost perpendicular earth walls.

It was a perfect hiding-place. No one ever came there, not even the village boys of Glen Ellen. Had this hole existed in the bed of a canyon a mile long, or several miles long, it would have been well known. But this was no canyon. From beginning to end the length of the stream was no more than five hundred yards. Three hundred yards above the hole the stream took its rise in a spring at the foot of a flat meadow. A hundred yards below the hole the stream ran out into open country, joining the main stream and flowing across rolling and grass-covered land.

My companion took a turn of the rope around a tree, and with me fast on the other end lowered away. In no time I was on the bottom. And in but a short while he had carried all the articles from the cache and lowered them down to me. He hauled the rope up and hid it, and before he went away called down to me a cheerful parting.

from Burning Daylight

This novel is one of London's many semi-autobiographical works. It portrays Elam Harnish—nicknamed Burning Daylight—in his quest for riches, first in the Yukon, then in the world of high finance. Success nearly ruins him, however, and he becomes a drunken, manipulative loner. Then he falls in love with his secretary, Dede Mason—another character patterned on Charmian. The strong young woman resists, saying "your money is destroying you." In the following scene, Harnish begins to rebuild his spirit on a ride up Sonoma Mountain: "It was as though he were going through a sort of cleansing bath. No room here for all the sordidness, meanness, and viciousness that filled the dirty pool of city existence." A changed man, he eventually wins Dede, and they move to a ranch in the Valley of the Moon, "the best soil in which their love would prosper." This novel was published in 1910.

Daylight's coming to civilization had not improved him. True, he wore better clothes, had learned slightly better manners, and spoke better English. As a gambler and a man-trampler he had developed remarkable efficiency. Also, he had become used to a higher standard of living, and he had whetted his wits to razor sharpness in the fierce, complicated struggle of fighting males. But he had hardened, and at the expense of his old-time, whole-souled geniality. Of the essential refinements of civilization he knew nothing. He did not know they existed. He had become cynical, bitter, and brutal. Power had its effect on him that it had on all men. Suspicious of the big exploiters, despising the fools of the exploited herd, he had faith only in himself. This led to an undue and erroneous exaltation of his ego, while kindly consideration of others—nay, even simple respect—was destroyed, until naught was left for him but to worship at the shrine of self.

186

Physically, he was not the man of iron muscles who had come down out of the Arctic. He did not exercise sufficiently, ate more than was good for him, and drank altogether too much. His muscles were getting flabby, and his tailor called attention to his increasing waistband. In fact, Daylight was developing a definite paunch. This physical deterioration was manifest likewise in his face. The lean Indian visage was suffering a city change. The slight hollows in the cheeks under the high cheekbones had filled out. The beginning of puff-sacks under the eyes was faintly visible. The girth of the neck had increased; and the first crease and fold of a double chin were becoming plainly discernible. The old effect of asceticism, bred of terrific hardships and toil, had vanished; the features had become broader and heavier, betraying all the stigmata of the life he lived, advertising the man's self-indulgence, harshness, and brutality.

Even his human affiliations were descending. Playing a lone hand, contemptuous of most of the men with whom he played, lacking in sympathy or understanding of them, and certainly independent of them, he found little in common with those to be encountered, say at the Alta-Pacific. In point of fact, when the battle with the steamship companies was at its height and his raid was inflicting incalculable damage on all business interests, he had been asked to resign from the Alta-Pacific. The idea had been rather to his liking, and he had found new quarters in clubs like the Riverside, organized and practically maintained by the city bosses. He found that he really liked such men better. They were more primitive and simple, and they did not put on airs. They were honest buccaneers, frankly in the game for what they could get out of it, on the surface more raw and savage, but at least not glossed over with oily or graceful hypocrisy. The Alta-Pacific had suggested that his resignation be kept a private matter, and then had privily informed the newspapers. The latter had made great capital out of the forced resignation, but Daylight had grinned and silently gone his way, though registering a black mark against more than one club member who was destined to feel, in the days to come, the crushing weight of the Klondiker's financial paw.

The storm-center of a combined newspaper attack lasting for months, Daylight's character had been torn to shreds. There was no fact in his history that had not been distorted into a criminality or a vice. This public making of him over into an iniquitous monster had pretty well crushed any lingering hope he had of getting acquainted with Dede Mason. He felt that there was no chance for her ever to look kindly on a man of his caliber, and, beyond increasing her salary to seventy-five dollars a month, he proceeded gradually to forget about her. The increase was made known to her through Morrison, and later she thanked Daylight, and that was the end of it.

One weekend, feeling heavy and depressed and tired of the city and its ways, he obeyed the impulse of a whim that was later to play an important part in his life. The desire to get out of the city for a whiff of country air and for a change of scene was the cause. Yet, to himself, he made the excuse of going to Glen Ellen for the purpose of inspecting the brickyard with which Holdsworthy had goldbricked him.

He spent the night in the little country hotel, and on Sunday morning, astride a saddle horse rented from the Glen Ellen butcher, rode out of the village. The brickyard was close at hand on the flat beside the Sonoma Creek. The kilns were visible among the trees, when he glanced to the left and caught sight of a cluster of wooded knolls half a mile away, perched on the rolling slopes of Sonoma Mountain. The mountain, itself wooded, towered behind. The trees on the knolls seemed to beckon to him. The dry, early-summer air, shot through with sunshine, was wine to him. Unconsciously he drank it in in deep breaths. The prospect of the brickyard was uninviting. He was jaded with all things business, and the wooded knolls were calling to him. A horse was between his legs—a good horse, he decided; one that sent him back to the cayuses he had ridden during his eastern Oregon boyhood. He had been somewhat of a rider in those

early days, and the champ of bit and crack of saddle-leather
sounded good to him now.

Resolving to have his fun first, and to look over the brickyard
afterward, he rode on up the hill, prospecting for a way across
country to get to the knolls. He left the country road at the first gate
he came to and cantered through a hayfield. The grain was waist-
high on either side the wagon road, and he sniffed the warm aroma
of it with delighted nostrils. Larks flew up before him, and from
everywhere came mellow notes. From the appearance of the road
it was patent that it had been used for hauling clay to the now idle
brickyard. Salving his conscience with the idea that this was part of
the inspection, he rode on to the clay-pit—a huge scar in a hillside.
But he did not linger long, swinging off again to the left and leaving the road. Not a farmhouse was in sight, and the change from
the city crowding was essentially satisfying. He rode now through
open woods, across little flower-scattered glades, till he came upon
a spring. Flat on the ground, he drank deeply of the clear water,
and looking about him, felt with a shock the beauty of the world.
It came to him like a discovery; he had never realized it before, he
concluded, and also, he had forgotten much. One could not sit in
at high finance and keep track of such things. As he drank in the
air, the scene, and the distant song of larks, he felt like a poker-
player rising from a nightlong table and coming forth from the
pent atmosphere to taste the freshness of the morn.

At the base of the knolls he encountered a tumble-down
stake-and-rider fence. From the look of it he judged it must be forty
years old at least—the work of some first pioneer who had taken
up the land when the days of gold had ended. The woods were very
thick here, yet fairly clear of underbrush, so that, while the blue sky
was screened by the arched branches, he was able to ride beneath.
He now found himself in a hook of several acres, where the oak
and manzanita and madroño gave way to clusters of stately redwoods. Against the foot of a steep-sloped knoll he came upon a
magnificent group of redwoods that seemed to have gathered
about the tiny gurgling spring.

He halted his horse, for beside the spring uprose a wild California lily. It was a wonderful flower, growing there in the cathedral nave of lofty trees. At least eight feet in height, its stem rose straight and slender, green and bare, for two-thirds its length, and then burst into a shower of snow-white waxen bells. There were hundreds of these blossoms, all from the one stem, delicately poised and ethereally frail. Daylight had never seen anything like it. Slowly his gaze wandered from it to all that was about him. He took off his hat, with almost a vague religious feeling. This was different. No room for contempt and evil here. This was clean and fresh and beautiful—something he could respect. It was like a church. The atmosphere was one of holy calm. Here man felt the prompting of nobler things. Much of this and more was in Daylight's heart as he looked about him. But it was not a concept of his mind. He merely felt it without thinking about it at all.

On the steep incline above the spring grew tiny maiden-hair ferns, while higher up were larger ferns and brakes. Great, moss-covered trunks of fallen trees lay here and there, slowly sinking back and merging into the level of the forest mould. Beyond, in a slightly clearer space, wild grape and honeysuckle swung in green riot from gnarled old oak trees. A gray Douglas squirrel crept out on a branch and watched him. From somewhere came the distant knocking of a woodpecker. This sound did not disturb the hush and awe of the place. Quiet woods' noises belonged there and made the solitude complete. The tiny bubbling ripple of the spring and the gray flash of tree-squirrel were as yardsticks with which to measure the silence and motionless repose.

"Might be a million miles from anywhere," Daylight whispered to himself.

But ever his gaze returned to the wonderful lily beside the bubbling spring.

He tethered the horse and wandered on foot among the knolls. Their tops were crowned with century-old spruce trees, and their sides clothed with oaks and madroños and native holly. But to the perfect redwoods belonged the small but deep canyon that threaded its way among the knolls. Here he found no passage out for his horse, and he returned to the lily beside the spring. On foot, tripping, stumbling, leading the animal, he forced his way up the hillside. And ever the ferns carpeted the way of his feet, ever the forest climbed with him and arched overhead, and ever the clean joy and sweetness stole in upon his senses.

On the crest he came through an amazing thicket of velvet-trunked young madroños, and emerged on an open hillside that led down into a tiny valley. The sunshine was at first dazzling in its brightness, and he paused and rested, for he was panting from the exertion. Not of old had he known shortness of breath such as this, and muscles that so easily tired at a stiff climb. A tiny stream ran down the tiny valley through a tiny meadow that was carpeted knee-high with grass and blue and white nemophila. The hillside was covered with mariposa lilies and wild hyacinth, down through which his horse dropped slowly, with circumspect feet and reluctant gait.

Crossing the stream, Daylight followed a faint cattle-trail over a low, rocky hill and through a wine-wooded forest of manzanita, and emerged upon another tiny valley, down which filtered another spring-fed, meadow-bordered streamlet. A jackrabbit bounded from a bush under his horse's nose, leaped the stream, and vanished up the opposite hillside of scrub oak. Daylight watched it admiringly as he rode on to the head of the meadow. Here he startled up a many-pronged buck, that seemed to soar across the meadow, and to soar over the stake-and-rider fence, and, still soaring, disappeared in a friendly copse beyond.

Daylight's delight was unbounded. It seemed to him that he had never been so happy. His old woods' training was aroused, and he was keenly interested in everything—in the moss on the trees and branches; in the bunches of mistletoe hanging in the oaks; in the nest of a wood rat; in the watercress growing in the sheltered eddies of the little stream; in the butterflies drifting through the rifted sunshine and shadow; in the blue jays that flashed in splashes of gorgeous color across the forest aisles; in the tiny birds, like wrens, that hopped among the bushes and imitated certain minor quail calls; and in the crimson-crested woodpecker that ceased its knocking and cocked its head on one side to survey him. Crossing the stream, he struck faint vestiges of a wood-road, used, evidently, a generation back, when the meadow had been cleared of its oaks. He found a hawk's nest on the lightning-shattered tipmost top of a six-foot redwood. And to complete it all, his horse stumbled upon several large broods of half-grown quail, and the air was filled with the thrum of their flight. He halted and watched the young ones "petrifying" and disappearing on the ground before his eyes, and listening to the anxious calls of the old ones hidden in the thickets.

"It sure beats country places and bungalows at Menlo Park," he communed aloud, "and if ever I get the hankering for country life, it's me for this every time."

The old wood-road led him to a clearing, where a dozen acres of grapes grew on wine-red soil. A cow-path, more trees and thickets, and he dropped down a hillside to the southeast exposure. Here, poised above a big forested canyon, and looking out upon Sonoma Valley, was a small farmhouse. With its barn and outhouses it snuggled into a nook in the hillside, which protected it from west and north. It was the erosion from this hillside, he judged, that had formed the little level stretch of vegetable garden. The soil was fat and black, and there was water in plenty, for he saw several faucets running wide open.

Forgotten was the brickyard. Nobody was at home, but Daylight dismounted and ranged the vegetable garden, eating strawberries and green peas, inspecting the old adobe barn and the rusty plough and harrow, and rolling and smoking cigarettes while he watched the antics of several broods of young chickens and the mother hens. A foot-trail that led down the wall of the big canyon invited him, and he proceeded to follow it. A waterpipe, usually above ground, paralleled the trail, which he concluded led upstream to the bed of the creek. The wall of the canyon was several hundred feet from top to bottom, and so magnificent were the untouched trees that the place was plunged in perpetual shade. He measured with his eye spruces five and six feet in diameter and red-woods even larger. One such he passed, a twister that was at least ten or eleven feet through. The trail led straight to a small dam where was the intake for the pipe that watered the vegetable gar-den. Here, beside the stream, were alders and laurel trees, and he walked through fern-brakes higher than his head. Velvety moss was everywhere, out of which grew maiden-hair and gold-back ferns.

Save for the dam, it was a virgin wild. No axe had invaded, and the trees died only of old age and stress of winter storm. The huge trunks of those that had fallen lay moss-covered, slowly resolving back into the soil from which they sprang. Some had lain so long that they were quite gone, though their faint outlines, level with the mould, could still be seen. Others bridged the stream, and from beneath the bulk of one monster half a dozen younger trees, overthrown and crushed by the fall, growing out along the ground, still lived and prospered, their roots bathed by the stream, their upshooting branches catching the sunlight through the gap that had been made in the forest roof.

Back at the farmhouse, Daylight mounted and rode on away from the ranch and into the wilder canyons and steeper steeps beyond. Nothing could satisfy his holiday spirit now but the ascent of Sonoma Mountain. And here on the crest, three hours afterward, he emerged, tired and sweaty, garments torn and face and hands scratched, but with sparkling eyes and an unwonted zestfulness of expression. He felt the illicit pleasure of a schoolboy playing tru-ant. The big gambling table of San Francisco seemed very far away. But there was more than illicit pleasure in his mood. It was as though he were going through a sort of cleansing bath. No room here for all the sordidness, meanness, and viciousness that filled the dirty pool of city existence. Without pondering in detail upon the matter at all, his sensations were of purification and uplift. Had he been asked to state how he felt, he would merely have said that he was having a good time; for he was unaware in his self-con-sciousness of the potent charm of nature that was percolating

through his city-rotted body and brain—potent, in that he came of
an abysmal past of wilderness dwellers, while he was himself coat-
ed with the thinnest rind of crowded civilization.

There were no houses in the summit of Sonoma Mountain,
and, all alone under the azure California sky, he reined in on the
southern edge of the peak. He saw open pasture country, intersect-
ed with wooden canyons, descending to the south and west from
his feet, crease on crease and roll on roll, from lower level to lower
level, to the floor of Petaluma Valley, flat as a billiard table, a card-
board affair, all patches and squares of geometrical regularity
where the fat freeholds were farmed. Beyond, to the west, rose
range on range of mountains cuddling purple mists of atmosphere
in their valleys; and still beyond, over the last range of all, he saw
the silver sheen of the Pacific. Swinging his horse, he surveyed the
west and north, from Santa Rosa to Mount St. Helena, and on to
the east, across Sonoma Valley, to the chaparral-covered range that
shut off the view of Napa Valley. Here, part way up the eastern wall
of Sonoma Valley, in range of a line intersecting the little village of
Glen Ellen, he made out a scar upon a hillside. His first thought
was that it was the dump of a mine tunnel, but remembering that
he was not in gold-bearing country, he dismissed the scar from his
mind and continued the circle of his survey to the southeast,
where, across the waters of San Pablo Bay, he could see, sharp and
distant, the twin peaks of Mount Diablo. To the south was Mount
Tamalpais, and, yes, he was right, fifty miles away, where the
draughty winds of the Pacific blew in the Golden Gate, the smoke
of San Francisco made a low-lying haze against the sky.

"I ain't seen so much country all at once in many a day," he
thought aloud.

He was loath to depart, and it was not for an hour that he was
able to tear himself away and take the descent of the mountain.
Working out a new route just for the fun of it, late afternoon was
upon him when he arrived back at the wooded knolls. Here, on the
top of one of them, his keen eyes caught a glimpse of a shade of
green sharply differentiated from any he had seen all day. Studying

it for a minute, he concluded that it was composed of three cypress trees, and he knew that nothing else than the hand of man could have planted them there. Impelled by curiosity purely boyish, he made up his mind to investigate. So densely wooded was the knoll, and so steep, that he had to dismount and go up on foot, at times even on hands and knees struggling hard to force a way through the thicker underbrush. He came out abruptly upon the cypresses. They were enclosed in a small square of ancient fence; the pickets he could plainly see had been hewn and sharpened by hand. Inside were the mounds of two children's graves. Two wooden headboards, likewise hand-hewn, told the story: *Little David, born 1855, died 1859;* and *Little Lily, born 1853, died 1860.*

"The poor little kids," Daylight muttered.

The graves showed signs of recent care. Withered bouquets of wildflowers were on the mounds, and the lettering on the headboards was freshly painted. Guided by these clues, Daylight cast about for a trail, and found one leading down the side opposite to his ascent. Circling the base of the knoll, he picked up with his horse and rode on to the farmhouse. Smoke was rising from the chimney, and he was quickly in conversation with a nervous, slender young man, who, he learned, was only a tenant on the ranch. How large was it? A matter of one hundred and eighty acres, though it seemed much larger. This was because it was so irregularly shaped. Yes, it included the clay-pit and all the knolls, and its boundary that ran along the big canyon was over a mile long.

"You see," the young man said, "it was so rough and broken that when they began to farm this country the farmers bought in the good land to the edge of it. That's why its boundaries are all gouged and jagged."

Oh, yes, he and his wife managed to scratch a living without working too hard. They didn't have to pay much rent. Hillard, the owner, depended on the income from the clay-pit. Hillard was well off, and had big ranches and vineyards down on the flat of the valley. The brickyard paid ten cents a cubic yard for the clay. As for the rest of the ranch, the land was good in patches, where it was

cleared, like the vegetable garden and the vineyard, but the rest of
it was too much up-and-down.

"You're not a farmer," Daylight said.

The young man laughed and shook his head.

"No; I'm a telegraph operator. But the wife and I decided to
take a two years' vacation, and...here we are. But the time's about
up. I'm going back into the office this fall after I get the grapes off."

Yes, there were about eleven acres in the vineyard—wine
grapes. The price was usually good. He grew most of what they ate.
If he owned the place, he'd clear a patch of land on the sidehill
above the vineyard and plant a small home orchard. The soil was
good. There was plenty of pasturage all over the ranch, and there
were several cleared patches, amounting to about fifteen acres in
all, where he grew as fine mountain hay as could be found. It sold
for three to five dollars more a ton than the rank-stalked valley hay.

As Daylight listened, there came to him a sudden envy of this
young fellow living right in the midst of all this which Daylight
had travelled through the last few hours.

"What in thunder are you going back to the telegraph office
for?" he demanded.

The young man smiled with a certain wistfulness.

"Because we can't get ahead here..." (he hesitated an instant),
"and because there are added expenses coming. The rent, small as
it is, counts; and besides, I'm not strong enough to effectually farm
the place. If I owned it, or if I were a real husky like you, I'd ask
nothing better. Nor would the wife." Again the wistful smile hovered on his face. "You see, we're country born, and after bucking
with cities for a few years, we kind of feel we like the country best.
We've planned to get ahead, though, and then some day we'll buy
a patch of land and stay with it."

The graves of the children? Yes, he had relettered them and
hoed the weeds out. It had become the custom. Whoever lived on
the ranch did that. For years, the story ran, the father and mother
had returned each summer to the graves. But there had come a
time when they came no more, and then old Hillard started the

custom. The scar across the valley? An old mine. It had never paid. The men had worked on it, off and on, for years, for the indication had been good. But that was years and years ago. No paying mine had ever been struck in the valley, though there had been no end of prospect-holes put down, and there had been a sort of rush there thirty years back.

A frail looking young woman came to the door to call the young man to supper. Daylight's first thought was that city living had not agreed with her. And then he noted the slight tan and healthy glow that seemed added to her face, and he decided that the country was the place for her. Declining an invitation to supper, he rode on for Glen Ellen, sitting slack-kneed in the saddle and softly humming forgotten songs. He dropped down the rough, winding road, through oak-covered pasture, with here and there thickets of manzanita and vistas of open glades. He listened greedily to the quail calling, and laughed outright, once, in sheer joy, at a tiny chipmunk that fled scolding up a bank, slipping on the crumbly surface and falling down, then dashing across the road under his horse's nose and, still scolding, scrambling up a protecting oak.

Daylight could not persuade himself to keep to the travelled roads that day, and another cut across country to Glen Ellen brought him upon a canyon that so blocked his way that he was glad to follow a friendly cow-path. This led him to a small frame cabin. The doors and windows were open, and a cat was nursing a litter of kittens in the doorway, but no one seemed at home. He descended the trail that evidently crossed the canyon. Part way down, he met an old man coming up through the sunset. In his hand he carried a pail of foamy milk. He wore no hat, and in his face, framed with snow-white hair and beard, was the ruddy glow and content of the passing summer day. Daylight thought that he had never seen so contented-looking a being.

"How old are you, daddy?" he queried.

"Eighty-four," was the reply. "Yes, sirree, eighty-four, and spryer than most."

"You must a' taken good care of yourself," Daylight suggested.

"I don't know about that. I ain't loafed none. I walked across the Plains with an ox-team and fit Injuns in '51, and I was a family man then with seven youngsters. I reckon I was as old then as you are now, or pretty nigh on to it."

"Don't you find it lonely here?"

The old man shifted the pail of milk and reflected.

"That all depends," he said oracularly. "I ain't never been lonely except when the old wife died. Some fellers are lonely in a crowd, and I'm one of them. That's the only time I'm lonely, is when I go to 'Frisco. But I don't go no more, thank you 'most to death. This is good enough for me. I've ben right here in this valley since '54—one of the first settlers after the Spaniards."

Daylight started his horse, saying: "Well, good night, daddy. Stick with it. You got all the young bloods skinned, and I guess you've sure buried a mighty sight of them."

The old man chuckled, and Daylight rode on, singularly at peace with himself and all the world. It seemed that the old contentment of trail and camp he had known on the Yukon had come back to him. He could not shake from his eyes the picture of the old pioneer coming up the trail through the sunset light. He was certainly going some for eighty-four. The thought of following his example entered Daylight's mind, but the big game of San Francisco vetoed the idea.

"Well, anyway," he decided, "when I get old and quit the game, I'll settle down in a place something like this, and the city can go to hell."

Instead of returning to the city on Monday, Daylight rented the butcher's horse for another day and crossed the bed of the valley to its eastern hills to look at the mine. It was dryer and rockier here than where he had been the day before, and the ascending slopes supported mainly chaparral—scrubby and dense and impossible to penetrate on horseback. But in the canyons water was plentiful and also a luxuriant forest growth. The mine was an abandoned affair, but he enjoyed the half-hour's scramble around.

He had had experience in quartz-mining before he went to Alaska, and he enjoyed the recrudescence of his old wisdom in such matters. The story was simple to him: good prospects that warranted the starting of the tunnel into the sidehill; the three months' work and the getting short of money; the lay-off while the men went away and got jobs; then the return and a new stretch of work, with the "pay" ever luring and ever receding into the mountain, until after years of hope, the men had given up and vanished. Most likely they were dead by now, Daylight thought, as he turned in the saddle and looked back across the canyon at the ancient dump and dark mouth of the tunnel.

As on the previous day, just for the joy of it, he followed cattle-trails at haphazard and worked his way up toward the summits. Coming out on a wagon-road that led upward, he followed it for several miles, emerging in a small, mountain-encircled valley, where half a dozen poor ranchers farmed the wine grapes on the steep slopes. Beyond, the road pitched upward. Dense chaparral covered the exposed hillsides, but in the creases of the canyons huge spruce trees grew, and wild oats and flowers.

Half an hour later, sheltering under the summits themselves, he came out on a clearing. Here and there, in irregular patches where the steep and the soil favored, wine grapes were growing. Daylight could see that it had been a stiff struggle, and that wild nature showed fresh signs of winning—chaparral that had invaded the clearings; patches and parts of patches of vineyard, unpruned, grassgrown, and abandoned; and everywhere old stake-and-rider fences vainly striving to remain intact. Here, at a small farmhouse surrounded by large outbuildings, the road ended. Beyond, the chaparral blocked the way.

He came upon an old woman forking manure in the barn-yard, and reined in by the fence.

"Hello, mother," was his greeting; "ain't you got ary men-folk around to do that for you?"

She leaned on her pitchfork, hitched her skirt in at the waist, and regarded him cheerfully. He saw that her toil-worn, weather-exposed hands were like a man's, calloused, large-knuckled, and gnarled, and that her stockingless feet were thrust into heavy man's brogans.

"Nary a man," she answered. "And where be you from, and all the way up here? Won't you stop and hitch and have a glass of wine?"

Striding clumsily but efficiently, like a laboring-man, she led him into the largest building, where Daylight saw a handpress and all the paraphernalia on a small scale for the making of wine. It was too far and too bad a road to haul the grapes to the valley wineries, she explained, and so they were compelled to do it themselves. "They," he learned, were she and her daughter, the latter a widow of forty-odd. It had been easier before the grandson died and before he went away to fight savages in the Philippines. He had died out there in battle.

Daylight drank a full tumbler of excellent Riesling, talked a few minutes, and accounted for a second tumbler. Yes, they just managed not to starve. Her husband and she had taken up this government land in '57 and cleared it and farmed it ever since, until he died, when she had carried it on. It actually didn't pay for the toil, but what were they to do? There was the wine trust, and wine was down. That Riesling? She delivered it to the railroad down in the valley for twenty-two cents a gallon. And it was a long haul. It took a day for the roundtrip. Her daughter was gone now with a load.

Daylight knew that in the hotels, Riesling, not quite so good even, was charged from a dollar and a half to two dollars a quart. And she got twenty-two cents a gallon. That was the game. She was one of the stupid lowly, she and her people before her—the ones that did the work, drove their oxen across the Plains, cleared and broke the virgin land, toiled all days and all hours, paid their taxes, and sent their sons and grandsons out to fight and die for the flag that gave them such ample protection that they were able to sell their wine for twenty-two cents. The same wine was served to him at the St. Francis for two dollars a quart, or eight dollars a short gallon. That was it.

Between her and her handpress on the mountain clearing and him ordering his wine in the hotel was a difference of seven dollars and seventy-eight cents. A clique of sleek men in the city got between her and him to just about that amount. And, besides them, there was a horde of others that took their whack. They called it railroading, high finance, banking, wholesaling, real estate, and such things, but the point was that they got it, while she got what was left—twenty-two cents. Oh, well, a sucker was born every minute, he sighed to himself, and nobody was to blame; it was all a game, and only a few could win, but it was damned hard on the suckers.

"How old are you, mother?" he asked.

"Seventy-nine come next January."

"Worked pretty hard, I suppose?"

"Sence I was seven. I was bound out in Michigan state until I was woman-grown. Then I married, and I reckon the work got harder and harder."

"When are you going to take a rest?"

She looked at him, as though she chose to think his question facetious, and did not reply.

"Do you believe in God?"

She nodded her head.

"Then you get it all back," he assured her; but in his heart he was wondering about God, that allowed so many suckers to be born and that did not break up the gambling game by which they were robbed from the cradle to the grave.

"How much of that Riesling you got?"

She ran her eyes over the casks and calculated. "Just short of eight hundred gallons."

He wondered what he could do with all of it, and speculated as to whom he could give it away.

"What would you do if you got a dollar a gallon for it?" he asked.

"Drop dead, I suppose."

"No; speaking seriously."

"Get me some false teeth, shingle the house, and buy a new wagon. The road's mighty hard on wagons."

"And after that?"

"Buy me a coffin."

"Well, they're yours, mother, coffin and all."

She looked her incredulity.

"No; I mean it. And there's fifty to bind the bargain. Never mind the receipt. It's the rich ones that need watching, their memories being so infernal short, you know. Here's my address. You've got to deliver it to the railroad. And now, show me the way out of here. I want to get up to the top."

On through the chaparral he went, following faint cattle-trails and working slowly upward till he came out on the divide and gazed down into Napa Valley and back across to Sonoma Mountain.

"A sweet land," he muttered, "an almighty sweet land."

Circling around to the right and dropping down along the cattle-trails, he quested for another way back to Sonoma Valley; but the cattle-trails seemed to fade out, and the chaparral to grow thicker with a deliberate viciousness, and even when he won through in places, the canyon and small feeders were too precipitous for his horse, and turned him back. But there was no irritation about it. He enjoyed it all, for he was back at his old game of bucking nature. Late in the afternoon he broke through, and followed a well-defined trail down a dry canyon. Here he got a fresh thrill. He had heard the baying of the hound some minutes before, and suddenly, across the bare face of the hill above him, he saw a large buck in flight. And not far behind came the deer-hound, a magnificent animal. Daylight sat tense in his saddle and watched until they disappeared, his breath just a trifle shorter, as if he, too, were in the chase, his nostrils distended, and in his bones the old hunting ache and memories of the days before he came to live in cities.

The dry canyon gave place to one with a slender ribbon of running water. The trail ran into a wood-road, and the wood-road emerged across a small flat upon a slightly travelled county road. There were no farms in this immediate section, and no houses. The soil was meagre, the bedrock either close to the surface or constituting the surface itself. Manzanita and scrub oak, however, flourished and walled the road on either side with a jungle growth. And out a runway through this growth a man suddenly scuttled in a way that reminded Daylight of a rabbit.

He was a little man, in patched overalls; bareheaded, with a cotton shirt open at the throat and down the chest. The sun was ruddy-brown in his face, and by it his sandy hair was bleached on the ends to peroxide blonde. He signed to Daylight to halt, and held up a letter.

"If you're going to town, I'd be obliged if you mail this," he said.

"I sure will." Daylight put it into his coat pocket. "Do you live hereabouts, stranger?"

But the little man did not answer. He was gazing at Daylight in a surprised and steadfast fashion.

"I know you," the little man announced. "You're Elam Harnish—Burning Daylight, the papers call you. Am I right?"

Daylight nodded.

"But what under the sun are you doing here in the chaparral?"

Daylight grinned as he answered, "Drumming up trade for a free rural delivery route."

"Well, I'm glad I wrote that letter this afternoon," the little man went on, "or else I'd have missed seeing you. I've seen your photo in the papers many a time, and I've a good memory for faces. I recognized you at once. My name's Ferguson."

"Do you live hereabouts?" Daylight repeated his query.

"Oh, yes. I've got a little shack back here in the bush a hundred yards, and a pretty spring, and a few fruit trees and berry bushes. Come in and take a look. And that spring is a dandy. You never tasted water like it. Come in and try it."

Walking and leading his horse, Daylight followed the quick-stepping, eager little man through the green tunnel and emerged abruptly upon the clearing, if clearing it might be called, where wild nature and man's earth-scratching were inextricably blended. It was a tiny nook in the hills, protected by the steep walls of a canyon mouth. Here were several large oaks, evidencing a richer soil. The erosion of ages from the hillside had slowly formed this deposit of fat earth. Under the oaks, almost buried in them, stood a rough, unpainted cabin, the wide veranda of which, with chairs and hammocks, advertised an out-of-doors bedchamber. Daylight's keen eyes took in everything. The clearing was irregular, following the patches of the best soil, and every fruit tree and berry bush, and even each vegetable plant, had the water personally conducted to it. The tiny irrigation channels were everywhere, and along some of them the water was running.

Ferguson looked eagerly into his visitor's face for signs of approbation.

"What do you think of it, eh?"

"Hand-reared and manicured, every blessed tree," Daylight laughed, but the joy and satisfaction that shone in his eyes contented the little man.

"Why, d'ye know, I know every one of those trees as if they were sons of mine. I planted them, nursed them, fed them, and brought them up. Come on and peep at the spring."

"It's sure a hummer," was Daylight's verdict, after due inspection and sampling, as they turned back for the house.

The interior was a surprise. The cooking being done in the small, lean-to kitchen, the whole cabin formed a large living room. A great table in the middle was comfortably littered with books and magazines. All the available wall space, from floor to ceiling, was occupied by filled bookshelves. It seemed to Daylight that he had never seen so many books assembled in one place. Skins of wildcat, 'coon, and deer lay about on the pine-board floor.

"Shot them myself, and tanned them, too," Ferguson proudly asserted.

The crowning feature of the room was a huge fireplace of rough stones and boulders.

"Built it myself," Ferguson proclaimed, "and, by God, she drew! Never a wisp of smoke anywhere save in the appointed channel, and that during the big southeasters, too."

Daylight found himself charmed and made curious by the little man. Why was he hiding away here in the chaparral, he and his books? He was nobody's fool, anybody could see that. Then why? The whole affair had a tinge of adventure, and Daylight accepted an invitation to supper, half prepared to find his host a raw-fruit-and-nut-eater, or some similar sort of health faddist. At table, while eating rice and jackrabbit curry (the latter shot by Ferguson), they talked it over, and Daylight found the little man had no food "views." He ate whatever he liked, and all he wanted, avoiding only such combinations that experience had taught him disagreed with his digestion.

Next, Daylight surmised that he might be touched with religion; but, quest about as he would, in a conversation covering the most divergent topics, he could find no hint of queerness or unusualness. So it was, when between them they had washed and wiped the dishes and put them away, and had settled down to a comfortable smoke, that Daylight put his question.

"Look here, Ferguson. Ever since we got together, I've been casting about to find out what's wrong with you, to locate a screw loose somewhere, but I'll be danged if I've succeeded. What are you doing here, anyway? What made you come here? What were you doing for a living before you came here? Go ahead and elucidate yourself."

Ferguson frankly showed his pleasure at the questions.

"First of all," he began, "the doctors wound up by losing all hope for me. Gave me a few months at best, and that, after a course in sanatoriums and a trip to Europe and another to Hawaii. They tried electricity, and forced feeding, and fasting. I was a graduate of about everything in the curriculum. They kept me poor with their bills, while I went from bad to worse. The trouble with me was twofold: first, I was a born weakling; and next, I was living unnaturally—too much work, and responsibility, and strain. I was managing editor of the *Times-Tribune*—"

Daylight gasped mentally, for the *Times-Tribune* was the biggest and most influential paper in San Francisco, and always had been so.

"—and I wasn't strong enough for the strain. Of course my body went back on me, and my mind, too, for that matter. It had to be bolstered up with whiskey, which wasn't good for it any more than was the living in clubs and hotels good for my stomach and the rest of me. That was what ailed me; I was living all wrong."

He shrugged his shoulders and drew at his pipe.

"When the doctors gave me up, I wound up my affairs and gave the doctors up. That was fifteen years ago. I'd been hunting through here when I was a boy, on vacations from college, and when I was all down and out it seemed a yearning came to me to go back to the country. So I quit, quit everything, absolutely, and came to live in the Valley of the Moon—that's the Indian name, you know, for Sonoma Valley. I lived in the lean-to the first year; then I built the cabin and sent for my books. I never knew what happiness was before, nor health. Look at me now and dare to tell me that I look forty-seven. "

"I wouldn't give a day over forty," Daylight confessed.

"Yet the day I came here I looked nearer sixty, and that was fifteen years ago."

They talked along, and Daylight looked at the world from new angles. Here was a man, neither bitter nor cynical, who laughed at the city-dwellers and called them lunatics; a man who did not care for money, and in whom the lust for power had long since died. As for the friendship of the city-dwellers, his host spoke in no uncertain terms.

"What did they do, all the chaps I knew, the chaps in the clubs, with whom I'd been cheek by jowl for heaven knows how long? I was not beholden to them for anything, and when I slipped out there was not one of them to drop me a line and say, 'How are you, old man? Anything I can do for you?' For several weeks it was: 'What's become of Ferguson?' After that I became a reminiscence and a memory. Yet every last one of them knew I had nothing but my salary and that I'd always lived a lap ahead of it."

"But what do you do now?" was Daylight's query. "You must need cash to buy clothes and magazines?"

"A week's work or a month's work, now and again, ploughing in the winter, or picking grapes in the fall, and there's always odd jobs with the farmers through the summer. I don't need much, so I don't have to work much. Most of my time I spend fooling around the place. I could do hackwork for the magazines and newspapers; but I prefer the ploughing and the grape picking. Just look at me and you can see why. I'm hard as rocks. And I like the work. But I tell you a chap's got to break in to it. It's a great thing when he's learned to pick grapes a whole long day and come home at the end of it with that tired happy feeling, instead of being in a state of physical collapse. That fireplace—those big stones—I was soft, then, a little, anemic, alcoholic degenerate, with the spunk of a rabbit and about one percent as much stamina, and some of those big stones nearly broke my back and my heart. But I persevered, and used my body in the way Nature intended it should be used—not bending over a desk and swilling whiskey . . . and, well, here I am, a better man for it, and there's the fireplace, fine and dandy, eh?

"And now tell me about the Klondike, and how you turned San Francisco upside down with that last raid of yours. You're a bonny fighter, you know, and you touch my imagination, though my cooler reason tells me that you are a lunatic like the rest. The lust for power! It's a dreadful affliction. Why didn't you stay in your Klondike? Or why don't you clear out and live a natural life, for instance, like mine? You see, I can ask questions, too. Now you talk and let me listen for a while."

It was not until ten o'clock that Daylight parted from Ferguson. As he rode along through the starlight, the idea came to him of buying the ranch on the other side of the valley. There was no thought in his mind of ever intending to live on it. His game was in San Francisco. But he liked the ranch, and as soon as he got back to the office he would open up negotiations with Hillard. Besides, the ranch included the clay-pit, and it would give him the whip-hand over Holdsworthy if he ever tried to cut up any didoes.

CHARACTER
AND CHARACTERS

from White Fang

According to the author, this novel was written as "a complete antithesis [and] companion book" to The Call of the Wild *(1903). In that work, a Santa Clara Valley ranch dog kidnapped to the Klondike must return to its wolf roots to survive. In* White Fang *(1906), the wolf of that name—after enduring many trials—is domesticated through kindness, ending up on a California ranch. White Fang was "not alone...in the geographical Southland," explains London, "for he was in the Southland of life." In the novel's anti-climax, however, White Fang must defend his owner, Judge Scott, against Jim Hall, one of Jack's most indelible minor characters—a man turned into a beast by social conditions. The larger point of the novel, illustrated by both wolf and man, was summarized by London when he wrote, "I have always been impressed with the awful plasticity of life, and I feel that I can never lay enough stress upon the marvelous power and influence of environment."*

It was about this time that the newspapers were full of the daring escape of a convict from San Quentin prison. He was a ferocious man. He had been ill-made in the making. He had not been born right, and he had not been helped any by the moulding he had received at the hands of society. The hands of society are harsh, and this man was a striking sample of its handiwork. He was a beast—a human beast, it is true, but nevertheless so terrible a beast that he can best be characterized as carnivorous.

In San Quentin prison he had proved incorrigible. Punishment failed to break his spirit. He could die dumb-mad and fighting to the last, but he could not live and be beaten. The more fiercely he fought, the more harshly society handled him, and the only effect of harshness was to make him fiercer. Straitjackets, starvation, and beatings and clubbings were the wrong treatment for Jim Hall; but it was the treatment he received. It was the treatment he had received from the time he was a little pulpy boy in a San Francisco slum—soft clay in the hands of society and ready to be formed into something.

It was during Jim Hall's third term in prison that he encountered a guard that was almost as great a beast as he. The guard treated him unfairly, lied about him to the warden, lost him his credits, persecuted him. The difference between them was that the guard carried a bunch of keys and a revolver. Jim Hall had only his naked hands and his teeth. But he sprang upon the guard one day and used his teeth on the other's throat, just like any jungle animal.

After this, Jim Hall went to live in the incorrigible cell. He lived there three years. The cell was of iron, the floor, the walls, the roof. He never left this cell. He never saw the sky nor the sunshine. Day was a twilight and night was a black silence. He was in an iron tomb, buried alive. He saw no human face, spoke to no human thing. When his food was shoved in to him, he growled like a wild animal. He hated all things. For days and nights he bellowed his rage at the universe. For weeks and months he never made a sound, in the black silence eating his very soul. He was a man and a monstrosity, as fearful a thing of fear as ever gibbered in the visions of a maddened brain.

And then, one night, he escaped. The warden said it was impossible, but nevertheless the cell was empty, and half in, half out of it, lay the body of a dead guard. Two other dead guards marked his trail through the prison to the outer walls, and he had killed with his hands to avoid noise.

He was armed with the weapons of the slain guards—a live arsenal that fled through the hills pursued by the organized might of society. A heavy price of gold was upon his head. Avaricious farmers hunted him with shotguns. His blood might pay off a mortgage or send a son to college. Public-spirited citizens took down their rifles and went out after him. A pack of bloodhounds followed the way of his bleeding feet. And the sleuth-hounds of the law, the paid fighting animals of society, with telephone, and tele-graph, and special train, clung to his trail night and day.

Sometimes they came upon him, and men faced him like heroes, or stampeded through barbwire fences to the delight of the commonwealth reading the account at the breakfast table. It was after such encounters that the dead and wounded were carted back to the towns, and their places filled by men eager for the man-hunt.

And then Jim Hall disappeared. The bloodhounds vainly quested on the lost trail. Inoffensive ranchers in remote valleys were held up by armed men and compelled to identify themselves; while the remains of Jim Hall were discovered on a dozen moun-tainsides by greedy claimants for blood-money.

In the meantime the newspapers were read at Sierra Vista, not so much with interest as with anxiety. The women were afraid. Judge Scott pooh-poohed and laughed, but not with reason, for it was in his last days on the bench that Jim Hall had stood before him and received sentence. And in open courtroom, before all men, Jim Hall had proclaimed that the day would come when he would wreak vengeance on the judge that sentenced him.

For once, Jim Hall was right. He was innocent of the crime for which he was sentenced. It was a case, in the parlance of thieves and police, of "railroading." Jim Hall was being "railroaded" to prison for a crime he had not committed. Because of the two prior convictions against him, Judge Scott imposed upon him a sentence of fifty years.

Judge Scott did not know all things, and he did not know that he was party to a police conspiracy, that the evidence was hatched and perjured, that Jim Hall was guiltless of the crime charged. And Jim Hall, on the other hand, did not know that Judge Scott was merely ignorant. Jim Hall believed that the judge knew all about it and was hand in glove with the police in the perpetration of the monstrous injustice. So it was, when the doom of fifty years of liv-ing death was uttered by Judge Scott, that Jim Hall, hating all things in the society that misused him, rose up and raged in the courtroom until dragged down by half a dozen of his blue-coated enemies. To him, Judge Scott was the keystone in the arch of injustice, and upon Judge Scott he emptied the vials of his wrath and hurled the threats of his revenge yet to come. Then Jim Hall went to his living death...and escaped.

Of all this White Fang knew nothing. But between him and Alice, the master's wife, there existed a secret. Each night, after Sierra Vista had gone to bed, she arose and let in White Fang to sleep in the big hall. Now White Fang was not a house-dog, nor was he permitted to sleep in the house; so each morning, early, she slipped down and let him out before the family was awake.

On one such night, while all the house slept, White Fang awoke and lay very quietly. And very quietly he smelled the air and read the message it bore of a strange god's presence. And to his ears came sounds of the strange god's movements. White Fang burst into no furious outcry. It was not his way. The strange god walked softly, but more softly walked White Fang, for he had no clothes to rub against the flesh of his body. He followed silently. In the Wild he had hunted live meat that was infinitely timid, and he knew the advantage of surprise.

The strange god paused at the foot of the great staircase and listened, and White Fang was as dead, so without movement was he as he watched and waited. Up that staircase the way led to the love-master and to the love-master's dearest possessions. White Fang bristled, but waited. The strange god's foot lifted. He was beginning the ascent.

Then it was that White Fang struck. He gave no warning, with no snarl anticipated his own action. Into the air he lifted his body in the spring that landed him on the strange god's back. White Fang clung with his fore-paws to the man's shoulders, at the same time burying his fangs into the back of the man's neck. He clung on for a moment, long enough to drag the god over backward. Together they crashed to the floor. White Fang leaped clear, and, as the man struggled to rise, was in again with the slashing fangs.

Sierra Vista awoke in alarm. The noise from downstairs was as that of a score of battling fiends. There were revolver shots. A man's voice screamed once in horror and anguish. There was a great snarling and growling, and over all arose a smashing and crashing of furniture and glass.

But almost as quickly as it had arisen, the commotion died away. The struggle had not lasted more than three minutes. The frightened household clustered at the top of the stairway. From below, as from out of an abyss of blackness, came up a gurgling sound, as of air bubbling through water. Sometimes this gurgle became sibilant, almost a whistle. But this, too, quickly died down and ceased. Then naught came up out of the blackness save a heavy panting of some creature struggling sorely for air.

Weedon Scott pressed a button, and the staircase and downstairs hall were flooded with light. Then he and Judge Scott, revolvers in hand, cautiously descended. There was no need for this caution. White Fang had done his work. In the midst of the wreckage of overthrown and smashed furniture, partly on his side, his face hidden by an arm, lay a man. Weedon Scott bent over, removed the arm, and turned the man's face upward. A gaping throat explained the manner of his death.

"Jim Hall," said Judge Scott, and father and son looked significantly at each other.

Then they turned to White Fang. He, too, was lying on his side. His eyes were closed, but the lids slightly lifted in an effort to look at them as they bent over him, and the tail was perceptibly agitated in a vain effort to wag. Weedon Scott patted him, and his throat rumbled an acknowledging growl. But it was a weak growl at best, and it quickly ceased. His eyelids drooped and went shut, and his whole body seemed to relax and flatten out upon the floor.

"He's all in, poor devil," muttered the master.

"We'll see about that," asserted the Judge, as he started for the telephone.

"Frankly, he has one chance in a thousand," announced the surgeon, after he had worked an hour and a half on White Fang.

Dawn was breaking through the windows and dimming the electric lights. With the exception of the children, the whole family was gathered about the surgeon to hear his verdict.

"One broken hind-leg," he went on. "Three broken ribs, one at least of which has pierced the lungs. He has lost nearly all the blood in his body. There is a large likelihood of internal injuries. He must have been jumped upon. To say nothing of three bullet holes clear through him. One chance in a thousand is really optimistic. He hasn't a chance in ten thousand."

"But he mustn't lose any chance that might be of help to him," Judge Scott exclaimed. "Never mind expense. Put him under the X-ray—anything. Weedon, telegraph at once to San Franciso for Doctor Nichols. No reflection on you, doctor, you understand; but he must have the advantage of every chance."

The surgeon smiled indulgently. "Of course I understand. He deserves all that can be done for him. He must be nursed as you would nurse a human being, a sick child. And don't forget what I told you about temperature. I'll be back at ten o'clock again."

White Fang received the nursing. Judge Scott's suggestion of a trained nurse was indignantly clamored down by the girls, who themselves undertook the task. And White Fang won out on the one chance in ten thousand denied him by the surgeon.

The latter was not to be censured for his misjudgment. All his life he had tended and operated on the soft humans of civilization, who lived sheltered lives and had descended out of many sheltered generations. Compared with White Fang, they were frail and flabby, and clutched life without any strength in their grip. White Fang had come straight from the Wild, where the weak perish early and shelter is vouchsafed to none. In neither his father nor his mother was there any weakness, nor in the generations before them. A constitution of iron and the vitality of the Wild were White Fang's inheritance, and he clung to life, the whole of him and every part of him, in spirit and in flesh, with the tenacity that of old belonged to all creatures.

Bound down a prisoner, denied even movement by the plaster casts and bandages, White Fang lingered out the weeks. He slept long hours and dreamed much, and through his mind passed an unending pageant of Northland visions. All the ghosts of the past arose and were with him. Once again he lived in the lair with Kiche, crept trembling to the knees of Gray Beaver to tender his allegiance, ran for his life before Lip-lip and all the howling bedlam of the puppy-pack.

He ran again through the silence, hunting his living food through the months of famine; and again he ran at the head of the team, the gut-whips of Mit-sah and Gray Beaver snapping behind, their voices crying "Raa! Raa!" when they came to a narrow passage and the team closed together like a fan to go through. He lived again all his days with Beauty Smith and the fights he had fought. At such times he whimpered and snarled in his sleep and they that looked on said that his dreams were bad.

But there was one particular nightmare from which he suffered—the clanking, clanging monsters of electric cars that were to him colossal screaming lynxes. He would lie in a screen of bushes, watching for a squirrel to venture far enough out on the ground from its tree-refuge. Then, when he sprang out upon it, it would transform itself into an electric car, menacing and terrible, towering over him like a mountain, screaming and clanging and spitting fire at him. It was the same when he challenged the hawk down out of the sky. Down out of the blue it would rush, as it dropped upon him changing itself into the ubiquitous electric car. Or again, he would be in the pen of Beauty Smith. Outside the pen, men would be gathering, and he knew that a fight was on. He watched the door for his antagonist to enter. The door would open, and thrust in upon him would come the awful electric car. A thousand times this occurred, and each time the terror it inspired was as vivid and great as ever.

Then came the day when the last bandage and the last plaster cast were taken off. It was a gala day. All Sierra Vista was gathered around. The master rubbed his ears, and he crooned his love-growl. The master's wife called him the "Blessed Wolf," which name was taken up with acclaim and all the women called him the Blessed Wolf.

He tried to rise to his feet, and after several attempts fell down from weakness. He had lain so long that his muscles had lost their cunning, and all the strength had gone out of them. He felt a little shame because of his weakness, as though, forsooth, he were failing the gods in the service he owed them. Because of this he made heroic efforts to arise, and at last he stood on his four legs, tottering and swaying back and forth.

"The Blessed Wolf!" chorused the women.

Judge Scott surveyed them triumphantly.

"Out of your own mouths be it," he said. "Just as I contended right along. No mere dog could have done what he did. He's a wolf."

"A Blessed Wolf," amended the Judge's wife.

"Yes, Blessed Wolf," agreed the Judge. "And henceforth that shall be my name for him."

"He'll have to learn to walk again," said the surgeon; "so he might as well start in right now. It won't hurt him. Take him outside."

And outside he went, like a king, with all Sierra Vista about him and tending on him. He was very weak, and when he reached the lawn he lay down and rested for a while.

Then the procession started on, little spurts of strength coming into White Fang's muscles as he used them and the blood began to surge through them. The stables were reached, and there in the doorway lay Collie, a half-dozen pudgy puppies playing about her in the sun.

White Fang looked on with a wondering eye. Collie snarled warningly at him, and he was careful to keep his distance. The master with his toe helped one sprawling puppy toward him. He bristled suspiciously, but the master warned him that all was well. Collie, clasped in the arms of one of the women, watched him jealously and with a snarl warned him that all was not well.

The puppy sprawled in front of him. He cocked his ears and watched it curiously. Then their noses touched, and he felt the warm little tongue of the puppy on his jowl. White Fang's tongue went out, he knew not why, and he licked the puppy's face.

Hand-clapping and pleased cries from the gods greeted the performance. He was surprised, and looked at them in a puzzled way. Then his weakness asserted itself, and he lay down, his ears cocked, his head on one side, as he watched the puppy. The other puppies came sprawling toward him, to Collie's great disgust; and he gravely permitted them to clamber and tumble over him. At first, amid the applause of the gods, he betrayed a trifle of his old self-consciousness and awkwardness. This passed away as the puppies' antics and mauling continued, and he lay with half-shut, patient eyes, drowsing in the sun.

from The Star Rover

Based in part on the actual experiences of Ed Morrell, who spent years locked up in San Quentin Prison, The Star Rover (1915), explores a remarkable character named Darrell Standing and his ability, though astral projection, to travel in time and space. As once happened to Morrell (who, incidentally, appears as a character in the novel), Standing is strapped into a straitjacket. He eventually learns to release his spirit and to experience some of his past lives—as, among other things, a boy killed in the infamous Mountain Meadows Massacre, a castaway living on a desert island, a fourth-century Christian ascetic dwelling in a cave, and a Roman soldier during the time of Jesus. While those stories are told, Darrell remains imprisoned, and the chapter that follows explains why. London once told Morrell, "It has been my ambition to put across a staggering punch against the whole damnable rotten American Jail System." He didn't achieve that in The Star Rover but, as biographer Clarice Stasz observes, he did present an argument "that the spirit is real and outlives matter."

I am Darrell Standing. They are going to take me out and hang me pretty soon. In the meantime I say my say, and write in these pages of the other times and places.

After my sentence, I came to spend the rest of my "natural life" in the prison of San Quentin. I proved incorrigible. An incorrigible is a terrible human being—at least such is the connotation of "incorrigible" in prison psychology. I became an incorrigible because I abhorred waste motion. The prison, like all prisons, was an affront and a scandal of waste motion. They put me in the jute mill. The criminality of wastefulness irritated me. Why should it not? Elimination of waste motion was my specialty. Before the invention of steam or steam-driven looms, three thousand years before, I had rotted in prison in old Babylon; and, trust me, I speak the truth when I say that in that ancient day we prisoners wove more efficiently on handlooms than did the prisoners in the steam-powered loom rooms of San Quentin.

The crime of waste was abhorrent. I rebelled. I tried to show the guards a score or so of more efficient ways. I was reported. I was given the dungeon and the starvation of light and food. I emerged and tried to work in the chaos of inefficiency of the loom rooms. I rebelled. I was given the dungeon plus the strait jacket. I was spread-eagled, and thumbed-up, and privily beaten by the stupid guards whose totality of intelligence was only just sufficient to show them that I was different from them and not so stupid.

Two years of this witless persecution I endured. It is terrible for a man to be tied down and gnawed by rats. The stupid brutes of guards were rats, and they gnawed the intelligence of me, gnawed all the fines nerves of the quick of me and of the consciousness of me. And I, who in my past have been a most valiant fighter, in this present life was no fighter at all. I was a farmer, an agriculturist, a desk-tied professor, a laboratory slave, interested only in the soil and the increase of the productiveness of the soil.

I fought in the Philippines because it was the tradition of the Standings to fight. I had no aptitude for fighting. It was all too ridiculous, the introducing of disruptive foreign substances into the bodies of little black menfolk. It was laughable to behold Science prostituting all the might of its achievement and the wit of its inventors to the violent introducing of foreign substances into the bodies of black folk.

As I say, in obedience to the tradition of the Standings I went to war and found that I had no aptitude for war. So did my officers find me out, because they made me a quartermaster's clerk, and as a clerk at a desk I fought through the Spanish-American War.

So it was not because I was a fighter but because I was a thinker that I was enraged by the motion wastage of the loom rooms and was persecuted by the guards into becoming an "incorrigible." One's brain worked and I was punished for its working. As

I told Warden Atherton, when my incorrigibility had become so notorious that he had me in on the carpet in his private office to plead with me; as I told him then:

"It is so absurd, my dear Warden, to think that your rat throttlers of guards can shake out of my brain the things that are clear and definite in my brain. The whole organization of this prison is stupid. You are a politician. You can weave the political pull of San Francisco saloon men and ward heelers into a position of graft such as this one you occupy; but you can't weave jute. Your loom rooms are fifty years behind the times..."

But why continue the tirade? For tirade it was. I showed him what a fool he was, and as a result he decided that I was a hopeless incorrigible.

Give a dog a bad name—you know the saw. Very well. Warden Atherton gave the final sanction to the badness of my name. I was fair game. More than one convict's dereliction was shunted off on me, and was paid for by me in the dungeon on bread and water, or in being triced up by the thumbs on my tiptoes for long hours, each hour of which was longer than the memory of any life I have ever lived.

Intelligent men are cruel. Stupid men are monstrously cruel. The guards and the men over me, from the warden down, were stupid monsters. Listen, and you shall learn what they did to me. There was a poet in the prison, a convict, a weak-chinned, broad-browed degenerate poet. He was a forger. He was a coward. He was a snitcher. He was a stool—strange words for a professor of agronomics to use in writing, but a professor of agronomics may well learn strange words when pent in prison for the term of his natural life.

This poet-forger's name was Cecil Winwood. He had had prior convictions, and yet, because he was a sniveling cur of a yellow dog, his last sentence had been only for seven years. Good credits would materially reduce this time. My time was life. Yet this miserable degenerate, in order to gain several short years of liberty for himself, succeeded in adding a fair portion of eternity to my own lifetime term.

I shall tell what happened the other way around, for it was only after a weary period that I learned. This Cecil Winwood, in order to curry favor with the Captain of the Yard, and thence the warden, the Prison Directors, the Board of Pardons, and the Governor of California, framed up a prison break. Now note three things: (a) Cecil Winwood was so detested by his fellow convicts that they would not have permitted him to bet an ounce of Bull Durham on a bedbug race—and bedbug racing was a great sport with the convicts; (b) I was the dog that had been given a bad name; (c) for his frame-up, Cecil Winwood needed the dogs with bad names, the lifetimers, the desperate ones, the incorrigibles.

But the lifers detested Cecil Winwood and, when he approached them with his plan of a wholesale prison break, they laughed at him and turned him away with curses for the stool that he was. But he fooled them in the end, forty of the bitterest-wise ones in the pen. He approached them again and again. He told of his power in the prison by virtue of his being trusty in the warden's office, and because of the fact that he had the run of the dispensary.

"Show me," said Long Bill Hodge, a mountaineer doing life for train robbery, and whose whole soul for years had been bent on escaping in order to kill the companion in robbery who had turned state's evidence on him.

Cecil Winwood accepted the test. He claimed that he could dope the guards the night of the break.

"Talk is cheap," said Long Bill Hodge. "What we want is the goods. Dope one of the guards tonight. There's Barnum. He's no good. He beat up that crazy Chink yesterday in Bughouse Alley …when he was off duty, too. He's on the night watch. Dope him tonight an' make him lose his job. Show me, and we'll talk business with you."

All this Long Bill told me in the dungeons afterward. Cecil Winwood demurred against the immediacy of the demonstration. He claimed that he must have time in which to steal the dope from the dispensary. They gave him the time, and a week later he announced that he was ready. Forty hard-bitten lifers waited for the guard Barnum to go to sleep on his shift. And Barnum did. He was found asleep, and he was discharged for sleeping on duty.

Of course, that convinced the lifers. But there was the Captain of the Yard to convince. To him, daily, Cecil Winwood was reporting the progress of the break—all fancied and fabricated in his own imagination. The Captain of the Yard demanded to be shown. Winwood showed him, and the full details of the showing I did not learn until a year afterward, so slowly do the secrets of prison intrigue leak out.

Winwood said that the forty men in the break, in whose confidence he was, had already such power in the prison that they were about to begin smuggling in automatic pistols by means of the guards they had bought up.

"Show me," the Captain of the Yard must have demanded.

And the forger-poet showed him. In the bakery, night work was a regular thing. One of the convicts, a baker, was on the first nightshift. He was a stool of the Captain of the Yard, and Winwood knew it.

"Tonight," he told the captain, "Summerface will bring in a dozen '44 automatics. On his next time off he'll bring in the ammunition. But tonight he'll turn the automatics over to me in the bakery. You've got a good stool there. He'll make you his report tomorrow."

Now Summerface was a strapping figure of a bucolic guard who hailed from Humboldt County. He was a simple-minded, good-natured dolt and not above earning an honest dollar by smuggling in tobacco for the convicts. On that night, returning from a trip to San Francisco, he brought in with him fifteen pounds of prime cigarette tobacco. He had done this before, and delivered the stuff to Cecil Winwood. So, on that particular night, he, all unwitting, turned the stuff over to Winwood in the bakery. It was a big, solid, paper-wrapped bundle of innocent tobacco. The stool baker, from concealment, saw the package delivered to Winwood and so reported to the Captain of the Yard next morning.

But in the meantime the poet-forger's too-lively imagination ran away with him. He was guilty of a slip that gave me five years of solitary confinement and that placed me in this condemned cell in which I now write. And all the time I knew nothing about it. I did not even know of the break he had inveigled the forty lifers into planning. I knew nothing, absolutely nothing. And the rest knew little. The lifers did not know he was giving them the cross. The Captain of the Yard did not know that the cross was being worked on him. Summerface was the most innocent of all. At the worst, his conscience could have accused him only of smuggling in some harmless tobacco.

And now to the stupid, silly, melodramatic slip of Cecil Winwood. Next morning, when he encountered the Captain of the Yard, he was triumphant. His imagination took the bit in its teeth.

"Well, the stuff came in all right as you said," the Captain of the Yard remarked.

"And enough of it to blow half the prison sky high," Winwood corroborated.

"Enough of what?" the captain demanded.

"Dynamite and detonators," the fool rattled on. "Thirty-five pounds of it. Your stool saw Summerface pass it over to me."

And right there the Captain of the Yard must have nearly died. I can actually sympathize with him—thirty-five pounds of dynamite loose in the prison.

They say that Captain Jamie—that was his nickname—sat down and held his head in his hands.

"Where is it now?" he cried. "I want it. Take me to it at once."

And right there Cecil Winwood saw his mistake.

"I planted it," he lied—for he was compelled to lie because, being merely tobacco in small packages, it was long since distributed among the convicts along the customary channels.

"Very well," said Captain Jamie, getting himself in hand. "Lead me to it at once."

But there was no plant of high explosives to lead him to. The thing did not exist, had never existed save in the imagination of the wretched Winwood.

In a large prison like San Quentin there are always hiding places for things. And as Cecil Winwood led Captain Jamie he must have done some rapid thinking.

As Captain Jamie testified before the Board of Directors, and as Winwood also testified, on the way to the hiding place Winwood said that he and I had planted the powder together.

And I, just released from five days in the dungeons and eighty hours in the jacket; I, whom even the stupid guards could see was too weak to work in the loom room; I, who had been given the day off to recuperate—from too terrible punishment—I was named as the one who had helped hide the nonexistent thirty-five pounds of high explosive!

Winwood led Captain Jamie to the alleged hiding place. Of course they found no dynamite in it.

"My God!" Winwood lied. "Standing has given me the cross. He's lifted the plant and stowed it somewhere else."

The Captain of the Yard said more emphatic things than "My God!" Also, on the spur of the moment but cold-bloodedly, he took Winwood into his own private office, locked the doors, and beat him up frightfully—all of which came out before the Board of Directors. But that was afterward. In the meantime, even while he took his beating, Winwood swore by the truth of what he had told.

What was Captain Jamie to do? He was convinced that thirty-five pounds of dynamite were loose in the prison and that forty desperate lifers were ready for a break. Oh, he had Summerface in on the carpet and, although Summerface insisted the package contained tobacco, Winwood swore it was dynamite and was believed.

At this stage I enter...or, rather, I depart; for they took me away out of the sunshine and the light of day to the dungeons, and in the dungeons and in the solitary cells, out of the sunshine and the light of day, I rotted for five years.

I was puzzled. I had only just been released from the dungeon, and was lying pain-wracked in my customary cell, when they took me back to the dungeon.

"Now," said Winwood to Captain Jamie, "though we don't know where it is, the dynamite is safe. Standing is the only man who does know, and he can't pass the word out from the dungeon. The men are ready to make the break. We can catch them red-handed. It is up to me to set the time. I'll tell them two o'clock tonight, and tell them that, with the guards doped, I'll unlock their cells and give them their automatics. If at two o'clock tonight you don't catch the forty I shall name with their clothes on and wide awake, then, Captain, you can give me solitary for the rest of my sentence. And with Standing and the forty tight in the dungeons, we'll have all the time in the world to locate the dynamite."

"If we have to tear the prison down stone by stone," Captain Jamie added valiantly.

That was six years ago. In all the intervening time they have never found that nonexistent explosive, and they have turned the prison upside down a thousand times in searching for it. Nevertheless, to his last day in office Warden Atherton believed in the existence of that dynamite. Captain Jamie, who is still Captain of the Yard, believes to this day that the dynamite is somewhere in the prison. Only yesterday, he came all the way up from San Quentin to Folsom to make one more effort to get me to reveal the hiding place. I know he will never breathe easy until they swing me off.

Amateur Night

*This story about writing reveals one rule that London himself fre-
quently observed, especially in his early stories: "Tell it all in the opening paragraph as advertisement of contents, and in the contents tell it
all over again." Notwithstanding that, in "Amateur Night"—originally published in* Moon Face and Other Stories *(1906)—the author
works more subtly, employing an omniscient narrator and emphasizing
character traits, while revealing his knowledge of another favorite topic,
show business. For writers, though, his major message—one that his
own career exemplified—is the necessity of perseverance.*

The elevator boy smiled knowingly to himself. When he took her
up, he had noted the sparkle in her eyes, the color in her cheeks.
His little cage had quite warmed with the glow of her repressed
eagerness. And now, on the down trip, it was glacierlike. The
sparkle and the color were gone. She was frowning, and what little
he could see of her eyes was cold and steel-gray. Oh, he knew the
symptoms, he did. He was an observer, and he knew it, too, and
some day, when he was big enough, he was going to be a reporter,
sure. And in the meantime he studied the procession of life as it
streamed up and down eighteen skyscraper floors in his elevator
car. He slid the door open for her sympathetically and watched her
trip determinedly out into the street.

There was a robustness in her carriage which came of the soil
rather than of the city pavement. But it was a robustness in a finer
than the wonted sense, a vigorous daintiness, it might be called,
which gave an impression of virility with none of the womanly left
out. It told of a heredity of seekers and fighters, of people that

228

worked stoutly with head and hand, of ghosts that reached down out of the misty past and moulded and made her to be a doer of things.

But she was a little angry, and a great deal hurt. "I can guess what you would tell me," the editor had kindly but firmly interrupted her lengthy preamble in the long-looked-forward-to interview just ended. "And you have told me enough," he had gone on (heartlessly, she was sure, as she went over the conversation in its freshness). "You have done no newspaper work. You are undrilled, undisciplined, unhammered into shape. You have received a high-school education, and possibly topped it off with normal school or college. You have stood well in English. Your friends have all told you how cleverly you write, and how beautifully, and so forth and so forth. You think you can do newspaper work, and you want me to put you on. Well, I am sorry, but there are no openings. If you knew how crowded—"

"But if there are no openings," she had interrupted, in turn, "how did those who are in, get in? How am I to show that I am eligible to get in?"

"They made themselves indispensable," was the terse response. "Make yourself indispensable."

"But how can I, if I do not get the chance?"

"Make your chance."

"But how?" she had insisted, at the same time privately deeming him a most unreasonable man.

"How? That is your business, not mine," he said conclusively, rising in token that the interview was at an end. "I must inform you, my dear young lady, that there have been at least eighteen other aspiring young ladies here this week, and that I have not the time to tell each and every one of them how. The function I perform on this paper is hardly that of instructor in a school of journalism."

She caught an outbound car, and ere she descended from it she had conned the conversation over and over again. "But how?" she repeated to herself, as she climbed the three flights of stairs to the rooms where she and her sister "bach'ed."

"But how?" And so she continued to put the interrogation, for the stubborn Scotch blood, though many times removed from Scottish soil, was still strong in her. And, further, there was need that she should learn how. Her sister Letty and she had come up from an interior town to the city to make their way in the world. John Wyman was land-poor. Disastrous business enterprises had burdened his acres and forced his two girls, Edna and Letty, into doing something for themselves. A year of school-teaching and of night-study of shorthand and typewriting had capitalized their city project and fitted them for the venture, which same venture was turning out anything but successful. The city seemed crowded with inexperienced stenographers and typewriters, and they had nothing but their own inexperience to offer. Edna's secret ambition had been journalism; but she had planned a clerical position first, so that she might have time and space in which to determine where and on what line of journalism she would embark. But the clerical position had not been forthcoming, either for Letty or her, and day by day their little hoard dwindled, though the room rent remained normal and the stove consumed coal with undiminished voracity. And it was a slim little hoard by now.

"There's Max Irwin," Letty said, talking it over. "He's a journalist with a national reputation. Go and see him, Ed. He knows how, and he should be able to tell you how."

"But I don't know him," Edna objected.

"No more than you knew the editor you saw today."

"Y-e-s," (long and judicially), "but that's different."

"Not a bit different from the strange men and women you'll interview when you've learned how," Letty encouraged.

"I hadn't looked at it in that light," Edna conceded. "After all, where's the difference between interviewing Mr. Max Irwin for some paper, or interviewing Mr. Max Irwin for myself? It will be practice, too. I'll go and look him up in the directory."

"Letty, I know I can write if I get the chance," she announced decisively a moment later. "I just *feel* that I have the feel of it, if you know what I mean."

And Letty knew and nodded. "I wonder what he is like?" she asked softly.

"I'll make it my business to find out," Edna assured her; "and I'll let you know inside forty-eight hours."

Letty clapped her hands. "Good! That's the newspaper spirit! Make it twenty-four hours, and you are perfect!"

"And I am sorry to trouble you," she concluded the statement of her case to Max Irwin, famous war correspondent and veteran journalist.

"Not at all," he answered, with a deprecatory wave of the hand. "If you don't do your own talking, who's to do it for you? Now I understand your predicament precisely. You want to get on the *Intelligencer*, you want to get on at once, and you have had no previous experience. In the first place, then, have you any pull? There are a dozen men in the city, a line from whom would be an open-sesame. After that you would stand or fall by your own ability. There's Senator Longbridge, for instance, and Claus Inskeep the streetcar magnate, and Lane, and McChesney—" He paused, with voice suspended.

"I am sure I know none of them," she answered despondently.

"It's not necessary. Do you know any one that knows them? or any one that knows any one else that knows them?"

Edna shook her head.

"Then we must think of something else," he went on, cheerfully. "You'll have to do something yourself. Let me see."

He stopped and thought for a moment, with closed eyes and wrinkled forehead. She was watching him, studying him intently, when his blue eyes opened with a snap and his face suddenly brightened.

"I have it! But no, wait a minute."

And for a minute it was his turn to study her. And study her he did, till she could feel her cheeks flushing under his gaze.

"You'll do, I think, though it remains to be seen," he said enigmatically. "It will show the stuff that's in you, besides, and it will be a better claim upon the *Intelligencer* people than all the lines from all the senators and magnates in the world. The thing for you is to do Amateur Night at the Loops."

"I—I hardly understand," Edna said, for his suggestion conveyed no meaning to her, "What are the 'Loops'? and what is 'Amateur Night'?"

"I forgot you said you were from the interior. But so much the better, if you've only got the journalistic grip. It will be a first impression, and first impressions are always unbiased, unprejudiced, fresh, vivid. The Loops are out on the rim of the city, near the Park—a place of diversion. There's a scenic railway, a water toboggan slide, a concert band, a theatre, wild animals, moving pictures, and so forth and so forth. The common people go there to look at the animals and enjoy themselves, and the other people go there to enjoy themselves by watching the common people enjoy themselves. A democratic, fresh-air-breathing, frolicking affair, that's what the Loops are.

"But the theatre is what concerns you. It's vaudeville. One turn follows another—jugglers, acrobats, rubber-jointed wonders, fire-dancers, coon-song artists, singers, players, female impersonators, sentimental soloists, and so forth and so forth. These people are professional vaudevillists. They make their living that way. Many are excellently paid. Some are free rovers, doing a turn wherever they can get an opening, at the Obermann, the Orpheus, the Alcatraz, the Louvre, and so forth and so forth. Others cover circuit pretty well all over the country. An interesting phase of life, and the pay is big enough to attract many aspirants.

"Now the management of the Loops, in its bid for popularity, instituted what is called 'Amateur Night'; that is to say, twice a week, after the professionals have done their turns, the stage is given over to the aspiring amateurs. The audience remains to criticize. The populace becomes the arbiter of art—or it thinks it does, which is the same thing; and it pays its money and is well pleased with itself, and Amateur Night is a paying proposition to the management.

"But the point of Amateur Night, and it is well to note it, is that these amateurs are not really amateurs. They are paid for doing their turn. At the best, they may be termed 'professional amateurs.' It stands to reason that the management could not get people to face a rampant audience for nothing, and on such occasions the audience certainly goes mad. It's great fun—for the audience. But the thing for you to do, and it requires nerve, I assure you, is to go out, make arrangements for two turns, (Wednesday and Saturday nights, I believe), do your two turns, and write it up for the *Sunday Intelligencer.*"

"But—but," she quavered, "I—I—" and there was a suggestion of disappointment and tears in her voice.

"I see," he said kindly. "You were expecting something else, something different, something better. We all do at first. But remember the admiral of the Queen's Navy, who swept the floor and polished up the handle of the big front door. You must face the drudgery of apprenticeship or quit right now. What do you say?"

The abruptness with which he demanded her decision startled her. As she faltered, she could see a shade of disappointment beginning to darken his face.

"In a way it must be considered a test," he added encouragingly. "A severe one, but so much the better. Now is the time. Are you game?"

"I'll try," she said faintly, at the same time making a note of the directness, abruptness, and haste of these city men with whom she was coming in contact.

"Good! Why, when I started in, I had the dreariest, deadliest details imaginable. And after that, for a weary time, I did the police and divorce courts. But it all came well in the end and did me good. You are luckier in making your start with Sunday work. It's not particularly great. What of it? Do it. Show the stuff you're made of, and you'll get a call for better work—better class and better pay.

Now you go out this afternoon to the Loops, and engage to do two turns."

"But what kind of turns can I do?" Edna asked dubiously.

"Do? That's easy. Can you sing? Never mind, don't need to sing. Screech, do anything—that's what you're paid for, to afford amusement, to give bad art for the populace to howl down. And when you do your turn, take someone along for chaperon. Be afraid of no one. Talk up. Move about among the amateurs waiting their turn, pump them, study them, photograph them in your brain. Get the atmosphere, the color, strong color, lots of it. Dig right in with both hands, and get the essence of it, the spirit, the significance. What does it mean? Find out what it means. That's what you're there for. That's what the readers of the *Sunday Intelligencer* want to know.

"Be terse in style, vigorous of phrase, apt, concretely apt, in similitude. Avoid platitudes and commonplaces. Exercise selection. Seize upon things salient, eliminate the rest, and you have pictures. Paint those pictures in words and the *Intelligencer* will have you. Get hold of a few back numbers, and study the *Sunday Intelligencer* feature story. Tell it all in the opening paragraph as advertisement of contents, and in the contents tell it all over again. Then put a snapper at the end, so if they're crowded for space they can cut off your contents anywhere, re-attach the snapper, and the story will still retain form. There, that's enough. Study the rest out for yourself."

They both rose to their feet, Edna quite carried away by his enthusiasm and his quick, jerky sentences, bristling with the things she wanted to know.

"And remember, Miss Wyman, if you're ambitious, that the aim and end of journalism is not the feature article. Avoid the rut. The feature is a trick. Master it, but don't let it master you. But master it you must; for if you can't learn to do a feature well, you can never expect to do anything better. In short, put your whole self into it, and yet, outside of it, above it, remain yourself, if you follow me. And now good luck to you."

They had reached the door and were shaking hands.

"And one thing more," he interrupted her thanks, "let me see your copy before you turn it in. I may be able to put you straight here and there."

Edna found the manager of the Loops a full-fleshed, heavy-jowled man, bushy of eyebrow and generally belligerent of aspect, with an absentminded scowl on his face and a black cigar stuck in the midst thereof. Symes was his name, she had learned, Ernst Symes.

"Whatcher turn?" he demanded, ere half her brief application had left her lips.

"Sentimental soloist, soprano," she answered promptly, remembering Irwin's advice to talk up.

"Whatcher name?" Mr. Symes asked, scarcely deigning to glance at her.

She hesitated. So rapidly had she been rushed into the adventure that she had not considered the question of a name at all.

"Any name? Stage name?" he bellowed impatiently.

"Nan Bellayne," she invented on the spur of the moment. "B-e-l-l-a-y-n-e. Yes, that's it."

He scribbled it into a notebook. "All right. Take your turn Wednesday and Saturday."

"How much do I get?" Edna demanded.

"Two-an'-a-half a turn. Two turns, five. Getcher pay first Monday after second turn."

And without the simple courtesy of "Good day," he turned his back on her and plunged into the newspaper he had been reading when she entered.

Edna came early on Wednesday evening, Letty with her, and in a telescope basket her costume—a simple affair. A plaid shawl borrowed from the washerwoman, a ragged scrubbing skirt borrowed from the charwoman, and a gray wig rented from a costumer for twenty-five cents a night, completed the outfit; for Edna had elected to be an old Irish-woman singing broken-heartedly after her wandering boy.

Though they had come early, she found everything in uproar. The main performance was under way, the orchestra was playing and the audience intermittently applauding. The infusion of the amateurs clogged the working of things behind the stage, crowded the passages, dressing rooms, and wings, and forced everybody into everybody else's way. This was particularly distasteful to the professionals, who carried themselves as befitted those of a higher caste, and whose behavior toward the pariah amateurs was marked by hauteur and even brutality. And Edna, bullied and elbowed and shoved about, clinging desperately to her basket and seeking a dressing room, took note of it all.

A dressing room she finally found, jammed with three other amateur "ladies," who were "making up" with much noise, high-pitched voices, and squabbling over a lone mirror. Her own make-up was so simple that it was quickly accomplished, and she left the trio of ladies holding an armed truce while they passed judgment upon her. Letty was close at her shoulder, and with patience and persistence they managed to get a nook in one of the wings which commanded a view of the stage.

A small, dark man, dapper and debonair, swallow-tailed and top-hatted, was waltzing about the stage with dainty, mincing steps, and in a thin little voice singing something or other about somebody or something evidently pathetic. As his waning voice neared the end of the lines, a large woman, crowned with an amazing wealth of blond hair, thrust rudely past Edna, trod heavily on her toes, and shoved her contemptuously to the side. "Bloomin' hamateur!" she hissed as she went past, and the next instant she was on the stage, graciously bowing to the audience, while the small, dark man twirled extravagantly about on his tiptoes.

"Hello, girls!"

This greeting, drawled with an inimitable vocal caress in every syllable, close in her ear, caused Edna to give a startled little jump. A smooth-faced, moon-faced young man was smiling at her good-naturedly. His "make-up" was plainly that of the stock tramp of the stage, though the inevitable whiskers were lacking.

"Oh, it don't take a minute to slap 'm on," he explained, divining the search in her eyes and waving in his hand the adornment in question. "They make a fellar sweat," he explained further. And then, "What's yer turn?"

"Soprano—sentimental," she answered, trying to be offhand and at ease.

"Whata you doin' it for?" he demanded directly.

"For fun; what else?" she countered.

"I just sized you up for that as soon as I put eyes on you. You ain't graftin' for a paper, are you?"

"I never met but one editor in my life," she replied evasively, "and I, he—well, we didn't get on very well together."

"Hittin' 'm for a job?"

Edna nodded carelessly, though inwardly anxious and cudgelling her brains for something to turn the conversation.

"What'd he say?"

"That eighteen other girls had already been there that week."

"Gave you the icy mit, eh?" The moon-faced young man laughed and slapped his thighs. "You see, we're kind of suspicious. The Sunday papers'd like to get Amateur Night done up brown in a nice little package, and the manager don't see it that way. Gets wild-eyed at the thought of it."

"And what's your turn?" she asked.

"Who? me? Oh, I'm doin' the tramp act tonight. I'm Charley Welsh, you know."

She felt that by the mention of his name he intended to convey to her complete enlightenment, but the best she could do was to say politely, "Oh, is that so?"

She wanted to laugh at the hurt disappointment which came into his face, but concealed her amusement.

"Come, now," he said brusquely, "you can't stand there and tell me you've never heard of Charley Welsh? Well, you must be young. Why, I'm an Only, the Only amateur at that. Sure, you must have seen me. I'm everywhere. I could be a professional, but I get more dough out of it by doin' the amateur."

"But what's an 'Only'?" she queried. "I want to learn."

"Sure," Charley Welsh said gallantly. "I'll put you wise. An 'Only' is a nonpareil, the feller that does one kind of a turn better'n any other feller. He's the Only, see?"

And Edna saw.

"To get a line on the biz," he continued, "throw yer lamps on me. I'm the Only all-round amateur. Tonight I make a bluff at the tramp act. It's harder to bluff it than to really do it, but then it's acting, it's amateur, it's art. See? I do everything, from Sheeny monologue to team song and dance and Dutch comedian. Sure, I'm Charley Welsh, the Only Charley Welsh."

And in this fashion, while the thin, dark man and the large, blond woman warbled dulcetly out on the stage and the other professionals followed in their turns, did Charley Welsh put Edna wise, giving her much miscellaneous and superfluous information and much that she stored away for the *Sunday Intelligencer*.

"Well, tra la loo," he said suddenly. "There's his highness chasin' you up. Yer first on the bill. Never mind the row when you go on. Just finish yer turn like a lady."

It was at that moment that Edna felt her journalistic ambition departing from her, and was aware of an overmastering desire to be somewhere else. But the stage manager, like an ogre, barred her retreat. She could hear the opening bars of her song going up from the orchestra and the noises of the house dying away to the silence of anticipation.

"Go ahead," Letty whispered, pressing her hand; and from the other side came the peremptory "Don't flunk!" of Charley Welsh.

But her feet seemed rooted to the floor, and she leaned weakly against a shift scene. The orchestra was beginning over again, and a lone voice from the house piped with startling distinctness:

"Puzzle picture! Find Nannie!"

A roar of laughter greeted the sally, and Edna shrank back. But the strong hand of the manager descended on her shoulder, and with a quick, powerful shove propelled her out on to the stage. His hand and arm had flashed into full view, and the audience, grasping the situation, thundered its appreciation. The orchestra was drowned out by the terrible din, and Edna could see the bows scraping away across the violins, apparently without sound. It was impossible for her to begin in time, and as she patiently waited, arms akimbo and ears straining for the music, the house let loose again (a favorite trick, she afterward learned, of confusing the amateur by preventing him or her from hearing the orchestra).

But Edna was recovering her presence of mind. She became aware, pit to dome, of a vast sea of smiling and fun-distorted faces, of vast roars of laughter, rising wave on wave, and then her Scotch blood went cold and angry. The hard-working but silent orchestra gave her the cue, and, without making a sound, she began to move her lips, stretch forth her arms, and sway her body, as though she were really singing. The noise in the house redoubled in the attempt to drown her voice, but she serenely went on with her pantomime. This seemed to continue an interminable time, when the audience, tiring of its prank and in order to hear, suddenly stilled its clamor, and discovered the dumb show she had been making. For a moment all was silent, save for the orchestra, her lips moving on without a sound, and then the audience realized that it had been sold, and broke out afresh, this time with genuine applause in acknowledgment of her victory. She chose this as the happy moment for her exit, and with a bow and a backward retreat, she was off the stage in Letty's arms.

The worst was past, and for the rest of the evening she moved about among the amateurs and professionals, talking, listening, observing, finding out what it meant and taking mental notes of it all. Charley Welsh constituted himself her preceptor and guardian angel, and so well did he perform the self-allotted task that when it was all over she felt fully prepared to write her article. But the proposition had been to do two turns, and her native pluck forced her to live up to it. Also, in the course of the intervening days, she discovered fleeting impressions that required verification; so, on Saturday, she was back again, with her telescope basket and Letty.

The manager seemed looking for her, and she caught an expression of relief in his eyes when he first saw her. He hurried up, greeted her, and bowed with a respect ludicrously at variance with his previous ogrelike behavior. And as he bowed, across his shoulders she saw Charley Welsh deliberately wink.

But the surprise had just begun. The manager begged to be introduced to her sister, chatted entertainingly with the pair of them, and strove greatly and anxiously to be agreeable. He even went so far as to give Edna a dressing room to herself, to the unspeakable envy of the three other amateur ladies of previous acquaintance. Edna was nonplussed, and it was not till she met Charley Welsh in the passage that light was thrown on the mystery.

"Hello!" he greeted her. "On Easy Street, eh? Everything slidin' your way."

She smiled brightly.

"Thinks yer a female reporter, sure. I almost split when I saw 'm layin' himself out sweet an' pleasin'. Honest, now, that ain't yet graft, is it?"

"I told you my experience with editors," she parried. "And honest now, it was honest, too."

But the Only Charley Welsh shook his head dubiously. "Not that I care a rap," he declared. "And if you are, just gimme a couple of lines of notice, the right kind, good ad, you know. And if yer not, why yer all right anyway. Yer not our class, that's straight."

After her turn, which she did this time with the nerve of an old campaigner, the manager returned to the charge; and after saying nice things and being generally nice himself, he came to the point.

"You'll treat us well, I hope," he said insinuatingly. "Do the right thing by us, and all that?"

"Oh," she answered innocently, "you couldn't persuade me to do another turn; I know I seemed to take and that you'd like to have me, but I really, really can't."

"You know what I mean," he said, with a touch of his old bulldozing manner.

"No, I really won't," she persisted. "Vaudeville's too—too wearing on the nerves, my nerves, at any rate."

Whereat he looked puzzled and doubtful, and forbore to press the point further.

But on Monday morning, when she came to his office to get her pay for the two turns, it was he who puzzled her.

"You surely must have mistaken me," he lied glibly. "I remember saying something about paying your car fare. We always do this, you know, but we never, never pay amateurs. That would take the life and sparkle out of the whole thing. No, Charley Welsh was stringing you. He gets paid nothing for his turns. No amateur gets paid. The idea is ridiculous. However, here's fifty cents. It will pay your sister's car fare also. And,"—very suavely—"speaking for the Loops, permit me to thank you for the kind and successful contribution of your services."

That afternoon, true to her promise to Max Irwin, she placed her typewritten copy into his hands. And while he ran over it, he nodded his head from time to time, and maintained a running fire of commendatory remarks: "Good!—that's it!—that's the stuff!—psychology's all right!—the very idea!—you've caught it!—excellent!—missed it a bit here, but it'll go—that's vigorous!—strong!—vivid!—pictures!—pictures!—excellent!—most excellent!"

And when he had run down to the bottom of the last page, holding out his hand: "My dear Miss Wyman, I congratulate you. I must say you have exceeded my expectations, which, to say the least, were large. You are a journalist, a natural journalist. You've got the grip, and you're sure to get on. The *Intelligencer* will take it, without doubt, and take you too. They'll have to take you. If they don't, some of the other papers will get you."

"But what's this?" he queried, the next instant, his face going serious. "You've said nothing about receiving the pay for your turns, and that's one of the points of the feature. I expressly mentioned it, if you'll remember."

"It will never do," he said, shaking his head ominously, when she had explained. "You simply must collect that money somehow. Let me see. Let me think a moment."

"Never mind, Mr. Irwin," she said. "I've bothered you enough. Let me use your phone, please, and I'll try Mr. Ernst Symes again."

He vacated his chair by the desk, and Edna took down the receiver.

"Charley Welsh is sick," she began, when the connection had been made. "What? No! I'm not Charley Welsh. Charley Welsh is sick, and his sister wants to know if she can come out this afternoon and draw his pay for him?"

"Tell Charley Welsh's sister that Charley Welsh was out this morning, and drew his own pay," came back the manager's familiar tones, crisp with asperity.

"All right," Edna went on. "And now Nan Bellayne wants to know if she and her sister can come out this afternoon and draw Nan Bellayne's pay?"

"What'd he say? What'd he say?" Max Irwin cried excitedly, as she hung up.

"That Nan Bellayne was too much for him, and that she and her sister could come out and get her pay and the freedom of the Loops, to boot."

"One thing more," he interrupted her thanks at the door, as on her previous visit. "Now that you've shown the stuff you're made of, I should esteem it, ahem, a privilege to give you a line myself to the *Intelligencer* people."

from The Little Lady of the Big House

This remains in some ways London's most difficult novel, in large measure because it promises much but doesn't fully deliver. Reviewers and readers in 1916 found its frank sexual imagery and adulterous plot outrageous; one described the novel as "erotomania." Set on a California ranch—the big house of the title is the hacienda—this is the story of Dick and Paula Forrest, who at first seem to be an ideal modern couple. It soon becomes clear, however, that Dick is all efficiency, a great manager but not in touch with his emotions (Paula says that her only rival is the ranch). His wife, though immature, is passionate and wishes for a more fulfilling relationship. Both want a child. Into this mix comes Evan Graham, a friend of Dick's, and as the excerpt that follows reveals, he falls in love with Paula, bringing unspoken tensions into the open. "Deep down she was conscious of her own recklessness and madness," writes London, "and of an end to it all that could not but be dreadful to some one of them or all of them." Although he continues conducting ranch business as usual, Dick demands that Paula decide between Evan and him. When Paula makes her decision, the novel ends in an event that renders her earlier perception prophetic.

But it is not the way for a man and a woman, in propinquity, to maintain a definite, unwavering distance asunder. Imperceptibly Paula and Graham drew closer. From lingering eye-gazings and hand-touchings the way led to permitted caresses, until there was a second clasping in the arms and a second kiss long on the lips. Nor this time did Paula flame in anger. Instead, she commanded:

"You must not go."

"I must not stay," Graham reiterated for the thousandth time. "Oh, I have kissed behind doors, and been guilty of all the rest of the silly rubbish," he complained. "But this is you, and this is Dick."

"It will work out, I tell you, Evan."

"Come with me then and of ourselves work it out. Come now."

She recoiled.

"Remember," Graham encouraged, "what Dick said at dinner the night Leo fought the dragons—that if it were you, Paula, his wife, who ran away he would say 'Bless you, my children.'"

"And that is just why it is so hard, Evan. He is Great Heart. You named him well. Listen—you watch him now. He is as gentle as he said he would be that night—gentle toward me, I mean. And more. You watch him—"

"He knows?—he has spoken?" Graham broke in.

"He has not spoken, but I am sure he knows, or guesses. You watch him. He won't compete against you—"

"Compete!"

"Just that. He won't compete. Remember at the rodeo yesterday. He was breaking mustangs when our party arrived, but he never mounted again. Now he is a wonderful horse-breaker. You tried your hand. Frankly, while you did fairly well, you couldn't touch him. But he wouldn't show off against you. That alone would make me certain that he guesses."

"Listen. Of late haven't you noticed that he never questions a statement you make, as he used to question, as he questions every one else. He continues to play billiards with you, because there you best him. He fences and singlesticks with you—there you are even. But he won't box or wrestle with you."

"He *can* out-box and out-wrestle me," Graham muttered ruefully.

"You watch and you will see what I mean by not competing. He is treating me like a spirited colt, giving me my head to make a mess of things if I want to. Not for the world would he interfere. Oh, trust me, I know him. It is his own code that he is living up to. He could teach the philosophers what applied philosophy is.

"No, no; listen," she rushed over Graham's attempt to interrupt. "I want to tell you more. There is a secret staircase that goes up from the library to Dick's work room. Only he and I use it, and his secretaries. When you arrive at the head of it, you are right in his room, surrounded by shelves of books. I have just come from there. I was going in to see him when I heard voices. Of course it was ranch business, I thought, and they would soon be gone. So I waited. It *was* ranch business, but it was so interesting, so, what Hancock would call, illuminating, that I remained and eavesdropped. It was illuminating of Dick, I mean.

"It was the wife of one of the workmen Dick had on the carpet. Such things do arise on a large place like this. I wouldn't know the woman if I saw her, and I didn't recognize her name. She was whimpering out her trouble when Dick stopped her. 'Never mind all that,' he said. 'What I want to know is, did you give Smith any encouragement?'

"Smith isn't his name, but he is one of our foremen and has worked eight years for Dick.

"'Oh, no, sir,' I could hear her answer. 'He went out of his way from the first to bother me. I've tried to keep out of his way, always. Besides, my husband's a violent-tempered man, and I did so want him to hold his job here. He's worked nearly a year for you now, and there aren't any complaints, are there? Before that it was irregular work for a long time, and we had real hard times. It wasn't his fault. He ain't a drinking man. He always—'

"'That's all right,' Dick stopped her. 'His work and habits have nothing to do with the matter. Now you are sure you have never encouraged Mr. Smith in any way?' And she was so sure that she talked for ten minutes, detailing the foreman's persecution of her. She had a pleasant voice—one of those sweet, timid, woman's voices, and undoubtedly is quite attractive. It was all I could do to resist peeping. I wanted to see what she looked like.

"'Now this trouble yesterday morning,' Dick said. 'Was it general? I mean, outside of your husband, and Mr. Smith, was the scene such that those who live around you knew of it?'

"'Yes, sir. You see, he had no right to come into my kitchen. My husband doesn't work under him anyway. And he had his arm around me and was trying to kiss me when my husband came in. My husband has a temper, but he ain't overly strong. Mr. Smith would make two of him. So he pulled a knife, and Mr. Smith got him by the arms, and they fought all over the kitchen. I knew there was murder going to be done and I run out screaming for help. The folks in the other cottages'd heard the racket already. They'd smashed the window and the cook stove, and the place was filled with smoke and ashes when the neighbors dragged them away from each other. I'd done nothing to deserve all that disgrace. You know, sir, the way the women will talk—'

"And Dick hushed her up there, and took all of five minutes more in getting rid of her. Her great fear was that her husband would lose his place. From what Dick told her, I waited. He had made no decision, and I knew the foreman was next on the carpet. In he came. I'd have given the world to see him. But I could only listen.

"Dick jumped right into the thick of it. He described the scene and uproar, and Smith acknowledged that it had been riotous for a while. 'She says she gave you no encouragement,' Dick said next.

"'Then she lies,' said Smith. 'She has that way of looking with her eyes that's an invitation. She looked at me that way from the first. But it was by word-of-mouth invitation that I was in her kitchen yesterday morning. We didn't expect the husband. But she began to struggle when he hove in sight. When she says she gave me no encouragement—'

"'Never mind all that,' Dick stopped him. 'It's not essential.' 'But it is, Mr. Forrest, if I am to clear myself,' Smith insisted.

"'No; it is not essential to the thing you can't clear yourself of,' Dick answered, and I could hear that cold, hard, judicial note come into his voice. Smith could not understand. Dick told him. 'The thing you have been guilty of, Mr. Smith, is the scene, the disturbance, the scandal, the wagging of the women's tongues now

going on forty to the minute, the impairment of the discipline and
order of the ranch, all of which is boiled down to the one grave
thing, the hurt to the ranch efficiency.'

"And still Smith couldn't see. He thought the charge was of
violating social morality by pursuing a married woman, and tried
to mitigate the offense by showing the woman encouraged him
and by pleading: 'And after all, Mr. Forrest, a man is only a man,
and I admit she made a fool of me and I made a fool of myself.'

"'Mr. Smith,' Dick said. 'You've worked for me eight years.
You've been a foreman six years of that time. I have no complaint
against your work. You certainly do know how to handle labor.
About your personal morality I don't care a damn. You can be a
Mormon or a Turk for all it matters to me. Your private acts are
your private acts, and are no concern of mine as long as they do not
interfere with your work or my ranch. Any one of my drivers can
drink his head off Saturday night, and every Saturday night. That's
his business. But the minute he shows a hold-over on Monday
morning that is taken out on my horses, that excites them, or
injures them, or threatens to injure them, or that decreases in the
slightest the work they should perform on Monday, that moment
it is my business and the driver goes down the hill.'

"'You, you mean, Mr. Forrest,' Smith stuttered, 'that, that I'm
to go down the hill?' 'That is just what I mean, Mr. Smith. You are
to go down the hill, not because you climbed over another man's
fence—that's your business and his; but because you were guilty of
causing a disturbance that is an impairment of ranch efficiency.'

"Do you know, Evan," Paula broke in on her recital, "Dick
can nose more human tragedy out of columns of ranch statistics
than can the average fiction writer out of the whirl of a great city.
Take the milk reports—the individual reports of the milkers—so
many pounds of milk, morning and night, from cow so-and-so, so
many pounds from cow so-and-so. He doesn't have to know the
man. But there is a decrease in the weight of milk. 'Mr. Parkman,'
he'll say to the head dairyman, 'Is Barchi Peratta married?' 'Yes, sir.'
'Is he having trouble with his wife?' 'Yes, sir.'

"Or it will be: 'Mr. Parkman, Simpkins has the best longtime record of any of our milkers. Now he's slumped. What's up?' Mr. Parkman doesn't know. 'Investigate,' says Dick. 'There's something on his chest. Talk to him like an uncle and find out. We've got to get it off his chest.' And Mr. Parkman finds out. Simpkins' boy, working his way through Stanford University, has elected the joy-ride path and is in jail waiting trial for forgery. Dick put his own lawyers on the case, smoothed it over, got the boy out on probation, and Simpkins' milk reports came back to par. And the best of it is, the boy made good, Dick kept an eye on him, saw him through the college of engineering, and he's now working for Dick on the dredging end, earning a hundred and fifty a month, married, with a future before him, and his father still milks."

"You are right," Graham murmured sympathetically. "I well named him when I named him Great Heart."

"I call him my Rock of Ages," Paula said gratefully. "He is so solid. He stands in any storm—Oh, you don't really know him. He is so sure. He stands right up. He's never taken a cropper in his life. God smiles on him. God has always smiled on him. He's never been beaten down to his knees…yet. I…I should not care to see that sight. It would be heartbreaking. And, Evan—" Her hand went out to his in a pleading gesture that merged into a half-caress. "—I am afraid for him now. That is why I don't know what to do. It is not for myself that I back and fill and hesitate. If he were ignoble, if he were narrow, if he were weak or had one tiniest shred of meanness, if he had ever been beaten to his knees before, why, my dear, my dear, I should have been gone with you long ago."

Her eyes filled with sudden moisture. She stilled him with a pressure of her hand, and, to regain herself, she went back to her recital:

"'Your little finger, Mr. Smith, I consider worth more to me and to the world,' Dick told him, 'than the whole body of this woman's husband. Here's the report on him: willing, eager to please, not bright, not strong, an indifferent workman at best. Yet you have to go down the hill, and I am very, very sorry.'

"Oh, yes, there was more. But I've given you the main of it. You see Dick's code there. And he lives his code. He accords latitude to the individual. Whatever the individual may do, so long as it does not hurt the group of individuals in which he lives, is his own affair. He believed Smith had a perfect right to love the woman, and to be loved by her if it came to that. I have heard him always say that love could not be held nor enforced. Truly, did I go with you, he would say, 'Bless you, my children.' Though it broke his heart he would say it. Past love, he believes, gives no hold over the present. And every hour of love, I have heard him say, pays for itself, on both sides, quittance in full. He claims there can be no such thing as a love-debt, laughs at the absurdity of love-claims."

"And I agree with him," Graham said. "'You promised to love me always,' says the jilted one, and then strives to collect as if it were a promissory note for so many dollars. Dollars are dollars, but love lives or dies. When it is dead how can it be collected? We are all agreed, and the way is simple. We love. It is enough. Why delay another minute?"

His fingers strayed along her fingers on the keyboard as he bent to her, first kissing her hair, then slowly turning her face up to his and kissing her willing lips.

"Dick does not love me like you," she said, "not madly, I mean. He has had me so long, I think I have become a habit to him. And often and often, before I knew you, I used to puzzle whether he cared more for the ranch or more for me."

"It is so simple," Graham urged. "All we have to do is to be straightforward. Let us go."

He drew her to her feet and made as if to start.

But she drew away from him suddenly, sat down, and buried her flushed face in her hands.

"You do not understand, Evan. I love Dick. I shall always love him."

"And me?" Graham demanded sharply.

"Oh, without saying," she smiled. "You are the only man, besides Dick, that has ever kissed me this...way, and that I have kissed this way. But I can't make up my mind. The triangle, as you call it, must be solved for me. I can't solve it myself. I compare the two of you, weigh you, measure you. I remember Dick and all our past years. And I consult my heart for you. And I don't know. I don't know. You are a great man, my great lover. But Dick is a greater man than you. You—you are more clay, more—I grope to describe you—more human, I fancy. And that is why I love you more...or at least I think perhaps I do.

"But wait," she resisted him, prisoning his eager hand in hers. "There is more I want to say. I remember Dick and all our past years. But I remember him today, as well, and tomorrow. I cannot bear the thought that any man should pity my husband, that you should pity him, and pity him you must when I confess that I love you more. That is why I am not sure. That is why I so quickly take it back and do not know.

"I'd die of shame if through [an] act of mine any man pitied Dick. Truly, I would. Of all things ghastly, I can think of none so ghastly as Dick being pitied. He has never been pitied in his life. He has always been top-dog—bright, light, strong, unassailable. And more, he doesn't deserve pity. And it's my fault...and yours, Evan."

She abruptly thrust Evan's hand away.

"And every act, every permitted touch of you, does make him pitiable. Don't you see how tangled it is for me? And then there is my own pride. That you should see me disloyal to him in little things, such as this—" (she caught his hand again and caressed it with soft fingertips) "—hurts me in my love for you, diminishes me, must diminish me in your eyes. I shrink from the thought that my disloyalty to him in this I do—" (she laid his hand against her cheek) "—gives you reason to pity him and censure me."

She soothed the impatience of the hand on her cheek, and, almost absently, musingly scrutinizing it without consciously seeing it, turned it over and slowly kissed the palm. The next moment she was drawn to her feet and into his arms.

"There, you see," was her reproach as she disengaged herself.

The Mexican

In this, among his most admired stories, London managed to combine two of his enduring themes: atavism and social justice. Assigned to cover the Mexican Revolution for the Hearst syndicate in 1911, the egalitarian London found himself identifying with the "chicken thieves and outlaws" struggling to overthrow the dictator Porfirio Díaz. He also presented his vision in fiction—"The Mexican" was included in The Night-Born *(1913)—creating Felipe Rivera, a character both atavistic and utterly dedicated to the cause. Felipe also illustrates the author's ability to embody abstract ideas in palpably real figures; he "is power,— he is the primitive, the wild wolf,—the striking rattlesnake, the stinging centipede....He is the Revolution incarnate." He is also a boxer (one more of the author's longtime interests) and his epic match with Danny Ward—another unforgettable minor character—shows Jack at his best as a writer of action.*

Nobody knew his history—they of the Junta least of all. He was their "little mystery," their "big patriot," and in his way he worked as hard for the coming Mexican Revolution as did they. They were tardy in recognizing this, for not one of the Junta liked him. The day he first drifted into their crowded, busy rooms they all suspected him of being a spy—one of the bought tools of the Díaz secret service. Too many of the comrades were in civil and military prisons scattered over the United States, and others of them, in irons, were even then being taken across the border to be lined up against adobe walls and shot.

At the first sight the boy did not impress them favorably. Boy he was, not more than eighteen and not overlarge for his years. He announced that he was Felipe Rivera, and that it was his wish to work for the revolution. That was all—not a wasted word, no further explanation. He stood waiting. There was no smile on his lips, no geniality in his eyes. Big, dashing Paulino Vera felt an inward shudder. Here was something forbidding, terrible, inscrutable. There was something venomous and snakelike in the boy's black eyes. They burned like cold fire, as with a vast, concentrated bitterness. He flashed them from the faces of the conspirators to the typewriter which little Mrs. Sethby was industriously operating. His eyes rested on hers but an instant—she had chanced to look up—and she, too, sensed the nameless something that made her pause. She was compelled to read back in order to regain the swing of the letter she was writing.

Paulino Vera looked questioningly at Arrellano and Ramos, and questioningly they looked back and to each other. The indecision of doubt brooded in their eyes. This slender boy was the Unknown, vested with all the menace of the Unknown. He was unrecognizable, something quite beyond the ken of honest, ordinary revolutionists whose fiercest hatred for Díaz and his tyranny after all was only that of honest and ordinary patriots. Here was something else, they knew not what. But Vera, always the most impulsive, the quickest to act, stepped into the breach.

"Very well," he said coldly. "You say you want to work for the revolution. Take off your coat. Hang it over there. I will show you—come—where are the buckets and cloths. The floor is dirty. You will begin by scrubbing it, and by scrubbing the floors of the other rooms. The spittoons need to be cleaned. Then there are the windows."

"Is it for the revolution?" the boy asked.

"It is for the revolution," Vera answered.

Rivera looked cold suspicion at all of them, then proceeded to take off his coat.

"It is well," he said.

And nothing more. Day after day he came to his work—sweeping, scrubbing, cleaning. He emptied the ashes from the stoves, brought up the coal and kindling, and lighted the fires before the most energetic one of them was at his desk.

"Can I sleep here?" he asked once.

Aha! So that was it—the hand of Díaz showing through! To sleep in the rooms of the Junta meant access to their secrets, to the lists of names, to the addresses of comrades down on Mexican soil. The request was denied, and Rivera never spoke of it again. He slept they knew not where, and ate they knew not where nor how. Once Arrellano offered him a couple of dollars. Rivera declined the money with a shake of the head. When Vera joined in and tried to press it upon him, he said: "I am working for the revolution."

It takes money to raise a modern revolution, and always the Junta was pressed. The members starved and toiled, and the longest day was none too long, and yet there were times when it appeared as if the revolution stood or fell on no more than the matter of a few dollars. Once, the first time, when the rent of the house was two months behind and the landlord was threatening dispossession, it was Felipe Rivera, the scrub boy in the poor, cheap clothes, worn and threadbare, who laid sixty dollars in gold on May Sethby's desk. There were other times. Three hundred letters, clicked out on the busy typewriters (appeals for assistance, for sanctions from the organized labor groups, requests for square news deals to the editors of newspapers, protests against the high-handed treatment of revolutionists by the United States courts), lay unmailed, awaiting postage. Vera's watch had disappeared—the old-fashioned gold repeater that had been his father's. Likewise had gone the plain gold band from May Sethby's third finger. Things were desperate. Ramos and Arrellano pulled their long mustaches in despair. The letters must go off, and the post office allowed no credit to purchasers of stamps. Then it was that Rivera put on his hat and went out. When he came back he laid a thousand two-cent stamps on May Sethby's desk.

"I wonder if it is the cursed gold of Díaz?" said Vera to the comrades.

They elevated their brows and could not decide. And Felipe Rivera, the scrubber for the revolution, continued, as occasion arose, to lay down gold and silver for the Junta's use.

And still they could not bring themselves to like him. They did not know him. His ways were not theirs. He gave no confidences. He repelled all probing. Youth that he was, they could never nerve themselves to dare to question him.

"A great and lonely spirit, perhaps, I do not know, I do not know," Arrellano said helplessly.

"He is not human," said Ramos.

"His soul has been seared," said May Sethby. "Light and laughter have been burned out of him. He is like one dead, and yet he is fearfully alive."

"He has been through hell," said Vera. "No man could look like that who has not been through hell—and he is only a boy."

Yet they could not like him. He never talked, never inquired, never suggested. He would stand listening, expressionless, a thing dead, save for his eyes, coldly burning, while their talk of the revolution ran high and warm. From face to face and speaker to speaker his eyes would turn, boring like gimlets of incandescent ice, disconcerting and perturbing.

"He is no spy," Vera confided to May Sethby. "He is a patriot—mark me, the greatest patriot of us all. I know it, I feel it, here in my heart and head I feel it. But him I know not at all."

"He has a bad temper," said May Sethby.

"I know," said Vera with a shudder. "He has looked at me with those eyes of his. They do not love; they threaten; they are savage as a wild tiger's. I know, if I should prove unfaithful to the cause, that he would kill me. He has no heart. He is pitiless as steel, keen and cold as frost. He is like moonshine in a winter night when a man freezes to death on some lonely mountaintop. I am not afraid of Díaz and all his killers; but this boy, of him am I afraid. I tell you true. I am afraid. He is the breath of death."

Yet Vera it was who persuaded the others to give the first trust to Rivera. The line of communication between Los Angeles and Lower California had broken down. Three of the comrades had dug their own graves and been shot into them. Two more were United States prisoners in Los Angeles. Juan Alvarado, the federal commander, was a monster. All their plans did he checkmate. They could no longer gain access to the active revolutionists, and the incipient ones, in Lower California.

Young Rivera was given his instructions and dispatched south. When he returned, the line of communication was re-established, and Juan Alvarado was dead. He had been found in bed, a knife hilt-deep in his breast. This had exceeded Rivera's instructions, but they of the Junta knew the times of his movements. They did not ask him. He said nothing. But they looked at one another and conjectured.

"I have told you," said Vera. "Díaz has more to fear from this youth than from any man. He is implacable. He is the hand of God."

The bad temper, mentioned by May Sethby, and sensed by them all, was evidenced by physical proofs. Now he appeared with a cut lip, a blackened cheek, or a swollen ear. It was patent that he brawled, somewhere in that outside world where he ate and slept, gained money, and moved in ways unknown to them. As the time passed he had come to set type for the little revolutionary sheet they published weekly. There were occasions when he was unable to set type, when his knuckles were bruised and battered, when his thumbs were injured and helpless, when one arm or the other hung wearily at his side while his face was drawn with unspoken pain.

"A wastrel," said Arrellano.

"A frequenter of low places," said Ramos.

"But where does he get the money?" Vera demanded. "Only today, just now, have I learned that he paid the bill for white paper—one hundred and forty dollars,"

"There are his absences," said May Sethby. "He never explains them."

"We should set a spy upon him," Ramos propounded.

"I should not care to be that spy," said Vera. "I fear you would never see me again, save to bury me. He has a terrible passion. Not even God would he permit to stand between him and the way of his passion."

"I feel like a child before him," Ramos confessed.

"To me he is power—he is the primitive, the wild wolf, the striking rattlesnake, the stinging centipede," said Arrellano.

"He is the revolution incarnate," said Vera. "He is the flame and the spirit of it, the insatiable cry for vengeance that makes no cry but that slays noiselessly. He is a destroying angel moving through the still watches of the night."

"I could weep over him," said May Sethby. "He knows nobody. He hates all people. Us he tolerates, for we are the way of his desire. He is alone...lonely." Her voice broke in a half sob and there was dimness in her eyes.

Rivera's ways and times were truly mysterious. There were periods when they did not see him for a week at a time. Once he was away a month. These occasions were always capped by his return, when, without advertisement or speech, he laid gold coins on May Sethby's desk. Again, for days and weeks, he spent all his time with the Junta. And yet again, for irregular periods, he would disappear through the heart of each day, from early morning until late afternoon. At such times he came early and remained late. Arrellano had found him at midnight, setting type with fresh-swollen knuckles, or mayhap it was his lip, new-split, that still bled.

The time of the crisis approached. Whether or not the revolution would be depended upon the Junta, and the Junta was hard-pressed. The need for money was greater than ever before, while money was harder to get. Patriots had given their last cent and now could give no more. Section-gang laborers—fugitive peons from Mexico—were contributing half their scanty wages. But more than that was needed. The heartbreaking, conspiring, undermining toil of years approached fruition. The time was ripe. The revolution hung on the balance. One shove more, one last heroic effort, and it would tremble across the scales to victory. They knew their Mexico. Once started, the revolution would take care of itself. The whole Díaz machine would go down like a house of cards. The border was ready to rise. One Yankee, with a hundred I.W.W. men, waited the word to cross over the border and begin the conquest of Lower California. But he needed guns. And clear across to the Atlantic, the Junta in touch with them all and all of them needing guns, mere adventurers, soldiers of fortune, bandits, disgruntled American union men, socialists, anarchists, roughnecks, Mexican exiles, peons escaped from bondage, whipped miners from the bullpens of Coeur d'Alene and Colorado who desired only the more vindictively to fight—all the flotsam and jetsam of wild spirits from the madly complicated modern world. And it was guns and ammunition, ammunition and guns—the unceasing and eternal cry.

Fling this heterogeneous, bankrupt, vindictive mass across the border, and the revolution was on. The customhouse, the northern ports of entry, would be captured. Díaz could not resist. He dared not throw the weight of his armies against them, for he must hold the south. And through the south the flame would spread despite. The people would rise. The defenses of city after city would crumple up. State after state would totter down. And at last, from every side, the victorious armies of the revolution would close in on the city of Mexico itself, Díaz's last stronghold.

But the money. They had the men, impatient and urgent, who would use the guns. They knew the traders who would sell and deliver the guns. But to culture the revolution thus far had exhausted the Junta. The last dollar had been spent, the last resource and the last starving patriot milked dry, and the great adventure still trembled on the scales. Guns and ammunition! The ragged battalions must be armed. But how? Ramos lamented his confiscated estates. Arrellano wailed the spendthriftness of his youth. May Sethby wondered if it would have been different had they of the Junta been more economical in the past.

"To think that the freedom of Mexico should stand or fall on a few paltry thousands of dollars," said Paulino Vera.

Despair was in all their faces. José Amarillo, their last hope, a recent convert who had promised money, had been apprehended at his hacienda in Chihuahua and shot against his own stable wall. The news had just come through.

Rivera, on his knees, scrubbing, looked up, with suspended brush, his bare arms flecked with soapy, dirty water.

"Will five thousand do it?" he asked.

They looked their amazement. Vera nodded and swallowed. He could not speak, but he was on the instant invested with a vast faith.

"Order the guns," Rivera said, and thereupon was guilty of the longest flow of words they had ever heard him utter. "The time is short. In three weeks I shall bring you the five thousand. It is well. The weather will be warmer for those who fight. Also, it is the best I can do."

Vera fought his faith. It was incredible. Too many fond hopes had been shattered since he had begun to play the revolution game. He believed this threadbare scrubber of the revolution, and yet he dared not believe.

"You are crazy," he said.

"In three weeks," said Rivera. "Order the guns."

He got up, rolled down his sleeves, and put on his coat.

"Order the guns," he said. "I am going now."

After hurrying and scurrying, much telephoning and bad language, a night session was held in Kelly's office. Kelly was rushed with business; also, he was unlucky. He had brought Danny Ward out from New York, arranged the fight for him with Billy Carthey, the date was three weeks away, and for two days now, carefully concealed from the sporting writers, Carthey had been lying up, badly injured. There was no one to take his place. Kelly had been burning the wires east to every eligible lightweight, but they were tied up with dates and contracts. And now hope had revived, though faintly.

"You've got a hell of a nerve," Kelly addressed Rivera, after one look, as soon as they got together.

Hate that was malignant was in Rivera's eyes, but his face remained impassive.

"I can lick Ward," was all he said.

"How do you know? Ever see him fight?"

Rivera shook his head.

"He can beat you up with one hand and both eyes closed."

Rivera shrugged his shoulders.

"Haven't you got anything to say?" the fight promoter snarled.

"I can lick him."

"Who'd you ever fight, anyway?" Michael Kelly demanded. Michael was the promoter's brother, and ran the Yellowstone Poolrooms, where he made goodly sums on the fight game.

Rivera favored him with a bitter, unanswering stare.

The promoter's secretary, a distinctively sporty young man, sneered audibly.

"Well, you know Roberts." Kelly broke the hostile silence. "He ought to be here. I've sent for him. Sit down and wait, though from the looks of you, you haven't got a chance. I can't throw the public down with a bum fight. Ringside seats are selling at fifteen dollars, you know that."

When Roberts arrived it was patent that he was mildly drunk. He was a tall, lean, slack-jointed individual, and his walk, like his talk, was a smooth and languid drawl.

Kelly went straight to the point.

"Look here, Roberts, you've been braggin' you discovered this little Mexican. You know Carthey's broke his arm. Well, this little yellow streak has the gall to blow in today and say he'll take Carthey's place. What about it?"

"It's all right, Kelly," came the slow response. "He can put up a fight."

"I suppose you'll be sayin' next that he can lick Ward," Kelly snapped.

Roberts considered judicially.

"No, I won't say that. Ward's a topnotcher and a ring general. But he can't hash-house Rivera in short order. I know Rivera. Nobody can get his goat. He ain't got a goat that I could ever discover. And he's a two-handed fighter. He can throw in the sleepmakers from any position."

"Never mind that. What kind of a show can he put up? You've been conditioning and training fighters all your life. I take off my hat to your judgment. Can he give the public a run for its money?"

"He sure can, and he'll worry Ward a mighty heap on top of it. You don't know that boy. I do. I discovered him. He ain't got a goat. He's a devil. He's a wizzy-wooz if anybody should ask you. He'll make Ward sit up with a show of local talent that'll make the rest of you sit up. I won't say he'll lick Ward, but he'll put up such a show that you'll all know he's a comer."

"All right." Kelly turned to his secretary. "Ring up Ward. I warned him to show up if I thought it worth while. He's right across at the Yellowstone, throwin' chests and doing the popular." Kelly turned back to the conditioner. "Have a drink?"

Roberts sipped his highball and unburdened himself.

"Never told you how I discovered the little cuss. It was a couple of years ago he showed up out at the quarters. I was getting Prayne ready for his fight with Delaney. Prayne's wicked. He ain't got a tickle of mercy in his make-up. He'd chopped up his pardners something cruel, and I couldn't find a willing boy that'd work with him. I'd noticed this little starved Mexican kid hanging around, and I was desperate. So I grabbed him, slammed on the gloves, and put him in. He was tougher'n rawhide, but weak. And he didn't know the first letter in the alphabet of boxing. Prayne chopped him to ribbons. But he hung on for two sickening rounds, when he fainted. Starvation, that was all. Battered? You couldn't have recognized him. I gave him half a dollar and a square meal. You oughta seen him wolf it down. He hadn't had a bite for a couple of days.

That's the end of him, thinks I. But next day he showed up, stiff an' sore, ready for another half and a square meal. And he done better as time went by. Just a born fighter, and tough beyond belief. He hasn't a heart. He's a piece of ice. And he never talked eleven words in a string since I know him. He saws wood and does his work."

"I've seen 'm," the secretary said. "He's worked a lot for you."

"All the big little fellows has tried out on him," Roberts answered. "And he's learned from 'em. I've seen some of them he could lick. But his heart wasn't in it. I reckoned he never liked the game. He seemed to act that way."

"He's been fighting some before the little clubs the last few months," Kelly said.

"Sure. But I don't know what struck 'm. All of a sudden his heart got into it. He just went out like a streak and cleaned up all the little local fellows. Seemed to want the money, and he's won a bit, though his clothes don't look it. He's peculiar. Nobody knows his business. Nobody knows how he spends his time. Even when he's on the job, he plumb up and disappears most of each day soon as his work is done. Sometimes he just blows away for weeks at a time. But he don't take advice. There's a fortune in it for the fellow that gets the job of managin' him, only he won't consider it. And you watch him hold out for the cash money when you get down to terms."

It was at this stage that Danny Ward arrived. Quite a party it was. His manager and trainer were with him, and he breezed in like a gusty draft of geniality, good nature, and all-conqueringness. Greetings flew about, a joke here, a retort there, a smile or a laugh for everybody. Yet it was his way, and only partly sincere. He was a good actor, and he had found geniality a most valuable asset in the game of getting on in the world. But down underneath he was the deliberate, cold blooded fighter and businessman. The rest was a mask. Those who knew him or trafficked with him said that when it came to brass tacks he was Danny on the Spot. He was invariably present at all business discussions, and it was urged by some that his manager was a blind whose only function was to serve as Danny's mouthpiece.

Rivera's way was different. Indian blood, as well as Spanish, was in his veins, and he sat back in a corner, silent, immobile, only his black eyes passing from face to face and noting everything.

"So that's the guy," Danny said, running an appraising eye over his proposed antagonist. "How de do, old chap."

Rivera's eyes burned venomously, but he made no sign of acknowledgment. He disliked all gringos, but this gringo he hated with an immediacy that was unusual even in him.

"Gawd!" Danny protested facetiously to the promoter. "You ain't expectin' me to fight a deef mute." When the laughter subsided he made another hit. "Los Angeles must be on the dink when this is the best you can scare up. What kindergarten did you get 'm from?"

"He's a good little boy, Danny, take it from me," Roberts defended. "Not as easy as he looks."

"And half the house is sold already," Kelly pleaded. "You'll have to take 'm on, Danny. It's the best we can do."

Danny ran another careless and unflattering glance over Rivera and sighed.

"I gotta be easy with 'm, I guess. If only he don't blow up."

Roberts snorted.

"You gotta be careful," Danny's manager warned. "No taking chances with a dub that's likely to sneak a lucky one across."

"Oh, I'll be careful all right, all right," Danny smiled. "I'll get 'm at the start an' nurse 'm along for the dear public's sake. What d'ye say to fifteen rounds, Kelly—an' then the hay for him?"

"That'll do," was the answer. "As long as you make it realistic."

"Then let's get down to biz." Danny paused and calculated. "Of course, sixty-five percent of gate receipts, same as with Carthey. But the split'll be different. Eighty will just about suit me." And to his manager, "That right?"

The manager nodded.

"Here, you, did you get that?" Kelly asked Rivera.

Rivera shook his head.

"Well, it's this way," Kelly exposited. "The purse'll be sixty-five percent of the gate receipts. You're a dub, and an unknown. You and Danny split, twenty percent goin' to you, an' eighty to Danny. That's fair, isn't it, Roberts?"

"Very fair, Rivera," Roberts agreed. "You see, you ain't got a reputation yet."

"What will sixty-five percent of the gate receipts be?" Rivera demanded.

"Oh, maybe five thousand, maybe as high as eight thousand," Danny broke in to explain. "Something like that. Your share'll come to something like a thousand or sixteen hundred. Pretty good for takin' a licking from a guy with my reputation. What d'ye say?"

Then Rivera took their breaths away.

"Winner takes all," he said with finality.

A dead silence prevailed.

"It's like candy from a baby," Danny's manager proclaimed.

Danny shook his head.

"I've been in the game too long," he explained. "I'm not casting reflections on the referee or the present company. I'm not sayin' nothing about bookmakers an' frame-ups that sometimes happen. But what I do say is that it's poor business for a fighter like me. I play safe. There's no tellin'. Mebbe I break my arm, eh? Or some guy slips me a bunch of dope." He shook his head solemnly. "Win or lose, eighty is my split. What d'ye say, Mexican?"

Rivera shook his head.

Danny exploded. He was getting down to brass tacks now.

"Why, you dirty little greaser! I've a mind to knock your block off right now."

Roberts drawled his body to interposition between hostilities.

"Winner takes all," Rivera repeated sullenly.

"Why do you stand out that way?" Danny asked.

"I can lick you," was the straight answer.

Danny half started to take off his coat. But, as his manager knew, it was a grandstand play. The coat did not come off, and Danny allowed himself to be placated by the group. Everybody sympathized with him. Rivera stood alone.

"Look here, you little fool," Kelly took up the argument. "You're nobody. We know what you've been doing the last few months—putting away little local fighters. But Danny is class. His next fight after this will be for the championship. And you're unknown. Nobody ever heard of you out of Los Angeles."

"They will," Rivera answered with a shrug, "after this fight."

"You think for a second you can lick me?" Danny blurted in. Rivera nodded.

"Oh, come; listen to reason," Kelly pleaded. "Think of the advertising."

"I want the money," was Rivera's answer.

"You couldn't win from me in a thousand years," Danny assured him.

"Then what are you holding out for?" Rivera countered. "If the money's that easy, why don't you go after it?"

"I will, so help me!" Danny cried with abrupt conviction. "I'll beat you to death in the ring, my boy—you monkeyin' with me this way. Make out the articles, Kelly. Winner take all. Play it up in the sportin' columns. Tell 'em it's a grudge fight. I'll show this fresh kid a few."

Kelly's secretary had begun to write, when Danny interrupted.

"Hold on!" He turned to Rivera. "Weights?"

"Ringside," came the answer.

"Not on your life, fresh kid. If winner takes all, we weigh in at 10 a.m."

"And winner takes all?" Rivera queried.

Danny nodded. That settled it. He would enter the ring in his full ripeness of strength.

"Weigh in at ten," Rivera said.

The secretary's pen went on scratching.

"It means five pounds," Roberts complained to Rivera. "You've given too much away. You've thrown the fight right there. Danny'll be as strong as a bull. You're a fool. He'll lick you sure. You ain't got the chance of a dewdrop in hell."

Rivera's answer was a calculated look of hatred. Even this gringo he despised, and him had he found the whitest gringo of them all.

Barely noticed was Rivera as he entered the ring. Only a very slight and very scattering ripple of halfhearted handclapping greeted him. The house did not believe in him. He was the lamb led to slaughter at the hands of the great Danny. Besides, the house was disappointed. It had expected a rushing battle between Danny Ward and Billy Carthey, and here it must put up with this poor little tyro. Still further, it had manifested its disapproval of the change by betting two, and even three, to one on Danny. And where a betting audience's money is, there is its heart.

The Mexican boy sat down in his corner and waited. The slow minutes lagged by. Danny was making him wait. It was an old trick, but ever it worked on the young, new fighters. They grew frightened, sitting thus and facing their own apprehensions and a callous, tobacco-smoking audience. But for once the trick failed. Roberts was right. Rivera had no goat. He, who was more delicately coordinated, more finely nerved and strung than any of them, had no nerves of this sort. The atmosphere of foredoomed defeat in his own corner had no effect on him. His handlers were gringos and strangers. Also they were scrubs—the dirty driftage of the fight game, without honor, without efficiency. And they were chilled, as well, with certitude that theirs was the losing corner.

"Now you gotta be careful," Spider Hagerty warned him. Spider was his chief second. "Make it last as long as you can—them's my instructions from Kelly. If you don't, the papers'll call it another bum fight and give the game a bigger black eye in Los Angeles."

All of which was not encouraging. But Rivera took no notice. He despised prizefighting. It was the hated game of the hated gringo. He had taken up with it, as a chopping block for others in the training quarters, solely because he was starving. The fact that he was marvelously made for it had meant nothing. He hated it. Not until he had come in to the Junta had he fought for money, and he had found the money easy. Not first among the sons of men had he been to find himself successful at a despised vocation.

He did not analyze. He merely knew that he must win this fight. There could be no other outcome. For behind him, nerving him to this belief, were profounder forces than any the crowded house dreamed. Danny Ward fought for money and for the easy ways of life that money would bring. But the things Rivera fought for burned in his brain—blazing and terrible visions, that, with eyes wide open, sitting lonely in the corner of the ring and waiting for his tricky antagonist, he saw as clearly as he had lived them.

He saw the white-walled, water-power factories of Rio Blanco. He saw the six thousand workers, starved and wan, and the little children, seven and eight years of age, who toiled long shifts for ten cents a day. He saw the perambulating corpses, the ghastly death's heads of men who labored in the dye rooms. He remembered that he had heard his father call the dye rooms the "suicide holes," where a year was death. He saw the little patio, and his mother cooking and toiling at crude housekeeping and finding time to caress and love him. And his father he saw, large, big-mustached, and deep-chested, kindly above all men, who loved all men and whose heart was so large that there was love to overflowing still left for the mother and the little *muchacho* playing in the corner of the patio. In those days his name had not been Felipe Rivera. It had been Fernandez, his father's and mother's name. Him had they called Juan. Later he had changed it himself, for he had found the name of Fernandez hated by prefects of police, *jefes politicos,* and *rurales.*

Big, hearty Joaquin Fernandez! A large place he occupied in Rivera's visions. He had not understood at the time, but, looking back, he could understand. He could see him setting type in the little printery, or scribbling endless hasty, nervous lines on the much-cluttered desk. And he could see the strange evenings, when workmen, coming secretly in the dark like men who did ill deeds, met with his father and talked long hours where he, the *muchacho*, lay not always asleep in the corner.

As from a remote distance he could hear Spider Hagerty saying to him: "No layin' down at the start. Them's instructions. Take a beatin' an' earn your dough."

Ten minutes had passed, and he still sat in his corner. There were no signs of Danny, who was evidently playing the trick to the limit.

But more visions burned before the eye of Rivera's memory. The strike, or, rather, the lockout, because the workers of Rio Blanco had helped their striking brothers of Puebla. The hunger, the expeditions in the hills for berries, the roots and herbs that all ate and that twisted and pained the stomachs of all of them. And then the nightmare; the waste of ground before the company's store; the thousands of starving workers; General Rosalio Martinez and the soldiers of Porfirio Díaz; and the death-spitting rifles that seemed never to cease spitting, while the workers' wrongs were washed and washed again in their own blood. And that night! He saw the flatcars, piled high with the bodies of the slain, consigned to Vera Cruz, food for the sharks of the bay. Again he crawled over the grisly heaps, seeking and finding, stripped and mangled, his father and his mother. His mother he especially remembered— only her face projecting, her body burdened by the weight of dozens of bodies. Again the rifles of the soldiers of Porfirio Díaz cracked, and again he dropped to the ground and slunk away like some hunted coyote of the hills.

To his ears came a great roar, as of the sea, and he saw Danny Ward, leading his retinue of trainers and seconds, coming down the center aisle. The house was in wild uproar for the popular hero who was bound to win. Everybody proclaimed him. Everybody was for him. Even Rivera's own seconds warmed to something akin to cheerfulness when Danny ducked jauntily through the ropes and entered the ring. His face continually spread to an unending succession of smiles, and when Danny smiled he smiled in every feature, even to the laughter wrinkles of the corners of the eyes and into the depths of the eyes themselves. Never was there so genial a fighter. His face was a running advertisement of good feeling, of good-fellowship. He knew everybody. He joked, and laughed, and greeted his friends through the ropes. Those farther away, unable to suppress their admiration, cried loudly: "Oh, you Danny!" It was a joyous ovation of affection that lasted a full five minutes.

Rivera was disregarded. For all that the audience noticed, he did not exist. Spider Hagerty's bloated face bent down close to his.

"No gettin' scared," the Spider warned. "An' remember instructions. You gotta last. No layin' down. If you lay down, we got instructions to beat you up in the dressing rooms. Savvy? You just gotta fight."

The house began to applaud. Danny was crossing the ring to him. Danny bent over, caught Rivera's right hand in both his own and shook it with impulsive heartiness. Danny's smile-wreathed face was close to his. The audience yelled its appreciation of Danny's display of sporting spirit. He was greeting his opponent with the fondness of a brother. Danny's lips moved, and the audience, interpreting the unheard words to be those of a kindly-natured sport, yelled again. Only Rivera heard the low words.

"You little Mexican rat," hissed from between Danny's gaily smiling lips, "I'll fetch the yellow outa you."

Rivera made no move. He did not rise. He merely hated with his eyes.

"Get up, you dog!" some man yelled through the ropes from behind.

The crowd began to hiss and boo him for his unsportsman-like conduct, but he sat unmoved. Another great outburst of applause was Danny's as he walked back across the ring.

When Danny stripped, there were ohs! and ahs! of delight. His body was perfect, alive with easy suppleness and health and strength. The skin was white as a woman's, and as smooth. All grace, and resilience, and power resided therein. He had proved it in scores of battles. His photographs were in all the physical-culture magazines.

A groan went up as Spider Hagerty peeled Rivera's sweater over his head. His body seemed leaner because of the swarthiness of the skin. He had muscles, but they made no display like his opponent's. What the audience neglected to see was the deep chest. Nor could it guess the toughness of the fiber of the flesh, the instantaneousness of the cell explosions of the muscles, the fineness of the nerves that wired every part of him into a splendid fighting mechanism. All the audience saw was a brown-skinned boy of eighteen with what seemed the body of a boy. With Danny it was different. Danny was a man of twenty-four, and his body was a man's body. The contrast was still more striking as they stood together in the center of the ring receiving the referee's last instructions.

Rivera noticed Roberts sitting directly behind the newspapermen. He was drunker than usual, and his speech was correspondingly slower.

"Take it easy, Rivera," Roberts drawled. "He can't kill you, remember that. He'll rush you at the go-off, but don't get rattled. You just cover up, and stall, and clinch. He can't hurt you much. Just make believe to yourself that he's choppin' out on you at the trainin' quarters."

Rivera made no sign that he had heard.

"Sullen little devil," Roberts muttered to the man next to him. "He always was that way."

But Rivera forgot to look his usual hatred. A vision of countless rifles blinded his eyes. Every face in the audience, far as he could see, to the high dollar seats, was transformed into a rifle. And he saw the long Mexican border arid and sun-washed and aching, and along it he saw the ragged bands that delayed only for the guns.

Back in his corner he waited, standing up. His seconds had crawled out through the ropes, taking the canvas stool with them. Diagonally across the squared ring, Danny faced him. The gong struck, and the battle was on. The audience howled its delight. Never had it seen a battle open more convincingly. The papers were right. It was a grudge fight. Three-quarters of the distance Danny covered in the rush to get together, his intention to eat up the

Mexican lad plainly advertised. He assailed with not one blow, nor two, nor a dozen. He was a gyroscope of blows, a whirlwind of destruction. Rivera was nowhere. He was overwhelmed, buried beneath avalanches of punches delivered from every angle and position by a past master in the art. He was overborne, swept back against the ropes, separated by the referee, and swept back against the ropes again.

It was not a fight. It was a slaughter, a massacre. Any audience, save a prizefighting one, would have exhausted its emotions in that first minute. Danny was certainly showing what he could do—a splendid exhibition. Such was the certainty of the audience, as well as its excitement and favoritism, that it failed to take notice that the Mexican still stayed on his feet. It forgot Rivera. It rarely saw him, so closely was he enveloped in Danny's man-eating attack. A minute of this went by, and two minutes. Then, in a separation, it caught a clear glimpse of the Mexican. His lip was cut, his nose was bleeding. As he turned and staggered into a clinch the welts of ooz-ing blood, from his contacts with the ropes, showed in red bars across his back. But what the audience did not notice was that his chest was not heaving and that his eyes were coldly burning as ever. Too many aspiring champions, in the cruel welter of the training camps, had practiced this man-eating attack on him. He had learned to live through for a compensation of from half a dollar a go up to fifteen dollars a week—a hard school, and he was schooled hard.

Then happened the amazing thing. The whirling, blurring mix-up ceased suddenly. Rivera stood alone. Danny, the redoubtable Danny, lay on his back. His body quivered as con-sciousness strove to return to it. He had not staggered and sunk down, nor had he gone over in a long slumping fall. The right hook of Rivera had dropped him in midair with the abruptness of death. The referee shoved Rivera back with one hand and stood over the fallen gladiator counting the seconds. It is the custom of prize-fighting audiences to cheer a clean knockdown blow. But this audi-ence did not cheer. The thing had been too unexpected. It watched the toll of the seconds in tense silence, and through this silence the voice of Roberts rose exultantly:

"I told you he was a two-handed fighter!"

By the fifth second Danny was rolling over on his face, and when seven was counted he rested on one knee, ready to rise after the count of nine and before the count of ten. If his knee still touched the floor at "ten" he was considered "down" and also "out." The instant his knee left the floor he was considered "up," and in that instant it was Rivera's right to try and put him down again. Rivera took no chances. The moment that knee left the floor he would strike again. He circled around, but the referee circled in between, and Rivera knew that the seconds he counted were very slow. All gringos were against him, even the referee.

At "nine" the referee gave Rivera a sharp thrust back. It was unfair, but it enabled Danny to rise, the smile back on his lips. Doubled partly over, with arms wrapped about face and abdomen he cleverly stumbled into a clinch. By all the rules of the game the referee should have broken it, but he did not, and Danny clung on like a surf-battered barnacle and moment by moment recuperated. The last minute of the round was going fast. If he could live to the end, he would have a full minute in his corner to revive. And live to the end he did, smiling through all desperateness and extremity.

"The smile that won't come off!" somebody yelled, and the audience laughed loudly in its relief.

"The kick that greaser's got is something God-awful," Danny gasped in his corner to his adviser while his handlers worked frantically over him.

The second and third rounds were tame. Danny, a tricky and consummate ring general, stalled and blocked and held on, devoting himself to recovering from that dazing first-round blow. In the fourth round he was himself again. Jarred and shaken, nevertheless his good condition had enabled him to regain his vigor. But he tried no man-eating tactics. The Mexican had proved a tartar. Instead he brought to bear his best fighting powers. In tricks and skill and experience he was the master, and though he could land nothing vital, he proceeded scientifically to chop and wear down his opponent. He landed three blows to Rivera's one, but they were punishing blows only, and not deadly. It was the sum of many of them that constituted deadliness. He was respectful of this two-handed dub with the amazing short-arm kicks in both his fists.

In defense Rivera developed a disconcerting straight left. Again and again, attack after attack he straight-lefted away from him with accumulated damage to Danny's mouth and nose. But Danny was protean. That was why he was the coming champion. He could change from style to style of fighting at will. He now devoted himself to infighting. In this he was particularly wicked, and it enabled him to avoid the other's straight left. Here he set the house wild repeatedly, capping it with a marvelous lock-break and lift of an inside uppercut that raised the Mexican in the air and dropped him to the mat. Rivera rested on one knee, making the most of the count, and in the soul of him he knew the referee was counting short seconds on him.

Again, in the seventh, Danny achieved the diabolical inside uppercut. He succeeded only in staggering Rivera, but in the ensuing moment of defenseless helplessness he smashed him with another blow through the ropes. Rivera's body bounced on the heads of the newspapermen below, and they boosted him back to the edge of the platform outside the ropes. Here he rested on one knee, while the referee raced off the seconds. Inside the ropes, through which he must duck to enter the ring, Danny waited for him. Nor did the referee intervene or thrust Danny back.

The house was beside itself with delight.

"Kill 'm, Danny, kill 'm!" was the cry.

Scores of voices took it up until it was like a war chant of wolves.

Danny did his best, but Rivera, at the count of eight, instead of nine, came unexpectedly through the ropes and safely into a clinch. Now the referee worked, tearing him away so that he could be hit, giving Danny every advantage that an unfair referee can give.

But Rivera lived, and the daze cleared from his brain. It was all of a piece. They were the hated gringos and they were all unfair.

And in the worst of it visions continued to flash and sparkle in his brain—long lines of railroad track that simmered across the desert; *rurales* and American constables; prisons and calabooses; tramps at water tanks—all the squalid and painful panorama of his odyssey after Rio Blanco and the strike. And, resplendent and glorious, he saw the great red revolution sweeping across his land. The guns were there before him. Every hated face was a gun. It was for the guns he fought. He was the guns. He was the revolution. He fought for all Mexico.

The audience began to grow incensed with Rivera. Why didn't he take the licking that was appointed him? Of course he was going to be licked, but why should he be so obstinate about it? Very few were interested in him, and they were the certain, definite percentage of a gambling crowd that plays long shots. Believing Danny to be the winner, nevertheless they had put their money on the Mexican at four to ten and one to three. More than a trifle was up on the point of how many rounds Rivera could last. Wild money had appeared at the ringside proclaiming that he could not last seven rounds, or even six. The winners of this, now that their cash risk was happily settled, had joined in cheering on the favorite.

Rivera refused to be licked. Through the eighth round his opponent strove vainly to repeat the uppercut. In the ninth Rivera stunned the house again. In the midst of a clinch he broke the lock with a quick, lithe movement, and in the narrow space between their bodies his right lifted from the waist. Danny went to the floor and took the safety of the count. The crowd was appalled. He was being bested at his own game. His famous right uppercut had been worked back on him. Rivera made no attempt to catch him as he arose at "nine." The referee was openly blocking that play, though he stood clear when the situation was reversed and it was Rivera who required to rise.

Twice in the tenth Rivera put through the right uppercut, lifted from waist to opponent's chin. Danny grew desperate. The smile never left his face, but he went back to his man-eating rushes. Whirlwind as he would, he could not damage Rivera, while Rivera, through the blur and whirl, dropped him to the mat three times in succession. Danny did not recuperate so quickly now, and by the eleventh round he was in a serious way. But from then till the fourteenth he put up the gamest exhibition of his career. He stalled and blocked, fought parsimoniously, and strove to gather strength. Also he fought as foully as a successful fighter knows how. Every trick and device he employed, butting in the clinches with the seeming of accident, pinioning Rivera's glove between arm and body, heeling his glove on Rivera's mouth to clog his breathing. Often, in the clinches, through his cut and smiling lips he snarled insults unspeakable and vile in Rivera's ear. Everybody, from the referee to the house, was with Danny and was helping Danny. And they knew what he had in mind. Bested by this surprise box of an unknown, he was pinning all on a single punch. He offered himself for punishment, fished, and feinted, and drew, for that one opening that would enable him to whip a blow through with all his strength and turn the tide. As another and greater fighter had done before him, he might do—a right and left, to solar plexus and across the jaw. He could do it, for he was noted for the strength of punch that remained in his arm as long as he could keep his feet.

Rivera's seconds were not half caring for him in the intervals between rounds. Their towels made a showing but drove little air into his panting lungs. Spider Hagerty talked advice to him, but Rivera knew it was wrong advice. Everybody was against him. He was surrounded by treachery. In the fourteenth round he put Danny down again, and himself stood resting, hands dropped at side, while the referee counted. In the other corner Rivera had been noting suspicious whisperings. He saw Michael Kelly make his way to Roberts and bend and whisper. Rivera's ears were a cat's, desert-trained, and he caught snatches of what was said. He wanted to hear more, and when his opponent arose he maneuvered the fight into a clinch over against the ropes.

"Got to," he could hear Michael, while Roberts nodded. "Danny's got to win—I stand to lose a mint. I've got a ton of money covered—my own. If he lasts the fifteenth I'm bust. The boy'll mind you. Put something across."

And thereafter Rivera saw no more visions. They were trying to job him. Once again he dropped Danny and stood resting, his hands at his side. Roberts stood up.

"That settled him," he said. "Go to your corner."

He spoke with authority, as he had often spoken to Rivera at the training quarters. But Rivera looked hatred at him and waited for Danny to rise. Back in his corner in the minute interval, Kelly, the promoter, came and talked to Rivera.

"Throw it, damn you," he rasped in a harsh low voice. "You gotta lay down, Rivera. Stick with me and I'll make your future. I'll let you lick Danny next time. But here's where you lay down."

Rivera showed with his eyes that he heard, but he made neither sign of assent nor dissent.

"Why don't you speak?" Kelly demanded angrily.

"You lose anyway," Spider Hagerty supplemented. "The referee'll take it away from you. Listen to Kelly and lay down."

"Lay down, kid," Kelly pleaded, "and I'll help you to the championship."

Rivera did not answer.

"I will, so help me, kid."

At the strike of the gong Rivera sensed something impending. The house did not. Whatever it was, it was there inside the ring with him and very close. Danny's earlier surety seemed returned to him. The confidence of his advance frightened Rivera. Some trick was about to be worked. Danny rushed, but Rivera refused the encounter. He sidestepped away into safety. What the other wanted was a clinch. It was in some way necessary to the trick. Rivera backed and circled away, yet he knew, sooner or later, the clinch and the trick would come. Desperately he resolved to draw it. He made as if to effect the clinch with Danny's next rush. Instead, at the last instant, just as their bodies should have come together, Rivera darted nimbly back. And in the same instant Danny's corner raised a cry of foul. Rivera had fooled them. The referee paused irresolutely. The decision that trembled on his lips was never uttered, for a shrill boy's voice from the gallery piped, "Raw work!"

"Why don't you fight" it demanded wrathfully of Rivera. "You're yellow! You're yellow!" "Open up, you cur! Open up!" "Kill 'm, Danny! Kill 'm!" "You sure got 'm! Kill 'm!"

In all the house, bar none, Rivera was the only cold man. By temperament and blood he was the hottest-passioned there; but he had gone through such vastly greater heats that this collective passion of ten thousand throats, rising surge on surge, was to his brain no more than the velvet cool of a summer twilight.

Into the seventeenth round Danny carried his rally. Rivera, under a heavy blow, drooped and sagged. His hands dropped helplessly as he reeled backward. Danny thought it was his chance. The boy was at his mercy. Thus Rivera, feigning, caught him off his guard, lashing out a clean drive to the mouth. Danny went down. When he arose Rivera felled him with a down-chop of the right on neck and jaw. Three times he repeated this. It was impossible for any referee to call these blows foul.

"Oh, Bill! Bill!" Kelly pleaded to the referee.

"I can't," that official lamented back. "He won't give me a chance."

Danny, battered and heroic, still kept coming up. Kelly and others near to the ring began to cry out to the police to stop it, though Danny's corner refused to throw in the towel. Rivera saw the fat police captain starting awkwardly to climb through the ropes, and was not sure what it meant. There were so many ways of cheating in this game of the gringos. Danny, on his feet, tottered groggily and helplessly before him. The referee and the captain were both reaching for Rivera when he struck the last blow. There was no need to stop the fight, for Danny did not rise.

"Count!" Rivera cried hoarsely to the referee.

And when the count was finished Danny's seconds gathered him up and carried him to his corner.

"Who wins?" Rivera demanded.

Reluctantly the referee caught his gloved hand and held it aloft.

There were no congratulations for Rivera. He walked to his corner unattended, where his seconds had not yet placed his stool. He leaned backward on the ropes and looked his hatred at them, swept it on and about him till the whole ten thousand gringos were included. His knees trembled under him, and he was sobbing from exhaustion. Before his eyes the hated faces swayed back and forth in the giddiness of nausea. Then he remembered they were the guns. The guns were his. The revolution could go on.

Selected Bibliography of London's Work

Fiction (in chronological order)

The Son of the Wolf. Boston: Houghton Mifflin, 1900.
The God of His Fathers. New York: McClure, Phillips, 1901.
Children of the Frost. New York: Macmillan, 1902.
The Cruise of the Dazzler. New York: Century, 1902.
A Daughter of the Snows. Philadelphia: J. B. Lippincott, 1902.
The Call of the Wild. New York: Macmillan, 1903.
The Faith of Men. New York: Macmillan, 1904.
The Sea-Wolf. New York: Macmillan, 1904.
The Game. New York: Macmillan, 1905.
Tales of the Fish Patrol. New York: Macmillan, 1905.
Moon Face and Other Stories. New York: Macmillan, 1906.
White Fang. New York: Macmillan, 1906.
Before Adam. New York: Macmillan, 1907.
Love of Life and Other Stories. New York: Macmillan, 1907.
The Iron Heel. New York: Macmillan, 1908.
Martin Eden. New York: Macmillan, 1909.
Lost Face. New York: Macmillan, 1910.
Burning Daylight. New York: Macmillan, 1910.
When God Laughs and Other Stories. New York: Macmillan, 1911.
Adventure. New York: Macmillan, 1911.
South Sea Tales. New York: Macmillan, 1911.

The House of Pride and Other Stories of Hawaii. New York: Macmillan, 1912.
A Son of the Sun. Garden City, NY: Doubleday, Page, 1912.
Smoke Bellew. New York: Century, 1912.
The Night-Born. New York: Century, 1913.
The Abysmal Brute. New York: Century, 1913.
The Valley of the Moon. New York: Macmillan, 1913.
The Strength of the Strong. New York: Macmillan, 1914.
The Mutiny of the Elsinore. New York: Macmillan, 1914.
The Scarlet Plague. New York: Macmillan, 1915.
The Star Rover. New York: Macmillan, 1915.
The Little Lady of the Big House. New York: Macmillan, 1916.
The Turtles of Tasman. New York: Macmillan, 1916.
Jerry of the Islands. New York: Macmillan, 1917.
Michael Brother of Jerry. New York: Macmillan, 1917.
The Red One. New York: Macmillan, 1918.
On the Makaloa Mat. New York: Macmillan, 1919.
Hearts of Three. New York: Macmillan, 1920.
Dutch Courage and Other Stories. New York: Macmillan, 1922.

Drama (in chronological order)

Scorn of Women. New York: Macmillan, 1906.
Theft: A Play in Four Acts. New York: Macmillan, 1910.
The Acorn-Planter: A California Forest Play. New York: Macmillan, 1916.
The Birth Mark. In *The Human Drift.* New York: MacMillan, 1917.
A Wicked Woman. In *The Human Drift.* New York: Macmillan, 1917.

Nonfiction (in chronological order)

The Kempton-Wace Letters. New York: Macmillan, 1903.

The People of the Abyss. New York: Macmillan, 1903.

War of the Classes. New York: Macmillan, 1905.

The Road. New York: Macmillan, 1907.

Revolution and Other Essays. New York: Macmillan, 1910.

The Cruise of the Snark. New York: Macmillan, 1911.

John Barleycorn. New York: Century, 1913.

The Human Drift. New York: Macmillan, 1917.

Letters from Jack London. Edited by King Hendricks and Irving Shepard. New York: Odyssey, 1965.

Jack London Reports: War Correspondence, Sports Articles, and Miscellaneous Writings. Edited by King Hendricks and Irving Shepard. Garden City, NY: Doubleday, 1970.

No Mentor but Myself: A Collection of Articles, Essays, Reviews and Letters, by Jack London, on Writing and Writers. Edited by Dale L. Walker. Port Washington, NY: Kennikat, 1979.

Jack London on the Road: The Tramp Diary and Other Hobo Writings. Edited by Richard W. Etulain. Logan, UT: Utah State University Press, 1979.

Recommended Readings
about London

Auerbach, Jonathan. *Male Call: Becoming Jack London*. Durham, NC: Duke University Press, 1996.

Cassuto, Leonard, and Jeanne Campbell Reesman. *Rereading Jack London*. Stanford, CA: Stanford University Press, 1996.

Foner, Philip S., ed. *Jack London, American Rebel: A Collection of His Social Writings Together with an Extensive Study of the Man and His Times*. New York: Citadel, 1947.

Geismar, Maxwell. "Jack London: The Short Cut." In *Rebels and Ancestors: The American Novel, 1890–1915*. Boston: Houghton Mifflin, 1953.

Kingman, Russ. *A Pictorial Life of Jack London*. New York: Crown, 1979.

Labor, Earle. *Jack London*. New York: Twayne, 1974.

London, Charmian K. *The Book of Jack London*. 2 vols. New York: Century, 1921.

London, Joan. *Jack London and His Daughters*. Berkeley, CA: Heyday Books, 1990.

_____. *Jack London and His Times: An Unconventional Biography*. New York: Doubleday, Doran, 1939; rpt. Seattle: University of Washington Press, 1968.

McClintock, James I. *White Logic: Jack London's Short Stories*. Grand Rapids, MI: Wolf House Books, 1975.

Nuernberg, Susan, ed. *The Critical Response to Jack London.* Westport, CT: Greenwood Press, 1995.

Ownbey, Ray Wilson, ed. *Jack London: Essays in Criticism.* Santa Barbara, CA: Peregrine Smith, 1978.

Powell, Lawrence Clark. "Martin Eden." In *California Classics.* Los Angeles: The Ward Ritchie Press, 1971.

Rather, Lois. *Jack London, 1905.* Oakland, CA: The Rather Press, 1974.

Sinclair, Andrew. *Jack: A Biography of Jack London.* New York: Harper & Row, 1977.

Starr, Kevin. "The Sonoma Finale of Jack London, Rancher." In *Americans and the California Dream, 1850–1915.* New York: Oxford University Press, 1973.

Stasz, Clarice. *American Dreamers: Charmian and Jack London.* New York: St. Martin's Press, 1988.

Tavernier-Courbin, Jacqueline, ed. *Critical Essays on Jack London.* Boston: G. K. Hall, 1983.

Walcutt, Charles Child. *Jack London.* University of Minnesota Pamphlets on American Writers. Minneapolis: University of Minnesota Press, 1966.

Walker, Dale L. *The Alien Worlds of Jack London.* Grand Rapids, MI: Wolf House Books, 1973.

Walker, Franklin. *Jack London and the Klondike.* San Marino, CA: Huntington Library, 1966.

_____. *The Seacoast of Bohemia: An Account of Early Carmel.* San Francisco: The Book Club of California, 1966; enlarged ed., Santa Barbara, CA: Peregrine Smith, 1973.

Watson, Bruce. "Jack London Followed His Muse into the Wild." *Smithsonian.* February 1998, 104–113.

Watson, Charles N., Jr. *The Novels of Jack London: A Reappraisal.* Madison, WI: University of Wisconsin Press, 1983.

Bibliographies

Sherman, Joan R. *Jack London: A Reference Guide*. Boston: G. K. Hall, 1977.

Sisson, James E., III, and Robert W. Martens, comps. *Jack London First Editions—Illustrated—A Chronological Reference Guide*. Oakland, CA: Star Rover House, 1979.

Walker, Dale L., and James E. Sisson, III, eds. *The Fiction of Jack London: A Chronological Bibliography*. El Paso, TX: Texas Western Press, 1972.

Woodbridge, Hensley C., John London, and George H. Tweney, comps. *Jack London: A Bibliography*. Georgetown, CA: Talisman, 1966; enlarged ed., Millwood, NY: Kraus, 1973.

About the Editor

Gerald Haslam is the author and editor of more than twenty books, including fiction such as *Condor Dreams & Other Fictions* (University of Nevada Press, 1994) and non-fiction such as *Workin' Man Blues: Country Music in California* (University of California Press, 1999). He most recently edited the second, expanded edition of *Many Californias: Literature from the Golden State* (University of Nevada Press, 1999) and, with Alexandra R. Haslam, *Where Coyotes Howl and Wind Blows Free: Growing Up in the West* (University of Nevada Press, 1995). His books have won a Bay Area Book Reviewers' Award, a Commonwealth Club Medal, and a Benjamin Franklin Award, among other honors.